THE
SILVER WELL

THE KINGDOM OF GEMS TRILOGY

BOOK 1: *Candara's Gift*

BOOK 2: *The Silver Well*

BOOK 3: *The Glass Prison*

ANOTHER BOOK
BY JASPER COOPER ~ *GORDO*

A thrilling fictional adventure based upon the launch of the first monkey into space in 1958.

Gordo, a little squirrel monkey, is the object of several sinister plots.

Fortunately, thirteen year old Jamie and his cousin Rachel are ready to fight for him.

When others around him are determined to achieve their selfish aims,

drastic measures are needed...

www.GordoMonkey.com

THE KINGDOM OF GEMS TRILOGY

~ BOOK 2 ~

THE SILVER WELL

Jasper Cooper

Illustrations by Jasper Cooper

SILVERWELL PUBLISHING

For more information on Jasper and his books, visit:
www.TheKingdomOfGems.com
www.JasperCooper.com
www.GordoMonkey.com

First published in 2010 by SilverWell Publishing
12, Mount Road, Canterbury, Kent CT1 1YD   UK

Reprinted in 2014

3 5 7 9 10 8 6 4

ISBN
978-0-9551653-1-3

Printed and bound in Great Britain by
CPI Group (UK) Ltd, Croydon, CR0 4YY.

To get updates of Jasper's new books and other exciting news, make sure you sign up for his updates and newsletter here:

www.TheKingdomOfGems.com/updates

CONTENTS

TIMELINE

Covering events that happened in and around *The Kingdom Of Gems*

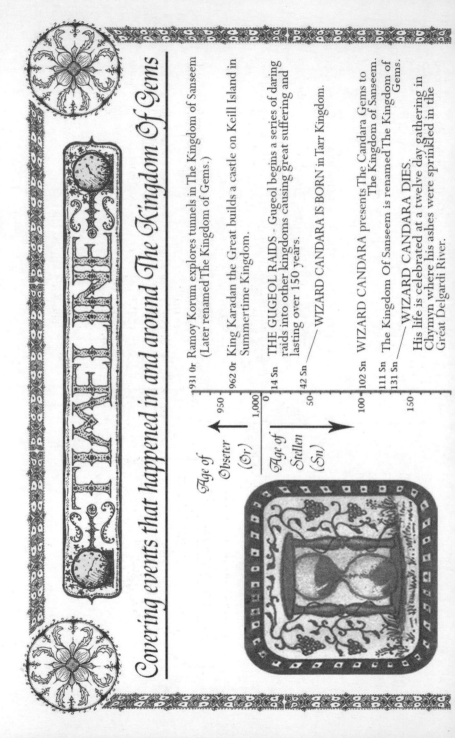

Age of Obseter (Or)

931 Or — Ramoy Korum explores tunnels in The Kingdom of Sanseem (Later renamed The Kingdom of Gems.)

962 Or — King Karadan the Great builds a castle on Keill Island in Summertime Kingdom.

Age of Stellen (Sn)

14 Sn — THE GUGEOL RAIDS - Gugeol begins a series of daring raids into other kingdoms causing great suffering and lasting over 150 years.

42 Sn — WIZARD CANDARA IS BORN in Tarr Kingdom.

102 Sn — WIZARD CANDARA presents The Candara Gems to The Kingdom of Sanseem.

111 Sn — The Kingdom Of Sanseem is renamed The Kingdom of Gems.

131 Sn — WIZARD CANDARA DIES.
His life is celebrated at a twelve day gathering in Chymyn where his ashes were sprinkled in the Great Delgardi River.

950

1,000

0

50

100

150

200 — 201 Sn **GUGEOL ARISES** and invades the surrounding kingdoms of Glyfild, Bortell, Urlom, Fantem South and Hesteri.

227 Sn **GUGEOL** occupies many kingdoms between the two Great Oceans but not The Kingdom of Gems which is protected by the Candara Gems.

250 — 259 Sn **ARAM & HALO** awaken to protect The Kingdom of Gems against an invasion of evil Troublers sent by Gugeol.

300 — 308 Sn **THE FIRE CREATURES OF RUDDHA** join forces with Gugeol.

339 Sn **THE TWENTY DAY HAROOR UPRISING** in the Kingdom of Mardice is quashed by Gugeol.

350 — 376 Sn Widespread famine caused by a massive volcano eruption in the Heldfore Mountains in the Kindom Of Agulta. The Kingdom Of Gems is protected from this by the Candara Gems.

400 —

450 — 447 Sn **THE GREAT INVASION** - Gugeol is defeated and forced back. The Fire Creatures return to Ruddha deep beneath the earth. The Dark Ages end.

470 Sn — The **FORENTONE BEARS** attack the wolves in Juran Forest in Summertime Kingdom, and start their territorial war.

500 — 511 Sn—**THE GLYFILD BELL** is cast by Gugeol in the iron mines of Glyfild.

528 Sn **GUGEOL INVADES SUMMERTIME KINGDOM** and casts a spell with the Glyfild Bell.

550 — 553 Sn—**THE MUNDEN REBELLION** led by Hawkeye. Gugeol retreats.

567 Sn — The **Dark Wizard Troubler** enters The Kingdom of Gems.

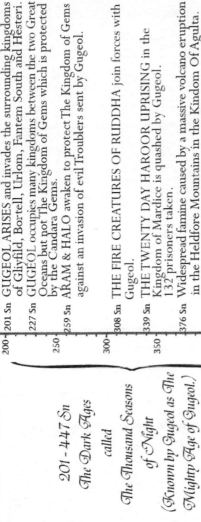

201 - 447 Sn
The Dark Ages
called
The Thousand Seasons
of Night
(Known by Gugeol as The Mighty Age of Gugeol.)

The 7 Eras of Known History
each lasting 1,000 years.

Shair Era
Fenair Era
Saltone Era
Ealume Era
Pumat Era
Obseter Era
Srellen Era

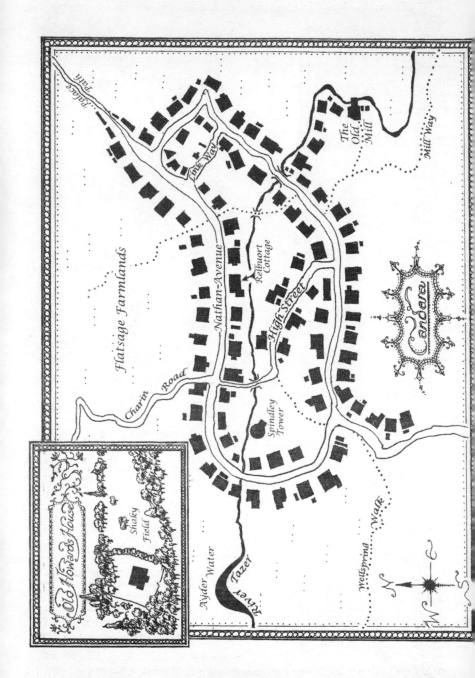

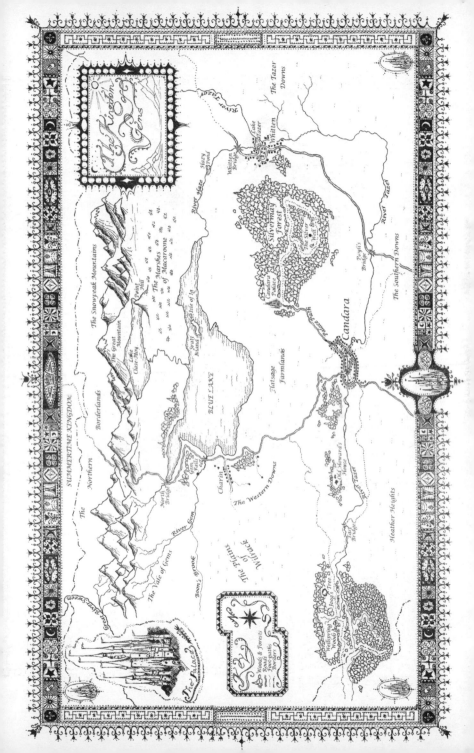

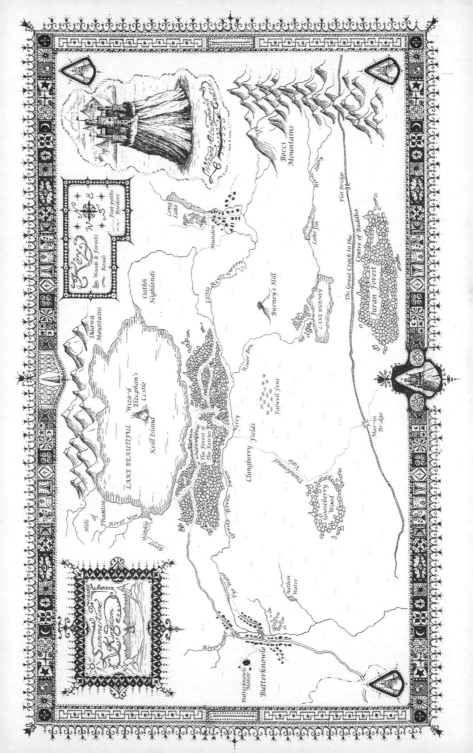

This book is dedicated to Sarah, my wife.

Chapter 1

~ The Trap ~

The Forest of the Fairies was wrapped in semi-darkness. Under a clear night sky, moonlight bathed the tops of the trees and touched the forest floor where it found gaps through the branches and leaves. The air was still and warm. A tender woodland scent filled the forest and nocturnal animals could be heard rustling among the ferns and undergrowth.

Princess Amalek, Prince Seph and Neville the albatross had settled down for the night. They were comfortable on a bed of leaves under an overhanging rock. Just a few trees away, high up on a branch of an elm, were the two old ravens Crayle and Jum. Earlier they had listened to the voices of the children below and realized with glee that they had found who they were looking for. Then, after a while, the voices had stopped and the ravens had remained silent and still. For half an hour they had watched and listened without speaking. Then Jum spoke.

"I think we…" she began.

"Sshh!" Crayle jerked his head towards her. They were sitting side by side and with his sudden movement his beak knocked into her head and made her lose balance. She nearly fell off the branch but managed to flap her wings and settle down again.

"Sorry," he whispered, "But we must keep quiet... they mightn't be asleep yet. And if they are asleep we mustn't wake 'em up."

"I know, dear," she whispered back, "But I think they

are sleeping. They've been silent now for some time. So, what do we do now?"

Crayle thought for a moment.

He tilted his head on one side so that he was looking down. He only had one eye and he continually had to make jerky movements with his head in order to see. "I'll go down and take a look."

"Now what's the point in that?" whispered Jum, "You're not as young as you used to be, my dear... you might crash and wake them up."

"Don't be silly," Crayle lifted his head up and tried to look sprightly, "Just 'cos I hit the General that time..." he whispered.

He jumped off the branch and swooped down into the deeper darkness beneath the trees. Jum heard a rustle as he clipped a bush with his wings and then a moment later he was back and perched beside her again. He landed the wrong way around so that they were facing opposite directions. He shuffled around, first turning one way to find his tail was in the way and then managing to turn in the other direction until he was the right way round again.

"Asleep," he announced, "Not a sound."

Jum shook her head, "Yes, but your hearing, Crayle! How can you tell with your bad hearing? What's got into you? This whole thing has gone to your head. You're trying to act like a young bird again." She lifted her beak and a distant look clouded her eyes. "Now when you *were* a young bird, and in your prime, well, to see you in flight, shiny wings an' all, now that was something. It turned my heart…"

"We'll stalk 'em," Crayle whispered, ignoring her, "When they wake and get moving again, we'll stalk 'em."

Jum said nothing as she was still dreaming of the memory of Crayle as a young bird.

"Jum!" he whispered loudly and nudged her with his beak, "Are you listening to me?"

This shook her out of her reverie and she said absentmindedly, "What's that, my dear?"

"I said," Crayle snapped, "We'll stalk 'em when they wake, OK?"

"OK," whispered Jum, "And after that? After we've stalked 'em, then what?"

"We'll… um," he began, "We'll… well, we'll decide that later…"

Jum turned to face him, "Don't you think we should tell the General?"

"Of course... then we'll be heroes!" Crayle announced, "Heroes, that's what we'll be. Heroes!" Then he thought for a moment. "We must tell the General... but the problem is... how do we do that and still stalk the enemy?"

"Well, it's obvious, isn't it?" Jum looked surprised, "We split up... one stalks and the other flies off and tells the General."

Crayle looked concerned, "But I don't want to leave you by yourself with the enemy, so I'll have to keep stalking 'em while you go and tell the General."

"But not yet. You need sleep. I've slept already, so you sleep now, OK?"

He did feel very tired and sleepy so he welcomed the idea.

"OK," whispered Crayle.

They leant together on the branch. Crayle closed his eyes to sleep and Jum watched and listened.

It was just after midnight. Joog kept his distance as he followed Old Howard who was plodding towards Burney's Hill. The old man had retraced his steps, crossing the Great River Sween and then the Little River Sween as he headed southwards. Once again he could feel water in his boots from crossing the rivers on a raft but he did not care. He just had one task to complete now; the Dark Wizard Troubler had instructed him to kill the cat and had promised to reward him. This meant that he would get more gold.

Occasionally, in his excitement, he smiled to himself and even whistled a few random notes. Now and again his hand slipped into his pocket to run his fingers over the gold bar that he kept there and this fuelled his greed even more. He was eager to claim his reward.

Joog kept his distance as he dipped skilfully behind trees and skimmed across open areas, staying close to the ground. His soft white feathers fanned the air with silent ease. His excellent owl's eyes could pick out Old Howard at a distance and the old man had no idea he was being followed.

When Old Howard was approaching the rickety shack at the foot of Burney's Hill, Joog flew off to his left, making a wide circle and flashing through the trees like a silver dart. Losing sight of Old Howard, he swung around until he was behind the shack, gliding in to perch in an overhanging tree. He was hidden in the shadowy leaves and his patterned feathers disguised him well. He gazed through the branches and found he had an excellent view to see Old Howard's rotund body plodding wearily in his direction. In the pale moonlight Joog also saw the sack hanging by a rope on a nearby tree and wondered. He knew that Flop and Miriam had been captured in a sack and this one was bulging with a shape about the size of a cat. Then he heard Flop's voice.

"We're in here," he said softly.

Joog's heart leapt with joy. They were alive. He saw a hole in the back of the sack and realized they were trying to escape. What a shame they had not made it before Old Howard returned. Joog wanted to reply but Old Howard was too close now, trudging towards him, the sound of his steps clear in the quiet night air. A moment later, he had arrived and he stopped walking, pausing in front of the sack and gazing at it. A few drops of sweat ran down his forehead.

"Roight, cat," he said decisively, "First, oy'll deal with you. I hope yer're enjoyin' yerself in there, 'cos it's the last few seconds of yer loife."

He thought for a moment and then went into the shack, reappearing a minute later with a lighted oil lamp and a bag which he dropped onto the grass. He lifted the lamp to his head's height and looked at the sack. Then he saw the hole.

"What?!" he bellowed, "So you've been troying to escape 'ave you? Well, oy don't approve of that at all!"

His face became an expression of fury. His fists clenched tightly as he glared at the sack that hung at about the same level as his head.

"Kill the cat now," said a sinister voice from nowhere.

Old Howard jumped as the phantom Dark Wizard Troubler suddenly materialized right in front of him. The old man was still staring at the sack but now through the ghostly figure that glared back at him intently. The phantom Troubler was transparent, a mere outline in the mellow lamp-light, staring with a sinister expression at Old Howard.

"Do it now," the phantom hissed, "Right now! Do you here me? No more of your delays."

Old Howard's eyes opened wide as he stepped back in fear and stammered, "Alroyt, alroyt! Oy…oy 'adn't forgotten, 'ad oy?"

The phantom shimmered, growing slightly more solid. "Let's see some action then."

Old Howard nodded, held by the phantom's penetrating stare. He had agreed to work for the Troubler for payment of gold, but now he was terrified of his threats. Fear sat in the pit of his stomach.

The phantom scowled at him and then snapped, "Go on then. What are you waiting for?"

Old Howard stepped forwards, carrying the lamp in one hand, and passed straight through the phantom who swung around to watch the old man.

Joog tensed. He crouched lower with his wings half outstretched, ready to leap off and defend his friends. Before he could act Old Howard suddenly lunged forwards, almost falling, and took a great swing at the sack with a clenched fist, pummelling into it with all his might.

"Aaaaahhhh!" screamed Old Howard.

He had been expecting the soft feeling of a furry cat, but this was something hard, very hard. His round face screwed up in pain as he clutched his injured hand with the other.

"Moy 'and! Oh moy 'and!" he yelled.

"Where's the cat?" demanded the phantom sternly.

"Oy don't know! Can't you see oy'm in pain?"

Old Howard was now holding his hand up and opening and closing it very slowly while moaning in pain.

"Find the cat," hissed the phantom, "Look for it now. It might still be close by."

"And if it is?" asked Old Howard.

"Catch it and kill it of course," the phantom growled, shimmering again in anger, growing even more solid and then fading back again, "But check the sack first."

Old Howard moved beside the sack, held up the lamp

and looked in through the hole. "Stones!" he exclaimed, "It's got stones in it, but no cat!"

"Show me," commanded the phantom.

Old Howard put his good hand in and grabbed a large stone. As he did the rope holding the sack loosened and the sack fell, landing hard on one of his feet.

"Oowww!" he screeched, once again feeling intense pain and dropping the oil lamp, which landed the right way up on the ground but tilted at an angle.

Then an even more extraordinary thing happened. As he reached down to try to move the sack off his foot the ground gave way underneath him, a pit opened up and he fell in. In a split-second, before he could do anything about it, he was in it up to his chest. Immediately the loose earth tumbled in around him and gripped his body until only his head and shoulders, with his arms flailing frantically around, were left above.

"What's goin' on?!" he wailed.

"You've been made to look ridiculous," sneered the phantom who hissed out the words with anger, "By a cat!"

The phantom laughed eerily.

"You idiot! You should have finished off the cat when you had the chance. I told you to kill it! If you had followed my instructions you wouldn't be in the mess you're in now, would you?"

Old Howard was panicking. He pushed down hard with his arms, straining to free his stout body but the earth around him was packed tightly. If he had been slightly stronger or slightly less round he might have lifted himself out, but he found to his dismay that he was firmly stuck. His temper boiled over and he thumped his fists hard on the ground, forgetting about his injured hand, and he cried out again in pain as it hit the earth.

Joog watched in amazement from the tree, his calm mind trying to work out what had happened and whether he should do something. Then he noticed that the phantom Troubler was becoming even fainter.

"Get me out!" shouted Old Howard, sounding desperate, "Don't leave me 'ere loike this! Why ar'yer fading?"

"I can't help that at the moment. I can't stay now," it said, all the time becoming fainter and softer, "I'll be back and I'll find a way to get you out... that's if I choose." The phantom was now barely visible, "I think I will free you because you can still be of use to me. Oh, and one more thing, old man," and it laughed cruelly, "Don't run away!"

As it laughed it flickered and grew slightly clearer and then faded quickly until it was gone completely.

Joog glided down and landed on the grass.

"Where are you?" Joog called.

"In this bush!" called Flop, who walked casually out of his hiding place just beside the tree where the sack had been hanging. Miriam was on his back.

"Flop! Miriam!" said Joog, "I thought you were in the sack. I was so frightened for you."

"So we tricked you as well!" said Flop, picking up the lamp in his mouth and putting it down again where the ground was flatter, "Did you like our little trap?"

"It was brilliant, but how did you do it?"

Before Flop could answer Old Howard interrupted.

"But... but you're dead!" he exclaimed, looking at Joog with an expression that was thunderous with anger, "I saw you crushed and washed away boi the wave. I saw it 'appen!"

"You're easily fooled, Old Howard," said Joog shaking his head, "You thought I was dead, but I escaped."

Flop lifted the lamp with a paw and placed it on a log where it shed a better light.

"And... well..." Old Howard blurted out, "What about... what about the others then?"

Joog dropped his head slightly, looked down and spoke earnestly. "Where's your sense of guilt? Have you no shame about what you've done? How could they survive a wave like that?"

Joog glanced at Flop and Miriam, hoping that his look would tell them that really Seph, Amalek and Neville were all alive.

"Look..." pleaded Old Howard, "Listen. Oy am ashamed. Oy'm sorry about the others, really oy am. It was 'im, that thing," and he pointed at the place where the phantom had been. "Get me out of 'ere... please."

"You're in no position to demand anything," stated Joog.

"But..." objected Old Howard.

"Now be quiet," snapped Joog with such authority that Old Howard just clenched his teeth and growled in anger and frustration.

Then he shook his head and let his chin drop onto his chest in despair. Just when things seemed to be going better and he was having some success this had happened. He felt like a broken man.

Joog turned to Flop again. "So... tell me how you did it?"

"Well, to start with," began Flop, sitting down and curling his tail tidily around his side, "Miriam bit the hole in the sack for us to escape and while I was in the sack I had time for thinking. That's when I dreamt up this plan to stop any other schemes that Old Howard might have. Once we were out we put the plan into action."

"But how did you do it?" asked Joog.

Flop smiled with contentment. "I carried all those stones up the tree in my mouth and dropped them through the hole into the sack. Then Miriam got to work."

Miriam piped up with a squeak and said in her high-pitched voice, "I bit almost through the rope to leave the sack hanging by a few strands."

"And then the masterstroke!" exclaimed Flop, standing up, "As Old Howard stood under the sack Miriam bit through the last threads of the rope... and down came the sack of stones! It was meant to hit him on the head and knock him out, and trap him in the pit, and when the sack missed his head we thought it had all gone wrong. But then the hole opened up and in he fell."

"That's brilliant!" said Joog his eyes shining brightly in the lamplight, "But how did you dig the pit?"

"Oh, the pit?" squeaked Miriam, "A young hare appeared to help us. He's called Tally and he's going to Wizard Elzaphan to offer his help. He came just at the right time and helped us by digging the pit... with a few other hares and other animals... he got them to help too. He said he saw us from the top of Burney's Hill."

"Huh! How fortunate!" commented Joog, "It's amazing sometimes how help comes in the most surprising ways... and at just the right time."

He looked around.

"And where is he now? I'd like to meet him."

"He's gone," Flop explained, "Once he'd dug the pit he went off on his journey to Wizard Elzaphan."

Joog nodded. "I see. So it was a real team effort. And the pit did the job perfectly." Then he turned to Old

Howard. "Didn't it?"

Old Howard made an angry growl at him.

"That's so ingenious," said Joog, "It's... brilliant!"

Joog took off and glided a little distance away.

"Come over here, Flop. I want to tell you something... in private."

Flop trotted over to Joog with Miriam on his back.

"They're all fine," said Joog.

"Everyone?" asked Flop excitedly.

"Yes!" exclaimed Joog. Then he glanced at Old Howard and lowered his voice, "The ones in the boat that Old Howard saw were dummies... just copies of Seph, Amalek and all of us. I'll tell you more about it later."

"Oh! That's such a relief," Miriam squeaked.

Joog glided back to Old Howard and Flop followed. They looked at the pitiful sight of the poor old man trapped in the earth.

"Well, Old Howard," said Joog, "We must get going..."

"Help me!" cried Old Howard suddenly, "Please, oy'm sorry about what oy've done. And Oy'm sorry 'bout yer friends. Oy told you it was 'im. You should be blaming 'im not me! Please 'elp me out of here. You can't just leave me 'ere."

They could not help feeling sorry for Old Howard as he hung his head despondently. He looked a sad spectacle in the dull lamplight. They wondered what they should do about him. Suddenly the old man's hand jerked out and grabbed at Flop, catching him by the tail and swinging him into his body. Old Howard pulled his other arm around Flop and held him tightly.

"Got yer!" he shouted defiantly, and then desperately, "If you want him back get me out of 'ere."

For a moment everyone froze. Then Flop started wriggling frantically with all his strength, his sharp claws scrabbling at Old Howard arms.

"Keep still!" Old Howard shouted, gripping with all his might.

Joog took his chance, leapt into the air and his skilful flight was just a flash of white feathers. In an instant he was gripping Old Howard's arm like a branch, his sharp talons piercing the skin, and his beak pecking hard on the old man's hand. Old Howard cried out in pain and tried to shake the owl off. Flop wriggled free and fell to the ground, springing away in one jump. Joog released his grip and landed. They were all out of reach now and all Old Howard could do was to scowl at them and rub his bleeding arms.

"We'd better go," said Joog, "Even when he's trapped like that he's still trying to harm us. And the phantom wizard could reappear any second."

Flop was licking his fur, but he suddenly stopped and looked around. "And the ravens..."

"Yes, come on," Joog urged, taking to the air, "Quick! We must get to Keill Island and Wizard Elzaphan."

Miriam climbed onto Flop's back and he hurried off, running into the trees. Joog glided in the air above. They headed east, towards the River Ben, leaving Old Howard half buried in the earth, a forlorn and miserable sight, completely unable to free himself and wishing that he had not fallen for the trap.

The conversation a little earlier between Old Howard and the phantom Troubler was secretly overheard. Of course Joog, Flop and Miriam had listened to it from their hiding places, but there were two other eavesdroppers that none of them were aware of at all. For these covert listeners it was not easy to hear. In fact they missed most of the words and found it difficult to really work out what it was all about. The difficulty was that they were listening through the glass of a window. They were far away in The Kingdom of Gems where the night embraced the frozen land with a heavy darkness.

The two listeners were standing in the deep snow outside Old Howard's house. They were looking through the condensation that was misting up the window on the inside and into a room lit by a flickering oil-lamp resting on the wooden floor. Their eyes were fixed on the cloaked figure of the Dark Wizard Troubler as he stood in front of the cabinet mirror that was placed on a table. He stared intently into it. Through the mirror he was able to materialize in Summertime Kingdom, although it took great energy for him to achieve it. He was concentrating hard as he spoke to the image of Old Howard in the mirror. The two eavesdroppers were unicorns, one gold and the other silver. It was Aram and Halo.

By the house they were sheltered from the powerful wind as the large snowflakes danced and whirled around them.

"We've got to do something," whispered Halo.

"I know," Aram replied, "But we need to take care... great care."

"Yes, you're right," Halo whispered into his ear, "I wish we could hear what he's saying. Is that an old man in the mirror?"

"It's hard to see from here, especially with the window misted up," whispered Aram, moving his great head closer to the window, "It is an old man, and it looks like he's half buried!"

A glint of something bright on the other side of the room caught Aram's eye.

"Look at that…" he whispered, "over there. Look! It's a block of gold! I wonder why he's got that."

Halo looked and saw the large block by the far wall catching the flickering light of the lamp. She shook her head and her long mane shed a sprinkling of tiny bright silver sparks.

"I don't know…" she said, "We need to know more, don't we? We're having to guess."

Just then the image in the mirror faded, the wizard stepped back and turned his head towards the window. The two unicorns were not ready to confront the evil wizard, not yet, so they jerked their heads back quickly and Halo's nose brushed against the window pane.

"Let's go," she whispered urgently, "Quick!"

Aram glanced across the snow in the back garden.

"Oh no!" he exclaimed, "He'll see our tracks!"

The unicorns lowered their magic alicorns to point them at the tracks and smooth the snow, but at that moment the Troubler moved. In three strides he was beside the window and staring out.

"Quick!" whispered Aram.

The snow shifted and smoothed.

The Troubler thought he saw something move in the dark and lifted a hand to wipe away the condensation. He looked out again, his face close to the glass. Aram and Halo were just to his right, leaning as close to the wall as they could. One glance to the right and he would see them. He turned, grabbed the lamp and holding it up at the window cupped his hand by his eyes to shield them from the reflection.

"I'm slipping," whispered Halo.

She was leaning against Aram who was right against the wall and one of her hooves was slipping in the snow. Aram leant away from the wall to help Halo, and her balance held.

The wizard still had his face right against the window and the lamp was now blocking his view of the unicorns. He gazed with puzzlement at the snow which stretched away to the deep darkness of the trees at the end of the garden. He saw a few birds frozen in mid-air and now coated with snow, caught in flight when the spell was cast. They were completely still.

Had he seen something move? He could not be sure. However, he knew he had heard something, which is what brought him to the window. There should be nothing moving in the Kingdom of Gems, nothing at all. He had frozen all living things in his spell so there was nothing left that was free to move.

He stared out of the window, through the falling snow to the end of the garden and into the night. The unicorns kept as still as they could. As he peered out he squinted and moved the lamp up and down.

The only movement he could see was the swirling of the snow flakes. For a few moments he stared out as his black, ruthless eyes scanned and searched. Suddenly, he saw a movement in the trees at the end of the garden. His eyes widened to see some snow slipping off a branch and landing on the smooth carpet of snow below with a muffled noise. He relaxed, satisfied that he had found the source of the sound.

Tiredness washed through him. He desperately needed to rest after his time at the mirror. He walked back to his chair, collapsed into it and thought about the recent events.

The two magnificent unicorns breathed freely again and moved slowly along the wall of the house. They passed through some trees that formed the garden boundary to the east of Old Howard's house and into the full blast of the icy wind. As they walked across Shaky Field and headed for Candara they were a beautiful sight, expressing an exquisite balance of grace and power as they lifted their legs above the smooth snow in stately silence. Their manes shook and rippled in the snow-laden air which rushed by.

When they had crossed Shaky Field they turned and pointed their magic alicorns. Their tracks disappeared leaving the snow as smooth as a tabletop.

Halo nudged closer to Aram and spoke softly, "Do you think he saw us?"

"No," replied Aram. He lifted his head slightly and looked back at the house, "I don't think so."

They stood still and stared back across Shaky Field to check. The house was now a dark shape in the night. The wind drove large snowflakes into their gold and silver bodies, clinging and whitening their skin.

"We've been lucky," Halo concluded.

"Yes," agreed Aram, "We don't want him suspecting that we're here. He probably thinks we're in Summertime Kingdom with the others."

"And that..." added Halo, "That gives us the advantage of surprise."

Aram nodded. "Yes, and we'll have to work out how best to surprise him."

They turned and continued walking through the driving snow and the wintry landscape towards Candara.

Soon after Old Howard had been left alone, he heard sounds in the air behind him. He was unable to twist his head around enough to see them, but he recognized their raucous noises and knew it was the ravens. The sounds became louder and soon they were all landing around him, busy black shapes in the dark, the whole of the Female Squadron of over fifty ravens. They stared at him in amazement, and laughed, and pointed with their wings by the dim flickering light of the oil lamp. One raven even landed on Old Howard's head much to the amusement of the others. The old man scowled and swept it off with a wave of his uninjured hand. He looked around at the ravens as they cackled and laughed at him.

"Alroyt, alroyt," said Old Howard, his face turning red with growing frustration. He had been filled with self-pity until the arrival of these ravens and now the sharp edge of anger was welling up inside him. "Oy know it looks funny," he snapped. "But it ain't very noyce stuck 'ere in all this earth."

This just made the ravens laugh at him even more and a couple of them pecked at him from behind.

"Instead of laughing, get me out!" he bellowed.

With his sudden shout the laughing stopped and they fell quiet. Searle stepped forwards. She was the proud Captain of the Female Squadron.

"Now, Old Howard," she began, "We could get you

out or we could not. It all depends on what you tell us."

"That's right," said Urrg, stepping forwards as well. She had been upset since the General had sacked her and appointed Searle in her place. "Last time you tricked us - sent us the wrong way." Searle was watching her intently as she spoke. "You sent us south beyond Burney's Hill instead…"

"Get back in the ranks!" shouted Searle.

"But I can help," said Urrg, "I want to hel…"

"Now!" Searle snapped and Urrg reluctantly stepped back, glaring at Searle with envy and hate. Searle stared back with equal venom and then said sharply, "Remember what the General said? I'm to tell him if you give me any trouble? Now… where was I?" She turned back to face Old Howard. "Oh yes, I know. We could help you out if we want to. But we need some information first."

"Then oy'll tell yer," said Old Howard desperately, "You ask an' oy'll tell yer."

"Where is she?" asked Searle.

"Who?"

"The Princess of course, and the birds," Searle sounded impatient.

"*She's* dead. I saw 'er washed away by the wave… remember? You were there too."

"The Prince is dead, yes, but not the Princess. She seemed dead, but no, they tricked you and she got away to travel in this direction. I think you know. Now tell us!"

"Oy don't know, oy tell yer. Oy think you've got it wrong. She is dead. But the cat, mouse and the owl, I seen 'em 'an they did this to me!"

"The cat and the mouse? Oh yes… yes… I remember now… we heard that you'd captured a cat. And there's a mouse as well, is there? Hmm… and both killed I presume?" Searle enquired.

"Oy did capture 'em! But they escaped an' did this to me. Now get me out!"

"Not so fast," said Searle thoughtfully, and she shook her head as she thought it through. This was complicated and she was struggling to grasp it all. "The most important question of all is this; where are they now?"

"Will you get me out if oy tell yer?"

"Of course," Searle nodded.

"They went west, not too long ago. That way." He pointed with a grimy hand. "Now will yer get me out?" he pleaded.

"Yes, but you have to earn it," said Searle.

Old Howard scowled in anger, "You jus' said you'd get me out!"

"We will," she said calmly, "But, as I said, you have to earn it."

Old Howard screwed up his face in frustration.

"What now?" he grumbled.

"If we find them, then we will come back and free you. If we don't, we will still come back and punish you for your trickery."

"Look, oy am tellin' the truth," he pleaded, but Searle was no longer listening to him.

"Females," shouted Searle, "Attennnnnn…tion."

They all stood still with their beaks pointing forwards.

"Take off!"

"Why would oy lie to yer?" Old Howard shouted.

The ravens were taking off now, and quickly disappearing into the night.

"Come back! Come back!" he yelled after them.

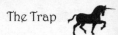

Once again, he slammed a fist, this time just the uninjured one, into the earth that held him prisoner.

Chapter 2

~ Jamaar's Journey ~

Jamaar's journey through the Kingdom of Gems was not an easy one. He had been sent by his master, the Dark Wizard Troubler, on a journey into Summertime Kingdom. His mission was to hunt for any survivors of the great wave and if he found any he must kill them.

Night surrounded him and the cold wind pushed hard against him, whipping the driving snow into his face. The snow fell layer upon layer and it was such a depth now that most of the time it was about as high as his neck and he had to use his chest to plough through as best he could. He found, however, that his mighty legs were so strong that he hardly felt tired and he began to enjoy it. At times he could run, but sometimes the snow would tumble in around him and he would have to fight his way free. Then suddenly, where the snow was deeper, he would find he was actually making a tunnel under it as he ran, but soon it would compact in front of him and he would have to dig out.

Every so often he stopped briefly to rest and check that he was travelling in the right direction because he had added a plan of his own to the instructions of his master. This plan involved a detour from the direct northerly route he had been ordered to take.

The black compass, which hung around his neck on a chain, was glowing slightly in the dark. The Troubler had told him it was a guide and certainly the light it was shedding was allowing him to see a few steps ahead. It was guiding him through the dark and moonless night and he would have been far more hesitant without it.

He was heading for Silvermay Forest. It was not much of a detour and afterwards he would soon be able to get back on route, but he wanted to check something that was important to him. After all he was sure that the Troubler would never know that he was deviating from his commands. So he headed off into the heart of the forest and towards the Silver Well where he had buried some treasured possessions just under the ground. He was particularly glad now that he had chosen this spot because the snow made every place look the same, but the Silver Well would stand out and be easy to find, even in the dark.

He followed a path through the trees. He was out of breath after all the exertion and his heaving chest blew air in and out, making small clouds around his head. Snow clung to his black fur but he was warm after running. He knew the forest well because when he was a wandering stray he often ran through the forest hunting for small animals to eat.

After a while he came to the clearing, ducked under a bird frozen in mid-air and stopped to gaze across the smooth blanket of snow. The compass glowed softly, lighting up the area dimly, and in the semi-light he saw the glittering of silver. Stepping forwards with his paw slipping into the snow with a gentle crunch, he could clearly see the Silver Well. It shone here and there where the silver was exposed.

Trees sheltered the clearing from the bitter wind and snow fell gently in large flakes. Jamaar stood for a brief moment staring across the open space and at the well. It was a large well and the hole in the middle was exceptionally wide. A snow-covered wooden roof sheltered it and this was supported by two wooden posts. There was no bucket or pulley any more because it had not been used for drawing water for many years. It was deep, dropping to a great distance below the ground.

After Jamaar's frantic efforts through the snow, the clearing was strangely still. There was snow piled up against one side of the well where it had drifted in the wind and snow was layered on the top of the circular silver wall like a fluffy ermine scarf. He jumped the last few steps to the well and stood beside it. He took three paces towards a particular tree, followed by another half step and then stopped. Then he remembered how he had grown bigger and stronger which made his strides bigger too and so he stepped backwards half a step. He decided this was the place and began to dig furiously.

Snow flew through the air like a fountain and once he had broken through the frozen crust of earth, then soil followed as he scrabbled away with remarkable energy.

Suddenly, he stopped. He nodded slowly with pleasure as he looked down at the shallow hole he had dug.

"Ah, yes," he said softly to himself.

His hard work had revealed three small waterproof canvas bags rolled up to keep the contents safe inside. He lifted them out of the hole with his mouth and placed them carefully on the snow.

He opened the first bag, nudging it across the snow with his nose until it had unrolled. He pushed open the mouth of the bag with his muzzle and pulled out a bone. He could not resist a couple of quick chews before he put it to one side. Then he sniffed inside the bag and the wonderful smell of his favourite dog biscuits filled his nostrils. He wagged the remainder of his tail, now just a short stump since Horrik, his master's komodo dragon, had spat at him in the cellar of Old Howard's house. Her bacterial saliva had hit his tail and over half of it had fallen off but there was still enough left to wag.

He had stolen this food and buried it in case of an emergency. But now, on smelling it, and the bone, he felt that he could not resist eating it. He smelled them again and nearly began eating but decided he would save it until he had opened the other bags.

He unrolled the next bag with his front paws this time and again nuzzled into the top with his nose to open it. He looked inside to check the contents: two gold necklaces, half a dozen rings of gold and silver, some earrings and three broaches with precious stones decorating them. These were stolen from the people of Candara and he gazed greedily into the bag like a miser selfishly enjoying his worldly wealth. He took them out, gripping them one by one in his teeth, laid them carefully on top of the bag and admired them glimmering and sparkling in the light of the compass around his neck.

Then he came to the third and last bag. The content of this bag was also stolen and again from someone in the town; it was the object that he had stolen when he crept into Darsan and Harraine Lopery's house bent on revenge. He had been foraging in Darsan's desk for something to steal and had found it in a drawer. At the time, he had considered his theft almost a complete failure but after recent events he realized that it might have great significance. He needed to see the object again and check that what he suspected was correct.

He felt a sense of anticipation and excitement as he unrolled the third canvas bag. The thought of what this was thrilled him and frightened him at the same time and he held his breath as the bag opened. Fluffy flakes of snow settled in white dots on the bag as he pushed his muzzle in, gently grasped the object in his teeth and lifted out a small item wrapped in a black velvet bag. The edge of the bag was decorated with a delicate pattern of fine silver thread. He laid it carefully on the snow and then slipped it out of the bag.

There it was, just as he remembered, a black compass on a black chain. He let the one around his neck dangle down beside it to compare and just as he had thought they were identical. He looked from one to the other, comparing and checking to make absolutely sure. There was no doubt about it and this made his feelings of excitement and fear intensify. He turned it over and there was the coat of arms, his master's coat of arms, etched in silver on the back. He lowered his great head to study it more carefully and a shiver of uneasiness ran down his spine. He shook his head in disbelief as he observed to his surprise that the coat of arms was *not* the same! It was indeed almost identical but something was different. It had the same sinister gloom about it and the symbols were also the same - except for one - but in the dim light he could not see what it was.

"What does it mean?" he thought, *"What have I found? Why did Darsan Lopery have it? Has it got some special powers? How can I use it?"*

He felt confused, puzzled and afraid, but also elated at the mysterious object that was now in his possession. He studied the coat of arms again, dropping his head even lower so that he could pick out all the detail. Then he received yet another shock. There, clearly engraved in the top right section, was a komodo dragon.

The compass suddenly made a small movement and Jamaar jerked his head up in surprise. Then a clinking sound behind him made him jump and he spun around. Horrik was bearing down on him. Her mighty jaws were open with poisonous saliva dribbling around her rows of dagger-like teeth and hanging from her mouth. The remains of the chain, which had tethered her for so long, were still hanging around her thickset neck and it shook whenever she moved.

Jamaar managed somehow, using all his strength, to leap back as the massive jaws snapped at him, missing him by a whisker. He felt a few drops of the deadly saliva sprinkle his face so he shook his head hoping to shake it off but immediately smelt burning fur.

Horrik stared at Jamaar. Her eyes, usually deep black, were now reflecting the glow of the compass like discs of light in the darkness. Her long, thin, forked tongue shot out of her mouth and in again. Saliva hung down from her massive jaws.

"I hate you!" she roared, "And now you'll pay!" She glanced at the jewellery lying on the bag just in front of her. "And what's this!" she exclaimed, "Is this yours?"

She scooped up the jewellery and the bag in her great mouth and swallowed. Jamaar looked on in horror.

"Were those important to you?" she asked.

She had swallowed everything except for one silver necklace which had caught on her teeth and hung out of her mouth. She jerked her head up and back and swallowed again.

"Well…" she sneered, "Now your little collection of riches has gone. And you're next!"

"What have I done?" Jamaar shouted back, totally shocked to see her and wondering how she had escaped.

"Everything," she roared, "You took my place!"

"I'm sure we can work it out," pleaded Jamaar.

"No! I've suffered too much due to you. You took my place!" Her eyes looked wild and filled with disgust. "You tried to kill me with that fire, remember? Well… now it's my turn! I've been listening to you padding around to your master's every beck and call for too long." Then she added, her voice loaded with sarcasm. "Do you get his slippers for him?"

As she spoke she jerked towards Jamaar who retreated towards the well.

Suddenly, Horrik lunged at him again and as she did she stumbled over the other bags and the chain of the black compass became tangled around the claws of one of her front feet. Jamaar barked fiercely and bared his teeth, his fur standing on end on his back.

"You don't frighten me at all!" said Horrik, consumed by anger as she lunged towards him, "Just a lot of noise. I could eat you for breakfast!"

"And you don't scare me!" Jamaar shouted back as he stepped towards the well.

But he was lying. He was terrified by this massive vicious creature, even with his new strong body. She made him feel weak. Jamaar retreated again and jumped onto the wall of the well to try to get a position of advantage. Snow sprayed off the wall and tumbled into it. He was now under the wooden roof and felt protected because she was too big to fit under it. He looked down at Horrik and barked ferociously.

She made a terrific leap at him, smashing into one of the wooden posts. The roof collapsed and shattered, parts of it falling down the well and other bits flying off and landing in the snow. Jamaar reacted by jumping off the wall, once again just in time to avoid another snap of the huge, venomous jaws. Horrik's huge frame landed on the well. She spanned across the gaping hole, with her two front feet on one side and her back feet on the other. Her forked tongue repeatedly flashed in and out of her mouth as she glared at Jamaar with loathing and roared at him.

Jamaar began a rapid retreat across the snow, whilst looking back at the dragon over his shoulder. Then something extraordinary happened. The black compass that was still tangled around Horrik's leg, started glowing and then, amazingly, began to tug at her. Horrik was surprised and momentarily distracted, so Jamaar plucked up courage and took his opportunity. He rushed past Horrik who was shaking a leg to try to get the compass off. In a flash he was behind her and snapping at her. At the second attempt, his sharp teeth sank into her tail, piercing through the rugged scaly skin.

Horrik roared in pain and shook her massive tail to

get free, but Jamaar held on with brawny tenacity. Then he pulled with all his might and with a jerk her front legs slipped off the wall, her claws scraping downwards on the silver on the inside of the wall with her head dropping into the hole. Her whole body tilted like a see-saw, pulling Jamaar upwards until he was clinging on with only his back legs on the snowy ground. Then he realized that by holding on he was stopping her falling in and instantly he let go.

Fear flashed in Horrik's eyes as she realized with a pang of horror what was happening and there was nothing she could do to stop it. She was falling into the well.

With another great roar of anguish, her head descended further as her long tail lifted up. She just fitted into the cavernous hole. As she fell her feet scrabbled hopelessly at the slippery, rock walls with her tough claws scraping on the sides and trying to find a grip in vain. Despite her frantic efforts, the great weight of her massive body was unstoppable. As she fell, her agonized roar echoed around the walls of the well and Jamaar stared in astonishment. He kept still, listening. The sounds of her roar, as well as her feet scraping against the sides, faded away and then there was silence.

Horrik had plummeted into the depths. Jamaar listened and heard nothing.

He jumped to his feet and stepped through the snow to the well. He stood on his back legs to lean against the silver wall and cautiously peeped over. He was panting after the fight and felt cold flakes of snow landing on his tongue and dissolving. He almost expected Horrik to rise up and snap at him with her massive jaws. He looked over the wall, down the hole and into the darkness far below. She was gone. Relief flooded his mind. He felt a couple of scales from Horrik's tail in his mouth and spat them out and down the well in a gesture of contempt.

It had all happened so quickly. Jamaar felt stunned by the vicious attack that had taken him completely by surprise. He was also bewildered by the revelation of the black compass, not only that it was in fact the same as the one around his neck at the moment, but there were also other mysteries surrounding it. Why was the coat of arms similar but different? Why did Darsan Lopery have possession of it? It must have some sort of special powers. With his head spinning with questions that he could not answer, he stood in the falling snow by the well. The compass was gone now anyway, caught around Horrik's leg as she fell to her doom.

Everything seemed so still after the furious activity of the fight. He peered cautiously over the wall again, with his front paws resting on the silver. Once again he half expected Horrik to rise out and attack. He gazed down into the dark depths and thought.

After a few moments he let his front paws drop onto the snow and breathed a sigh of relief in the satisfaction that Horrik had gone. Then he remembered the bag of delicious dog biscuits and the bone. He sniffed around in the snow and quickly found it, pulled it out and guzzled them greedily in a few seconds. Then he attacked the bone with equal enthusiasm. He crunched it in his powerful jaws until it had all gone.

He was beginning to feel cold so he shook his body rigorously to release the snow frozen to his fur. It sprayed off like sparks from a firework and splattered onto the soft snow.

Feeling a slight burning sensation on his head he

remembered the saliva that had flown out of Horrik's massive jaws and onto his head. It was only a matter of tiny droplets but the stinging was growing so he rubbed his head vigorously in the snow. The stinging faded, soothed by the snow as the deadly saliva was washed away.

He looked around to get his bearings. By the light of the compass around his neck he could just see the trees at the edge of the clearing. The snow descended steadily and silently, a mass of flakes, gray in the dim light, gusting just slightly here and there, playing around each other as they filled the air. He turned his mind away from Horrik and the fight and back to his journey. He knew he must set off again.

Glancing back he saw the two remaining canvas bags, already nearly hidden by the falling snow. They were both empty now. In the past few minutes he had lost all his secret possessions. It had taken him some years to build up his collection of jewellery and in one moment they were all gone. He released a little howl of pain as he thought about it.

Then there was the compass. He sensed that this was a special find, a rare and possibly very powerful instrument. This was gone too. At least he had enjoyed the biscuits and the bone.

The compass around his neck gave a little jerk making him jump with surprise. Jamaar tilted his head on one side.

"What was that for?" he asked the compass.

He walked across the clearing towards the trees, his great paws gently crunching into the snow. He took one last fleeting look back at the well and then ran off between the trees and along the snow covered forest paths to continue his journey. As he ran, he thought about the black compasses. He tried to work out what it all meant but found that he did not have enough information and that all he could do was try to guess.

He noticed that the compass hanging around his thick-set neck was not only glowing but it was now warm. As he ran, it pulled slightly forwards in a northerly direction and every so often it made a little jump towards the north. Just as the Troubler had said it would, it was guiding him.

Flop, Miriam and Joog wanted to hide their plans from Old Howard and make him think that they were travelling west, so as soon as they felt they were definitely well clear, they stopped and followed the River Ben southwards. Then they turned and circled around Burney's Hill until they were due north of the place where Old Howard was trapped in the earth. They started moving northwards towards the Little River Sween and when they reached its banks they turned left to follow it to the meeting of the two Sween rivers, the little and the great. It was now deep into the night and the moon looked down on them from the black starry sky like a pale watchful eye. They were feeling tired.

As they traveled along the southern bank of the Little River Sween the sound of gently splashing water grew louder. It was the place where the two rivers joined and the merging of the waters agitated the surface creating a multitude of little frothy waves and whirlpools.

When they reached this place, Joog landed on a rock

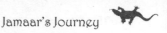

and Flop stood beside him. Miriam had been asleep on Flop's neck and woke up at the sound of their voices. She peeped out from his fur.

"Where are we?" she squeaked, "Where are we?"

"The Great River Sween," Flop replied as he gazed across the water.

The moon's reflection shimmercd on the black water, broken up into a million sparkles of light. It was a peaceful scene.

"We ought to sleep," Joog announced, "We could get a few hours before dawn."

"Definitely," Flop agreed, sitting down and purring, "It's beautifully warm here... lovely. But I'm so tired."

"We all are," added Joog, "And when we've slept then we'll continue with the plan in the morning."

Miriam turned to Joog. "What plan?" she asked.

"Oh, yes," Joog said, blinking slowly, "Flop and I made a plan but you missed it whcn you were sleeping. We'll tell you in a minute."

He lifted a wing to point.

"There," he continued, "The perfect place for you two." He was pointing at a nearby prickly bush. "And I'll keep watch."

Flop walked over to the bush to investigate.

"Yes, perfect," he agreed and slipped through the branches. He was completely concealed inside. Then his head poked out. "If you need some sleep after a couple of hours, Joog, I can take over the watch."

Miriam peeped out, "I'll help too," she said.

"I'll be fine," answered Joog, "I can maybe doze a little. Good night."

"Good night," chorused Flop and Miriam together.

Flop explained the plan to Miriam and then they

quickly slipped into a restful sleep.

Hopping along the northern bank of the Great River Sween was a young mountain hare. It was Tally who had left his home high in the Becci Mountains with his strong young heart set upon helping the fight against the Dark Wizard Troubler. His old grandfather, Hawkeye, had given him encouragement as well as wise advice before he had set out on his adventure.

Pale moonlight lit the scene along the Great River Sween, falling upon her banks like the soft and tender touch of an artist's hand. A shimmering path of light, the moon's reflection, rested on the darkness of the wide waters as the current sped westward. Further down the river to the west, after the place where Old Howard had created the great wave, all the plants and flowers had been flattened, but here the banks were still adorned with moon-lit flowers. The scene was beautiful and calm.

Tally was heading for Wizard Elzaphan's Castle to offer his help to the great wizard. On his way he had spotted Flop from the top of Burney's Hill, saw he was in trouble, and went to help. Having dug the pit for Flop and Miriam he left to continue his journey. With his large feet and strong rear legs he was a good powerful swimmer and able to cross the two rivers, the Little Sween and then the Great Sween, without too much trouble.

As he sped along the bank, the warm air blew past his face and quickly dried his fur. He knew that he would have to turn northward and pass through the Forest of the

Fairies and he was just beginning to worry that he may have gone too far. The last thing he wanted was to lose his direction and get lost. He felt tired and uncertain. He skidded to a halt and sniffed the air, his nose twitching as he tried to pick up a scent. His mind was turning with thoughts. He had been so calm and clear before, but now doubt was clouding his awareness.

"KYWAY."

The word rang clearly in the air around him. He looked around. Then he heard it again.

"KYWAY, Tally, KYWAY."

He realized it was in his mind too. It was the gentle loving sound of Hawkeye's voice, the voice of his grandfather. There was no doubt about it. He had heard it several times before on this journey and he instantly remembered what it meant: Keep Your Wits About You. Now, as before, a refreshing wave of clarity washed through him. His senses opened out. Now he could smell clearly. His sight was sharp. He paused, feeling strong again.

All of a sudden he knew what to do. He had to turn now and he knew the direction too. This knowledge, totally absent a few moments before, was now clear and certain.

He turned north away from the river, hopped over a fallen branch and into the darkness of the forest. He moved quickly through the ever-thickening ferns and as he travelled further into the forest the trees became denser and the shadows deepened. The moon shone through the small gaps in the branches and leaves above, throwing occasional patches of pale light on the ground below.

Tally had good young eyes and found that he could see well enough in the scanty light. Since he had heard his grandfather's voice he felt happy again. His youthful heart was lifted.

He travelled for a while before he spotted a suitable place to rest. It was a hollow tree trunk with a hole in the bark of just the right size for him to squeeze in. He snuggled down inside and quickly drifted off to sleep.

From his home high above the snow line in the Becci Mountains, Hawkeye gazed out over the moonlit scene. He was old now, the oldest hare in the whole group, but his eyesight was still better than any of the others. Years ago, when he was very young and just learning his first few words, he had spotted a hunting hawk before any of the other hares and raised the alarm.

"Hawk! Hawk! Hawk!" he had cried.

None of the others believed him and they laughed in fun at the playful imagination of the baby hare, until the hawk attacked and carried off one of them. Since that day he was famous for his extraordinary ability to see great distances and the other Hares began to call him Hawkeye. Today, as the curtain of time began to draw closed on his life, he could see as well as ever.

The passing years had made him wise. This was not only due to his rich experience of life but because he had lived well. He had always followed what he believed to be right and faced difficult situations with a strong and happy heart. But he was also humble and sensitive to others. He was not the official leader of the group of seventy three hares living here, but he was the wisest.

Hawkeye had awoken in the night with a feeling of concern for Tally and had immediately climbed out of his burrow. Since Tally had left he had been mapping the young hare's journey in his mind and now he looked towards the place where he thought he might be.

He looked out beyond the falling slopes of the mountains and towards Burney's Hill. The pale moonlight shone down on the land spread out in front of him, taming the darkness and glittering on the surface of Lake Jin. But he could see no further than this.

As he gazed at the scene he thought of Tally, his grandson who he had brought up and who he loved so dearly, and wondered how he was faring in his journey to Wizard Elzaphan. He felt so close to him that he would sometimes speak aloud to him when he felt instinctively that Tally needed help.

After a while the feeling of concern for Tally that had woken him up, grew stronger.

"KYWAY," he had said.

A tear of love had trickled from his eye. He wished he could be there to help his grandson.

"KYWAY, Tally, KYWAY."

Then, almost straight away, his heart lightened. He knew Tally was alright. Tally was fine.

He turned slowly with a contented feeling in his heart and went back into his burrow.

Jamaar was very pleased when he finally reached the border. He had become used to running through the snow and his muscular legs carried him with powerful strides. Soon he was racing along at a strong pace through the fierce wintry blizzard that surrounded him.

He knew the Snowpeak Mountains well and had stayed in the valleys until he had entered the great Mularn Tunnel. He had discovered the hidden entrance to this ancient route accidentally a few months earlier and lived there for a whole week before returning to his wandering life of scavenging around the kingdom. By running through the Mularn Tunnel and so avoiding the blizzard he made his journey much faster. It was dark but fortunately the light of the compass shed a pale glow and showed him the tunnel floor a few steps ahead which was all he needed. Soon he had emerged onto the flat Northern Borderlands, leaving him in sight of Summertime Kingdom.

When he reached the border he stopped and paused. Snow whipped past him in the icy, howling gale. For a moment he stood in the snow, panting heavily with his tongue lolling out of his mouth. Behind him, beyond the Northern Borderlands, rose the great masses of the Snowpeak Mountains, while in front Summertime Kingdom stretched away in gently undulating slopes. It was an extraordinary contrast.

Then he spotted a frozen bird just above the snow and not far from him along the border. He jumped through the deep snow until he was right next to it. He was hungry and this was not a small bird but quite a reasonable size; it was a magpie. He opened his mouth and tried to bite into it, tentatively at first and then harder. He heard his teeth grind on the rock-hard surface. Straight away he gave up and looked across the border again. The magpie had disappointed him but he was immediately cheered up when he realized that across the border everything was normal. He could find something to eat there.

Just a few feet away the snow ended abruptly. He walked forwards and then jumped across, out of the stormy snow-filled land and into the balmy still air of Summertime Kingdom. The sound of the howling blizzard had suddenly gone and was replaced by a silence that seemed tangible.

The night air felt beautifully warm and he flopped down to enjoy a moment of rest that he felt he had well deserved. He lay there panting on the grass for a few minutes as the snow on his fur melted quickly. Standing up he checked his compass by clicking it open and holding it flat on a paw. He remembered that the needle always pointed north and he turned slightly to align his body with it, pointing his nose directly north. Then he snapped it shut and let it hang again around his brawny neck. It jerked northward.

"Right," he said.

He headed off on his hunting mission, quickly settling into a steady comfortable trot across the dark and quietly rolling slopes of Summertime Kingdom.

Old Howard had never felt so frustrated. He felt abandoned, firstly by the ravens who were supposed to be on his side and now by the Dark Wizard Troubler. The wizard had said he would return in his ghostly form to get him out and now all Old Howard could do was wait. His predicament had left him completely helpless. The lamp flickered and dimmed as the oil ran out, until the flame died and he was plunged into darkness.

The pallid light of the moon tamed the night but the shadows were deep. He could hear the sounds of nocturnal creatures without seeing what was making the noises. His imagination ran riot as he twitched and turned, thinking that he would be attacked at any moment. In this way the night passed without Old Howard getting even a wink of sleep.

He was extremely relieved when he saw the dawn light begin to brighten the sky, but his relief was short-lived as the frustration rose in him again. He was getting desperate. Where was the Troubler when he needed him? Would he come back at all? He imagined that he must have gone to rest and regain his power but he wished he would appear again. Old Howard was beginning to lose feeling in his legs now. The rising sun reflected brightly on his forehead and beads of sweat ran down his face.

Suddenly the frustration grew too much and he clenched his teeth together in anger and closed his eyes tightly. Then he opened his mouth wide and let out a great cry of anguish.

"Old Howard," said the calm, quiet voice of the phantom Troubler.

Old Howard opened his eyes to see the phantom right in front of him.

"Stop your grumbling and shouting, old man."

The phantom looked much more solid than before but was still see-through.

"I'm so glad yer back," Old Howard blurted out, looking very relieved, "Now you can get me out, can't yer?"

"Not so fast, my friend..."

"Oh no!" he groaned, his face wrinkling up again in

disappointment, "What is it now? What d'yer mean 'not so fast'?"

"Be quiet," hissed the phantom, "It seems..."

"You promised," interrupted Old Howard, "You promised to get me..."

"Stop all your silly babbling!" the phantom snapped. His words stabbed into Old Howard like poisonous darts. The old man stopped instantly, frightened by the wizard, and listened. "I am extremely concerned about your failure to complete the tasks I give you successfully. At Marrin Bridge they got away... failure..."

"But not all of 'em," blurted Old Howard, "The unicorns... oy got 'em both..."

"Maybe," the phantom said slowly, "Maybe you did and maybe you didn't... we don't know do we? You didn't see them fall into the crack did you? You're just guessing. Maybe they did fall in but on the other hand, if they didn't, they could be anywhere and that is a matter of concern to me..."

"The Princess," Old Howard interrupted desperately, "Oy got 'er didn't oy? Before the magic got 'er out? But that's not moy fault is it."

He looked at the phantom with pleading eyes.

"As you yourself say, she got out, so even *that* failed. When I sent you to catch the Prince you came back with that stupid cat... failure. The Princess would have done, but no, you come back with a cat! Then, after that, you don't kill the cat when I tell you to... failure. And then it escapes... failure again. And then, unbelievably, they even trap you... yet another failure."

Old Howard shook his head and frowned.

"What about the wave?" he shouted, "That worked! They were drowned. Oy saw 'em washed away by the

wave! Oy know that the owl escaped 'cos oy saw it...
and the ravens mentioned the Princess... but the rest...
all dead. Oy saw it!"

"Well..." and then the phantom lowered his voice to
almost a whisper, his words hissing out with venom,
"This is interesting... the Princess and the owl escaped.
Who told you?"

"The ravens... some of them... the females... they
told me."

"So... *that*... the great wave... was a failure too!"
The wizard's words cut into Old Howard who cringed
inside. "That is the worst of all, at the river, where the
wave was meant to finish them off, well they tricked you
again... failure."

"But... but..." stammered Old Howard in fear, "The
Prince is dead."

"Yes," the phantom said, shimmering in anger until it
was a little more solid, "It is good that the Prince is dead,
but you were meant to deal with them all." The Troubler
glared with even more intensity at Old Howard. "I cannot
get the Candara Gems until they are all dead...
understand?"

Old Howard nodded.

"I need those gems and now you have failed to kill
the Princess... *and* the cat... *and* the owl. Even the
unicorns may be alive."

Old Howard looked stunned and pale.

The phantom continued with his eyes fixed on the old
man. "It's a sad story of failures. One after the other.
Your record of failures is extraordinary and I have a good
mind to leave you here to rot!"

"No!" Old Howard looked terrified.

"But, this time, I will give you another chance... but

only one. One… more… chance. Do you understand?"

"Yeah," Old Howard said, grumpily.

"I don't know why I'm so generous," the phantom hissed, "But this time you must succeed. Will you try harder?"

"Yeah, yeah, oy'll try 'arder," said the frightened old man. The phantom stared at him until he added, "Oy'll try *much* 'arder."

"Alright then, I'll get you out, then I'll set you your next task, but this time, you must not fail me!"

Old Howard nodded in resigned agreement. At that moment they both looked up as they heard the cackling sounds of a flock of ravens approaching and swooping down towards them. The phantom turned back to Old Howard.

"Good," he said, "So that's agreed. These ravens will dig you out."

Old Howard sighed with great relief in the knowledge that in the next few minutes he would be freed from his earthy prison.

Flop woke to the sound of singing birds against the background of the splashing and gurgling of the meeting of flowing waters. They had slept just south of the place where the Great River Sween joined the Little River Sween. The dawn chorus filled the warm air as the bright new day banished the night. A light mist hung above the water and reached up over the grassy banks.

"Miriam? Are you awake?" Flop said.

He felt a movement in the fur on the back of his neck.

"I am now," she replied.

Flop stretched his front legs and looked out of the bush. He saw Joog standing on the rock and gazing the other way. Joog's head turned 180° and looked straight at Flop with his great watchful eyes.

"I was just thinking about waking you two," he said happily, "Because I need to get going."

"The sooner the better," said Flop, now stretching his back legs.

"I shouldn't be long, but what about you?"

"We'll be alright," said Flop brightly, "We'll just wait here until you get back."

"Alright," Joog replied cheerily, "But be careful. Those ravens could be anywhere."

"Do you think he'll still be there?" asked Miriam.

"Most likely," Joog replied, "He is a ferryman so let's hope so. If not then we'll have to change our plans and cut up through the Forest of the Fairies."

"I wonder what's happened to the others," Miriam said anxiously as she looked towards the forest.

"Oh, they're probably well on their way by now," Joog said, stretching out his wings, "On their way to Wizard Elzaphan, I mean. I hope so. Anyway, I'd better go. I won't be long."

With a couple of flaps of his strong wings he took off and flew west directly above the Great River Sween.

A few hours earlier, at midnight, Jamaar had decided to

sleep for about four hours and then he had resumed his journey at a steady pace. He headed directly northwards as he had been told, stopping only occasionally. The first time was to drink some water from a pool and quench his thirst. As he was drinking, a passing vole caught his eye. He sprang after it, ambushed it by a tree and devoured it quickly.

After his meal he travelled on with extra vigour, stopping again after a while to rest and check the direction on the black compass just to make sure he was still heading north. He was beginning to trust the jerky little movements of the compass more and more. As he ran it was still pulling forwards, guiding him in the right direction. He was extremely pleased with his strong muscular legs as they carried him along relentlessly to his destination.

When dawn arrived he was feeling as strong as ever and it was not long before he heard the sound that told him he could begin the hunt. It was the sound of the Great River Sween. He carried on pounding the ground with his sturdy legs until it came into view and then he slowed down to a walk to approach it with caution.

He sniffed the air and thought he caught a scent. For a moment he stood still and then crouched low into the long grass. Slowly he began to approach the river. The compass jerked to the right. At first he ignored it, but when it juddered even harder he turned, still hiding in the grass, and started creeping eastwards along the river. Again his sensitive nose picked up a scent in the air and then he heard a sound. It was the sound of something splashing. He stood still and listened... splash... splash... splash. Then he recognized it. It was the clear distinctive rhythm of oars dipping in and out of the water. There was no doubt about it.

Very slowly he raised his head above the grass and

saw a boat heading upstream, already past him, and speeding away quickly. He saw a hooded figure rowing and the back of an owl, a snowy owl, sitting opposite the rower, facing each other. They were deep in conversation. He quickly dipped his head into the grass and out of sight; he did not want to be seen.

"Quick!" he thought as his saliva began to run, *"I must follow… a snowy owl, yes! I have found a survivor, the one most likely if any to survive a great wave. Why not? If he had just got air-borne somehow… it makes sense. Also the compass has guided me to them! Yes, I must hunt them. My master said hunt thoroughly!"*

He started following, hiding in the grass and behind trees and bushes, but keeping them in sight. He knew that a good hunter waited for the right opportunity and did not strike too early. This is what he would do. He would wait until exactly the right time, the right opportunity, and then he would strike. After that he would return to his master with his trophy.

Flop and Miriam looked anxiously along the Great River Sween. Surely Joog should be back by now. The sun was rising in the sky and it bathed everything below in warmth and light. Flop would have loved to stretch out on the grass and soak up the heat, but he knew they could not relax for a moment. They felt, somehow, that they were being watched and so they needed to stay alert at all times. The ravens might suddenly appear and swoop down upon them and Flop knew that they were easy to spot from above.

"We ought to hide, Miriam," he said.

"Back in the bush?" she asked.

Before Flop could reply they heard a noise behind them. They spun around and what they saw made them jump with surprise. There, just emerging from the shade of a tree, walking towards them, padding gently along, was a young elephant. It looked older than a baby elephant but not fully grown with the height of its head about five feet and its trunk swinging playfully as it approached them. Two canvas bag hung by its sides, supported by two straps which rested across its broad back. They could hardly believe their eyes as it drew near and they were not sure what they should do.

"Hello," said the elephant in a very friendly way.

Flop crouched low to the ground, alert and ready to spring into action.

"Don't be afraid," the elephant said, slowing her walk as she came closer.

She stopped a few feet away and turned her head slightly to look at them with one eye and they saw it was a most extraordinary bright blue. Everything about her was friendly. The kind look in her eye, the sound of her voice, even the way she had moved towards them, placing her feet so gently down on the grass. She seemed to hold no threat.

Flop relaxed and was just about to say "Hello" back when something made him crouch again. His sharp eyes had spotted something else.

"Look!" he exclaimed.

He was staring back in the direction of Burney's Hill. Flying towards them was a great flock of black ravens. Flop shuddered with fear. He knew they should have hidden whilst they had the chance but now it was too late.

"Under the elephant," squeaked Miriam, "Quick!"

Flop jumped up and ran under the young elephant. It was the perfect hiding place. The elephant stood still and spoke quietly to them.

"Just keep still," she said, "And I'll stay still too. I'm Lazuli." Then she whispered to them, "I'm on your side."

As the ravens approached they heard them cackling in harsh, callous voices.

"Search," screeched Searle, the captain of the Female Squadron, "Search for the enemy. Scan, scan, scan the ground."

"Scan the ground!" echoed another.

Then Flop, Miriam and Lazuli heard the swishing of wings overhead. Again Searle addressed her squadron. This time her voice was close and clear.

"The enemy are cunning. The enemy are slinking around somewhere. They're…"

"Hang on," interrupted Urrg, "What's that! There!"

One of them laughed, "That's an el…e…phant!" it mocked, "Ever heard of an el…e…phant? Where have you lived?"

Laughter rippled through the flock.

Urrg shook her head with embarrassment, "No, I didn't mean…"

"And," began another loudly, "Have you only just seen it? We all saw it back there!"

"Way back there!" called out another.

The whole group burst into cackling laughter as they circled above. Then Urrg's voice rose above the laughter.

"Let's not fly around laughing. Let's go down and ask it about the enemy then. It might have seen them."

The laughter petered out and there were sounds of agreement.

"Yesss! Let's go down."

"Yesss!"

They began to swoop down towards Lazuli. One descended faster than the others and was soon above her head. Lazuli suddenly lifted her head and swiped upward at it with her trunk, hitting it and sending it spinning away. It regained its flight, turned again and was joined by several others.

"Stop!" shouted Searle, very cross with Urrg for giving a command, "I make the decisions! We have a job to do for the Master. Now let's do it."

The ravens reluctantly abandoned Lazuli, swooping past her head and then rising again into the air. Soon they were all gathered together in one flock again.

"Right," announced Searle angrily, frustrated that she had lost control, "That's better. I never gave the order to go down, did I?"

"Urrg did!" shouted one.

"I know!" Searle screeched, "Urrg?!"

Urrg was flying just beneath her and looked up.

Searle dropped slightly and pecked Urrg hard on the back. "Have you forgotten your station?" she snapped, "I'm in charge now... remember?"

Urrg looked cross but did not answer and so Searle assumed she had made her point.

"Now," she announced, "Let's go and do our job as instructed by our Master. No more delays."

The swishing sounds of their wings grew softer as they headed towards the Forest of the Fairies. As they left, Flop, Miriam and Lazuli heard a painful moan coming from among the mass of black feathers.

"What was that?" exclaimed Miriam.

Flop peeped out to see the ravens speeding away.

"Miriam," he said, "Look! They're carrying something, aren't they?"

"Oh, yes," Miriam squeaked.

"But what is it?" Flop said, fixing his eyes on the ravens.

The great flock of birds was definitely carrying something, but as it was in among the swirling mass they could not see what it was.

"I can't see," Miriam replied, "They're too far away. But whatever it was... or whoever it was... it wasn't happy."

Flop walked out from beneath the elephant and looked up at her.

"I'm Flop and this is Miriam," said Flop gazing up at her at her huge head, "And thank you."

Lazuli dropped her head down to study the tiny mouse. "And you're hiding from the ravens," she said, "So you must be from the Kingdom of Gems."

"That's right," squeaked Miriam.

They immediately liked this young elephant who towered above them. She seemed huge to them. She was so powerful that with just one step she could crush them both and yet she moved and spoke with such gentle care.

She lifted her head again. "Wizard Elzaphan sent Neville to our herd as his messenger to ask for help. Did Neville find you?"

"Yes," replied Flop, sitting down on the grass, "He's been helping us."

Lazuli looked anxious, "Where is he now then?"

"We think... we hope... he's with Seph and Amalek somewhere."

"Ah... the Prince and Princess," said Lazuli, "You see Neville told us all about it when he visited the herd.

We live near the Daawa Mountains over there." She waved her trunk to the north. "It was all in Wizard Elzaphan's message to us. And he wanted one of the young elephants to volunteer to help you, so here I am."

Miriam's nose twitched and she nodded her tiny head, "You volunteered to help us! Well, thank you."

"But…" continued Lazuli, looking around, "But where are they now… the Prince and Princess… and Neville?"

"We were split up," explained Miriam, "We don't know where they are… but Joog reckons they should be somewhere in the Forest of the Fairies if all went well with them, and that's where those ravens were heading."

Miriam looked towards the forest, pointed her nose up in the air and sniffed a couple of times.

"Did you see what they were carrying?" Miriam asked her.

"No," replied Lazuli, "But who's Joog?"

Miriam looked up at the great creature towering over her, "Joog's an owl… a very wise snowy owl."

There was a pause as they all gazed towards the Forest of the Fairies.

"Those ravens are up to something… something against us no doubt," said Flop still gazing in the direction of the forest.

"Do you know about the Troubler?" squeaked Miriam.

"Yes. Neville said that a wizard, a fallen wizard, a dark wizard, had cast a spell to trap everyone and that you were in terrible danger."

Miriam's nose twitched again, this time nervously. "We're being hunted."

Lazuli nodded, "I can see that," she said gravely, "Those ravens! And you're trying to get to the castle?

Wizard Elzaphan's Castle?"

"Yes," chorused Flop and Miriam together.

"Well, that's my job," announced Lazuli, "To help you get there. And to look after the Prince and Princess."

"Good," said Flop, "And the best thing is that the ravens don't know you at all."

"And," added Miriam, "They don't know that you're helping us."

Lazuli swung her trunk backwards and up onto her back, clutching the straps and swinging the bags down onto the ground.

"Food," she announced, "There's food and drink for you in the bags. Help yourselves."

Flop began to purr and rubbed his body against one of Lazuli's legs.

"Look!" exclaimed Flop.

They all looked up to see Joog gliding gracefully down. He landed beside them and pointed down the river with his wing.

"He's coming," he said and as they watched they saw the boat appear, passing out into the early morning sunlight from the shade of overhanging trees.

There was the green-cloaked ferryman, with his back facing them and his hood around his head, rowing steadily upstream with great strength and purpose. His powerful arms pulled the oars with complete ease making the boat cut through the strong current of water that flowed against him.

As he approached they opened the bags and spread out the food and drink on the grass.

Chapter 3

~ Creatures of the Night ~

The Silver Well

The Dark Wizard Troubler was in a foul mood. His hand was still hurting where the skin had been blackened from the flash when he tried to steal the ruby, the protecting stone of the three magical Candara Gems. The wounds where his finger and thumb had been lost still ached from time to time, even though he had sped up the healing process with a magic spell.

He was greedy for total power and hence he was frustrated that there were still those who were challenging and resisting him. He believed that the Prince had died in the huge wave he created on the Great River Sween and wished that he could go to Summertime Kingdom and deal with the rest of his enemies himself but this held a great risk. He was confident that his ravens and Old Howard could kill them. He had sent Jamaar there as well now. If things became really desperate then he thought he may take the risk and go. Then he shuddered at the thought of losing everything he had gained, because if he left the Kingdom of Gems then the spell would be broken and he would have to start again.

He desperately wanted the gems, the three Candara Gems, which would give him so much extra power. He also wondered if maybe there was a way in which he could enter Summertime Kingdom without breaking the spell. He racked his brain for the answer. In extreme frustration he paced up and down in the dusty room in Old Howard's house trying to work it out.

In the back of his mind he was concerned about the unicorns. They had not been seen since the escape from the palace and he had assumed that they had left the kingdom with the others. He did not know that they could not leave the kingdom because if they did they would immediately turn back into statues. Their magical life was linked to the Candara Gems. Before the gems were given as a gift to the kingdom over four hundred and fifty years before by the great Wizard Candara, Aram and Halo were gold and silver statues on the pillars to the palace gates. With the gift of the gems Wizard Candara had given the unicorns the power to come to life when the kingdom was in danger. This had only happened once, over three hundred years before, to fight off a terrible invasion of Troublers.

The Dark Wizard Troubler knew nothing of this and so he thought that the unicorns had probably fallen to their death down the Great Crack to the Centre of Ruddha, but he could not rely upon this. If they were still alive they could be anywhere in Summertime Kingdom or even back in The Kingdom of Gems.

Ideas were swimming in his dark and evil mind when he remembered Horrik. She was a weapon that he had not used yet; a terrifying, powerful weapon that should not be wasted. He had been regularly throwing down ravens to feed the great animal but he had not descended the cellar steps to check how she was and to speak to her.

He crossed the dingy hall at the bottom of the stairs and passed through the door to the cellar. He could see his way down the steps by the light that streamed in through the door behind him. Down below the room was gently lit by the dim light coming in through the broken door. As he descended he felt a draught of cold air blowing through and hurried down to investigate.

"Horrik!" he exclaimed as he gazed at the remains of the broken chain in amazement.

He dashed to the broken door, stepped out and fought his way though the piled up snow to the top of the steps outside.

"Horrik!" he thundered, "Horrik!"

His voice echoed in the lifeless kingdom until the sound was drowned by the howl of the wind. The blustery weather caught his black cloak and it flapped vigorously as the driving snow dotted it with white. He saw Horrik's distinctive tracks, now covered with snow but still visible. Perhaps he could find her. He followed the tracks into the trees at the end of the garden hoping that she was sheltering there.

"Horrik!" he called.

He saw the tracks come out of the trees and join some more tracks; this was Jamaar's trail. He stared and wondered. Had Horrik joined Jamaar and they were travelling together? Or was Horrik following Jamaar? Horrik hated Jamaar.

He hesitated, standing in the deep snow and gazing along the tracks until they disappeared into the greyness of descending snowflakes. He could not follow now… maybe later. Anyway, Jamaar had left some time ago so they would have covered some distance.

He turned back to the house, striding through the snowstorm and up to the door. He had no idea that at this very moment he was being watched once again.

As he entered the house, he muttered to himself angrily through clenched teeth.

"That dragon will suffer for this. That's her second escape. What is she doing? Has she forgotten my rules?"

He slammed the door closed behind him.

Spindley Tower was the tallest building in the town of Candara and it was from this lookout point that the Troubler's movements were being watched by Aram and Halo. The two unicorns were in the tall tower, the finely decorated lookout that stood out among the other buildings; it was by far the highest building in Candara. The fine carvings that adorned it were partly hidden now, smoothed and softened by the flakes which slipped into every crevice they could find. Aram and Halo had made this their shelter and home since returning from the border.

The view from the tower was extraordinary. The snow had transformed the kingdom into a land gripped by a deep winter freeze. Snow was everywhere. It blanketed the ground with a deep smooth covering and dressed every tree with white, coating even the smallest twigs. Snow flakes filled the chilly air chasing on the strong wind as if they were eagerly rushing somewhere as fast as they could.

Aram and Halo were standing about three quarters of the way up the tower. They wanted to ascend to the top, to the highest balcony, but found that the winding staircase became too narrow for their bulky bodies. When they stepped out onto the third highest balcony they found that the view from this height was excellent. Each balcony was partially sheltered by a wooden roof but on the side they were standing they received the full blast of the icy wind. The snow was blowing heavily into their faces.

"I can't see him anymore," said Halo, "I think he must've gone back in."

She dipped her head and tapped a hoof on the wooden floor as the snow gusted into her face. Their flowing manes rippled in the blast releasing gold and silver sparks.

"What's he up to?" wondered Aram who was standing next to her.

"I don't know," she replied, "He must've gone out for something, but from here we can't see well enough. And I wish we knew what he was planning."

They had decided to watch Old Howard's House for they wanted to know what the Dark Wizard Troubler was doing. Now at last they had seen him. At times the falling snow had been too thick even to see the house but now, as it thinned a little, they could see it well. A moment earlier they had caught a glimpse of the wizard just beyond the house and in the back garden.

Aram shook his golden head and mane to disturb the snow that had settled on him. Melted snow dripped from their magical spiral alicorns as they glowed with warmth, the drips freezing into ice as the wind whipped them away.

He looked through the driving snow and blinked.

"We need to act soon," he commented.

"I know," agreed Halo, "And as he doesn't know we're here... or we think he doesn't know... so perhaps we can surprise him."

"I wish we knew what he's doing," Aram said anxiously, "We know he's using that mirror somehow... it seems he can see into Summertime Kingdom. And we know that he was talking to an old man. Now who was that? We need to find out more... we need to find out his plans."

Halo nodded, "We do, that's true. But how?"

"If we keep watching we may spot something," Aram replied, "But just watching is not enough. Let's go in and we'll think about it."

Aram started backing away from the balcony railings.

"We need to act soon and we need to work out a good plan. Come on."

The two stately unicorns backed through a door, turned and began to clatter down the spiral stairs.

Amalek, Seph and Neville had slept soundly through the night. Their hiding place beneath the overhanging rock was a cosy secluded den and they were undisturbed. Amalek had awoken first, rolling onto her front on the bed of leaves and resting her head on her hands as she looked out. All around she heard the dawn chorus which was particularly vibrant and uplifting in the Forest of the

Fairies. When they had arrived here the night before it had been too dark to see much and they were running to escape from the ravens as quickly as possible. Now she gazed out sleepily and in wonder at the beauty of the forest while the other two still slept.

Amalek's love for nature had grown when she was eight. The King, Queen and the Prince had been delayed on a trip to the north and had sent sparrow-messengers to tell her to stay with a wise, old woman called Pemima until they returned. The trip was meant to take a matter of days but various dangerous situations held them up and they not return for several weeks.

Pemima lived in Whitten and her wisdom lay in her special knowledge of nature and particularly wildlife. Day by day she taught Amalek, talking to her about many different animals and taking her for walks in Silvermay Forest where they met a variety of forest dwellers. Amalek enjoyed learning and her understanding of animals developed; she became an expert in how they thought and acted, as well as their habits. She also grew to love the forest and now, as she gazed out of the den, she felt delight at the scene in front of her.

The ground undulated gently with small dips and hollows among the trees. The forest floor was a carpet of golden leaves while here and there were patches of fern. Tree trunks rose from their rooted bases with sturdy strength, reaching up and spreading their branches to hang masses of delicate green leaves above. The low rising sun glanced through gaps, warm and bright. The forest scent was sweet and gentle and a stream was babbling nearby.

Hanging in the air, a light mist paled the more distant trees. It was a beautiful and enchanting scene.

Amalek's sleepy enjoyment of the forest scene was short-lived. She sighed deeply as her worries rose to fill her mind like a bitter taste that could not be ignored. She was heartbroken by the plight of her mother and father, frozen by the Troubler's spell, and this was almost more than she could bare. But this was not her only worry. She was concerned about Flop and Miriam. She feared their lives were in danger and the fact that Joog had flown off to find them and had not returned made her fear for him as well. To add to these concerns, they had left the Ferryman to face the evil ravens. All these thoughts grasped her and would not let go, feeding her anxious feelings. She dropped her head onto the leaves and began to cry.

She was a neat and tidy person who liked to have everything in the right place but her worries were out of control and she felt panic rising. She managed to restrain the feeling by taking three deep breaths and then three more. This was something her mother had taught her and it helped, but thoughts still swirled in her mind. She forced herself to lift her head and open her eyes. She must think it through. What could they do to help Flop, Miriam and Joog?

She climbed out of the leafy den, stretched her arms and brushed a few leaves off her clothes. She felt the pain of a blister on her foot which she had not noticed the day before. She slipped on her shoes and took a step. Not too bad.

She ran a comb through her long wavy hair, flicking her head back and hooking her hair behind her ears. Then she called to the others.

"Seph! Neville! Wake up!"

Neville appeared next, stumbling out clumsily and

stretching his massive wings. He shook his body which ruffled his feathers leaving them looking even more untidy than before.

"We needed that sleep," he said, and then turning back, "Seph, wake up!"

"He's always last," commented Amalek irritably, "It drives me crazy... I'm always waiting for him. Give him a peck, Neville."

Neville stretched his head back in and pecked Seph in the side. The leaves rustled as he turned over.

"Are you awake?" called Amalck.

There was another rustle and then a soft grunt from Seph.

"It's time to go, Seph. Get up!" she bossed.

He lifted his head and looked out with blurry eyes and dishevelled hair.

"Thanks," he mumbled sleepily and his head dropped back onto his pillow of leaves.

"He'll be out in a minute," Neville said to Amalek.

"I hope so," Amalek snapped.

Seph needed one more peck from Neville before he emerged, squinting his eyes in the morning light.

"At last!" called Amalek who was kneeling down beside a little stream, "Come over here, Seph."

Seph joined her, crouching beside his sister to reach down into the cool water to splash his face. Then they drank. The water tasted wonderfully fresh.

Neville paddled in the stream, first drinking and then splashing to wash his feathers. His magic stripy scarf draped in the water, rippling along its length as he shook, and when he clambered out with the help of the children, the scarf was completely dry. Amalek and Seph stood up.

"Seph," said Amalek, "I'm really worried about Flop

and Miriam… and Joog… and the Ferryman…"

"I know," replied Seph, "We talked it through already… remember?"

"Yes, but…" Amalek sighed, "We must do something… like try to find them…"

"The Ferryman ordered us not to go back," Seph said firmly, "We must follow what he said."

"I know," Amalek pleaded, "But what about the others?"

"We must get to the castle," Seph said decisively, "It's difficult to leave them behind, I know. But, anyway, we've got no idea where they are… we'd never find them. We can't go back… not now. If we start going back… well, think about it… it could mean disaster. *We* could be caught too. Imagine if no one reached Wizard Elzaphan to get his help! And Neville agrees."

Seph was looking directly at her, his big blue eyes steady and strong. She gazed back, tears just a tiny motion away. She battled inside but she knew he was right and although she found his words hard to accept, his strength was comforting. She blinked and released a single tear which trickled down her cheek.

"I know," she conceded.

Seph nodded.

"We'd better go then," he said standing up.

He turned and walked across the leaf-strewn ground and into a clearing.

"Come on, Ammey," he called back cheerily, "We need to get going. There's something not right here… I can feel it. Let's go."

"What is it? … ravens?" asked Amalek, looking around.

"Maybe… I don't know. Come on!"

"Horrible, creepy things," commented Amalek, shivering at the thought.

She caught up with Seph and they both stood still, looking up and scanning the branches of the trees above their heads. The cross feeling she had towards her brother had gone now and she felt calmer and stronger.

"I can't see any ravens," Amalek said quietly.

Seph pointed upward and asked in a whisper.

"What's that?"

Amalek peered upward moving her head to look through the leaves.

"It's not a raven," she replied, smiling, "Too small, silly! Can't you tell a blackbird from a raven?"

Seph stared at it and then smiled.

"Yes, you're right," he acknowledged. Then he was serious again. "But I still feel something. Let's just get going as quickly as possible. Come on Neville."

Neville realized that there should be enough space for him to get airborne. He started waddling across the leaves, looking like a clumsy goose. The children turned when they heard his feet rustling in the leaves.

"Seph," said Amalek, looking alarmed, "He's trying to take off! Quick, stop him!"

"Neville!" called Seph.

"Neville!" called out Amalek, "Stop! We can help you!"

"No," he replied as his waddling became faster, "I'm fine."

"Watch out for the trees then!" exclaimed Amalek.

They had witnessed Neville's attempt to take off on several occasions now. Although he was graceful in the air, his movement on the ground was ungainly and cumbersome. They watched as his waddling became a run, and as he gathered speed he bobbed up and down swaying jerkily from side to side. In the wake of this display of wobbly scrabbling, the leaves under his great webbed feet were being thrown up like a surfer's foam. A few feathers flew off spinning in the slipstream as he held his great wings out for his attempted lift off.

He dropped into a dip and then rose again. His stripy scarf flew out behind him, fluttering in the air. With his feet still running he began to leave the ground and flap his great wings slowly.

One of his wings clipped some ferns making him tilt precariously. He held control, turned to miss a tree narrowly at the end of the clearing and then he was up and gliding with perfect grace.

"I'm up!" he exclaimed happily, looking down at Amalek and Seph.

Amalek sighed with relief.

"Now that the entertainment is over..." called Seph, laughing and shaking his head, "can we carry on with our journey?"

Amalek turned to Seph. "He's great, isn't he?" she commented.

"He's such a good friend already," replied Seph.

"I know," Amalek glanced up to see him circling above, "And look at the size of him. It's not surprising he finds it hard to take off!"

They chatted as they walked through the trees. Amalek looked around, staying alert and aware, her sharp eyes scanning the area.

"It's strange," she said, "We haven't seen anyone else in this kingdom... any other people at all. It's weird. You'd think we'd have met someone as we travelled."

"Yes, I know," Seph shook his head and glanced

around nervously, "It's very strange."

"Not a soul," said Amalek, whispering now, "Except the Ferryman of course. But no one else."

Soon they were in among trees again. They stopped to drink some more fresh water from a stream and to put something on Amalek's blister to ease the pain and stop the rubbing, which they made by ripping one of the back pockets off Seph's trousers and folding it up. It eased Amalek's discomfort and they carried on. They were all hungry but decided to look out for some fruit trees or bushes as they traveled. Neville skilfully glided between the trees above their heads as they began their journey deeper into the forest.

At this moment Jum awoke.

"Crayle!" she said quietly, repeatedly bumping into him to shake him awake, "Crayle! Wake up!"

Crayle jerked his head up and shook it, "What?! What is it?"

"I fell asleep," she said, "And now it's daytime. We've both slept all through the night. What about the enemy?"

"Oh no!" he said jerking his head around to look with his one eye.

"I'm sorry, dear," Jum sighed.

Crayle looked at her crossly and then down at the overhanging rock. "What if they've gone?" he asked.

"Shhh," Jum held a wing to her beak. "Listen. Can you hear them?"

"No, not a thing, Jum."

He tilted his head to one side and they both listened for a moment more.

"I'll take a look," he said and jumped off the branch.

He was back very quickly, this time making a tidy

landing. This was more luck than skill but nevertheless he wobbled his head slightly in pride.

"Well?" asked Jum.

"Well what?"

"Have the enemy gone, Crayle?" she asked impatiently.

"They've gone," he said, sounding upset, "If only you hadn't fallen asleep."

"I was tired, dear," she said, trying to soften his anger towards her, "But they can't have gone far, can they?"

Crayle perked up, "Yes, that's true. Let's find 'em then. Now, which way would they go?"

"North, of course," she said, "Remember? They're heading for Wizard Elzaphan's castle."

"Yes, of course. Come on then. Let's go."

Together they took off and headed through the trees.

They had not been flying for a minute when Jum landed. Crayle was following her and landed beside her, bumping into her so that she had to flap her wings to stay on the branch.

"What is it?" he said.

"I heard something," she pointed her beak and nodded, "Through there. I heard voices. It's them, I think."

They flew from branch to branch with Crayle leading. Suddenly he darted into a richly leafed tree and landed on a branch. Jum followed and landed beside him.

"There," he whispered, jerking his beak to point, "Look, through those branches."

"It's them," agreed Jum, "The enemy… the prince and the princess. And there's the albatross."

"It's so big!" exclaimed Crayle, "Look at those wings! I won't be arguing with that in a hurry! Now we can follow 'em. Or at least I can. You need to go and tell the General."

"OK, but..." Jum hesitated, "but we don't know where he is, do we?"

Crayle thought for a moment.

"True," he said and pecked at the branch crossly. "I'd forgotten that." He peered through the leaves of the tree. "Look, they've gone! Follow me."

They flew to the next tree and then to the next.

"There they are," said Jum.

As they followed, the trees were becoming denser and the bushes larger. The ferns, which on the outskirts of the forest were patchy, now filled the ground everywhere. The ravens continued following, keeping their distance, with Crayle enjoying the challenge and feeling like a young bird again.

Down below Amalek and Seph were finding their journey through the forest slower than they had expected. They found a cluster of gooseberry bushes and quickly stuffed their pockets full of the delicious fruit to eat as they walked. They avoided the paths to stay hidden among the trees but the thicker undergrowth made travelling difficult. Neville flew in between the trees where possible but at times he had to rise above the treetops to find the space for his great wingspan.

As they moved Seph was uncomfortably aware of the watching power of the Dark Wizard Troubler. He stopped and stood still.

"I can still feel it," he said to his sister.

Amalek paused and closed her eyes. She knew Seph was more sensitive to things like this than her, but after a moment she felt it too.

"You're right, Seph," she said and shivered, opening

her eyes and looking at him with a worried expression, "Ravens?"

"Maybe, Ammey. We'll just keep moving. How's the blister."

"Not too bad," replied Amalek, "Your back pocket has helped."

They began walking again, accompanied by the sinister presence of the two old ravens. In this way they travelled in fear and kept dreading the attack of the great flock of evil ravens. This dwelt constantly in their minds like an unwelcome guest. As well as this, another thought which haunted them was Old Howard and the apprehension that he would suddenly appear out of the bushes and confront them. It seemed that the dull ache of the Troubler's shadow was pursuing them.

Neville was gliding just above there heads and suddenly began singing. Their feeling of doom lifted as he entertained them with another riddle-song.

"I am a wonder of the night,
a beauty of the day,
but my magic spell begins to tell
when the sun has gone away.

Just like a soldier on parade
called to serve his land
with no glance about, and without doubt,
upright and tall I stand.

When evening falls into the night
I put my night-cap on
tossed here and there in the gentle air,
a breeze - and it is gone!

You may think I'm shedding tears
as I dance and play,
but just observe it's you I serve
to help you find your way!"

"You'll have to sing it again!" called out Seph, and as they kept walking Neville sang it again and the Prince and Princess tried to solve it.

A few trees away Crayle and Jum sat on a high branch. They could see Seph and Amalek, and Neville too as he glided through the trees. The ravens were well hidden by a thick mass of leaves.

"What is it?" asked Jum quietly.

"I dunno," Crayle replied. He tilted his head to one side, "A soldier?"

"No, no," Jum said with certainty, "It says *like* a soldier. And anyway does a soldier cry and wear a night-cap?"

"It might…" he replied, "If it lost a battle… and then was sleeping."

"But…" Jum said, thinking it through, "But a soldier doesn't dance and play."

"You're right," Crayle agreed, nodding slowly, "We can count a soldier out."

"Yes, completely."

"You know what I think?" Crayle said, looking serious.

"What?" asked Jum as Crayle jumped off the branch to fly to the next tree.

Jum followed and landed beside Crayle.

"What do you think?" she asked.

"It's the moon, that's what it is," Crayle announced,

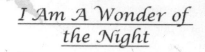

I Am A Wonder of the Night

"I am a wonder of the night,
a beauty of the day,
but my magic spell begins to tell
when the sun has gone away.

Just like a soldier on parade
called to serve his land
with no glance about, and without
doubt,
upright and tall I stand.

When evening falls into the night
I put my night-cap on
tossed here and there in the gentle air,
a breeze - and it is gone!

You may think I'm shedding tears
as I dance and play,
but just observe it's you I serve
to help you find your way!"

~ NEVILLE'S 4TH RIDDLE ~

"A wonder of the night. Well... what's that? It's the moon. It must be."

He preened his feathers with his beak as if he had solved it and now could get on with something else.

Jum thought for a moment as she listened to Neville singing the riddle again.

"In that case," she said, "How is the moon like a soldier, tall and upright?"

Crayle looked disappointed and sighed, "I've had enough of this. It's just rubbish. It probably isn't anything... just a load of muddled words. Anyway, why are we trying to solve a stupid riddle?" He jerked his head forwards. "Hey, where are they?"

They flew together into the next tree. Crayle again landed badly and the branch shook.

Just then Seph stopped and turned and seemed to look straight at them.

"Keep still," whispered Jum.

After a moment Crayle spoke. "He's looked away. Do you think he saw us?"

"I don't think so. Look he's walking again. Come on, we'll keep stalking 'em."

"You should go off to tell the General," Crayle said.

"I've been thinking about that," she said. They fluttered to the next tree and then she continued. "If I go and tell him... and you're still stalking and moving while I'm gone... then how can I tell him where you are? You'll have moved won't you?"

Crayle sighed and then pecked at the branch again in frustration.

"Sshh," Jum whispered crossly, "They'll hear us."

He stopped pecking, put his head to one side and thought about it.

"Yeah," he whispered, "You're right... it is a problem, but you can tell him roughly where I am, can't you? You know the direction they're travelling in. You can tell him that."

They flew to the next tree.

"In that case," Jum said, continuing the conversation, "You might as well come too. I'd worry about leaving you."

Crayle nodded slowly. He suddenly thought that if he was there when the General was first told, then he would receive the hero's welcome sooner. He could hardly wait.

"OK," he said, "Let's go then!"

"Hang on, dear," Jum said, "You've forgotten again, haven't you? We don't know where the General is do we?"

Crayle sighed again, "Oh, why isn't anything straightforwards?"

He hung his head despondently.

"Crayle, my dear," she said spreading out a wing and putting it around Crayle, "We'll fly off and try to find him. If they're on the wing then we'll see him easily. OK?"

Crayle did not answer.

"Come on, dear," Jum whispered tenderly.

Crayle lifted his head and nodded slowly. "OK," he said.

They jumped off the branch, rose up above the trees and then flew off southwards. If Neville had been above the trees at this moment he would probably have seen them, but he was weaving through the forest and above the heads of Amalek and Seph. They had solved the riddle and felt the atmosphere grow lighter as the two old ravens flew away.

The forest was a very interesting place. As they moved towards the centre, the trees became more dense, ferns and mosses covered the forest floor and thick bushes and plants made walking more difficult. Neville had to float up above the trees again. The children both picked up sticks to beat at tangled patches of undergrowth that blocked their way here and there.

The leaves of the trees created a canopy of green above the children which also became thicker as they journeyed on into the depths of the forest. The sun was high in the clear sky now but beneath this ceiling of leaves the light struggled to get through and they found themselves moving through semi-darkness. On the forest floor the mosses and ferns were all soaked with dew. Little streams trickled tunefully in the still air. Dripping water from the trees fell into little forest pools and the patchy light that pierced the gaps in the trees reflected in the drops making them shine like jewels.

As they moved deeper into the forest they became aware that the dripping water and trickling streams were releasing notes that blended together and created a beautiful sound. It formed a magical musical chorus that echoed around the entire forest. The birds were singing with it too; they were part of the music of the forest which all harmonized like a great symphony. It seemed perfect; there was not a note that sounded out of place. This was so beautiful that they stopped to listen and enjoy a moment's rest.

The trees had thinned slightly so that there was just enough room between the trunks for Neville to float above the children once more. He dropped down and decided to land on a branch. His great webbed feet slapped down above their heads in an elm tree and after a few wobbles and flaps he was reasonably stable.

After enjoying the music for a few minutes both children picked up their sticks and started walking again. Neville jumped off his branch to take to the air, but found himself plummeting instead.

"Neville!" shouted Seph, and both the children ran back towards him.

Neville needed some speed or some wind to lift him into the air and here he had neither. He held his wings out, but he was falling faster all the time and a crash seemed inevitable. He disappeared under the thick layer of ferns on the forest floor, but as he did he managed to pull out of the dive he was in and for a few feet he was swiftly gliding parallel with the ground and flattening a channel of ferns the width of his wingspan. Then he rose out majestically, managing to avoid hitting any trees and dragging a mass of broken ferns on his wings. He circled above Amalek and Seph.

"Hey!" he called out to them with a laugh, "How was that?"

"I've seen better," joked Seph.

Bits of fern fell from Neville's wings and dropped through the dim light.

Amalek and Seph continued forcing their way through thick undergrowth, but now the uncomfortable feeling that they were being watched arose again. They all felt it. They heard a few small noises close by. Then suddenly, they heard something rustling behind them.

Amalek and Seph spun around and stared into the undergrowth.

"What was that?" whispered Seph.

"I don't know," Amalek replied quietly, "We're being followed… I'm sure we are."

They stood still and gazed towards the sounds. Then they heard the eerie sound of someone else walking and rustling the leaves underfoot. The rustling stopped and a shiver of fear ran through them. They peered through the dappled pattern of the forest foliage and heard the rustling again and saw something move; a dark shape, and they stared even harder in the dim light to see what it was. It seemed to melt away into the background. They stood utterly still, frozen in terror, too afraid to move, listening, watching.

"There was something," Seph whispered to Amalek, "I'm sure I saw something… something moved… over there."

"We must stay close together," whispered Amalek, "It's so dark in here."

Then, suddenly, the music of the forest, the sounds of trickling streams and singing birds stopped and ghostly silence filled the air.

"What's happening?" whispered Amalek.

"I don't know," replied Seph, his eyes wide and alert, "But if anything does happen I've got the magic drop."

He reached into his pocket, turned out several gooseberries, and then clasped the magic drop.

"Good," Amalek whispered, looking slightly comforted, "Let's keep going then. The quicker we travel the quicker we can get out of here."

The magic drop in Seph's hand was golden unicorn blood. After Aram had been injured he had given one drop of his dried, golden blood to each of the children when they were entering Summertime Kingdom. The magic was only to be used in emergencies and Amalek had already used hers to save her from the Great Crack to the Centre of Ruddha. Now there was just one left.

Suddenly they heard a noise in the trees just behind them. Someone was taking a step, placing a foot on the leaves on the ground. The closeness of it made them jump with shock. Instinctively, as if all their energy was released by the sound, they began to scrabble frantically through the undergrowth of ferns and other plants, slipping, running a step or two, pushing through some bushes, doing anything to get away from that evil presence that was closing in on them. Their terror drove them on.

"Run!" cried Neville from above their heads. He was looking back as he flew. "Quick, run! It's Old Howard!"

Seph was faster than Amalek and she was struggling with her blistered foot as well.

"Come on!" he said to her as he stopped to reach back and grab her hand to pull her along.

Neville swooped at Old Howard and took him by surprise. He ducked to avoid the great bird. The end of Neville's scarf touched his cheek and he toppled backwards, crashing through the bushes and ferns.

"Aahh!" Old Howard cried as his ankle twisted and he hit the ground hard.

Momentarily he disappeared from sight, hidden by the foliage and when his head popped up through the ferns he saw Neville flying away.

"Oy'll get you!" he screamed, as he tried to stand up, "Aahh!" he cried as he fell down again and onto his knees.

He was still shaky after his flight with the Female Squadron of ravens who had carried him here, dropped him in the forest as instructed by the phantom Troubler and then flown off to meet the Male Squadron.

He jumped when he heard the voice of the Dark

Wizard Troubler in his mind, that voice that controlled him and gave him power.

"What!" it exclaimed, "The Prince! So he's not dead... well he won't be alive for long. Get them!" the voice said firmly, "Hold your compass... now!"

Old Howard had a black compass hanging around his neck and under his shirt. He gripped the chain to pull out the compass and grasped it. It felt warm.

"Now," the voice urged, "Point at them. Point at them now. Concentrate. Come on!"

Old Howard, still on his knees, lifted his arm and pointed a finger in the direction of Neville who was gliding between the trees but then passed out of sight.

"But oy can't see 'em," he said, "Where are they?"

"Point more to the right," said the voice, "Yes that's it! There. Now... concentrate... concentrate hard!"

Old Howard's hand and finger steadied as he obeyed the voice and concentrated.

"Now," continued the Dark Wizard Troubler, "Say these words."

Old Howard repeated them aloud as they sounded in his mind.

> "I summon creatures of the night
> from past and present to this time
> I summon you to turn and fight
> defeat all good, destroy things fine.
> Come from each leaf and show your strength,
> come creatures of the night, come hence!"

Amalek and Seph were still struggling through the forest in their efforts to escape, with Seph dragging his sister along. They heard Old Howard's gravely voice and this spurred them on. Neville was now overhead.

"I think he's injured," he called down to them, "But he's up to something!"

As Old Howard's words sounded all the leaves on the trees around them fell and tumbled lightly towards the forest floor. The Prince and Princess stopped in their tracks, wondering what was happening. The leaves fluttered and rustled as they descended through the air like a mass of butterflies. The children were surrounded by falling leaves and they both lifted their hands to brush leaves off their shoulders and heads. They looked up to see gaps appearing in the canopy of leaves above and for the first time for a while they could see the blue sky. However, down below the darkness persisted.

"Run!" shouted Seph, but before they could start something terrifying happened which again froze them to the spot in fear.

As the first leaf landed gently on the forest floor it turned into a massive two-tailed scorpion. The tails rose up above its body to hang forwards, each with a poison sac and long sharp sting on the end. As more leaves landed, they too transformed into two-tailed scorpions and in a moment there were ten, and then twenty, and soon there was a multitude of them. They were much bigger than the children. Some reared up as if getting ready to pounce upon their victims with their huge front claws open, stretching forwards and then snapping closed with a loud cracking sound. The still air was filled with the eerie clicking of their pincers and sharp scratching of their bony legs as they clambered over each other. They were dark brown, their hard shiny bodies gleaming in the dim light. One of them opened a huge pair of leathery wings and flapped them wildly. Others did the same as they danced around the Prince and Princess. It was a horrifying sight and took them completely by surprise.

Amalek grabbed Seph's hand again and kicked some leaves towards the creatures.

"Get away!" she shouted, trying to frighten them and Seph swept his stick through the air towards them.

This produced an immediate reaction from them. They reared back in surprise but then took a step towards the children and some of them opened their mouths wide to hiss threateningly. Just behind their heads, s their deadly stings hovered, ready to strike. Amalek and Seph glanced around, desperate for a way to escape, but they were trapped. The amazing creatures loomed closer in the shadows of the near-darkness and the children could see that each giant scorpion had a row of beady black eyes.

The children were completely surrounded and totally outnumbered; there seemed to be hundreds of them and now they were clambering over each other in an effort to be the first to reach their prey.

Amalek and Seph dropped to their knees and huddled together for protection. They crouched down, back to back, both holding their sticks out in front of them in case one of the ghastly hungry-looking creatures swung one of its tails towards them with its dangerous-looking sting. Neville floated just above their heads ready to dive and attack. In the semi-darkness the creatures' eyes glittered and their strange shapes looked hideous. They were almost upon the two children now.

Neville descended. His magic stripy scarf had grown much longer and it hung down and swept through the creatures causing an explosion of commotion among them. The scarf threw them aside as it carved a path through them. The children jumped up and ran into the gap but in a second the creatures had reformed a circle around them. Amalek and Seph cowered down again in fear. Neville turned in the air.

At that moment Seph suddenly stood up making the scorpions recoil slightly in surprise. He held the magic drop between his fingers.

"Rub the drop!" cried Amalek.

"I am… I am," exclaimed Seph frantically, "It's not working."

Amalek's eyes were wide in fear. The magic drop was their only chance.

"Keep rubbing," she cried out.

Seph rubbed it again. He looked desperate.

"It's not working… what shall I do?"

The scorpions moved in again to attack them, their mouths open, hissing threateningly. Seph swung his stick at one of the scorpions and the stick cracked into its great claw. The claw snapped around the stick and cut through it with a crunch. Then Neville swooped in again and headed for the creature closest to Amalek. He flew at its head but it swayed back swiftly to avoid Neville's beak and then stabbed at him with its sting. It missed and Neville shot past, his scarf again throwing creatures away but there were so many it hardly made any difference. In a moment they had recovered.

Amalek struck out with her stick, swinging it with all her might at a scorpion's head. It crunched as it hit, breaking and bouncing off in bits, leaving the scorpion unharmed. She was left holding just the remaining end of it. She flung it at them and it disappeared among their scrabbling legs.

A large scorpion, slightly bigger than all the rest,

clambered over the others and fell towards the children who were now side by side. Immediately it thrust its two front claws at Amalek and fixed its eyes on her. Then it attacked, stepping closer and jabbing with its sting. Seph threw himself in front of his sister and the sting stabbed into his arm sending him crashing backwards. He fell into Amalek and the magic drop flew from his hand.

"Aahh!" he cried as intense pain erupted in his arm.

Seph had knocked Amalek over leaving them both sprawling on the grass.

Neville swooped again, his scarf hitting the large scorpion and throwing it back but in a second it was moving in again. Amalek gazed up at it in terror. Seph felt his arm going numb as he looked frantically for the magic drop. It was gone.

Then he saw something glowing, buried in the blades of grass. He dived for it, snatching a handful of grass and ripping it away from the ground. Light streamed out between Seph's fingers and immediately the creatures hissed and stepped back. It shone brighter and brighter until it was sending out rays as bright as the sun. The surrounding forest lit up in its glow. As the light fell directly upon the large scorpion it turned back into a leaf. Then another of the hideous creatures changed, and then another as they panicked and scrambled over each other in their desperate efforts to escape.

Their sinister clicking echoed in the silent forest and gradually died away as they were turned back into leaves. In a moment there were none left. The leaves began to rise slowly and float back up to the trees and attach themselves once more to the branches. Seph and the golden drop had now dealt with every creature and the air was once again filled with fluttering dancing leaves.

"Look!" cried Princess Amalek, standing up, "See! Fairies... carrying the leaves!"

She turned to look for the Prince. He was behind her, collapsed onto the grass with his sleeve soaked in blood.

"I can't feel my arm," he moaned as he gripped it with his hand.

Amalek dropped onto her knees beside him.

"Seph, Seph," she cried, breathless with shock, "Your arm!"

She knelt down beside him, tears now running down her cheeks.

"It's numb," he said quietly, "It's spreading... I can feel it... it's in my shoulder now... "

"Alright, alright," she said, trying to calm herself down, "Hold on, Seph. Hang in there... and stay awake."

She looked around.

"Where's the drop?" she asked.

His eyelids were drooping now as the poison spread.

"I don't... know... I think..." he said, his voice petering out.

Amalek reached down and patted his face. He felt cold. Neville floated above.

"Stay awake," she said, and then louder, "Seph, stay awake!"

There was no response.

She looked desperately at Neville and pleaded, "What shall we do?"

"Quick! Find the magic drop," he replied.

Then she panicked.

She started scrambling in the grass for the magic drop and with her eyes streaming with tears she could hardly see.

"Amalek," said Neville, gliding down towards her,

"That will not help anyone... especially Seph. Calm down."

She obeyed and stopped her frantic scrambling. She knew he was right - she had to stay calm. She wiped her eyes and looked at the grass. Something made her stand up and take a step away from Seph. She saw a glow in the grass and reached her hand down. Nestled in the green blades was the magic drop. She reached in and picked it up. The glow began to fade. She quickly held it close to her brother's arm and a small patch of light lit up his blood-soaked clothes.

"Seph! Seph!" she cried.

She grabbed him with her free hand and shook. He opened his eyes and smiled at her.

"Seph!" she exclaimed, now with joy, "You're alive!"

"Of course I am," he said, looking pale, "A scorpion sting... ha, nothing!"

"Is it getting better?" she asked.

He smiled again, "Better... yes, much better."

He moved his arm slightly.

"It's coming back to life... yes, I can feel it tingling."

He opened and closed his hand. The music of the forest began again, at first just a few birds and then more until the forest echoed with their beautiful singing. Then the dripping sounds of water joined in and the glorious chorus was as rich as before.

Amalek blew out air in a long sigh. "That was close... I thought you were dead. Don't you ever do that to me again, Seph!"

She smiled at him.

"I don't intend to," he replied, smiling back at her, "It wasn't exactly enjoyable!"

Seph was lying on his back and looking straight up.

"Look at the fairies," he said, "They're amazing. They're so little! Look at their tiny wings."

Together they watched as the last few leaves floated up, each carried by a tiny glowing fairy whose fluttering wings caught the light here and there and shone with all the colours of the rainbow. Their ears were pointed as were their shoes and they seemed to be filled with delight as they performed their task beautifully. The children occasionally heard the tiniest of voices peal with delicate laughter. Soon all the leaves were back on the trees and the fairies had gone; some into holes in the trees; some hiding under the leaves and branches; and some had simply flown away.

They suddenly heard a noise in the bushes.

"Old Howard!" Amalek called up to Neville, "It's Old Howard."

Neville was circling above them and dodging in and out of the trees. He glided down.

"Where is he?" he asked.

"Over there," replied Amalek pointing, "I didn't see him… just heard a noise of someone in those bushes… but it must be him."

"I'll take a look," said Neville turning.

"Don't," said Seph, leaping up, "It's too dangerous… I'll go."

Neville was already flying in the direction of the bushes. "No, you need to recover, Seph. I'll just look to see what he's up to."

The children watched as Neville flew off between the trees until he was out of sight. A moment later he returned.

"It's him," Neville called out as he flew above their

heads, "But he's just hobbling away. I don't think we need to worry about him at the moment."

"Good," commented Amalek, "The traitor… as long as he doesn't try again."

Seph was regaining the colour in his cheeks.

"Huh," he chuckled, swinging his arm, "Look at that. It's fine now."

"Thanks to the magic drop," laughed Amalek.

She held it in the palm of her hand and looked at it. She passed it to Seph. It no longer glowed but he still slipped it back into his pocket.

"And you've ruined your sleeve," she joked, touching the torn, blood-soaked material.

"Thanks for saving me, Ammey," he said.

"It was easy," she smiled, "And thanks for saving me," she added.

"It's a fair exchange," he laughed, "If we keep saving each other we'll survive anything!"

His leap in front of Amalek to protect her felt like a natural thing to do and now he felt strong. It was the strength that arises through doing something totally for someone else. It had been instinctive at the time, without a thought of the danger to himself, and looking back now it surprised him. But in that moment of courage, he had grown stronger.

Amalek sighed again with deep relief that the danger had passed, "I'm glad *that's* over."

She was on her feet now and she held out a hand to Seph and pulled him up.

Neville glided just above their heads, "Wow! Those magic drops are good to have around, Seph!" he said, his calm clear voice seeming to blend in with the music of the forest, "Is that the last one?"

"Yes," replied Seph, "We only had two and we've used them both now."

"Well let's just hope…" Neville said, "that we don't get attacked again before we reach the castle."

Amalek glanced around nervously towards the bush where she had heard Old Howard moving, "Let's get going then before Old Howard comes back," she said.

They began to walk quickly though the ferns, Amalek hobbling but ignoring the pain of her blister. They each found a new stick to carry and use to beat their way through any dense patches of undergrowth.

"Neville?" called Seph, "Look out for Old Howard."

Neville looked down and dropped through the air until he was circling just above their heads.

"I will," Neville answered, "But I think he's gone. You just keep going and I'll look out for him."

He soared upwards and found a gap through the tops of the trees. He rose out of the mass of branches and leaves to look for ravens. Nothing. He felt uneasy about losing sight of the children even for a moment, especially with Old Howard somewhere close. After a quick glance all around he dropped back past the tops of the trees to glide above them.

Old Howard had watched with excited glee from the bush as the scorpions attacked the Prince and Princess but his glee had melted away into alarm and then anger as he saw the scorpions turn back into leaves. When the Prince recovered from the scorpion sting it was the final straw. He had scrambled to his feet, grabbed a stick to help him walk with his twisted ankle, and hobbled away into the forest.

Soon after, he had turned to walk towards the castle. He was furious that once again they had escaped by the skin of their teeth. Why did everything keep going wrong? He was more terrified than ever of the Dark Wizard Troubler and then he heard the voice in his head, cutting through his thoughts like an icy wind.

"Old Howard, you have failed me… again."

Old Howard shuddered at the sound of the evil voice.

"They have got away and that was your last chance. Now they are getting too close to the castle, to Wizard Elzaphan, and it gets much harder for me. The power is more difficult, but I am working on that and soon I will have the power… even in the castle. But… you… you… I have had more than enough of you and your failures."

"It was just a bit of good ol' bad luck," Old Howard said, trying to sound cheery as he struggled along, "It could've 'appened to anyone."

"But it happened to you," the voice punched out the words with venom, "And those who fail me, pay. I told you that was your last chance and I am a man to keep my word. So you will pay and suffer first… and then I have another task for you."

As Old Howard hobbled along the voice was getting softer.

"No! No!" said Old Howard, trying to stretch out the conversation, "Gimme just one more chance. Just one. Please."

"Enough," the voice was softer still, "I will not be argued with like some fool you can persuade."

"Oy would never think of you as a fool," Old

Howard said and kept hobbling.

He paused as he felt the black compass under his shirt jumping excitedly against his skin. He grasped the chain with shaking hands and pulled out the black compass with such impatience that he ripped his shirt. He lifted the chain over his head and flung it and compass away into the trees.

"No, my lord," he said, "You're not a fool. Not at all."

"Why are you growing softer?" said the voice, barely audible now, and Old Howard knew he was almost free from the Troubler's grasp.

"Am oy? You're as clear as day, moy lord," he shouted as he hobbled even faster.

"Are you going towards the castle?"

"No, moy lord," Old Howard panted.

"You're trying to escape me, aren't you?" the voice was shouting, but to Old Howard it was like the most distant voice now, "Well, you can't!"

Then he suddenly remembered something. Was the bar of gold still in his pocket or had it fallen out when he fell? He quickly put his hand in his pocket to check. Relief washed through him as he touched the cold surface of the bar of gold and ran his finger lovingly along the edge.

The voice was slightly louder, "You're getting closer to the castle, aren't you?"

Old Howard let go and the voice spoke again, softer once more.

"And the compass… you haven't got it anymore, have you? I can feel it."

Old Howard almost panicked. Why was the voice louder when he touched the gold? He could not understand it. Perhaps he should throw the gold away? He couldn't bear to think about losing it and anyway the voice was fainter again now.

"I advise you not to be so foolish," said the voice, growing fainter still as Old Howard staggered towards the castle, grimacing with the pain in his ankle, "You will pay for this mistake later on. Stop! I assure you that I will get you and then you will be sorry about this. You will regret this day, all the mistakes and most of all running away." The voice was barely audible now. "You must turn around now and then I will be more lenient on you. Believe me, I am growing more and more powerful. As soon as I have the power I will be back with you… talking to you again, like this, in your mind. You cannot escape for long. You'll be hearing me soon…" and it was gone.

Silence.

Old Howard leant his shoulder against a tree. Green moss layered the bark with a soft velvet surface. He lifted his injured ankle off the ground, closed his eyes and sighed. He felt a certain relief but it was only a partial relief. He was surprised at how easy it had been to escape from the Dark Wizard Troubler but he still feared him. The sound of the evil wizard's threatening voice still echoed in his memory and made him shudder. He felt that somehow he was not completely free and that the Troubler would suddenly find a way to reappear in his mind again as he said he would. Then he would be taken over once more with his cutting commands. But for the moment he was free.

He tentatively put his hand into his pocket, touched the gold bar and listened. Nothing.

Turning so that his back was against the tree trunk he

slipped down until he was sitting rather uncomfortably on a knobbly root but he was too tired to move. His breath was still heaving in his round body and his heart thumping with exertion and fear. He stretched out his legs in front of him, closed his eyes and wondered what to do next.

The power of the Dark Wizard Troubler possessed the entire Kingdom of Gems. The evil spell had seeped into everything, holding and gripping every rock, plant, animal and human, trapping the whole land and all its inhabitants.

In Candara, in Relbuort Cottage, 17, Nathan Avenue, where Darsan and Harraine Lopery lived, something stirred and broke free. For a split second the power of the spell was shaken and overcome. A moment later the sound of footsteps down the stairs broke the eerie hush of silence.

Chapter 4

~ Burney's Hill ~

The whole flock of ravens, the males and the females, were now gathered in some trees just outside Butterknowle, to the east of the town. Earlier, the phantom Dark Wizard Troubler had used the female raven squadron to dig with their bills and clawed feet until the earth was loose enough for Old Howard to wriggle out.

"Thank you, my great Lord," Old Howard had said to the phantom as he shifted from foot to foot to get the circulation flowing around his stiff legs.

He had been surrounded by ravens trying to get earth off their beaks and feet by wiping them on the grass. They complained and grumbled quietly about it to each other. One wiped its bill on Old Howard's trousers. This did not help at all because his trousers were covered with earth anyway. Old Howard irritably kicked the raven away. The phantom suddenly grew a little more solid.

"Searle... where are you?" the phantom hissed, as he looked for her among the mass of busy ravens.

Searle had stepped forwards towards the phantom and looked up at him. She still had some earth on her bill and head. The Phantom glared at her.

"We know that the Prince is dead, drowned by the wave, but the other wretched child, the Princess, could be anywhere. She tricked us, or rather she tricked *you*. You must do better than this."

The phantom glowered at Searle and she recoiled in fear.

"But where…" the phantom had said slowly, "Where is the Princess? We'll try the Forest of the Fairies first… that's the most direct route to Wizard Elzaphan's castle."

He paused for a moment and some of the ravens began to lose concentration, looking around and pecking on the ground.

"This is what you will do," he announced loudly and they all stared at him again, "You will carry *him*." He pointed directly at Old Howard with a long wiry finger. Old Howard scowled at this and looked shocked. "And you will put him down in the Forest of the Fairies. Fly as close to the castle as you dare but not too close because you will lose power and fall. Put him down gently. Try not to drop him en route, although if you do it will be no great loss to me… or anyone!"

"What?!" Old Howard exclaimed, looking terrified, "I'm not going!"

"You will do what I say!" the phantom commanded harshly, his words biting and cruel, "And when you are in the forest I will tell you what to do. Understand?"

"Oy do, Oy d… do understand," Old Howard stammered out, "But oy don't loike it at all. Why can't oy walk?"

"Pick him up!" the phantom commanded.

The ravens responded immediately and before Old Howard could do anything about it he was smothered by ravens grasping and grabbing at his clothes with their beaks and clawed feet.

"Help! Get off!" he had shouted.

"When you've got rid of him," the phantom said, "Join the male squadron. Work together."

A second later the mass of female ravens rose into the air. In the middle was Old Howard with his legs hanging down, not daring to struggle in case they dropped him. They headed in the direction of the Forest of the Fairies, passing over Lazuli who was hiding Flop and Miriam. In the forest they put Old Howard down and then flew off to join the male squadron. They found the males in the small wood just east of Butterknowle.

Now that they were all together again they chatted about each other's news until the General cawed loudly with a deep ringing tone to get all the ravens to look at him. His black compass hung around his neck and jiggled as he spoke.

"The situation is not good," he began, his thin nasal voice holding their attention as he looked around at his army, "Not good at all. We, the males, despite a thorough search, have not found the Princess. And the females..." he paused to glare angrily at a few of them, "The females have completely failed in their searching. I have heard from them the reliable information that even the cat has escaped and the owl is free and flying around wherever it wants to. The Princess tricked us with those stupid dummies, so she is totally free... and the albatross, with that ridiculous scarf, that stupid albatross, is gliding around a totally free bird. Even though the Prince is dead this situation is not good and definitely... definitely..."

he paused and spoke louder for emphasis, "Completely unsatisfactory! The females tell me that our Master is angry. He should be pleased with us but at the moment, I have to report to you, he is very disappointed. He wants all the enemy killed... not just the Prince. Now are we going to disappoint him further?"

He looked around expecting a response but none of them spoke, so he shouted.

"Well, are we?"

This time there was a great chorus of noise with most of them shouting, "No, sir!" but some shouting, "Are we *what?*"

"That's better," he said.

The sunlight flashed in metallic purple and green off one of his wings and the black compass bumped against his chest feathers. He thought he was beginning to get to know the compass and its movements. He opened his bill again and continued.

"The enemy is cunning... but they must be somewhere... which means that they can be found. We *must* find them and we *will* find them. So we search methodically. Where are you Searle...?"

Searle was in the next tree and called back, "Here, sir!"

"A special job for your Female Squadron. Go and search for the Princess north of here... Butterknowle, Tye Water and all around there. After that, when you've killed the Princess, then search diligently for the owl, the white, snowy owl, and the cat, black and white. I know they're hard to see but scan the ground... scan...scan... scan... all of you... and you will find them. As you know they were last seen by Old Howard going west from Burney's Hill, so start with the Clungberry Fields and around there. Don't bother with the Falwell Fens because no one can walk there... it's too marshy. Then work along the river, the Great River Sween."

He looked at Searle, "Orders understood?"

"Yes, sir,"

"When you've killed them report to me on Burney's Hill which we will now use as our base. Now go!"

"Yes, sir!" Searle replied, "Female Squadron! Attennnnnnnn...tion! Take off!"

All the females took off together with wings flapping quickly and the swishing sound of the movement of air. The General looked around at the remaining ravens.

"Now, males, we need to strike at the enemy... we will try seeking first in the Forest of the Fairies because that is where I think the Princess is. We will..." He stopped abruptly as one of them spotted Crayle and Jum flying towards them and screeched out.

"It's Crayle and Jum!"

They all turned their heads together and saw the two old birds approaching.

Some of them remembered the incident when Crayle hit the General's head when coming in to land on Tye Water. One of these shouted, "Look out, General!"

A loud cackle of laughter rippled through the group.

"Ah ha!" the General said, "They're the two deserters aren't they, Gerr?"

Gerr was young and enthusiastic. Before the raven army had left The Kingdom of Gems the Dark Wizard Troubler had picked him and Searle to find the Candara Gems. They had been successful in discovering them in the Brinscally Cave behind the Gem Falls, and Gerr had tried to steal the ruby. This resulted in a large flash leaving his beak badly singed at the end and cracked along the top.

He was ambitious and desperately wanted to be appointed second in command. He made sure he was always close to the General trying to please him and ready to assist him.

"I doubt if they deserted, sir," Gerr replied. "They're the two old ones, sir,"

"That doesn't stop them being deserters, does it?" the General snapped, "Just because they're one thing it doesn't stop them being another at the same time, does it?"

The General was always looking for opportunities to show his authority over the other birds. The black compass hanging around his neck bumped twice on his chest and he looked at it quizzically. Was it telling him he was wrong?

"Gerr?" the General whispered privately to him, "You don't think they're spies, do you?"

"No, sir."

"Hmm," the General sounded dubious, "Have you been looking out for spies as I asked you to?"

"Of course, sir."

"And what have you discovered then?" the General whispered.

The other birds were silent now as they tried to hear the conversation. Some of them shuffled closer.

"Nothing... yet, sir. But my investigations are continuing," he added. He had made no investigations but wanted to impress the General.

The General leant his head slightly towards Gerr, "Keep me posted."

"Yes, sir," Gerr whispered back, "I will, sir."

The General suddenly noticed the other birds trying

to listen and looked around crossly. They immediately tried to look innocent and glanced around randomly.

Crayle and Jum were close now and they glided through the trees.

"Get down!" shouted Iker, the youngest raven in the army. He was so young that he still had some fluffy baby feathers left. He was only in the army because he was the General's nephew, and the General had persuaded him to join. "It's Crayle," he shouted, "So if you value your life, get down!"

"Danger!" shouted another.

"Duck, General!" shouted one called Razz.

"Where?" said the General looking around.

Many of the ravens cackled with laughter. The General realized they were laughing at him, scowled at them and then bobbed his head down.

There was a flurry of movement as most of the ravens also bobbed their heads down and lowered their bodies close to the branches they were perched on. They spread their black wings as they cowered while keeping their eyes on the flight of the two old ravens.

Crayle was in front and struggling to stop in time, so while Jum landed Crayle had to circle around and swoop in again. His wings clipped some leaves and a raven's tail feathers before he landed beside Jum with a bump and nearly fell off. With some flapping he managed to balance. The flock of ravens relaxed, folded their wings again and raised their heads up. Crayle and Jum were just below the General who looked down at them with disdain.

"Deserting…" he began coldly, "Deserting is a serious crime. It is cowardly, against the spirit of war and a direct conflict with traditional age-tested army rules."

Iker turned around to the others behind him and said,

"Are we at war?"

The General jerked his head in his direction, "Of course we're at war! We're at war with the enemy!" Then he turned back to Crayle and Jum. "Where have you two been?"

Crayle puffed out his chest feathers proudly. "We've been stalking the enemy, sir."

"What?" the General exclaimed with excitement. He looked very surprised. "Where? When?"

Crayle moved his head around to look with his one eye at all the other ravens who were observing him closely. He was the centre of attention and this would be his proudest moment. Then he turned back to the General. "In the forest, sir. The Forest of the Fairies, sir. Over there, sir." He nodded in the direction.

"Good, good," said the General, "And when was this?"

"Just now, sir," Crayle replied perkily trying to impress the General as much as possible.

Then Jum spoke. "We picked 'em up last night and trailed 'em this morning when they woke. We kept hidden and trailed 'em… sir. We stalked 'em and then came to tell you, sir."

"Well," the General was clearly pleased, "Very good. And *who* are they?"

Crayle straightened up slightly with pride and announced slowly, "The Prince… the Princess…"

There was an excited murmuring from the crowd of ravens. The General looked astonished.

"The Prince!" he exclaimed, "But we know he's dead! Drowned in the big wave… that ferryman told us. Are you sure?"

"Yes, sir."

"But with only one eye… well you might have been mistaken."

Crayle felt insulted by this remark and said sharply, "I'm sure, sir."

The General looked at Jum. "Did you see the Prince?"

"Yes, sir," she confirmed.

The General looked puzzled and put his head on one side to think. Then Gerr spoke.

"Maybe… just maybe, sir… that ferryman licd to us about that."

The General's compass jumped about on its chain and he knew it was confirming Gerr's comment.

"You're right, Gerr. Possibly for the first time ever, you're right!"

Then Crayle raised his voice. "*And*… that overgrown seagull with the stripy scarf, sir."

The General nodded. "It's an albatross, old bird, an albatross."

The compass on the General's chest moved out as if by an invisible hand and spun around once before falling back. This sparked off a chorus of 'oos' from the ravens.

"Excellent," the General said as he nodded his approval, "So the Princess *and* the Prince are there, as well as the albatross. It does make me wonder where the others are. But… no… this is excellent. Can you lead us to them?"

"Yes, sir," said Crayle and Jum together.

"Crayle and Jum…" the General began, nodding at the two old birds. Crayle looked intently back at him with his one eye. He was filled with expectations for the praise that he felt he deserved and that he thought he was about to receive. "You two have…" the General continued slowly, "Somehow... although it must be said by complete accident... become..."

Crayle sat up expectantly.

The General continued, "You have become... heroes by accident. You are accidental heroes." Then the General looked thoughtful. "Just one thing though. It's most irregular that you, Jum, being a female, should fly with the Male Squadron. However, on this occasion, in view of the exceptional circumstances, and as a special favour, I shall turn a blind eye to it."

Some of the ravens sniggered at his final remark and pointed with their bills at the one-eyed Crayle. Jum had in fact flown with Crayle all the time but the General had not noticed and the other birds had not cared enough to say anything. Crayle looked extremely let down and muttered quietly to Jum.

"Accidental heroes indeed! That's very disappointing that is... and after all we've done. Accidental!"

Jum nestled towards him. "Never mind, Crayle."

The General looked thoughtful and then looked at Crayle with a cutting glare.

"What were you doing there... in the forest?" he snapped, "Why were you there when you should have been with us, the army?"

Crayle looked confused.

"We were... resting, sir. Yes... resting. We're old, sir, and..."

"Laziness!" the General interrupted crossly, "Sheer laziness and self indulgence! All the other old ones keep up, don't they?"

He paused to look around for an old raven to use as an example but he could not see one because there were not any. "Anyway... your laziness, by luck, happened to put you in the right place at the right time, but its still… *laziness.*"

Crayle felt the burden of failure fall upon him. The confident feeling he was enjoying just a few minutes before had gone and he huddled down onto the branch. His disappointment had turned into anger and he gripped his bill together in frustration.

"Now," the General continued, "We must act on this new information. We'll go straight there now… no time to collect the females, and anyway they're busy hunting over Butterknowle at the moment." Then he raised his voice and shouted, "Male Squadron… attennnnnn… tion! Take off!"

At the General's command they all took off. Then, flying rather slower than usual because they were following Crayle and Jum, they headed towards the Forest of the Fairies.

Amalek and Seph, with Neville gliding effortlessly above, continued travelling through the forest. They were aware that they must forge ahead as quickly as possible. Amalek was using her stick now to take some of the weight off her blistered foot.

The afternoon sun was hot, but the travellers were mostly shaded by the canopy of leaves above their heads. Rays of bright sunlight sloped through the gaps casting pools of light below and transforming deep greens into yellowish greens. As they moved through the ferns and trees they were aware again of the magical atmosphere of the forest. It was so very still that the sound of the trickling water echoed through the woodland scene like voices in a great building. It refreshed them and put their minds at ease after the frightening time before.

There was water dripping delicately into forest pools and there was the delightful babbling and bubbling of streams as they trickled over pebbles and rocks. As before, all the sounds harmonized like a symphony of perfect music and all held in the stillness that seemed to fill the whole forest and everything in it. They felt they were moving through a huge cathedral with an atmosphere of deep peace everywhere and the music echoing in it. It was delightful and magical.

They travelled steadily through the afternoon. The sun fell in the sky, evening drew in and the temperature dropped a little. They were just passing through a small clearing when suddenly Seph stopped walking and held Amalek's arm.

"Did you hear that?" he asked quietly, turning to Amalek.

"No," she replied, "What?"

"Something moving over there."

He pointed between some trees and across dappled shadows to some bushes.

"Nothing," said Amalek, "Let's go…"

Just then the bush shook.

"Old Howard," whispered Seph, "It must be. He's following."

An image of the terrifying creatures, fresh in both their memories, flashed into the minds of the two children and their breath shallowed. Their eyes were fixed on the bush. It rustled and shook again and then two long ears slowly rose out. The ears turned this way and that as if listening for something. Then the ears were followed by a head.

"It's only a rabbit," whispered Seph relaxing and breathing out, "A white rabbit."

"But what's a rabbit like that doing here?" Amalek queried, still whispering, "White rabbits live in the snow."

They watched as it leapt out of the bush and landed gently in some long grass. Neville was circling gracefully above.

"It's a hare," whispered Amalek, remembering the knowledge of animals that she had learnt from Pemima, "Look at its big back legs and long ears. It's a mountain hare... or maybe an arctic hare. See, it's all white it's a hare definitely."

The hare glanced to the right and then to the left as if checking that it was safe and then started lolloping towards them through some tall grass.

"Hey there!" he called out, pausing and standing up on his back legs, "You did well to get out of that one! I mean... that trouble with Old Howard."

The children were surprised by the young hare's comment and wondered how he knew.

"Back there," Tally continued, now lolloping once more through the grass, "Old Howard trying to get you!"

He emerged from the grass and hopped up to them. The Prince and Princess stepped back uneasily. Was this hare on their side or against them? He was right in front of them now, looking up at them with big brown eyes, and they saw how beautiful his pure white fur was. He was bubbling with youthful energy.

"It's alright," he said, "Relax... I'm here to help you."

The children were warming to him but with everything that had happened they were still suspicious. Tally realized that they just needed reassurance.

"I'm Tally," he said, "And I'm on my way to Wizard Elzaphan... to offer my help."

"How do you know all that about Old Howard?" asked Amalek.

"I was there," Tally said brightly, "In fact, I tripped him up. That's why he fell into the ferns and hurt his leg."

Amalek knelt down and reached out to stroke him on the head. His fur was thick and soft. She had a wide knowledge of many kinds of animals, including where they lived, what sort of homes they liked and the food they ate. All this she learnt from Memima. She had also learnt how to treat them. She had a special way with them, a way of understanding them because she knew how they felt inside. She could sense that Tally was a friend.

"What else do you know, Tally," she asked him.

"I know lots of things," Tally said, "And I know about the Dark Wizard Troubler who has cast a spell in the Kingdom of Gems... and how Old Howard is working for him."

Amalek smiled at him and stroked him again on his head.

"But how do you know all this?" she asked.

"Well, I'll explain..." said Tally.

The children sat down so that they were close to Tally. Neville circled watchfully just above their heads.

"I want to help," he said, speaking quickly and with a young playful tone to his words, "I actually live in the Becci Mountains not far from the border of your kingdom and everyone was talking about the snow and some spell in the Kingdom of Gems and I said that we, that's us mountain hares, there's seventy-three of us you know, should do something about it... you know, try to help. All those people and animals and birds and everything... all trapped."

His mood suddenly became sad and he shook his young head with heart-felt concern.

"It's terrible," said Seph, clearly touched by the young hare's willingness to help, "And we can do with all the help we can get."

"I know," Tally lifted a front paw and turned it out in a gesture of resignation, "But all the other hares weren't interested... except for my grandfather. He said I should go. He used to do things like this when he was younger... go on adventures and fight! But all the others... *all* of them... said they've got their own problems. So I decided to go to Wizard Elzaphan and offer my help. Hawkeye, that's my grandfather, said I should go. The others tried to stop me, but I had decided. When I reached the forest I slept. Then, when I woke and carried on, I picked up your scent. I was just catching up to you when I saw the old man... um... Old Howard, creeping along behind you."

Amalek looked thoughtful.

"But how did you know Old Howard?" she asked.

"Some friends of yours," said Tally, "A cat and a mouse. I helped them make a trap for him... to catch Old Howard."

Seph looked at Amalek with wide-eyed excitement and clapped his hands around her shoulders.

"They're alive!" he exclaimed, and then he turned back to Tally, "And have they escaped then?"

"Well, I hope so," said Tally, "You see it began when

I saw them from Burney's Hill, and by the time I was down they were creating the trap."

"That sounds like them," said Seph beaming with the joy of the good news.

"I wondered how I could help them, and then I got a brilliant idea. I got some other animals to help, a couple of hares, a family of badgers and a mole, and we tunnelled underground and made a hole for him, Old Howard, to fall into. It was a way of making their trap even better... but the fact that Old Howard is here... well, I don't know, perhaps the plan didn't work. I just hope they're alright..."

This quashed Amalek and Seph's excitement and their hearts sank. The uncomfortable sense of fear for their friends returned. They wanted to know that they were alright, and to see them again.

"Did you see a snowy owl?" asked Amalek.

"I don't think so," replied Tally with his nose twitching. He paused to think. "I saw one old tawny in the forest last night but that's all... no, no snowy owl I'm afraid. Sorry."

Seph looked around to scan the trees for ravens.

Neville saw him and called from above, "It's all clear."

Tally continued perkily. "When I saw Old Howard following you I was really shocked! I watched and waited for my chance. Then I crept up, hid under the ferns and tripped him, and he didn't even see me, but over he went!"

"That was brave," said Seph, "That was very brave and we're thankful... Old Howard is extremely dangerous."

"It was easy for me," said Tally quickly, "I can hide

under the ferns."

Seph nodded. "It was still brave," he said, and scratched Tally affectionately behind the ears.

"We ought to move on," Neville's friendly voice called out from above their heads, "You can chat as you walk."

"Shall we travel together, Tally?" Amalek asked.

Tally looked very pleased with this invitation and he sat up straight on his large back feet.

"I'll love to come with you," he said decisively, "And I can help you too because I know a way to cross the lake to Keill Isle."

"Let's go then," Neville said from above their heads where he was gliding to and fro.

No sooner had they begun walking than a little group of ten tiny fairies, with wings shimmering with many colours and eyes bright, fluttered out of the trees and danced in the air around them. They were pointing and beckoning to them.

"Hey!" exclaimed Amalek. "Aren't they beautiful! Do you think they're showing us the way?"

She held her hand out and one landed on it, pointed the direction, and then flitted into the air again.

Tally was hopping beside Seph.

"I know they are," Tally said, "My grandfather told me about these fairies. They always help anyone good passing through their forest."

Amalek was watching the fairies with a look of wonder in her eyes.

"They're beautiful!" she repeated.

As they travelled more and more tiny fairies joined them, leading them through the forest, until the air was filled with their quick darting movements and their quivering wings. They were so delicate that the stirring of a gentle breeze would blow them around in the air, and some little groups of them looked like shoals of fish moving in harmony. Their wings reflected rainbow colours while their bodies were as transparent as their wings. They were constantly smiling and laughing, and their presence lifted the spirits of the travellers and made them feel stronger and happier. The whole effect was a dancing shimmering display that held them fascinated as they followed them.

The children chatted to Tally as they walked and told him everything that had happened. The trees were thinning out now and the canopy of leaves lay against a background of blue sky. Bright beams of yellow sunlight streamed through. They were in daylight again.

They were treading along a little grassy path that ran through the ferns with Tally now hopping in front. The music of the forest sounded gently in their ears and they found themselves walking in time with the rhythm of it.

Seph suddenly stopped.

"I feel something again..." he said, looking around.

Amalek stood still and looked up into the trees above.

"Yes, now that you mention it, I do," she agreed, "I feel that presence again. Could it be Old Howard?"

Tally sat down on the grass beside them. His ears were flicking this way and that as he listened. He put his nose in the air to try to catch a scent.

"Old Howard was limping badly," he commented, "Too badly to keep up with us surely."

"Neville," called Seph, "Can you see anything?"

Neville was gliding above.

"No," he replied, "But let's not hang around to find

out."

He had barely finished his sentence when the sky darkened and the ravens arrived. There were over fifty of them, gliding and squawking right above their heads, like a living black ceiling. On the ground below, the friends looked up in horror. Through the branches of an oak tree they saw the great mass of ravens with outspread wings and black angular bodies.

"Where are they?" shouted the General, "They must be in here somewhere…"

Gerr was beside him and peering down through the trees.

"Crayle said they'd be around here, sir," he said, "But it's so dark down there… it's hard to see."

The light was fading with the sun low in the sky and casting a red hue over everything. The ravens were swirling around now in a great mass, weaving in and out of each other with amazing skill.

The General was cross. He called out to Gerr who had just drifted away on an air current.

"Ask Crayle again… or Jum…" He looked around. "But where are they? We should be following them!"

Gerr lifted a wing to adjust his flight and he was beside the General again. He turned his head to the General.

"They were so slow that we went past them, sir. Then they couldn't keep up, sir. They've dropped right behind."

A raven from somewhere in the swirling mass cried out, "Overgrown seagull, sir!"

"What!?" shouted the General, "Is it the albatross?"

"Yes, sir," replied the raven.

"Well spotted, that bird!" exclaimed the General with

enthusiasm, "Where is it?"

"Just ahead," squawked the reply.

"There!" said Gerr excitedly, as he caught sight of Neville, "Look! Down there through the trees, sir."

"Where?" snapped the General.

"It's hidden by leaves now, but it's there," Gerr pointed his beak, "Under that tree just ahead, sir."

"Well done, Gerr," the General said, "Male Squadron follow me and prepare for attack!"

The General dropped through the great throng of cackling ravens, emerging just below and in front of them and flew towards the tree.

Down below them, Neville had heard the shout of "Attack!"

"Look out!" shouted Neville down to the others, "They're going to attack!"

Seph began to run as fast as he could with Tally scampering along right behind them. Neville turned; he would do his best to defend his friends. He decided he would hold off the attack as long as possible.

Amalek hobbled along on her blistered foot so Seph stopped, grabbed her by the hand and pulled her.

Neville's multicoloured stripy scarf began to tingle, the magic gathering in it and concentrating. As he glided the scarf lengthened, flowing out behind him and shaking in the turbulent air. He glanced up and through the leaves. The sight was terrifying. Flying towards him were over fifty ravens, jagged black shapes, their noises raucous and harsh with vicious war-like cries of "Attack!", "Kill them!" and "No mercy!"

"Hold and gather!" shouted the General, "Glide together now… together! And follow me!"

A moment later, despite the General's command, two

of them, too eager to wait, burst through the higher branches of the trees and descended upon Neville. His scarf suddenly moved by itself, flicking at the end first, and then whipping up and around, swiping them away. One went spinning into a tree-trunk with a thud and plummeted to the ground below. The other was knocked back above the trees again and crashed into two others who were in the main group.

"What are you doing?!" cried one of these as their wings became momentarily caught together.

"The scarf hit me!" shouted the raven as it disentangled itself and dropped again, "Attack!" it screeched.

It fell beneath the top branches to chase Neville who was gliding away. The scarf grew longer still and then caught the raven, winding twice around its body. Then it unwound and sent the raven spinning away towards the ground, a black blur of feathers. Above the trees the General and all the rest of the raven army were following Neville below. As Neville swerved they swerved.

Gerr was still beside the General and suddenly spotted the children running below.

"The Prince and Princess are there too, sir!" he announced excitedly, "Trying to run away, sir!"

"Male Squadron!" the General screamed, "Prepare to annihilate the enemy! Ready now?"

"Yes, sir!" they all shouted.

"Wait for my order!" shouted the General, now in complete control of his great army. His black compass was like a medallion around his neck and was pulling him forwards and down.

"Descend!" he commanded, "Not too fast now. Follow me!"

Altogether, while still tracking Neville below, they gradually descended. The whole group were close now to the tops of the trees. They were poised for the final command from the General to release them into combat. Neville was gliding between the trees but knew that the strength of over fifty ravens would be far too much, even with his magic scarf. He would fight and sacrifice himself for his friends if necessary, just to give them time to get away.

Then some of the ravens slowed.

"Keep up!" the General commanded, "Keep up… do you hear…"

His voice faded, his wings drooped and he began to drop towards the ground. He looked alarmed and terrified.

A chorus of groans came from the swirling crowd of ravens as the whole group began to fall slowly through the air. They were making every effort to stay up but they were slowing and stalling, losing speed and strength. Some were falling onto others and were trying to rise by kicking down on their backs. This produced raucous cries of complaints. Some were panicking and flying around in small circles as they fell and a few were even flying upside-down as if this might help their plight. It was complete chaos.

"What's happening!" the General blurted out, "Stop all your stupid noise!"

With a huge effort he managed to gather his failing strength and regain his flight.

"It's the power," shouted Gerr, "It's that Wizard Elzaphan! We're too close to the castle!"

"Male Squadrons," announced the General, as he wheeled around in the air guided again by the black compass, "Follow me and retreat!"

At the General's command all the ravens tried to turn and for a few moments the flock was still a chaotic muddle with ravens bumping into each other with loud squawking and complaining. A couple of birds fell out of the group. Gerr spotted them.

"Shall we help them, sir?" he cried.

"No!" the General snapped, "Leave them. If they're too weak to fly in this they shouldn't be in the army in the first place!"

Gradually the great mass of birds regained some order until they were all following the General. They continued turning until they were flying south and away from the castle in the failing light. They quickly regained their strength.

"That is *extremely* disappointing," grumbled the General, "We had them in our sights, Gerr."

Gerr was right beside him as usual. "Yes, sir," he said, "We'll get them next time."

"But how, Gerr, how?" he exclaimed with frustration, "They're through now. Unless we find a way..."

"I'm sure we can, sir," Gerr said brightly, "We can find a way, sir."

"Hmm, I hope so. If not we'll get them when they try to travel back to the Kingdom of Gems. But there are the others. The cat and the owl."

As he said this the black compass started bobbing around excitedly. This encouraged him.

"We can still get them... if only we can find them."

"Yes, sir," agreed Gerr.

"You know, Gerr... this is the most frustrating mission I've ever known!"

"What shall we do now, sir?" asked Gerr.

The General thought for a few moments.

"We go to the best look-out post in this kingdom."

"Burney's Hill, sir?"

"Correct," he snapped. He seemed to have regained his composure. "But just the Male Squadron." He lowered his voice. "The females are searching. I still don't trust them mind you, after the mutiny, but Searle is now the captain. We'll see what she can do." Then he lowered his voice even more. "You know the spies, Gerr?"

Gerr looked surprised, "What spies, sir?"

"The spies you're supposed to be looking out for. Yes?"

"Oh... yes, sir," said Gerr, remembering about the Generals' suspicions.

"Watch carefully... especially the females when they're back with us again, Gerr. If the spies do exist I'll bet you my mother's tail feathers that they're females."

"But your mother's not alive, sir," said Gerr.

The General ignored Gerr's comment and bellowed, "Male Squadron... we'll head for Burney's Hill. As for the Female Squadron we'll leave them with their special job..."

He looked over towards Tye Water where they were still searching but it was hard to see now with the night closing in.

The great flock of ravens headed off towards Burney's Hill. Once again Crayle and Jum were left behind. They had become exhausted trying to keep up and had landed in a tree to rest. They watched as the group of ravens flew away.

"What do we do now, Crayle?" asked Jum.

Crayle shook his head, and turned to look at her with

his one eye, "Oh, I don't know… rest? I'm so tired."

Jum nodded, "OK."

"One thing I do know," said Crayle, turning his good eye towards Jum, "I'm getting more and more fed up with the General."

He was still seething with anger at the General for calling them 'accidental heroes.' They sank down onto the branch as the thin red crescent of the sun dipped out of sight on the horizon. They ruffled up their feathers and closed their eyes to sleep.

"That was lucky!" said Seph, his breathing beginning to ease now after sprinting away from the ravens.

A few moments earlier, after the ravens had turned back, Neville had called down to his friends below.

"All clear! They've gone!"

Amalek and Seph had stopped running straight away and collapsed in exhaustion. Tally sat down beside them and helped Amalek slip off her shoe by gripping it in his teeth and pulling. Then she removed her sock to look at her blister.

"How is it?" asked Seph.

"All that running did not help," replied Amalek, "And your pocket has slipped around."

She lay back among the ferns and wriggled her toes as she gazed up at the trees, now dark shapes in the dying embers of the day. Seph looked up too and they watched the great white wings of Neville as he circled above. After a few minutes of recovering Amalek sat up and worked at her shoe and sock so that the pocket was padding her blister. The children stood up and Tally sat on his haunches.

"What happened?" asked Amalek.

"It's Wizard Elzaphan," said Neville looking down at them, "He's so powerful that they can't approach close to his castle."

"So what happened to them?" Amalek asked, trying to tidy her long wavy hair with her hands.

"They went weak and started falling," replied Neville, "Did you hear the noises they made? They had to turn back, away from the castle."

"Well, I'm just *so* glad they've gone," said Amalek. She hooked some of her hair around one ear. "They are creepy, aren't they?"

Seph nodded. "But what's really good," he commented, "Is that they won't come back. They *can't* come back."

"So… Neville," said Amalek brightening up, "which way to Lake Beautiful?"

Neville pointed his long, hooked, yellowish-pink bill and gave a little nod. "That way. Are you ready?"

Seph looked at Tally and reached down to stroke his head. The young hare looked up.

"I'm ready," he said.

"Let's go then."

The sun had set, leaving behind a lingering crimson sunset, fading slowly a like dying fire. Underneath the spreading branches of the trees it was dark. They began walking again and soon fairies appeared and led the way. They were tiny, no bigger than a child's little finger, with slim legs and happy round faces. They were luminous, shedding a gentle light which glittered on their delicate wings as they fluttered and darted through the warm forest air and led the way to Lake Beautiful. Their movement was like a dance that followed the beautiful music of the babbling forest springs and streams.

Several times, as they journeyed on, the fairies disappeared, and they thought they had gone. Then they would appear again just behind their heads, or around their feet, or swooping down from above with little peals of giggles. The fairies were travelling so fast that at times the Prince and Princess had to jog to keep up. Tally made his hops larger.

As they travelled, Amalek and Seph told Tally all the things that had happened to them including the attack by the giant scorpions. When Tally heard about Seph's bravery he was full of admiration and started hopping beside him. He loved the tales his grandfather Hawkeye had told him about fighting for what was good and right, and where qualities of courage, bravery and honesty were so important. From time to time he would look up at Seph with respect.

Neville glided above them with just a slow smooth flap of his wings every now and again.

"Nearly there!" called out Neville all of a sudden, "Keep going!"

They passed through the last few trees and found themselves, to their delight, on a grassy bank by the lake's edge. They gazed across the water, shimmering gently with the pale red reflection of the last moments of the sunset. They realized why it was called Lake Beautiful. The water stretched before them for miles with a surface that was so still and calm that it looked almost like a flat, slippery floor that they could walk on and the Princess picked up a stone and tossed it into the lake just to make sure that it was in fact water. The stone dropped in and created circles of ripples that expanded and soon faded away.

Seph then picked up a flat stone and tossed it across the surface of the lake, spinning it to make it skim.

"One… two…" he counted, and then getting quicker and quicker, "Three, four, five. How's that!"

"Not bad," replied Amalek, looking for a flat stone.

She threw it over the water and counted to five as well. Tally had never seen stones skimming before and he looked on with interest. After a few stones had been thrown he started getting excited and rushed around to collect flat stones for the children to throw. Then he started counting the number of jumps the stones made, and when Seph spun one across the water that skimmed eleven times he jumped up and down in enjoyment.

"That's great!" Tally exclaimed, turning a full circle on the spot.

Seph was an excellent thrower. His skill had developed over the past two years, playing a game with a few other boys in the Southern Downs. They accidentally discovered a hole in a sheer rock face with magical properties. When a stone was thrown into it, a colourful flash would burst forth, like an erupting firework, an explosion of fiery light. After their discovery they regularly returned there to throw stones at the hole, enjoy the spectacular display and see who could get the most hits.

They had discovered the faint remnants of a magic power, left from almost 2,000 years before. There were several places like this in The Kingdom Of Gems, legacies from the distant past when the magic was full and strong, but now almost completely faded. This soon became a favourite game among the children and gave Seph plenty of throwing practice; his aim became accurate and his throw strong. He soon became the best.

After throwing skimming stones for a while, Seph collected a few pebbles and rolled them in his fingers. Then he held them out to show Amalek.

"Look how round these are," he said.

He slipped them into his pocket and they sat down on the grass and gazed across the wonderful expanse of water. They could just about see the silhouetted turrets of a castle on an island in the middle of the lake. At last they were in sight of the home of Wizard Elzaphan, his great castle, built on the top of an outcrop of rock called Keill Island and set against the background of the distant Daawa Mountains.

They were feeling very tired after the journey and decided to rest. They sat down on the grass and Amalek loosened her shoe to relieve the pain of her blister. They watched as the red sunset paled to pink and then grey as the light rapidly faded. The mountains, which rose impressively above the distant shore of the lake, became barely visible, their sharp outline fading into the darkening sky.

Neville landed clumsily in a tree with his wings flapping. One wing got tangled in some leaves and he shook it and pulled it to get it free. It jerked loose, his feet slipped and he ended up sitting on the branch with one leg hanging down each side. He blinked, looked down at the others sitting below on the grass and shrugged.

"Well…" he began, "This is actually quite comfortable."

He opened his long, hooked bill a little wider and started singing another riddle-song, which gave them some light relief as they listened and then puzzled over the meaning.

"We dwell in many houses,
most houses to be sure,
in houses tall and houses small,
in houses rich and poor.

We live in many numbers
in rows of two directions,
we're friends forever and stick together
and display a bright reflection.

We are of many colours
and in most cases square
and we are bright when cleaned with a wipe
and dirt is removed with care.

For 'though we dwell in your own home
we're not in every room,
and that's the last clue - good luck to you
and solve this riddle soon!"

"So, there are lots of them…" began Seph, "And they live in houses…"

Amalek was thinking, "And they're square…"

"In *most* cases," added Seph.

Amalek spread her hands, "And of many colours."

They thought for a moment.

"This is hard!" said Amalek, "Sing it again, Neville."

Neville sang it again but they still could not solve it so they decided they would hear it again another time.

Neville jumped out of the tree and then glided down,

We Dwell in Many Houses

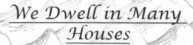

"We dwell in many houses,

most houses to be sure,

in houses tall and houses small,

in houses rich and poor.

We live in many numbers

in rows of two directions,

we're friends forever and stick together

and display a bright reflection.

We are of many colours

and in most cases square

and we are bright when cleaned with a wipe

and dirt is removed with care.

For 'though we dwell in your own home

we're not in every room,

and that's the last clue - good luck to you

and solve this riddle soon!"

~ NEVILLE'S 5TH RIDDLE ~

descending through the air like a huge paper plane. Still in motion, he touched down beside them, turned to look at them and then skidded past on the grass. A bump made him fall sideways and his skid turned into an ungainly, tumbling motion. He closed his eyes tightly as he rolled, his legs and wings thrashing around and around. He soon came to a halt and lay there on his back with his eyes closed and his bill pointing skywards.

"Are you alright?" called out Amalek.

Neville turned to face her and opened his eyes.

"Yes," he replied calmly, "Why?"

"Oh, Neville," Amalek smiled as she jokingly reprimanded him, "Your landings are atrocious!"

Neville managed to roll onto his feet and then waddled over until he was standing beside them.

"How," he asked calmly, "are you earth-bound creatures going to cross the lake?"

Tally smiled and took something out of a small pouch that was fixed to the fur on his belly. It was a piece of old paper, folded twice into a small rectangle. Time had faded it to a blotchy yellow-brown and he held it carefully between his paws like holding a fragile flower that could easily be damaged. The children looked at it with interest and could see that it was tattered at the edges and torn a little along the creases. He unfolded it carefully with his paws and laid it on the grass where they could see it. The children knelt down beside Tally and peered at it through the twilight.

"This," Tally stated, "Is a map of all the known tunnels in Summertime Kingdom. And look there." He pointed with a paw to Lake Beautiful on the map. "There's the tunnel under the lake to Keill Isle."

Amalek smiled.

"Excellent," she commented.

"That looks like a really old map, Tally," said Seph.

"It's older than my grandfather who gave it to me… his father gave it to him. My grandfather used it when he was younger and went on adventures. He said that a hare must have a tunnel map when travelling. He's too old to travel now so he gave me his maps and gave me some tips to help me my journey. He helped me with my route. He's very wise!"

"So," said Amalek pointing at the map, "There's the tunnel, and the entrance to it should be…" she looked up and pointed, "Just along there by those trees."

"Most tunnels are secret," said Tally, "They have to be else you'd have anyone using them. See that symbol there, that little door by that tree. Well, that means it's a hidden entrance, but I'll find it."

Seph yawned. "I think we're so tired," he said, "that we ought to sleep here first…"

"Or in the tunnel," added Amalek. In her mind she had already started planning. "We'd be safe in there."

"Good idea, Ammey," Seph agreed, "Over to you then, Tally."

He hopped off towards the clump of trees followed by Amalek and Seph. It was almost night now and just a few stars had appeared above. Neville waddled behind them. When they were among the trees Tally turned into a fury of activity, racing around the tree, sniffing the ground, digging a little bit with his paws, searching for the entrance.

"Here!" he called to the others, "I've found it!"

Amalek and Seph ran to Tally. The entrance had been hidden so well that they could see nothing.

"Where?" asked Seph.

"It's under here," Tally replied, pointed a paw at the grass at the foot of the tree, "It'll be a sliding door. Look!" He felt around on the bark until he found an opening near the roots that could be seen at the foot of the tree.

"Here it is!" he exclaimed triumphantly.

Neville waddled up eager to see the tunnel. Tally put his paw into the opening and pulled.

'Clunk.'

A large section of the grass dropped a little and then slid across, underneath the ground, leaving a large hole. As they peered into the darkness below they could see a platform and then steps leading downwards.

"I'll go by air," announced Neville, "See you over there."

He started waddling clumsily in the direction of the lake.

"Let us help you," called out Amalek, but again it was too late as he had started his attempt to take off with great enthusiasm.

"See you there!" called out Seph, as they all stood and watched nervously.

The grass sloped down to the surface and as it became steeper he sped up. His webbed feet were slapping the grass and sounding like rhythmic clapping and his head was wagging from side to side in the most ungainly way. Then he stretched out his great wings, but before he could get airborne he reached the earthy bank of the lake. Two steps later and the bank ended and he moved from land to lake.

For a moment he was running on the water, his large webbed feet splashing in rhythm as they beat downwards and propelled him along. He tried to run faster and gradually his feet were being lifted. The splashing became less and then stopped, and to the great relief of the others, he was airborne. He circled around effortlessly above their heads.

"See you at the castle!" he cried, and glided gracefully over the lake towards the castle.

"Right then," said Tally, "Let's go."

He hopped into the tunnel entrance and landed on the platform. Seph jumped down next and then Amalek.

They all paused and looked down the steps.

"I'll just close the door," said Tally, "It's easy."

He hopped up a few small steps and onto a little ledge underneath the sliding door. He lifted a paw and pushed gently on it. It moved smoothly and gathered speed.

A noise behind Amalek and Seph made them jump. They spun around and gazed into the dim shadows in the corner. They saw something move. At that moment the sliding door clunked into position and they were plunged into complete darkness. They stood motionless. Their fear was as deep as the darkness that suddenly surrounded them. They hardly dared breathe. Then a flickering light began to glow behind them and gradually light spread all around. They stared into the corner and saw, suspended on ropes, two heavy weights that must have dropped as they pulled the sliding door back into place. They smiled, and then laughed as they realized what had happened.

"That Troubler has set us all on edge," said Seph.

More lights began to glow and shed a flickering light along the tunnel. There were about twenty steps leading steeply down.

"The candles are sensitive to noises!" said Tally,

"They light up at the sound of footsteps. Most of the tunnels have no lighting but here Wizard Elzaphan has used his magic to create these."

They moved down the steps until the tunnel levelled off. The air was cool. They knew from the map that it twisted and turned as it made its way to the castle and when they had turned the first bend they knew that they must be under the lake itself. The candles came on as they walked and then faded out behind them, providing a gentle glimmering light that was sufficient to see where they were going.

The tunnel had been coarsely hewn out of rock and their footsteps and voices echoed around the damp walls that were green here and there where thick patches of moss had grown. Water dripped through from the ceiling and splattered in little pools that were dotted along the tunnel floor.

"We'll need something to sleep on," said Amalek, "Something soft."

They stopped walking.

Seph thought about it.

"All we've got is your bag…" he said, "Could be a pillow, I suppose."

"Yes, but we can't sleep on rock," said Amalek, shaking her head, "Well, we wouldn't sleep, would we? We'll have to go back up and collect some ferns to lie on."

"Good idea, Ammey," he agreed.

They turned back, with Tally following, and retraced their steps up the stairs, out through the door and collected as many ferns as they could carry. In a few minutes they were back in the tunnel with their arms stretched out to carry the huge bundles. They walked along to find a suitable place and after a while Amalek stopped and pointed down.

"We could sleep just here where it's dry and flat," she said.

They dropped the fern in a pile by the wall and then spread them around to make the best bed they could. When the two children lay down Tally hopped on and settled in between them and they found that the ferns worked quite well. Amalek was relieved to lie down at last and take the weight off her blistered foot. It had been a long and difficult day.

"It will be great to sleep without the fear of those ravens finding us, or Old Howard, or anyone," she said.

It was not comfortable but they were so exhausted that they were soon drifting into a well needed sleep.

Chapter 5

~ Triple-Cross ~

Night had descended, transforming Summertime Kingdom into a grey world of shadows, tenderly lit by soft moonlight. It was quiet along the Great River Sween with hardly any movement apart from the flowing of the water, the occasional small creature swimming or running along the river bank and the Ferryman's boat.

Flop was facing the front of the boat, towards the Ferryman, with Miriam nestled in his fur on the back of his neck. Joog sat on the prow as the boat sped along the Great River Sween. His powerful feet grasped the wood firmly, gripping with his sharp claws, and his golden-yellow eyes were alert and watchful. His white feathers looked grey in the moonlit night as they tremored in the warm air that rushed by. Lazuli was striding along on the grassy riverbank keeping pace perfectly with the boat. Her trunk swung playfully as she moved.

The Ferryman rowed in silence, his powerful arms pulling the oars through the water as the boat surged forwards against the current. Facing backwards as he rowed, he too was alert and watchful, but felt uneasy.

"Do you think we're being followed?" he asked the others, his deep voice gentle and rich.

Joog and Flop both turned to look through the dark and along the banks behind the boat, but before they had time to answer Flop raised a paw and pointed to the sky.

"Look!" exclaimed Flop, his night eyes piercing the darkness.

Joog turned his head to look behind him and saw it too; above the river behind them rose a black flock of ravens, swirling in one mass together. They flew above the river with all of them scanning intently below. They were silent and approaching fast.

"Hmm," said the Ferryman, "As I thought. Well, they're certainly persistent. I'll bet they spotted that my boat had gone and now they're searching for us."

He skilfully turned the boat towards the riverbank and rowed powerfully towards it.

"We must act quickly," he said, "Maybe they haven't seen us yet."

Flop looked anxious and kept his eyes fixed on the great flock of evil ravens as they worked their way along the river in their direction. He knew they were intent on killing them. Joog jumped off the boat and glided over to Lazuli who was watching from the riverbank.

"Lazuli," said Joog urgently, "Pull the boat out of the river."

The Ferryman stepped out and Lazuli reached down with her trunk over the water, grasped the boat, and as if it weighed almost nothing, pulled it onto the bank.

"Flop," said the Ferryman, "Hide in the trees over there, quick!"

Flop, with Miriam on his back, jumped out of the

boat, ran across the grass and hid. Joog glided above him, a silent, silver dart under the moon's tender rays. The boat lay on the bank tilted over and the Ferryman sat down beside it. Lazuli padded a little distance away and stood in the dark deep shadow under a tree.

The ravens were close now and suddenly they burst into a cacophony of rasping shouts when they saw the boat and the Ferryman.

In a moment they descended with great cackling noises and the sound of a hundred black wings beating the air. They landed all around the Ferryman, who was sitting in his boat with his hooded head resting on his arms. His body was shaking with sobbing and he seemed distraught about something.

"Why did you kill my brother!" he shouted at them, still sobbing as he lifted his hooded head.

His face, as always, could not be seen beneath his hood. He had turned his robe inside out, which made it now blue instead of green. Amazingly the voice was like a different person, so well had he changed it.

Flop and Miriam watched in amazement. Flop had climbed a tree and walked along a branch until he had found a place where they were well hidden by leaves. They looked out to see the Ferryman with the great mass of black ravens in front of him. Joog was beside Flop and as they watched they wondered at the skill of the Ferryman. He was clearly a master of disguise, a genius at hiding behind a cover of deception.

"What's he doing!" whispered Miriam.

"I don't know," replied Flop, "Shhh."

The Ferryman banged his fist angrily onto the side of the boat making the ravens jump in shock.

"Why did you do it?" he sobbed, "Why did you kill

him? He was only a simple ferryman like me!"

Searle stepped forwards from the mass of ravens.

"Who told you that we killed him?" she asked.

As she spoke the Ferryman knew that his disguise had completely fooled them.

"The one who's your leader told me," the Ferryman sobbed, "Where is he?"

"That's the General," she replied, "And he's not here."

"He said that *you* had my brother drowned," continued the Ferryman, "Said he tried to stop you, but you disobeyed."

"What?! The big liar!" Searle looked furious, "I've never trusted him."

"I hate the General!" shouted Urrg, who stepped forwards to be beside Searle, "I hate his bossy orders. He thinks he's so much better than us."

"Be quiet!" snapped Searle, jabbing her bill threateningly towards Urrg, "Although… I do agree with you." Then she turned back to the Ferryman. "I didn't have your brother killed, he did. The General, as he calls himself. How could I? He's taken charge and he did it. I'm not in charge, am I?"

She heard a noise behind her and jerked her head around quickly to look into the darkness. It was Jamaar sneaking closer, trying to get near enough to hear, and wondering whether to attack, but Searle could not see anything in the shadowy shapes of the bushes. Assuming it to be just a bird or some other harmless creature, she turned her attention back to the conversation.

"Look!" said Urrg, who was staring into the shadows under the trees, "There's that elephant again!"

Searle turned to her and spoke abruptly, "We have a

job to do and that does not include shouting out every time we see an elephant... it's just an elephant. OK?"

"But..." Urrg began, looking at Lazuli suspiciously and then back at Searle. She was about to say more but nodded reluctantly.

The Ferryman lifted a lamp from his boat and removed the glass cover. He struck a match and lit the wick, replacing the glass cover. He wanted to see their reactions and movements clearly.

"You're not in charge but you did it!" cried the Ferryman, "He told me!"

"But, listen to me," Scarle pleaded, "He lies! He tells lies! As I said, he's in charge. He makes the decisions, not me."

The Ferryman shook his head, "How do I know that you're not making it all up? Perhaps you're the liar!"

Searle looked down and pecked at the ground crossly. Then she looked up again.

"Look," she said sounding frustrated, but trying to control it, "Listen to me. Oh... how can I make you understand? He's the liar not me. It's *him*! Ask anyone here."

She looked around at the group of ravens who were all facing the Ferryman. They were standing on the ground and listening to the conversation.

"Well?" she snapped at them.

A murmuring of agreement gradually arose from them. Black feathers glistened metallic blue and green by the light of the lamp.

"There you are," announced Searle.

"Now I don't know who to believe," said the Ferryman shaking his head. He was gradually calming down.

There was a pause.

The Ferryman stopped sobbing and seemed to be thinking things out.

"Believe us then…" pleaded Searle, "It's the truth."

The Ferryman nodded slowly.

"Alright then," he said, "It makes sense… It does make sense… alright, I'll believe you."

Searle relaxed, "At last," she sighed.

The Ferryman nodded.

"Yes, it does make sense. I can see it now. So it was him, was it? I should have guessed. And there he is flying around the place blaming you! Trying to get you into trouble with the Guards of Summertime Kingdom. If Wizard Elzaphan hears he'll send the guards out and they'll be after whoever killed my brother, you know."

"Guards? What guards?" asked Searle, looking anxious.

"The Guards of Justice," the Ferryman said convincingly, and making it up as he went along, "They are fierce and ruthless and at the moment they may be thinking that you are the murderer!"

"But your brother did lie to us. He told us that the Princess was travelling west to Butterknowle, so the General went out that way and searched for the Princess and found nothing! Now we've just searched there too… she's not there."

"The General's using you!" said the Ferryman, "You said he's a liar yourself. Nevertheless, he didn't find the girl, because she didn't go that way. Not at all. My brother only said that because he was being tortured, and said something different to stop them. But the General went that way because he thought he *would* find her. Now he sent you there because he knows she's not there.

Don't you see? He always wants all the glory for himself! Am I right?"

"I… I…" began Searle, "I don't know. I'm confused…"

The Ferryman smiled knowing that they could not see his face. He wanted to confuse them. He wanted to control the conversation and them. He was definitely succeeding.

He paused to gather his thoughts. To have them in his power he had to convince them.

"But…" he continued, "She's actually hiding somewhere else now… right now… and I know where."

Searle stood taller in surprise and Urrg poked her head forwards with eager interest.

"Where?" she asked.

"Why do you want to know? She's only a girl! What's so special about her?"

"Nothing," Searle replied quickly, trying to look casual about it, "Nothing at all. As you say, just a girl. We only want to ask her some questions, that's all."

The Ferryman gazed at her from under his hood. He was wondering what to tell them next, he had to make up something quickly.

"Honestly," added Searle trying to convince him. She was even more desperate now to find the Princess and to do better than the General.

"Yes," said Urrg, who was equally keen to gain some glory and rewards, and put the General down. "We only want to ask her a few little questions." She took a couple of steps towards him and said, "Just a few little questions. Now what's wrong with that?"

Searle had stopped objecting to Urrg's comments now and was beginning to think that they could work together.

The Ferryman looked thoughtful. Suddenly it came to him and he knew what to say next, he just hoped it would work.

"Alright then, I'll tell you," he said, "Listen. You know the General?"

"Yes," said Searle and Urrg together, looking surprised.

"Well, he knows. He knows exactly where she's hiding. He told me that he knows where she's hiding when he told me that you killed my brother! Then he sent you over there," he waved an arm, "What did he tell you to look for?"

"The enemy," said Searle angrily, "The Princess."

"There you are! Did you find her there?"

"No," Searle replied.

"You see? She's *not* there and he knew it. He's not telling you everything at all. Then where did he send you after that?"

"To Tye Water and along this river," Searle was sounding more and more angry.

"Well, that's wild goose chase. He's had you chasing here and there after nothing! Think about it; wherever he has sent you never works, does it?"

Urrg sighed and shook her head. "I can't stand this. It's too complicated."

"But it's true," growled Searle, turning to Urrg, "It must be. It makes sense... well some sense... don't you think?"

"Well, I always thought the General was up to no good," snapped Urrg with anger welling up inside her, "That devious, two-timing, old..." she was so angry she could not finish her sentence.

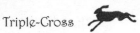

"You should follow him," continued the Ferryman, "Follow him and he'll lead you to the girl."

The Ferryman knew he had them under his control now. Their anger, hate and greed were possessing them.

"If he sees you he'll pretend otherwise. He'll try to put you off. He's been tricking you all along! He'll say he doesn't know. He'll say he's searching. He may fly this way and that, but don't trust him. You know how he hates you! Get the truth out of him. Don't let him get away with it any longer! Teach him a lesson. I hate him as much as you do because he killed my brother!"

"Well, thank you," said Searle angrily, "For a very interesting conversation! Female squadron!" she screamed, "Attennnnnnn...tion!"

They all looked alert and ready.

"Female squadron... fly low and out of sight to Burney's Hill... let's go!"

They took off with a great flurry of flapping wings and excited cackling and flew south, with anger and hate in their hearts, in pursuit of the General and his Male Squadron.

"Phew," sighed Miriam with relief, "They've gone."

Flop was keeping his eyes fixed on the ravens as they flew into the distance and disappeared into the night, "He's done it again," he said chuckling, "He's fooled those ravens and got them flying away just by speaking to them!"

"I couldn't follow it," Miriam laughed, "What he was saying was so difficult! No wonder they were confused."

Flop shook his head, "And I'm completely confused as well!"

"Yes, that was clever," Joog remarked, "He's a genius with words and disguises! And he's got rid of them, so we ought to get going. Come on!"

Joog spread his wings, glided down from the tree and landed by the boat. Flop climbed down, his sharp claws gripping the bark of the tree firmly, and Lazuli appeared from her hiding place. They walked together to join the Ferryman and Joog by the river.

Jamaar had watched and listened from the cover of the darkness in the bushes and from there he had tried to work out what was going on. He had not been able to hear all of the conversation, but only caught words here and there and parts of sentences. He knew the ravens were working for the Dark Wizard Troubler, but then why didn't they just kill the hooded rower who was obviously helping the enemy? Perhaps he was working for the ravens and had caught the cat and the owl. But, no, that did not make sense because he had seen the Ferryman talking to the owl. He could see the owl and the cat hiding from the ravens from the cover of a large clump of bushes under some trees.

What could it mean? He knew that if he just plunged in and attacked he would be lucky to catch anything as they would have too much warning; no, he had to stalk them carefully. And so he had decided to circle around behind the cat, who he knew was definitely the enemy, and he would catch it when it came down from the tree, kill it, have a small feast and then hunt down the owl and any others.

Just as he had circled around and had managed to get

behind his prey, the ravens had taken off. He was getting ready to attack when the cat, the elephant and the owl had come out of their hiding places and headed back towards the river. It had all gone wrong. He crouched down so that the long grass would conceal him and quickly tried to catch up to them. He paused to listen, then moved stealthily and quietly towards them. To attack by night was ideal. He wanted to surprise them.

All the time the compass was helping him with little movements. He had learnt that a quick jerk towards him meant 'stop'; he was either making too much noise or going the wrong way. A jerk forwards was the signal to continue. Now he stood still and listened.

"Brilliant!" said Flop to the Ferryman.

"How do you think of these things?" asked little Miriam.

"Well," began the Ferryman, laughing, "I always feel that if you can out-think the enemy it can save a lot of problems! Luckily the ravens are pretty stupid so it's not all that difficult. I think I just got them very confused!"

"Me too!" said Miriam.

Flop nodded and flicked the end of his tail. "You had me more confused than I've ever been!"

Joog stretched out his wings.

"Shall we go?" he asked.

"The sooner the better," Flop agreed, "Before they realize they've been tricked again and come back."

The Ferryman picked up the lamp and placed it in the boat.

Joog folded his wings and looked at Lazuli.

"And is this where you leave us, Lazuli?" he asked.

"Yes," Lazuli said, "But I'll help you with the boat first."

Flop looked up in surprise. "Where are you going?" he asked.

Lazuli looked down at him.

"To find the Prince and Princess," she answered.

She lifted the boat up with her strong trunk as if it was made of balsa wood and placed it carefully on the surface of the water where it rocked gently.

Jamaar crept forwards like a lion hunting, guided by the compass and still concealed in the long grass. He was almost close enough now to attack. His mouth watered with anticipation as he crouched lower still, muscles loaded and ready to explode into action. But he must wait for the right moment. The compass was still.

Lazuli padded off in the direction of Lake Beautiful.

Joog flew onto the prow of the boat and gripped the wood with his strong claws. The Ferryman held the rope attached to the boat as Flop jumped in, then he stepped in himself and took the oars.

Jamaar wondered if he had left it too late. The compass jerked forwards and he decided. He leapt out of the long grass like a spring being released and sprinted at his prey. Joog spotted Jamaar and dived at his head as Jamaar jumped over the bank and at the boat.

Joog's sudden movement had distracted the huge dog and he had to duck just as he jumped which made him slightly off balance. The Ferryman was ready too. He swung an oar through the air with tremendous strength and caught Jamaar on the jaw. There was a crack, and with the combination of Jamaar's speed and the crunching impact of the oar, Jamaar's great bulk was flung over the boat. He passed just above Flop and the black compass on the chain around his neck swung through the air and knocked Flop on the head.

"Ahh!" cried Flop in pain.

The blow to Jamaar's head with the oar had knocked him out and his limp body landed in the river with a great splash. He sank under the surface for a moment and then bobbed up again slightly downstream to float on the river's current. In a few seconds he was out of view.

The attack had been so sudden and over so quickly that for a few moments everyone was taken aback. The appearance of Jamaar, who they had not seen since they escaped from Candara Palace, had been a complete surprise and left them stunned. Joog broke the silence.

"Well done," he exclaimed, "That was close."

"All under control!" chuckled the Ferryman.

"Now *that* is a fierce dog," said Flop whose fur was still sticking up on his back. He was rubbing his furry head just above his eye with a paw. "Did you see the size of him?"

"Yes, but he was no match for us!" the Ferryman said with mock pride, "He'd need more than just brawn to fight against the likes of us!" Then he looked seriously at Flop. "Are you alright?"

Flop was looking dazed and lifted his paw again to his head. "Something hit me on the head…" he said. He shook his head weakly. "I feel…" he slurred, "I feel dizzy and…" His voice petered out and he fell back into the boat.

"He's hurt!" exclaimed Miriam peeping out from Flop's fluffy fur.

Joog hovered just above Flop and looked closely at his head where the fur was raised in two bumps which were close together. The Ferryman held up the lamp.

"It's swelling up fast," said Joog.

He landed on the side of the boat. Miriam climbed up

from Flop's back and onto his head. Using her tiny front paws she parted the fur, she studied the bumps while the others looked on.

"There are two marks," she said, "Look, there... right in the middle of each swelling... some blood as if something sharp pierced him."

The Ferryman stooped down to look at Flop.

"It looks just like two stings, doesn't it?" he said with concern, "Have a look at this, Joog?"

Joog hovered into the air again. "I see what you mean... it does look like stings... the swellings and those marks in the middle... it's just like stings."

Joog landed again on the side of the boat.

"How are you feeling, Flop?" he asked

Flop opened his eyes. "Not well... very groggy."

The Ferryman looked concerned.

"Flop," he said, "You must stay awake... do you hear?"

"I'll try," Flop replied weakly.

The Ferryman turned to the others. "Keep an eye on him you two. Make sure he stays conscious. We'll get going, though. I feel we're safer when we're on the move."

The Ferryman reached out, grasped the oars tightly and pulled. The boat surged into the current and they were on their way again.

The plan was to follow the river around until it met Lake Beautiful and then row across to Keill Island and Wizard Elzaphan's Castle. Flop looked weak as he lay on the seat next to Joog who kept him awake by talking to him, nudging him and even pecking him. His eyes, usually bright, were glazed with a distant look which alarmed the others. Miriam had been Flop's constant

companion. Their friendship had grown stronger as they had faced difficult situations together, particularly when they were kidnapped by Old Howard and trapped in the sack. She climbed onto his back and talked to him to keep him awake.

They had no idea how to treat Flop and no medicine to use anyway. They decided that the best thing they could do was to get to the castle as soon as possible and see Wizard Elzaphan. Perhaps he would know what to do.

The Ferryman rowed at a fast and steady pace. Joog and Miriam watched Flop while keeping a sharp lookout on the riverbanks. The boat moved fluently against the current, cutting through the water with ease.

The river twisted and turned as it weaved its way through the countryside. The moon rose higher in the sky, taming the deep night and sparkling on the rippling surface. Here and there, near the bank, there were clusters of reeds rising out of the water and swaying gently in the lightest of breezes. They saw mud flats in the deep elbows of the sharper turns and occasionally overhanging trees darkened the water beneath to a murky brown.

Joog observed all these things but something else was on his mind too. He was acutely alert with his watchful eyes scrutinizing the scene for the slightest sign that they were being followed.

The ride, around the winding turns of the Great River Sween, went smoothly and without incident. The river carried them northwards and then turned gradually to the west and towards Lake Beautiful. To their left the rounded hills of the Oathh Highlands looked down on them from moonlit, grassy slopes. There were patches of purple heather which added to the charm and beauty of the softly undulating hills and valleys.

To their right, the view was completely different. Here the land was flat and ran away from them to the foot of the Daawa Mountains. Trees dotted the expanse of level ground and groups of animals stood serenely here and there, some sleeping and some grazing. The mountains, great ghostly shapes, could just be seen in the on the dark horizon by the light of the moon.

They saw no sign of the ravens and now that they were approaching Lake Beautiful they felt relieved that they had almost completed their journey. Flop was slightly worse. Joog and Miriam had to work hard, chatting to him and nudging him to keep him awake. He was so dozy now that he was losing touch with his surroundings. Although the bumps had become more swollen and merged into one, at least it had stopped growing now. Joog had taken to gliding on ahead a little way now and again, to scout and then he would wait in a tree until they caught up.

The Ferryman seemed completely untiring and kept up a constant, steady pace. His strong black hands were wrinkled and old but they pulled the oars through the water with youthful energy. He manoeuvred the boat with great skill around every twist and turn. The occasional rock that stood above the surface was expertly avoided and he also seemed to be aware somehow of those that were hidden just underneath the water. Striking one of these could have pierced a hole in the floor of the wooden boat and caused disaster. There was a strength and wisdom about him that seemed as ancient as the hills.

They turned a bend in the river and there was the lake stretching out before them.

"Look!" cried little Miriam, "I can see the castle, Wizard Elzaphan's castle!"

It was an exciting moment. The Ferryman let the boat glide as he turned to look, and sure enough, just visible by the pale light of the moon, was the distinctive form of Keill Isle with the turreted castle perched on top. The lake was still. For the Ferryman one glance over his shoulder was enough and then he was rowing again and regaining speed as the boat slipped through the mouth of the river and out onto the lake.

Amalek woke first as usual. She had slipped partly off the ferns and was uncomfortable and slightly cold. The temperature had dropped in the night and it was completely dark. She sat up quickly and coughed to make the candles flicker on. Then she felt her neck. The muscles had tightened up on one side and she could only turn slightly to the left. She rubbed it, trying to ease the stiffness and looked along the tunnel.

The candles shed a pallid wavering light. Five of them were burning, one almost above her and two on each side of her along the tunnel. Beyond that the tunnel faded into gloomy darkness.

It was an eerie sight and as she gazed sleepily along the tunnel, back towards the entrance, she started imagining she saw shapes in the deep, shadowy dimness. Then she thought she saw a movement and the shock made her wake up fully.

It was still and silent; perhaps she was imagining it.

Then the candles went out.

"Seph!" she said softly, reaching down in the dark and feeling Tally's soft fur.

The candles lit again.

Tally stirred and then woke.

"Tally," she whispered, hooking a strand of hair behind one of her ears.

"Morning," he replied.

"Sshh," she whispered, "I thought I saw something move."

"Where?" he whispered quickly, opening his eyes and sitting up.

Amalek pointed down the tunnel, "Back there, in the dark."

He immediately hopped off the ferns and started moving cautiously along the tunnel towards the entrance.

"Tally, don't!" whispered Amalek, standing up.

"It's alright," he whispered back and carried on.

Amalek reached down and gave Seph a shake. There was no response.

"Wake up!" she whispered.

As Tally moved, the candles lit up further down the tunnel. There was no one there. Tally hopped back to the children.

"Nothing," he said, "We're safe down here... the tunnel's secret."

"Thanks, Tally," she said, sounding relieved and ruffling the fur on his back affectionately, "I must have imagined it." She waved a hand towards Seph. "You're far more use than this one!"

Seph was lying on his side still asleep and she stooped down and gave him another shake.

"Wake up!" she said loudly.

Seph stirred and turned over onto his back.

"I could do with some breakfast," he mumbled sleepily with his eyes still closed.

She stood up, dipped her hand into her pocket and produced an apple.

"Tadah!" she sang.

"Amalek!" exclaimed Tally, "Well done!"

She looked down at Seph.

"Come on!" she urged, "Come on, lazy bones, it's morning! And here's your breakfast."

She held an apple above him and then dropped it. When it hit his stomach he opened his eyes and clasped the apple with both hands.

"Breakfast is served," she announced.

"I've known better service," he said, "Kinder service. But when you're sleeping in a tunnel... Well I suppose I should be thankful."

"You should," said Amalek, "What better breakfast than an apple?"

He sat up and took a large crunchy bite.

"But, Ammey," he said, still not fully awake, "How do you know it's morning, anyway?"

"The temperature's dropped," she said, rubbing her neck, "And I've been waking up quite often so I sort of kept track. It must be morning by now."

"Are you alright?" asked Seph.

"Just a stiff neck," she replied, "To add to the blister!"

Amalek produced another two apples, this time dipping her hand into her bag which they had used as a pillow. She placed one in front of Tally so that he could grip it with his paws and nibble on it. Seph munched hungrily.

"While you've been sleeping, Seph," said Amalek in between bites, "Tally's been protecting us."

"Against what?" he asked, looking surprised.

"I thought I saw something move."

"Where?" he said quickly.

"Back there," she replied, pointing back along the tunnel.

Seph jumped up, now fully awake and stared along the tunnel.

"It alright," Amalek reassured him, smiling, "Sorry, I shouldn't be teasing you… I was trying to wake you up. There's no one there… it was nothing."

"Huh!" he laughed, "Well there's no point me waking up from a good deep sleep to protect us from nothing!"

He took a final bite of his apple and threw the core onto the ferns. When they had all finished eating they

began walking along the tunnel. Amalek was still using a stick to take some of the weight off her blistered foot. They felt relieved to be not far from their destination now and they walked quickly, chatting happily and kicking the odd stone they came across and seeing how far it would go along the tunnel. Tally was full of energy and would run along the tunnel and bring the stone back to the children.

They walked steadily without stopping for some hours until they turned a bend and saw a wonderful sight.

"Look!" Amalek's shout echoed around the tunnel, "We're there! There's the end of the tunnel!"

With this announcement a wave of excitement gripped the three young travellers and Seph and Tally broke into a run while Amalek hobbled as fast as she could after them. At the very end of the tunnel there was a large archway which curved above them as they passed under.

They found themselves in a short corridor where the only lighting came from the candles still alight in the tunnel behind them. They slowed to a walk until they reached the spiral stairs where they paused, wondering whether to go on through the corridor or go up the stairs. The candles behind them in the tunnel went out and in the darkness they noticed that a dim, hazy light shone down the stairwell above them.

"Which way shall we go, Ammey?" asked Seph, "Straight on or up the stairs?"

"Um…" replied Amalek, thinking about it, and then pointing up the stairs, "That could be daylight up there… I'll check the map first."

Amalek walked back down the corridor until she reached the doorway. The candles flickered back into life at the sound of her footsteps and she took the map out of her pocket. She unfolded it carefully and studied it.

"This corridor carries on right under the castle and then joins the tunnel under the lake to the other side," she called out to the others, "Those stairs must lead up to the castle," she explained, "Or at least to the grounds of the castle. So it's the stairs."

"Right," said Tally, "Up it is then."

He hopped up the first two steps.

Amalek walked to the foot of the stairs where she reached up and stroked Tally's back.

"Here's your map," she said to him.

"Thanks," said Tally as Amalek put it into his pouch.

"Right then," said Seph, turning to the stairs, and then with a smile he added, "We'll be meeting Wizard Elzaphan soon."

Amalek smiled back.

They started climbing towards the light above, their footsteps echoing around them. Down below the candlelight in the tunnel flickered and died.

"You know what my grandfather said about Wizard Elzaphan," said Tally. "He said he's a very great wizard, one of the greatest ever to live."

"Everyone says that about him," joined in Amalek, "And there are lots of stories about things he's done. Did you hear about…"

They carried on chatting as they climbed the stairs. It grew lighter until they could see the opening just a few steps above showing a round view of the blue sky.

Down below it was dark. Then the candlelight in the tunnel came on and shortly after went off again. Soft footsteps shuffled along the corridor.

Then it was silent.

Crouching down by the wall a dark figure hid in the shadows. It waited and listened. When the sounds of the three friends climbing the stairs faded away, the figure crept quietly forwards and started climbing.

Chapter 6

~ Harris and Quint ~

On the top of Burney's Hill, the fifty or so ravens of the Male Squadron perched in the highest branches of a cluster of old oak trees. They had slept through the night, the dawn had come and gone, and now they were chatting and preening their feathers. The General was in the middle, looking down on the others from the highest branch of the tallest tree. He cleared his throat ready to speak to them.

"Well, males," he began and then paused as their chatting to each other died down but not completely.

"Males," he continued, "I have been thinking about all this. The Dark Wizard, our Honoured Master, gave us a specific job to do and I get the feeling somehow that when he gives a job he expects it to be done. I don't want to have his wrath upon me and so we *must* complete the job for him. But how?"

He paused and looked around at the great flock, some of whom were still chattering quietly.

"We must assume now that the enemy, or at least

some of them, have got through and reached the castle. That is not good. In fact," then he shouted in anger, "It is a complete disaster!"

Now there was total silence.

"So, if we don't catch them before they reach the castle... and we will still try... then what do we do? What do we do next? We catch them as they return. What do we do?"

"We catch them, sir," they all echoed together, "as they return, sir!"

"And," he continued, "we stop them crossing the border."

"We stop them crossing the border, sir!" they chorused.

"That's right. That's us... the Male Squadron... the Females cannot be trusted."

"Females cannot be trusted, sir!"

The General shook his head despairingly, sighed and glared around at them crossly with a look of irritated disapproval. The black compass twitched as it hung around his neck. Then he snapped, "Stop repeating everything I say!"

"But some of the females," piped up Gerr who was still sticking to the General's side like a faithful dog at its master's heels, "some of them are our partners, sir."

"This privilege, of being our partners, they have lost," he growled, "We can get more partners later. These females... well, I just don't know... they are useless... they are not..."

He stopped abruptly when suddenly a great horde of frenzied ravens rose above the trees from below. The whole flock of females, like a great black cloud, and led by Searle and Urrg together, swirled up above the males and then showered upon them from above. They pointed their beaks downwards and descended like a hail of arrows. The Male Squadron was completely taken by surprise.

"Searle!" shouted the General, "What are you doing!"

"What we should have done a long time ago!" screamed Searle.

The Male Squadron just had time to rise from the branches before the females were upon them. The air was filled with cackling and shrieking, as well as the occasional deep honk as the two groups engaged in a tremendous air-borne battle. They used their remarkable flying skills to the full, darting here and there, changing direction and trying any acrobatic move to avoid attack and to attack the others. Wings flapped furiously as the birds twisted and turned above the trees. They pecked and scratched at each other as they grappled and fought. Bundles of ravens tumbled through the air with black feathers floating slowly down and drifting on the wind.

Occasionally, a raven would shoot out of the pack, pursued by another, and a few, including both Searle and Urrg, plummeted limply and crashed through the trees below. It was not long before the males began to win the battle and all of a sudden the General's voice rose above the commotion as he shouted a command.

"Female squadron, you are beaten! Surrender while you still live!"

Gradually the fighting petered out, until there were just two young females trying to bravely fight on. They were soon surrounded by males and had no choice but to give up. All the females then flew down to the trees below, most of them glad the fight was over. Some of them were whimpering softly in pain and looked timid and sheepish as they landed on the branches.

The males followed and intermingled with the females as they perched, as if to keep guard over them. Finally the General took up position again on the highest tree. They all looked extremely dishevelled with broken feathers sticking out at strange angles and blood dripping from the wounds they had received.

"That," he began, "was one of the stupidest things I have ever known! To attack your own army, and the superior half at that... well it's nothing short of ridiculous."

He looked proud as he spoke. He was enjoying the victory.

"I get the impression that you have learnt your lesson."

"Where's Searle and Urrg?" asked one of the males.

"Searle fell," said the General, "And good riddance to her!"

"I saw Urrg fall," said another raven.

"Shall we go and look for survivors?" asked Gerr.

"Are you stupid?" boomed the General "I'm quite sure there'll be no survivors after that fall." Then he turned his head to look down below and he thought for a moment. The compass bobbed around his neck. "But I suppose we ought to check just to make sure. A quick reconnoitre will do, and the criteria is: is there any life or not?"

The General looked at all the ravens gathered around him to choose one of them for the task.

"You," he nodded to one, but the keen Gerr had already jumped off his branch and was swooping down leaving the General looking down at him and shaking his head in despair.

Gerr glided between the trees and scanned the ground. Yes, he could see two ravens, then another, and another. Then he spotted two more making six altogether. He dived towards them to take a close look and then ascended again to report to the General.

"Well?" the General snapped.

"No sign of life, sir," Gerr replied, pleased to have completed the job well.

"How many?"

"How many what, sir?"

"What do you think... hamsters?" the General bellowed, "Ravens of course!"

Some of the ravens giggled and Gerr looked embarrassed.

"Six, sir," he replied.

"And next time, Gerr, wait to be asked."

"Yes, sir."

The General looked around at the others, and as he spoke he glared at the females.

"They are the casualties of battle and they should have known better than to challenge us. They are dead, and better off that way. Forget them."

He sounded angry, but paused to compose himself.

"At least this battle has established without doubt who is in charge around here."

He looked around at them all and took the silence to mean that they all agreed. He was the leader approved by all. The black compass hanging around his neck was his symbol of authority so he grasped the chain in his beak and held it out. All the birds stared at him as he flicked it with a claw making it ring and spin around. The Dark Wizard Troubler's coat of arms was etched in silver on one side and it flashed in the sunlight. He felt he had made his point. Then he continued.

"The question is what do we do? And I have decided. You four..." and he nodded at four male ravens who looked less injured than many others.

Once again Gerr had been hoping to be chosen and looked desperately disappointed.

"You four will fly back to the Kingdom of Gems, find the Master and ask him what we should do now. You'll find him, I think, most probably in Old Howard's house... you know, where we came from... then you speed back and tell me. Understand?"

"Yes, sir!" they said together.

"The rest of you stay here and recover with me."

He paused for a moment to think. His black compass hung around his neck. It had not been moving but suddenly it gave a little jerk which seemed to nudge the General into action.

"I need twelve volunteers to act as scouts," he ordered, "On this branch, now!"

He indicated a vacant branch with a point of his wing. Twelve tattered looking ravens fluttered onto the branch. He looked along the row inspecting them.

"You two are too injured. Two more please!"

With flapping wings, a few falling black feathers and some harsh cackling, they were replaced.

"Good, now you twelve go off in pairs and scout the area. And remember... don't go near the castle. If you do you will become weak and fall. Report to me in... say, two hours... OK?" They nodded in agreement. "Then, off you go!"

They flew off. The General's compass jiggled against his chest feathers as though it thought it was a good idea to send out the scouts. The General nodded to acknowledge it.

"No one else leaves, and when our orders come we will act as one army with one general in command and put an end to the enemy once and for all. This is an excellent lookout post. Any questions?"

No one spoke. Then he noticed that the four messengers were still there, waiting for the order to leave.

"What are you waiting for?!" he shouted at them, "Off you go then! Get moving!"

The four ravens flew off southwards towards the border while all the others were glad to stay in the trees and rest.

On the ground below the trees, beneath some ferns, a conversation was taking place.

"Are you alright?" whispered Searle.

"Yes, I think so," replied Urrg, "Just a bit bruised and scratched. No serious injuries."

"Good," whispered Searle.

She moved slowly over to Urrg, passing between two other ravens that were lying motionless on the ground. She chuckled quietly.

"That worked so well!" she whispered, "We fooled them all. But best of all, we fooled the General!" she whispered, "And, as a bonus, we have overheard what the General... I can hardly bare to call him that... is planning. In the meantime I have some plans of my own. Interested?"

"Very," whispered Urrg, "But what about the girl? We still don't know where she is."

"Well," began Searle, "The General isn't exactly rushing off to find her. I think that he doesn't know either, does he?"

"Then what was that ferryman on about?"

"I don't know. I really don't know," Searle shook her head and paused, "I can't work it out. It's all too confusing. Probably the General was tricking him! Anyway, we'll concentrate on my new plans. The only way now is for us to work alone because after this battle we are considered by the General to be rebels who have mutinied against his rule. If he thought we were alive he'd be hunting for us now and taking great pleasure in doing it! But he thinks we're dead! He's sure we're dead! So we'll work alone and he can't stop us."

"Tell me these plans," whispered Urrg, "And we'll work together."

The falling snow in The Kingdom of Gems was still steadily building up a deep blanket of whiteness throughout the land. The sunlight was dulled to a pale brightness reflecting off the smooth snow by the almost constant cloud cover. Very occasionally the clouds would part to let the sun through. It would sparkle in the icicles hanging from the guttering and window sills of the houses and cottages. Apart from these rare moments the sun would be hidden, shrouded by the persistent clouds and swirling snow of the sub-zero weather. Candara Palace overlooked all this from high up on the hill. It was a scene of stunning beauty.

The beauty of this dramatic wintry landscape contrasted starkly with the sinister atmosphere that hung across the land like an invisible mist. The dark presence of the spell was felt everywhere like a dull persistent ache that could not be avoided. It inhabited every frozen creature, every plant, every rock and every house. It filled everything.

Despite the seemingly invincible strength of the spell, something extraordinary had happened in Relbuort Cottage. Somehow, a powerful force had asserted itself and broken free from the crippling spell. Someone opened the front door and stepped out into the arctic scene.

During the night before, the strong current of the Great River Sween had swiftly carried the unconscious Jamaar on its flowing waters. The black compass had saved his life by pulling at his head and keeping his mouth out of the water. He was borne along, without knowing it, around all the twists and turns of the mighty river, through the turbulent waters where first the Little River Sween and then the River Ben join it, past the Forest of the Fairies which skirts its northern bank, until he came to a particularly sharp bend. This was shortly before Tye Water, and it was here that he was washed up, with some help from the compass that pulled in that direction, and he came to rest on a little gravel shelf right in the elbow of the turn.

He lay there unconscious and completely still so that at first glance it was hard to tell whether he was dead or alive. Now that the day had arrived his black fur was gradually drying in the hot sun. He was alive, but only just, his breath passing in and out slowly and steadily, while his heart beat weakly in his chest. The blow on his jaw from the Ferryman's oar had been a mighty one, but what had made it much worse was the fact that he was leaping at speed through the air so that when the oar hit his heavy jowl, the impact had been doubled. His jaw was broken and badly swollen. Blood still dribbled from his loosely open mouth, colouring the black fur of his chin and dripping onto the gravel.

Flying above were two of the raven scouts.

"Nothing," said one, "All this scouting, Forr, and we've seen nothing."

"Not yet," said Forr, "Not yet. You're too impatient, Akk."

"They've all gone. Let's go back and tell the General…"

"But it's not time yet, Akk," said Forr crossly, "He'd be furious…"

"Let's rest then," Akk suggested, "I'm tired. Let's rest in a tree for a bit… no harm in that, is there? The General wouldn't even know."

"We might be seen by…" began Forr, then stopping suddenly and adding, "Hang on… what's that, Akk?"

Akk gazed down.

"What?" he asked.

"Look, down there by the river. Something black. It could be something that we should investigate."

"It looks like just a dead dog to me. Yes, look, there's the head and there's the tail… a short tail, but definitely a tail. Just a dog… I'm sure that's what it is. Let's have a rest, Forr, come on."

"No!" Forr sounded cross and determined, "Listen, it

might be important. You never know. We should take a quick look. It'll only take a moment. Come on!"

They swooped down and landed by Jamaar and walked around him.

"It's breathing," said Forr, "But look at its jaw, Akk."

"And the tail!" Akk added, "That tail has met with an accident... it's only got half left... if that."

They walked around Jamaar, inspecting him.

"That," commented Akk, looking at the swollen jaw, "Is not good. It is alive though."

Forr said thoughtfully, "I don't think it's anything to do with the enemy, do you?"

"No," Akk was quick to agree, "We'd better take our rest. How about in that tree there?" He pointed with a wing. "Come on, Forr, let's go."

"OK," said Forr, "But not to rest... we'll carry on scouting..."

Then he suddenly stopped.

"Hang on! What's that?" he said.

He was looking at the compass around Jamaar's neck. It was almost concealed by his body. Akk stepped closer and dipped his head down to scrutinize it more carefully. He tugged at the chain with his beak to pull it out and into the sunlight.

Suddenly he jerked his head back in shock.

"It moved!" he exclaimed.

Forr gazed at it. It now lay completely still.

"Don't be stupid," he said, "It must have slipped or something."

He now stepped forwards and looked more closely at it.

"It looks like... the General's compass!"

"You're right!" said Akk, "It looks exactly the

same!"

"Which means," said Forr, now getting excited by his find, "it has come, probably, from the Kingdom of Gems! And even more important, remember where the General got his?"

"From the Master!" exclaimed Akk, leaning closer and touching it with his foot, "That's strange, it's warm."

"That's because it's lying in the sun, silly!"

"Oh yes, of course," said Akk, not entirely convinced. He turned it over with his claws. "Look! There's our Master's coat of arms on it!"

"Right!" said Forr, feeling very pleased with himself, "So, there is a connection somewhere, definitely. What should we do?"

He paused to think.

"I know," he announced, "I'll fly back and report to the General, and you guard the dog."

"And if it wakes up?" said Akk, not happy at all with Forr's plan, "What then?"

"Well, I don't know," replied Forr, getting ready to take off, "I'm sure you'll think of something."

"Look, that dog is fierce. Why don't *you* stay and…" began Akk.

"Stop grumbling. It can't do much attacking with a jaw like that, can it? Just stay close… watch from a tree and follow it if it moves. OK?"

Before Akk could reply Forr took off and headed back in a direct line to Burney's Hill. Akk flew up into a nearby tree and watched.

Crayle and Jum had flown to a group of trees just north of Munden. They found one that was particularly inviting with the trunk dividing into three large branches. This was high up in the tree and so the view of the land around was excellent. It created a bowl shape where some other birds must have nested previously as there were the remains of twigs, bits of wool and material. Jum was particularly taken with this.

"It's great, isn't it?" she said, settling down comfortably and lifting her head so that she could see the view, "The perfect place."

"For what?" asked Crayle.

"To settle down, dear. I've always wanted a more settled life, and now we're older, well, it's just the thing. Look, there'd be plenty of food for scavenging down there."

She nodded towards the village of Munden where people were busy with daily life.

"Jum," Crayle sighed, "We're in the army, remember? We are enrolled, enlisted and signed up good and proper. This is ideal for resting up here, catching up on some sleep, but then we must find the army again and serve the cause. I didn't lose this eye for nothing."

Crayle knew that this was his trump card. He knew that the combination of being so decisive so that there was no room for argument, together with appealing to her sympathy for his lost eye, always worked.

Jum looked fed up and did not reply. She settled down, closed her eyes and quickly drifted off to sleep.

During the night before, Lazuli had padded along between the northern fringe of the Forest of the Fairies and Lake Beautiful. She could run at a good pace through the long grass, only slowing when she met patches of trees growing down to the waterside. She stopped once to drink from the lake, drawing the clear water up through her trunk to pour it into her mouth. The lake in front of her was still and she tried to look out across the water where the moon reflected. Like all elephants, her eyesight was poor, so she could not see the castle.

She continued padding along and trying to watch out for the Prince, Princess and Neville because she knew that if they had got through safely they would need to cross the lake. She also knew about the tunnel. She had used it herself in the past, and although she had grown since then she thought she could still just about fit. Most importantly, she could show them the entrance and they could walk through.

She had ambled past the entrance without thinking that they may be in the tunnel at that very moment; she had no idea that they even knew about the tunnel.

As she padded along with her shuffling run she kept alert, listening for them with her large ears. After a while she reached the end of the southern bank of the lake where its shoreline started to turn north. Trying to scan up the western shore of the lake was difficult for her with her poor eyes. She gazed towards the little harbour where the waters of the River Hinkle and the River Wen flowed into the lake, but she could not see that far.

She thought that perhaps they had not even arrived at the lake yet.

She felt tired after running and fast walking for so long and decided to settle down for the night but first she was hungry. After spending a few minutes reaching up with her trunk to eat leaves from a tree and fanning her great ears to cool her down, she began to doze. Soon she had fallen fast asleep.

When she woke in the morning she began ambling back, re-tracing her steps. She found herself passing the clump of trees again that concealed the tunnel entrance and sat down beside it and wondered what to do.

She was beginning to feel that maybe the Prince and Princess had already crossed to the castle by boat, but decided that she would wait awhile in case they appeared. If they arrived she would take them through the tunnel and if not she would go through herself later in the morning and hopefully find them there already. If they were not there then she could then ask Wizard Elzaphan what to do.

She moved until she was under the shade of the tree near the tunnel entrance and stood in the long grass and waited.

After some time she walked to the entrance and reached down with her trunk to find the lever to open the door among the roots. One pull and the door slid open. She stepped down onto the platform leading to the steps. She was right; she could only just fit. She lifted up her trunk and gave the sliding door a gentle push and it slid easily until it closed with a click. The candles flickered to life as she descended the stairs and began the journey under the lake to the castle.

Amalek and Seph, with Tally leading the way, emerged from the winding stairs into the bright morning sunlight. Keill Isle rose above the lake on steep cliffs and the view was stunning across the water. They found themselves facing the lake where it stretched out below them to the southern shoreline.

As they looked around they began to realize that there was a deep quality of calmness here. Everything, all the things they could see, seemed wonderful and magical, bright and clear, intricate and perfect. Peace seemed to fill the atmosphere. Birds sang to the background of the tender rustle of leaves on the trees. Delicate scents of flowers floated to them on the warm gentle breeze. The touch of the air caressing their faces was delightful and in fact every sound seemed to convey a feeling of relaxed contentment.

When they turned to see the castle they gasped with wonder. It had a sturdy beauty about it and the three friends found their eyes attracted to it again and again. It was built with grey stone and its eight turrets reached up towards the sky. It was dotted with windows; some were mere slits, the type used for shooting arrows, and others were full rectangles with glass panes gleaming in the sunlight. The castle was surrounded by a moat, and a drawbridge led from one side to the other. It was a magnificent sight.

High on one of the turrets they saw Neville, who swooped down to meet them.

"What kept you?" he joked, staying airborne.

"Well," Seph replied, "We were followed by the Dark Wizard Troubler and had to fight him off. But of course, he was no match for us!"

"Come on," said Amalek laughing, "Let's go into the

castle."

It seemed as if the castle was pulling them to it. It was like the warm feeling of home after being away for some time. As they crossed the drawbridge their footsteps clattered on the wooden boards.

"At last," said Seph, "What a journey!"

They walked towards the great portcullis, which was raised already.

Neville swooped past their heads again and called out to two large golden eagles who were by the entrance.

"They've arrived!"

Then he glided upwards, towards the turrets.

The two eagles greeted them with a stately bow of their heads. They were perched on either side of the great entrance door beneath the raised portcullis. Their strong taloned feet grasped wooden posts, which were beautifully carved, and which placed them just higher than the heads of the children. Featured on the wooden posts were their names embedded in gold letters; one spelt Harris and the other Quint. Their feathers were a rich dark brown except for the backs of their heads where small golden feathers shone in the sun. They were the largest eagles the Prince and Princess had ever seen. They stood up so tall and straight and looked so watchful that it was obvious they were the castle guards. The two eagles looked down on the visitors and studied them carefully.

"Welcome," announced Harris, fixing his penetrating eyes on them.

"Thank you," replied Seph.

"You are very welcome," they said together.

"Thank you," said Amalek.

"We were expecting you," Harris said, "Wizard

Elzaphan told us all about your journey."

"And you must be tired," said Quint kindly. She shook her head, "It's a terrible thing that's happened in your kingdom... terrible."

"It's a shocking thing," agreed Harris.

"We're hoping," Amalek commented, "That Wizard Elzaphan will help us."

"He will," said Quint enthusiastically, "Of course he will."

Harris looked intently at them.

"I can see," he began, "That you have goodness in your hearts. Great goodness. Stand by it and it will blossom and then you will do well."

Quint nodded. "Without doubt," she said.

"You need to go in," Harris said decisively, "Wizard Elzaphan is expecting you."

He reached out with his beak and grabbed a chain that was hanging beside him. He pulled it twice.

A few seconds later the great door creaked open.

"Please enter," announced Harris.

"Thank you," said Amalek and Seph together.

They walked past the tall eagles, Amalek still using her stick, and looked through the door and into the castle where they were met by the sounds and smells of busy life. Seph led them through the door.

They found themselves in a large square courtyard with the walls of the castle on all four sides. The children paused to look around as Tally sat on his haunches beside Seph, his long white ears standing up. It had been quiet outside, in contrast with the busyness in the courtyard. Three cats looked down at them, two from the sills of windows, which were latticed with black lead, and the third from a high wooden walkway which spanned across the courtyard between the walls.

A flower bed ran around the courtyard near the wall, with a display of blooms that decorated the courtyard with many colours and lent their fragrance to the warm air. The floor was made of white shiny marble veined with blue which dipped in the centre to a shallow pool. A fountain rose in a single line of water high above their heads, spreading out and cascading down into the pool below.

Against the background of the sound of the fountain, a dozen people were talking and performing a variety of tasks. To the left near the flower bed, a carpenter worked attentively with a hammer and chisel to shape the leg of a chair. Beside him, a ladder leaned against the wall to support a man painting a window frame with a boy standing at the foot of the ladder to hold it steady.

On the right, close to the wall, a small apple tree stood, hung with red apples. In its shade sat two young ladies at a table who were carefully attending to some small golden boxes of various shapes and sizes. Just in front of them a small boy and girl played with two kittens, pulling a length of string across the marble for them to chase and pounce.

Just then a door in the wall on their right opened and several people emerged. They carried food provisions from the stores to the kitchens and walked in a line across the courtyard with various pots and packages of food. They chatted as they went.

At the far end a gardener was planting some fuchsias in the flower bed. He looked old and was being helped by a pair of red squirrels. One squirrel was passing the plants to him and the other was digging the holes. The sounds of all these tasks being done, together with the chatting of the people, filled the courtyard with a busy, happy atmosphere.

The old gardener glanced up to look at the new arrivals, smiled at them and then carried on with his work.

Neville flew down from above landing on the smooth marble floor and skidding out of control. Suddenly all the chatter and movement in the courtyard stopped as everyone there stared at Neville. A couple of people were forced to jump out of the way of his wing and one dropped a pot of honey which smashed on the hard marble floor.

"Wooah!" Neville exclaimed as he skidded past, "Sorry!"

He drew his wings in and tried to slow down, pushing one foot out in front and waggling it around. This hardly slowed him down at all and suddenly he was approaching the pool which he slid into with a great splash. Water splattered out over Tally who hopped into the air, and Amalek and Seph jumped back quickly to escape with wet feet only. The water surface settled down to leave Neville with just his head showing above. He bobbed up to the surface where he floated like a duck.

"Not too bad," he announced and then looking at the broken pot of honey, "Sorry about that."

As soon as the people realized that he was not hurt a ripple of clapping and laughter arose from them. Several of them started clearing up the mixture of honey and broken glass and in a few moments everyone had resumed their work.

Beyond the fountain a tall figure in a blue robe stood. Underneath a tall pointed hat they could see bushy white eyebrows, long white hair and beard. He turned to face the children and smiled.

"Hello," he called out to them, "It's marvellous to see you here."

It was a gentle voice, smooth and deep, that carried in it a profound feeling of strength.

He strode past Neville and through the fountain, giving the albatross an affectionate pat on the head on the way. The cascading water ran straight off his flowing robe leaving him completely dry. He emerged, silver and gold stars shining on his deep blue cloak, his arms outstretched and a welcoming smile on his face. In his right hand he held a wizard's staff made from dark wood and he used it like a stick as he walked towards them. It caught the children's attention because on the top was a great oval ammolite gemstone that was glowing very gently. It was translucent and as they gazed at it they saw many colours within it; there were hues of reds, yellow, blues and greens. The colours moved and swirled inside as if it was alive.

It was the great Wizard Elzaphan himself.

Chapter 7

~ Feeni's Betrayal ~

Wizard Elzaphan embraced the two children together, wrapping a robed arm around each of them. He greeted them with such affection that they felt as if they were his own family - his son and daughter. Then he picked up Tally and walked towards the apple tree stroking him on the head. The children followed. There was a spare chair in the shade of the tree so he sat down with Tally on his lap and looked at the work the two ladies were doing on the table. They were painting the little wooden boxes with gold paint and putting hinges on them.

"Very good," he commented to them, picking one up and running his finger over the embossed coat of arms on the lid. He held it out to show the children, "That's beautifully made, isn't it?"

They both nodded. They noticed that his wizard's coat of arms on the left of his cloak, embroidered in gold was the same as the one on the boxes.

"It's good to see you," said Wizard Elzaphan in his

deep gentle voice, putting down the box and turning his full attention to his visitors, "So you're Tally are you?"

Tally nodded.

"Neville has already told me about you before you

Omnia Vincit Amor

got here. You're very brave to leave your mountain home."

They felt that they were in the presence of a very great wizard.

"I'd like to help," Tally said with enthusiasm, "How can I help?"

The great wizard smiled, "You will help, Tally, and this will become clearer soon. For the moment you need to relax after your long journey."

Just then Neville waddled over with water dripping from his feathers. At the same time the old gardener walked towards them with a squirrel on each shoulder.

"Excuse me, sir..." he said when he was standing in front of them, and then he looked at Amalek and Seph and made a little bow with his head, "Welcome to the castle."

"This is Cedric," the wizard said to the children, "He's the gardener here, and much, much more. He's in charge of all the people working here."

Wizard Elzaphan smiled at Cedric. "Are you finishing your planting now?" he asked.

"I thought I would, sir, if that's alright. There's other work to do and Relly here has a thorn in her paw."

Relly lifted her paw up with a quick movement and gave it a shake.

Wizard Elzaphan nodded, "You go now. You must look after little Relly."

The gardener smiled, his wrinkled face lighting up and making him suddenly look much younger. Then he nodded.

"Thank you, sir. I will, sir."

The wizard looked across to the place where they had been working, "That's a splendid job your doing."

"Thank you, sir," said Cedric, "The fuchsias will be beautiful... they'll be flowering soon. They'll be a cascading waterfall of red!"

Then Cedric turned to the others and smiled at them again, "I hope you enjoy your stay."

"Thanks," they replied.

He made a little bow with his head and the two squirrels copied him and bowed too. Then he turned to go but paused and looked back at them.

"Oh, and if there's anything you want during your stay... well, just ask."

He turned again and left with the squirrels on his shoulders chatting to him as he walked.

"He's a good man," commented Wizard Elzaphan, turning back to the two children, "Now... you need to relax. But, Amalek, have you injured your leg?"

"Just a blister..." she replied.

"Ah, so nothing too serious. We can deal with that later. You've all done well... very well. You need to recount to me all about the unfortunate happenings in The Kingdom of Gems, and particularly..." He paused, and looked very serious. "Particularly tell me about the Dark Wizard Troubler. I need to know everything you can remember about him. But first you must be hungry. Come into the castle and we shall eat. Some friends of yours are here already."

"Who?" asked Amalek excitedly.

"Joog, Flop and Miriam," he replied, "They're all here."

The wizard's hazel eyes met Amalek's first and then he glanced at each of them in turn - Seph, Tally and Neville.

"And, of course, Simron," he continued, "He rowed

them across the lake."

They looked puzzled.

"Ah," said Elzaphan nodding, "You know him as the Ferryman, don't you? Some folks call him that, but his real name is Simron."

Amalek and Seph looked at each other and smiled. To hear that Joog, Flop and Miriam were all safe was the best news they could receive.

"Where are they," said Amalek, "Can we see them?"

"You'll see them in a minute," the wizard said, but then his expression changed, just like a shadow dimming bright colours to grey in the twilight. Now he looked grim.

"Well, you can see Joog, Miriam and Simron later... and also Flop, but I have to warn you... Flop's not well. It's not looking good at all. I'm afraid he might not survive."

Amalek felt her cheeks numb with shock as the colour drained from them.

"What happened?" she asked nervously.

They all stared at the wizard, mouths slightly open with the fear of the bad news.

"They were attacked by a dog. But it was no ordinary dog... it was unusually muscular and strong... and Joog says it's the same one that chased you from Candara Palace, which means it was sent by the Dark Wizard Troubler."

He looked at them for confirmation.

"Yes," agreed Seph, "The Troubler did have a dog, and it was very powerful and fierce."

"So, it seems certain."

Wizard Elzaphan scratched his beard thoughtfully.

"Anyway," he continued, "they managed to knock

the dog out but unfortunately it injured Flop first with a black object that was hanging around its neck. Poor Flop. He's not well. He has all the symptoms of being stung with deadly poison. It's strange though. It's a poison which also has a subtle invisible effect and therefore is not something you can cure completely with normal medicine. And we have a big problem... we don't know even what sort of sting it is. We've tried to help him but it needs some special kind of antidote, and he needs it soon. You must visit him later, but first let's have that meal. You need some food to strengthen you up."

He looked around, and then called out, "Spark!"

They heard a bark and then a most unusual dog came dashing towards them. The dog sat down at Wizard Elzaphan's feet wagging his short tail and looking up at him with eyes of complete devotion. He was a medium sized dog, with a friendly happy face, and he panted in the warmth of the sunny day. His fur was a deep blue colour and he was covered with silver and gold stars that sparkled and shone as brightly as those on Wizard Elzaphan's cloak. In fact he perfectly matched his master's cloak: he was a wizard dog. His fur was short, and later on the children found that when they patted him he felt especially soft to touch.

"Spark," said Wizard Elzaphan, "Show these good people up to the Dining Room, please."

"Right," said Spark, looking up eagerly at his master and jumping onto his feet. Then he looked at the others, "Follow me," he said.

Spark trotted across the courtyard, his claws clicking on the marble floor, to an entrance to the east wing of the castle. All the others followed with Neville waddling clumsily at the back. Spark lifted a paw and pointed it towards the door. A bright spark flew off his paw, hit the door-handle and the double doors swung open. They entered through the large, arched doorway and walked into a spacious hall. The floor was grey stone, smoothed by centuries of footsteps and dipping slightly in the centre where it had been walked on most of all.

Large tapestries hung on the walls, colourfully adorned with many scenes which told stories of events that had happened in Summertime Kingdom. Headings of just a few words had been woven into the material above each scene naming each event and giving the date as well. In between the tapestries were finely carved wood panels. Higher on the walls a row of flags ran right along the hall and displayed designs of many colours. The high ceiling was painted with the same deep blue as Wizard Elzaphan's cloak and dotted with silver and gold stars. It was an entrance hall that gave the feeling that this castle should be treated with deep respect, like the abode of a great king. At the same time they felt welcomed and honoured to be there.

When they reached the end of the hall, the Prince and Princess noticed Wizard Elzaphan's flag with his coat of arms and then paused to look at the tapestry facing them on the end wall. Tally lolloped up beside them and gazed up.

"Look!" Tally piped up with excitement. He was staring up at the tapestry. "There's my grandfather!"

Seph read the words above the picture out loud:

HAWKEYE LEADS THE MUNDEN REBELLION -553 SN

Seph then picked Tally up and held him in front of the tapestry and they all studied the picture. There was

Hawkeye, dressed in shiny armour, with his head held up and his mouth open giving a war-cry to a multitude of people and animals behind him. A massive iron bell was hanging from a tree surrounded by another large group of people and animals.

Tally pointed with his paw, "That's when he freed Summertime Kingdom."

Spark barked and ran up some wide wooden stairs to their right.

Amalek stroked Tally on his head.

"We'll look at it later," she said, "And you can tell us more about it."

They followed Spark up the stairs, along a wide hallway and then through some double-doors into a large room. An oblong table was set for lunch; on the polished wood lay large white plates, and beside these, knives, forks, spoons and blue napkins. Bowls of fruit, little silver dishes and several vases of flowers completed the inviting display. Two glittering chandeliers hung above the table at each end, with a ring of candles that were already lit. The walls were hung with paintings of different sizes and a large round mirror was on the other side of the room.

They walked in and across the wooden floor, and they felt that they had been invited to a banquet of great importance.

Joog was already sitting at the table on a perch, looking a bit like a headmaster calmly watching the whole scene. When he saw the Prince and the Princess enter the room excitement took over. Joog flapped off his perch and glided across the room to greet them and landed on Seph's shoulder. They were all overjoyed to meet again.

"We kept thinking about you," said Amalek, stroking Joog's wing, "It was difficult not knowing where you were... we kept wondering what was happening to you, and if you were alright."

Joog blinked. "There's quite a story to tell about that!"

"Where's Miriam?" asked Seph, looking around for her.

Joog looked serious. "She's with Flop. She won't leave him even for a moment. You've heard about poor Flop, have you?"

"Yes," said Amalek sadly. Just the thought of him being so ill upset her and she looked tearful, "Poor Flop."

Seph put a comforting arm around her shoulders, "At least he's in the best possible place, Ammey."

Joog fluttered onto Amalek's arm.

"What about the Ferryman?" Seph asked.

Joog turned to face him, "Oh, he's with Flop too."

They heard someone entering the room behind them and turned to see Neville waddling in. He had dropped behind as they were the climbing the stairs. For him each step was a major challenge. He had to jump up to the step above without his great webbed feet slipping back to the step below. However, in spite of flapping his wings and hooking his great bill over the next step to haul himself up, he had slipped back several times. It was a clumsy and cumbersome ascent punctuated with frantic scrabbling.

"Thanks for the help," he joked.

"Sorry," said Tally, who was able to hop up easily by standing up on his back legs, "If you will insist on being an albatross."

"I prefer flying. All this walking around is not for

me!"

"We've noticed this," said Tally.

On the far side of the room, beyond the table, a door opened and in walked Wizard Elzaphan with Spark following. A few of the silver stars fluttered down from the ceiling and danced in the air around him and Spark jumped up onto a chair at the table.

"Good, good," he said looking around at everyone, "Sit down. You must be very hungry."

Joog returned to his perch. The Prince and Princess helped Neville and Tally up and placed cushions on their chairs until they were the right height. Wizard Elzaphan sat down at the head of the table. The stars fluttered back up to the ceiling like butterflies, except for two which landed on his shoulders and settled there.

"Marvellous," said the wizard smiling warmly and looking around the table at his guests, "It's marvellous to have you all here, although the circumstances are grim. But, please, do not think about that now... we will talk about it later, and make decisions. But now we will enjoy eating. The food should arrive any minute..."

At that moment the door opened.

"Ahh," the wizard smiled, "Excellent. You'll notice how things tend to run very smoothly here... not always, but usually! And as you eat, Amalek, your blister will be sorted. Just take your shoe and sock off."

"I have a stiff neck too," Amalek added.

"I thought so... you have been in the wars! I think we can ease that too."

Two waiters and a waitress entered with two trolleys of food and drink and busied themselves serving. There was a varied choice that covered all their different tastes and soon they were all enjoying the first proper meal they had eaten for some days. The waiters and waitress stood watchfully over the meal and offered more when necessary.

Amalek felt a tickle on her foot and looked down to see two mice with a pot of ointment. They rubbed it on her blister and she felt the pain ease immediately. Then they climbed up her clothes to her neck and rubbed on the same ointment. A moment later they were climbing down to the floor and running away, towards a hole in the skirting board. They disappeared into it.

"It's Hutsel Oil from the Hutsel plants in the Daawa Mountains. It's wonderful stuff with magical healing powers… and it works quickly too."

Amalek turned her neck and found the movement much better.

A sound at the door made them all turn. Both doors swung open together and Lazuli entered. The doorway was an arch and Lazuli fitted under it perfectly.

"Lazuli!" exclaimed Wizard Elzaphan standing up, "So you *can* still fit through my doorways as I thought… and through the tunnel as well."

"Yes, but only just," she replied walking into the room and beside the table. Her great padded feet were almost silent on the wooden floor.

The wizard smiled at her, "*And* the winding stairs up from the tunnel?"

Lazuli nodded and swung her trunk playfully. "But that was tight… a *very* tight squeeze."

The Prince, Princess and Tally had not met Lazuli and were gazing at her in amazement.

"This is Lazuli," he announced to them, "She volunteered to help, just like you Tally."

Seph was closest to her and reached out and patted

her on her side. He had never touched an elephant before and held his hand there for a moment feeling the tough leathery skin.

The wizard turned to one of the waiters. "Can you fetch a large bowl, please, for our large guest. A very large bowl... for Lazuli. And fill it with food... she does eat rather more than us."

The waiter left and Lazuli stood by the table where a space had been made for her bowl. The large bowl arrived, filled with leaves, bark and roots. Lazuli used her trunk to scoop the food up and put it into her mouth and they all began to eat.

The meal continued with only a little conversation as they all enjoyed the delicious food and drink.

Keill Island was an unusual place; a high outcrop of flat land with cliffs dropping away steeply all around. It was the only island on Lake Beautiful and situated close to the centre. It was the ideal setting for a castle, naturally protected on all sides not only by the cliffs but also by the great expanse of water stretching away for some distance. The moat almost seemed like an unnecessary extra, but when it was built some six hundred years earlier, King Karadan the Great, the king of Summertime Kingdom at that time, felt that a castle was not complete without a moat and so one was dug around the castle. The traditional drawbridge over it was then completed with its system of ropes and pulleys for raising and dropping it. Beneath the castle the dungeons had housed prisoners from time to time but they had not been used now for many years.

The castle grounds extended a small distance from the castle to the precipitous cliff edge. There was just enough land for a few clusters of trees and bushes.

In one of these little copses of trees, a brown rabbit called Feeni was having a conversation. To an observer it would have appeared that she was talking to a bush because the owner of the other voice was well hidden among the branches and leaves.

"When?" asked Feeni, looking at the bush, "When do you want this to happen?"

Feeni listened to the answer which came in a soft whisper and nodded.

"Yes, alright," she said, "But if I do it, what do I get out of it?"

Again she listened to the answer.

"That's good," she nodded again, "But when do I get it?"

As she listened to the answer she looked around to check that no one was near.

"No!" she snapped, "I have to have it first! Before I do it, you understand. Otherwise the deal is off!"

She listened to the response.

"That's better. Alright then, we have an agreement?"

The response from the bush pleased her.

"Great! I'll see you here later on then?"

She listened, nodded at the answer and hopped off into the trees.

The meal in the castle was coming to a natural end and they all felt much better after the nourishment of the food. The waiters and waitresses quickly stacked all the plates and cutlery onto two trolleys. Soon the dark oak table was completely cleared and the trolleys were rolled out.

Amalek was gazing out of the window. The view looked eastwards over the lake where the distant Oathh Highlands reflected in the still water.

"Wizard Elzaphan?" she asked, "Has this castle ever been attacked?"

"Oh, yes," he replied, "I sometimes think that a castle is not the best place to live, because it's a castle! Castles tend to be attacked! We have avoided that for a few years, yes, but in the past... well this castle has seen its share of troubles alright. The tapestries in the Great Hall downstairs record a few stories."

He looked around at their faces, eager for exciting stories of attacks on the castle, of battles won and lost, of heroes and bravery.

He laughed and held up his hand. "Not now, dear friends, not now. I will tell you some time, but today we have more important things to discuss... yes, the terrible threat that is upon your kingdom. This present danger is pressing upon us. But there is more and you need to know about it all... "

He paused to rise up from his chair and walk to the window.

"Tomorrow," said the great wizard, "You will need to climb up the highest turret... right to the top... where you'll find the Golden Room. That is where magical items are invented and given their power. And there are some for you."

Amalek and Seph looked at each other.

"Now," said Wizard Elzaphan, his rich voice filling the room, "I need to hear your story. Simron and Miriam have explained what they know and now I need hear from you to fill in the gaps and complete it."

He sat down at the table again.

"Tell me everything from the start up until now. I need to hear it all."

Joog, helped by the others here and there, told Wizard Elzaphan the whole story starting with the night when everyone slept in The Kingdom of Gems while the Dark Wizard Troubler and his komodo dragon entered the kingdom, up to their arrival at Wizard Elzaphan's Castle. They explained about the ravens, Old Howard and the Troubler's dog. They made sure they described the Dark Wizard Troubler as clearly as they could remember.

Wizard Elzaphan knew a good deal of it already of course but with their explanation he heard details that the others had not covered. He listened very carefully to the description of the Dark Wizard Troubler and his evil spells.

When they had finished the wizard looked concerned.

"Thank you," he said, "You've explained it all well. You've certainly faced this with great courage. Well done all of you. I think it's remarkable that you managed to escape this dark wizard… and then avoid his ravens and everything else."

He looked around the table at them with an expression of kindness. The glance held a depth of warmth and they felt his love for them. It was love as free as the open sky and as real as the ground beneath their feet. They felt as if they had known him for a thousand years.

"So..." he continued decisively, "I need to speak to Seph, Amalek and Joog. And Tally as well please."

He stood up, pushing his chair away from the table.

"If you would come to the Reading Room in about ten minutes, please. It's out of that door and turn right. You'll find it down the corridor. The rest of you... well, Neville, I'd like you to do an important job. Can you look out from one of the towers, please?"

Neville nodded.

"Of course," he replied, "Yes. Which tower?"

"The east. The others are covered. Cedric will help you too... he's up there now and expecting you. His eyesight isn't so good now so he could do with your help. And Spark... you can take a walk in the grounds."

Spark wagged his tail.

"And take Lazuli with you... just relax."

Elzaphan turned to leave the room, but then hesitated.

"Anything you want to ask?"

They shook their heads.

The great wizard left the room leaving them to chat around the table for ten minutes while Spark was enjoying his walk the grounds. Lazuli had followed him down and was having a wash in the pool in the courtyard. Neville found Cedric and perched on the very top of the east turret where he could see across the lake to the Forest of the Fairies and beyond. Tally went down to look at the tapestry again for a few minutes and then rejoined them around the table.

When ten minutes had passed the Prince, Princess,

Joog and Tally left the room by the far door and turned right down the corridor. The first door they came to had bronze lettering on which announced:

THE READING ROOM

They entered to find themselves in a spacious lounge where Wizard Elzaphan was sitting on a soft pale blue armchair reading a large book. He looked up as they came in and watched them over his silver-rimmed glasses.

"Good," he said, as he closed the book and placed it on a small round table beside him. The gold letters of the title on the spine glittered in the sunlight:

A Comprehensive History Of Wizards and their Works

"Come and sit down," he said waving his hand at a sofa.

They sat down opposite him on the sofa, which matched his armchair. A long shelf of books ran the full length of the wall behind the wizard's head. The room was again partly panelled with carved wood with stone walls above, rising to the same blue ceiling sprinkled with shining stars. The floor was dark polished floorboards. On the small table beside him there was a glass vase of large purple lilies, beautiful in the evening rays of the sun, which sloped through a large open window crisscrossed with lead. On a desk against the wall behind them, there was a half written letter with a long white-feathered quill standing up in a bottle of black ink. There was also a sturdy chest of drawers with a large bowl of fruit resting on it. All the furniture was elaborately decorated with carvings and inlaid with mother of pearl.

In the corner sat Simron. He was between the desk and the chest of drawers and sitting very still on an upright chair that probably belonged to the desk. They did not notice him at first because he was sitting behind them in the dark corner but then he got up to greet them.

"Well done," he said from beneath his hood. As always, his face was hidden and his voice warm and friendly. "I'm so glad you're here."

They all turned and the children stood up. Amalek picked up Tally. Simron lifted a hand to pull back his hood and for the first time they saw his face. He was a handsome man much younger than they thought. His dark-skinned face carried the qualities of strength and tranquillity together. He smiled and then laughed at their surprise.

"You thought I was an old man!" he said cheekily, "Now you know. My disguise was for the ravens… and it worked. It was better that they thought I was just an old ferryman."

"You fooled us too," said Seph.

Amalek beamed at him. "And thanks for helping us," she said.

"I was happy to do it," he said with a chuckle, "I didn't do much… just fooled those ravens, that's all. And what's easier than that?"

Seph laughed.

"That was the best!" he said, "The very best!"

Simron sat down again and the four young visitors turned back to Wizard Elzaphan. They sat down as well, Joog perching on the back of the sofa with Amalek and Seph just in front of him on the soft cushions. Tally sat in between the children. They all looked at Wizard

Elzaphan and waited for him to speak.

"It's very good to have you here," he said slowly. His voice was deep and calm. "I wish you could just enjoy your stay, but we do need to talk about this Troubler and his spell… it's a serious matter."

He frowned and shook his head.

"It's very serious. I think I may know who this Dark Wizard Troubler is… and if I'm right he's powerful and extremely dangerous. He's what we call a fallen wizard. He has the powers of a wizard but he's turned evil… and power in the hands of evil is a shocking thing to see. It's an alarming danger to everyone. You have done well… extremely well. I'm amazed at how you've fought your way here. That Troubler has tried hard to get rid of you, but you foiled all his attempts. Excellent! Normally, of course, I would have met you on your journey and helped you more. You must have wondered why I didn't meet you and help you myself."

"Well, yes," answered Joog, "We did wonder. We thought there must be a good reason."

He smiled at them, then took off his glasses and slipped them into a large pocket in his robe.

"There is. I *had* to stay here."

The door opened and Spark entered. He pushed the door closed with a back leg and trotted over to sit at the wizard's feet.

"Are they alright?" asked Elzaphan, reaching down and patting Spark on his head.

"Yes," Spark said looking up, "Neville's on lookout as you suggested and the others are fine."

"Thank you, Spark. It's good for them to relax for a little while," he said and looked back at the four friends sitting on the settee, "To conquer such a fallen wizard who has taken over a kingdom is not easy, and it's up to you, I'm afraid."

He looked at Seph, Amalek, Tally and Joog each in turn.

"And you two, as Prince and Princess of the kingdom, have particular responsibility. You look strong and healthy, and you have help of course."

There was a pause for a moment when no one spoke. Just the thought of the Dark Wizard Troubler and his piercing black eyes filled them with fear. They all absorbed the enormity of what the wizard had just said.

"You'll be coming back with us, won't you?" asked Seph.

"No," the wizard's voice was firm.

"But we thought…" said Amalek her voice shaking with surprise and shock at the wizard's answer. This was something they did not expect. "We thought that you would come back and get rid of him and the spell."

Wizard Elzaphan brought his hands together and clasped them on his lap.

"It's not that simple, I'm afraid," he said grimly, "You see, I wish I could do that. I *could* do it, but I cannot risk it. And there are reasons why. The best way to really free a kingdom from this sort of evil wizard is by the people of the kingdom. It's better this way because then the strength is there in the kingdom itself. And then… well it makes it very hard to cast another spell in that kingdom for some years. It's no guarantee, but it makes the kingdom stronger in the future. Do you understand?"

He looked at them earnestly and they nodded.

"But there's something else," he said calmly but his voice was grave. They felt he was about to tell them something of great importance and they held their breath in nervous expectance of what it was. "A few weeks ago I travelled to Kneb... do you know the place?"

They all nodded.

"Yes," replied Joog, "I've seen it on maps but none of us have ever been there, have we?"

Joog looked at the others to check. They shook their heads.

Wizard Elzaphan continued, "Well it's east from here on the coast. It's a holiday place, and it's free... it's always been free... there are no taxes or tariffs for anything. No money even. Anyone can go there and be looked after for a while if they need to. So it's not a kingdom but a place that serves the creatures of all the surrounding kingdoms. I go there sometimes to make sure all's well, and I always find it peaceful and happy, but when I was there this time something had changed. Hard to say exactly what, but it was in the atmosphere. A sort of gloom about it... faint but definitely there in the background... and also, the birds were singing less, which is never a good sign. Now, south of Kneb is the Kingdom of Gliyfild, and south of that is Gugeol."

The Prince gasped.

"Gugeol!" he exclaimed, and the others looked equally shocked, "You don't think that..."

The great wizard shook his head gravely.

"Gugeol has a long history of evil ways..." he continued, "The Troublers that have come from there! And Gugeol was the force behind The Thousand Seasons of Night. I've heard that *they* call that terrible time The Mighty Age of Gugeol... a glorious name for a violent and cruel occupation. And before that, right at the beginning of Stellen, there were the dreadful Gugeol Raids. Then they tried again just a few years back."

He looked at Tally.

"Your Grandfather, Hawkeye, led the battle against them then. The King of Summertime Kingdom was killed by the invaders, and so too were your parents, Tally. And I took over afterwards because there was no heir to the throne and no one strong enough to take it on. But Hawkeye... well he led the fight against them. Did he tell you?"

"Well, sort of," said Tally, "He told me stories, and there is a poem called 'The Bell', but I didn't know it was all about him until just before I left."

Wizard Elzaphan smiled, "That's just like him... strong and brave, but modest. And if you've heard the poem you will know that the sound of that bell cast the terrible spell. I'm glad to say, thanks to your grandfather, Gugeol was defeated. The bell, the Glyifild Bell, is lost now and no one knows what happened to it. Anyway, I'd say the signs are that it may be Gugeol trying again. Or it might be another evil force, but something is definitely happening. No doubt about it."

He paused as if it hurt him to even mention the name of Gugeol and he needed to gather his strength to carry on. They waited until the great wizard was ready to continue.

"But there's more still, I fear." He ran his hand down his long white beard. "I am hearing rumours, almost daily now, of trouble from the other direction too, in the east... there's a creeping desert moving in this direction and affecting everything in its wake - buildings are in ruins, trees are dying and lakes and rivers are drying up. Many creatures are leaving the Kingdom of Moone to settle elsewhere. And there are other strange things which I can't go into now. But all this means that I cannot leave. I have to stay to protect the kingdom... because if Summertime was invaded... well, I'm sure you understand."

They nodded.

"And the people of Summertime Kingdom are afraid. Did you meet any people on the way?"

"No," replied Joog, "Not a soul. It was strange. All the paths were empty."

The wizard nodded. "No one's travelling at all... even short journeys. They're staying near their homes because they've heard the rumours and they're afraid. You see they remember what happened before. Those who live in Butterknowle and Munden don't venture into the open countryside any more."

He paused for a moment.

"But..." and now his eyes twinkled, "I will be with you. I will be helping you... and you will be able to use magic... I'll show you how. And you can take your excellent helpers with you. There's Lazuli and Neville. And there are other things to help you too."

Wizard Elzaphan's gentle voice somehow soothed their fears. The Prince and Princess looked at each other and Joog flew onto the Princess' shoulder.

"And Simron?" asked Joog, "He's helped us so much with his tricks and disguises." Joog turned his head to face the Ferryman. "Will you come with us?"

"It depends..." replied Simron. His voice resounded clearly from the dark corner of the room. "It depends on Wizard Elzaphan. I'll do what he says."

Joog turned his head to fix his eyes on the wizard again.

"Hmm..." the Wizard nodded thoughtfully, "He's a great person to have around and on your side, as you've found already. He's a Master of Disguise, you know. He can melt into the background and hide. He can use disguises better than anyone I know. And when it comes to out-thinking an enemy he's the best, as you have already found out. He learnt his art in the jungles in the Kingdom of Agulta in the south where he was born. But no, I'm afraid he has to stay with me... for the moment anyway. He's needed here."

He paused again and looked out of the window.

"If it is at all possible I'll send him."

There was a pause in the conversation. The air was filled with tension. The Prince and Princess wondered about the future and felt the burden of their daunting task.

"So," Wizard Elzaphan continued, "What do you say? Success is not certain in these cases, and if he won... well, who knows what he would do to you and the kingdom. He would claim the Candara Gems and that would make him much stronger. As soon as they are taken across the border of The Kingdom of Gems their protective power would be gone and the kingdom would fall completely. But you are young and strong and he has not been able to get the better of you yet. Your survival so far has stopped him from taking the gems... you are holding him at bay. I have every confidence in you. Are you willing to fight him? Are you willing to risk your lives for the Kingdom of Gems and your loved ones?"

Something arose in Seph, something strong and clear, as confident as the rising sun on a cloudless day. The decision formed in his mind and settled in his young heart. When he spoke the answer was without doubt.

"Yes," said Seph.

Amalek felt strengthened by her brother's plucky confidence.

"Yes," she said with absolutely certainty.

"Yes, of course," said Joog looking at Amalek and Seph. He felt filled with love and admiration for the two children. "The King and Queen would be proud of you two. You are really marvellous."

"I agree, Joog," said Wizard Elzaphan, "That's excellent. Good. You have chosen a hard and dangerous path, but it is the wise choice... and a generous one because you have put aside your own fears for others."

He looked at Tally intently.

"And you, Tally?" asked the wizard, "Are you ready to risk your life?"

"Yes," he replied, "I am."

Elzaphan smiled kindly at him.

"You're a brave hare," he said, "Your parents would be pleased, and so will Hawkeye."

"And..." began Seph, "Flop and Miriam would say 'yes' too. I know they would."

"I'm sure you're right, but they have to answer for themselves. Flop's in no fit state to be asked at the moment, unfortunately. Now... tomorrow," Wizard Elzaphan continued, "I will prepare you for your task and tell you the plan. Then you must return to the Kingdom of Gems and do your very best. But now, who would like some fun?"

This last question came as a surprise after the serious conversation before. They all nodded.

"Yes," said Amalek, "But can we see Flop and Miriam first?"

"Of course, but I must warn you, he's not well."

Seph stood up.

"We just want to see him," he said.

"Yes, I know," said Wizard Elzaphan, standing up

and placing his hand on Seph's shoulder. It felt warm and comforting, "I'll take you there now."

The Silver Well in the Silvermay Forest, in The Kingdom of Gems, dropped deep beneath the ground. After its long descent straight down through the rock, the well hole opened out into a massive cave nearly one hundred and eighty feet high. This cave had been named Korum's Cave by its discoverer Ramoy Korum, an explorer who mapped the underground tunnels and caves centuries earlier. There were several tunnels leading out of the cave and cradled in it were the deep waters of Lake Merlode. This large underground lake was usually fed by a labyrinth of underground streams to the west, but since the casting of the spell which had turned all the water into ice or snow, the tunnels were no longer flowing with water draining through from above. The level of the lake had only dropped slightly and water still ran out of it as streams flowing through the eastwards facing tunnels. These flowed underneath the Kingdom of Moone until eventually emptying into the Great Eastern Synamian Ocean.

Ramoy Korum had made a startling discovery among the meanderings of the natural underground tunnels. He had found a tunnel that was so unusually straight it must have been created by men. It ran into Lake Merlode and out the other side. It was roughly hewed, varying in width, and seemed like a natural tunnel except for its remarkable straightness. It made just one slight turn southeast of Korum's Cave and headed due east, out of the Kingdom of Gems. At the time when he was exploring, it carried water like the other tunnels and so he named it Ramoy's Canal. Whether it had been created to help the underground flow of water or for some other reason no one knew and now, once again, its existence had long been forgotten.

Ramoy Korum had suddenly abandoned his mapping of the tunnels before he had finished. He emerged from the tunnels with an expression of terror and a sickening, pale complexion. He looked like a broken man as he staggered weakly through the town of Candara, in those days called Naldo. Onlookers were amazed. Somehow he seemed to have aged about twenty years. No one knew what had happened to him but it had left him suffering from such extreme shock that he was unable even to speak. He had packed up the very next day and left the kingdom, never to return.

This mysterious event is briefly mentioned in the history books of the kingdom but there are no details because none were ever known. Ramoy Korum's Journal was lost and with it the underground map he was plotting. In his panic to leave the tunnels he dropped his bag containing the journal and his mapping pens and equipment.

In this underground world, deep beneath the surface in the Kingdom of Gems, Horrik was groping and scraping along a large, dark tunnel. Her strong legs propelled her forwards as she used her claws to grip the rough rocky floor. The tunnel was damp and cold. The chain, which had held her prisoner, was still around her neck and rattled as she moved. Also around her neck was the black compass hanging on its chain. It was glowing gently and lighting up the tunnel for a few feet ahead.

Her hate for Jamaar was so deep that she had been desperate to kill him and eat him. The meal would have been a welcome bonus and Jamaar's body would have provided a sizeable meal for her. Her last meal had consisted of about twenty ravens, not by choice but as a punishment that the Dark Wizard Troubler had forced upon her. She hated the taste of ravens but had to eat them to satisfy her hunger. The punishment only fuelled her anger at Jamaar, who had lied about her and got her in trouble.

When Horrik fell down the well she was confused and terrified. She was sure she was going to die. She had shaken Jamaar off her tail and then found herself falling head first. Her claws scraping against the sides of the well had helped slow her fall. It was dark and she braced herself for the impact not knowing when it would come. As she fell her claws began to catch on the rock and slow her down even more. Then when they had almost caught her, she had slipped slowly down the last few feet of the well-hole with her claws juddering against the rock wall.

Then the well-hole ended and she fell into Korum's Cave. In the darkness she could not see anything. She was petrified. A moment later she had splashed nose first into Lake Merlode, hitting the water with some force, her immense strength keeping her body firm. She plunged down as the water absorbed her speed. Then, just before hitting the rocky bottom of the lake, she had turned using her excellent swimming skills.

She had swum up to the surface and had rested there for a while floating on the water and recovering her strength. Above her, high in the roof of the cave, the well-hole provided a weak light. Then she had managed to pull herself out of the water, clambering over some loose rubble and rocks and into a large tunnel. She was in Ramoy's Canal which was so dark that she could not see anything.

A tug on her leg had made her jump with surprise. Looking down she saw to her astonishment that it was the black compass glowing gently and shedding a pale light. The chain was still caught around her claws but was pulling and jerking to get free. Horrik had lifted her leg, spreading her claws and the chain shook loose and lay there on the rocky floor of the tunnel.

For a moment she looked at it with admiration. She had seen the Dark Wizard Troubler wearing one around his neck and knew it had some special power. She had also seen the one hanging around Jamaar's neck. Now she had one herself. She reached down her rounded snout, picked it up in her teeth and flicked the chain over her head. It fell around her thick neck, clinking against the other chain as the compass hung down on her chest.

She wondered where the compass came from and how Jamaar had got it. But the most important thing was that it was now hers and it was already helping her by glowing in the dark. As it hung around her neck she could sense the power of it. She began to like the feeling.

By the light of the compass she wandered through the tunnels, trying in vain to find a way out. She could hear in the distance the faint sound of flowing water echoing along the tunnels but could not tell where it was coming from. After several hours she recognized the tunnel she was in and realized that she had gone around in a circle. She roared with frustration.

Setting off again she began to panic and rush. The tunnel soon thinned until she could only just fit.

Suddenly her head entered a cave the size of a large room with a ceiling about the height of two men. This cave had been named by the adventurer Ramoy Korum who called it Serinta's Cave after his wife.

Horrik stopped with her body still in the tunnel and her large scaly head in the cave. Her forked tongue snaked out of her mouth and back again.

In front of her was a mass of hanging stalactites, some of which had joined to make a curtain of rock, and from the floor of the cave rose collections of stalagmites of various sizes. In the soft glowing light of the compass, she could see they were stained green, pink and orange by minerals that had been deposited over the years by dripping water.

As she looked around the cave, something glittered in the light of the compass and caught her eye. It came from the wall beside her, so she turned her head to take a closer look. Embedded in the grey rock she could see streaks of gold sparkling in the dim glow. For a moment the smudges of bright gold held her attention and she paused. Her panic faded.

The compass jerked around her neck as if to pull her into the cave and so she entered, moving around the stalactite curtain and clambering over the rocky ground. She was near the middle when the compass pulled at her neck again. She took another step and bumped into something. She lifted her head to use the light of the compass to see what it was. She gasped with surprise. It was an old wooden ladder reaching up to the ceiling.

The ladder had obviously been there for many years; some of the wood was rotten and had flaked away. A couple of the rungs were missing and she saw them lying near one of her feet, together with a few other bits of wood. The ladder was encrusted with mineral deposits that looked like candle wax and were tinted with the same green, pink and orange hues that she had seen on the stalagmites.

She followed the ladder up with her eyes to see it enter a hole in the roof. She thought she could see the beginning of some steps, maybe two or three, until it faded into deep darkness.

"What luck!" she thought, *"Or was it the compass guiding me?"*

She placed a clawed foot on the lowest rung and pushed down twice to test the ladder. It held. She began to climb with her front legs, at first slowly and cautiously, then, gripped by her desperate urge to be free, she sped up. She used the claws of her front legs to grip the rungs as she pushed with her mighty back legs. She was soon moving up the ladder until she was leaning on it with her back legs still on the cave floor and her rounded snout not far from the hole above. She paused for a moment and gazed upwards. Now she could see further and there was no doubt about it. It was a stairway.

She pushed again and rose off the floor. Her snout entered the hole above and her forked tongue slipped out of her mouth to sample the air. These steps must lead upwards to the surface. Soon she would be free. Jamaar's face flashed into her mind; when she was free she would follow him and this time he would not escape.

Then there was a crack. The ladder snapped under her great weight like fragile matchsticks and she crashed to the floor of the cave. She landed on top of the splintered ladder.

Horrik roared in anger.

The roar echoed around the cave and along the

tunnels and then gradually faded. Horrik dropped her head in despair. She had been so close.

Then she heard something that sent chills shivering through her massive body; a distant screech. She lifted her head and listened. Was it the echo of her own roar? Surely it could not be; her own roar had faded into nothing and this was a different sound altogether. This sounded like the desperate cry of something tormented to utter frustration; it was a screech which expressed anguish and misery. She was not alone down here.

She listened for a while but it did not come again so she turned her mind back to her own situation and looked up at the hole in the roof. Her chance for escape had gone, at least for the moment. She looked around. There was space enough here for her to move around freely. She slipped off the broken pieces of the ladder and started to investigate in the darkness. Then she put her foot in a pool of water near the side of the cave. She dropped her great head until her lower jaw was in the water and she let the cool water run in. She tipped her head back and swallowed, repeating this several times until her thirst was quenched.

She was so tired now that her frustration at not being able to find a way out was beginning to fade. She realized that under normal circumstances she could enjoy this underground world, but there was a major problem; she was hungry. She needed food and in these tunnels she had seen no other living creatures. Her huge, scaly body slumped down flat on the rocky floor of the cave and drifted off to sleep.

A thick layer of snow rested on the circular glass roof of Spindley Tower. Flakes swirled around the tall building and filled every gap in its finely detailed carvings. Below, in the town of Candara, the icy wind swept the falling snow between the houses. Layer upon layer covered the streets and buildings. Normally the children of Candara would be outside, building snowmen and having snowball fights; but in Candara today, and in the whole of the kingdom, everyone was frozen. A few people were staring out through frosted windows but their eyes were glazed and unseeing; they were as still and lifeless as statues. The Dark Wizard Troubler had trapped everything in his evil spell.

High on Spindley Tower, however, there were two creatures who were not trapped by the spell. From the third balcony Aram and Halo had continued to watch Old Howard's house. They were watching and waiting for an opportunity to act. They had a plan and soon they would need to use it, but as yet they did not have much information to work with.

They also knew that the Troubler was probably still in the house so they watched in the hope of seeing him leave. They could not be sure he was there, however, because they could not watch all the time. There were also times when the driving snow was so thick that they could not see the house at all. As soon as the snow eased the house would again come into view.

The two unicorns stood side by side and watched. They blinked and fidgeted in the snow-storm, silver and golden sparks occasionally flying off their manes to dance among the snow flakes.

"He's powerful," said Halo, "Very powerful, so we need to act at the right time… and with great care."

"Yes," Aram agreed, "But we mustn't delay too long. The first thing…" he said thoughtfully, "The first thing is to destroy that mirror, don't you think?"

"Yes," Halo agreed, "That would be a good start. When shall we do it?"

Aram peered through the gusting snow and spoke earnestly, his deep voice strong but gentle. "Soon. But it would be best to break in when he's not there. So when we see him go out then we'll strike."

Chapter 8

~ Magic Rooms ~

Amalek and Seph felt shocked after visiting Flop.
They were shaken by seeing their friend so ill and all they
could do was hope that he would recover. They came
away with heavy hearts.

Wizard Elzaphan gathered them all together in the
courtyard. The man painting was now working at a
different window frame and the boy was still holding the
ladder. The girl and boy with the kittens were trying to
teach them how to climb the apple tree and were each
munching on apples they had picked. The ladies were no
longer working on the golden boxes and had gone inside.

On the table, the boxes were lined up carefully in a
row and glittered attractively in the sun. One of them
hovered just above the table and the children looked at it
with interest. Cedric the gardener sat on a chair near the
main entrance with the two squirrels on his lap.

"Where's Neville?" asked Wizard Elzaphan.

"I'm coming down!" shouted Neville looking down
on them from the high turret.

Everyone looked up with worried faces to see him

take to the air and begin his descent, circling within the walls of the courtyard.

"Stop!" called out Wizard Elzaphan, "I think it might be safer if you landed in the grounds and then came in by the door."

"What?!" Neville called back.

The wizard turned to Joog, "Can you tell him please… and quickly before it's too late. And tell him to be careful."

Joog took off and sped silently through the air and up to Neville. He passed on the message and swooped down to land again.

Neville made a small adjustment to the angle of his wings and began to rise.

A minute later there was the sound of his bill tapping on the great door. Cedric rose up out of his chair in response and the squirrels ran up his clothes like climbing a tree and settled on his shoulders. He opened the door and looked down at Neville, who waddled in with his feathers ruffled. A twig was caught on one of his folded wings and dragged behind him, so Amalek walked over to him, pulled loose the twig and smoothed his feathers.

"Good," said the wizard, smiling at Neville, "We are all here. Now for the fun… to help you relax, to cheer you up, something that will take your mind off the problem you are facing. The problem cannot be avoided but you need to be strong and refreshed to face it. So I think I have just the thing. Something I'm sure you will enjoy."

They all wondered what this could be.

"Right," said Wizard Elzaphan decisively.

He turned to Spark who was lying down with his

head on his paws watching the fountain.

"Spark!" he said.

"Yes," said Spark.

Instantly he jumped up and trotted over to sit at the feet of his master. He gazed up devotedly, through loving eyes, awaiting his instructions.

"Could you take our guests to the Magic Rooms, please?"

"I'd love to," said Spark, wagging his tail with enthusiasm.

Tally picked up Spark's excitement and jumped up and down on his huge long feet.

"Right then! This way," said Spark.

He led the way across the marble floor of the courtyard to the west wing. The stars on his fur sparkled brightly. As he approached the arched double doors he lifted a paw and sent a spark flying to the door handle to open it.

The whole party of six friends, Seph, Amalek, Lazuli, Joog, Neville and Tally, followed Spark.

Spark led them through wide halls, past many doors and up and down stairs. The castle was richly decorated with carved wooden panels, shelves with silver candlesticks and other ornaments, and many paintings and tapestries. Amalek and Seph helped Neville along by walking one on either side and doing their best to lift him when they could. Finally Spark stopped.

"Here we are," he said, with a voice as bright as his sparkling fur.

They were standing in front of a large heavy oak door with a shiny brass handle. On the door was an inscribed brass plate which read:

THE MAGIC ROOMS

The Prince turned the handle and pulled the door open. They walked into a long, wide hallway. The ceiling was deep blue and covered with stars. The walls were grey stone with a row of twelve arched double doors on each side, all made of dark oak with shiny brass handles.

"I suppose these doors lead into the Magic Rooms," said Neville whose long scarf was draping on the ground and twitching excitedly at the end.

"Yes," said Spark brightly, "Have fun! Good night!"

He trotted off happily around a corner and out of sight.

They were wondering which door to open first when something amazing happened. The floor of the hall turned into a rushing river and they were, all of a sudden, swept along on the surface. The water was so buoyant that they found they could sit on it without getting wet.

Several doors passed by as they drifted along. Just ahead they saw a pair of the double doors open and they sailed through. The doors closed behind them and all the water ran out leaving them completely dry. They were sitting on a red carpet. The Prince opened his mouth to speak, but instead of a word coming out as usual a bubble appeared. He had heard the word faintly, but the bubble had caught it, and now it was floating away with the word still inside.

The Princess said, "How did you do that?"

Once again the words were caught and out came another bubble. Joog and Lazuli tried to speak too, but not a sound emerged, only bubbles. Now there were five bubbles floating beautifully in the air and gleaming with a million different colours. One touched Joog's beak and popped.

"Look at that!" said Lazuli's voice. Then another

popped on the floor.

"Wow!" said the Prince's voice as the word was released from inside the bubble. Another bubble popped.

"How did you do that?" questioned the voice of the Princess.

Then they all began speaking, shouting and whispering and out came the bubbles until the Magic Room was filled with them, and the six friends were jumping up and popping them, and the words, whispers and shouts were sounding all in a jumble. This certainly was fun.

Suddenly, the water began flooding the room again and the excited friends were lifted off the carpet. The door opened and they were swept out into the hall and onto the surface of the rushing river once more. They passed two more doors before another opened and the water carried them in.

This time when the water had all drained out, they found they could walk up the walls and across the ceiling. After a while, the water seeped in under the doors, lifted them off the floor and they were swept out again. They entered Magic Room after Magic Room, each with a different magic spell.

One room kept changing shape from oblong to square to sphere; another had no walls or floor and they all floated around in the air like fish in the sea. In the next room they found they could turn into any animal they imagined. All of them, except Joog, turned into snowy owls and no one could tell which one was Joog, except for Joog himself who became a little monkey. In the next room they all became invisible but could still hear each other's voices. Yet another was a huge glass ball which rolled across a grassy field with them running inside like hamsters in a wheel.

The last Magic Room, at the end of the hallway, was a large bedroom with a sleeping area suitable for each of them. There was a young silver birch tree in a large pot for Joog to perch in and a pile of soft blankets for Neville in the corner of the room. Straw had been laid out at one side of the room for Lazuli and Tally. Amalek and Seph had beds, which they found wonderfully comfortable. The large window provided a beautiful view of the snow-peaked Daawa Mountains across the smooth lake, in which they were reflected perfectly.

A table with food for all of them sat in the corner. They feasted and chatted about their thrilling time in the Magic Rooms as the sun set, falling towards the mountains like a large red ball. They settled down after dinner and quickly drifted into a deep, restful slumber to the sound of Neville singing another riddle-song.

"We waken with the fresh day-break
when the morning sun shines new,
we slip into slumber as night-time's wonder
enfolds her arms around you.

With faces bright just like the sun
with hair as white as snow
with garments green, in Nature's great scheme,
we gaze up from below.

We are ignored by passers-by
who walk over unwittingly
to leave us down-trodden, and oft' forgotten,
as they fell us so casually!

but before a week has slipped away
we spring up for your delight,
a speckled show like the first flakes of snow
or like stars that appear in the night.

We're tipped with pink like clouds in the dawn,
we're white ships in a sea of green
we are specks of light sent, for the innocent
to enjoy just by being seen."

Most of the raven army were still regaining their strength after the battle between the males and the females. They were resting in the trees on the top of Burney's Hill as dusk slowly descended. The blazing red sunset which had lit up the sky moments earlier was fading now to leave a glowing, pink semi-light across the kingdom. The treetops swayed gently in the warm breeze and provided an excellent view of the surrounding land.

The four messengers had been dispatched to the Dark Wizard Troubler, and the twelve scouts were doing their job. The rest were preening their feathers and chatting.

Forr was the first scout to return. Several ravens started cackling and pointing with their wings when they saw him approaching by himself. He landed, out of breath, near the General.

"Where's Akk?" asked the General.

"He's watching the dog, sir!" panted Forr.

"Dog? What dog?" the General looked puzzled.

"It's a black dog, sir. A monster of a dog. He's lying

The Fresh Day-Break

"We waken with the fresh day-break
when the morning sun shines new,
we slip into slumber as night-time's wonder
enfolds her arms around you.

With faces bright just like the sun
with hair as white as snow
with garments green, in Nature's great scheme,
we gaze up from below.

We are ignored by passers-by
who walk over unwittingly
to leave us down-trodden, and oft' forgotten,
as they fell us so casually!

But before a week has slipped away
we spring up for your delight,
a speckled show like the first flakes of snow
or like stars that appear in the night.

We're tipped with pink like clouds in the dawn,
we're white ships in a sea of green
we are specks of light sent, for the innocent
to enjoy just by being seen."

~ NEVILLE'S 6TH RIDDLE ~

unconscious by the river, sir."

"Hmm," the General put his large head on one side. The compass twitched. "This sounds interesting. Large dog, you say?"

"Yes, sir," said Forr, pleased that the General considered it important.

"Black and brawny?"

"Yes, sir," Forr said, his breathing returning back to normal, "The sort of dog that you would like to have on your side in a fight, sir. And it's got a compass like yours, sir, 'round its neck."

"Ah Ha!" the General sat up straight, "It's Jamaar. Must be. The Master must've sent him here. You know, that great black dog. Didn't you see him in Old Howard's house?"

"No, sir," Forr replied, while some of the others called out that they had seen him.

"But you say he's unconscious?"

"Yes, sir. With a swollen jaw. He's either been in a fight, or an accident. It looks a real mess, sir."

"He's been attacked by the enemy," stated the General, "Or fought them probably. Where is he, Forr?"

"Just before Tye Water, sir… on a bit of gravel where the river turns."

"OK… OK," the General said slowly and then paused to think.

The black compass twitched again. He was proud to have it around his neck and considered it a mark of his status, like a medallion that announced his rank of general. He was still unsure what all its movements meant, but he was beginning to feel what it was feeling. When it was just making small twitchy movements, as it was at the moment, it was taking in information. Bigger movements were guidance. He looked at Forr.

"This is what we will do. You fly to Butterknowle, as fast as you can, and get a strong blanket. You'll need to take someone with you. How about you, Iker?"

There was no response from Iker, the General's nephew, who was dozing comfortably on a branch, almost hidden by a mass of leaves. He was a young bird, the youngest of all the ravens, almost fully grown but still with some of his fluffy feathers left from when he was a fledgling. He was well known among the others for misunderstanding what was happening or being said. When Iker did not respond the General glared at him and shouted to wake him up.

"Iker!"

There were a few disgruntled mumblings about the General only picking Iker because he was his nephew. Iker lifted his head slowly, looked out through the leaves and nodded sleepily. Some of the ravens giggled at him.

The General continued, "I have a job for you, Iker. A good fly should snap you out of your lazy sleeping. Go with Forr and get a blanket."

"A blanket?" asked Iker sleepily, "What for, uncle?"

"Call me sir!" snapped the General so abruptly that Iker jumped with surprise and opened his eyes wide, "Remember what I told you? You're in the army now! You must respect your superiors."

"Sir," said Iker slowly, "Why do we need a blanket?"

"Just do it!" yelled the General, "Forr, take him with you."

"Yes, sir," said Forr, "But how do we get a blanket?"

"I don't care!" he snapped, "Just get one… borrow it or steal it or something. Then meet me and the others by Jamaar. OK?"

"Yes, sir!" he said and he flew off with Iker.

"Right," the General snapped, "I need... let's say... ten good birds," and he nodded at them as he counted them out, "You four... you... you... you two... and you... and you. The rest of you stay here and keep a good look out. You lot, follow me!"

He flew off, with his compass bobbing forwards to show him the direction and the ten others trailing behind him in a broken black line, flying beak to tail, in a westerly direction over the River Ben.

The General descended from the darkening sky and landed beside Jamaar with the other ten landing in turn immediately afterwards. Jamaar was just coming around and had opened his eyes. The General walked across the gravel until he was right beside him and studied the black metal compass. It was indeed identical to his own, with the same coat of arms engraved in the centre. As he looked, his compass jiggled excitedly.

"Jamaar!" said the General by his ear, "What happened?"

"I ozsh achachkt," said Jamaar hardly able to move his swollen jaw.

"What did he say?" said the General turning to Akk who had flown down from the tree.

"I don't know, sir," Akk replied.

"Can you stand up?" the General asked Jamaar.

Jamaar moved and made an effort to raise himself, but all he could manage was his head, which quickly flopped down again.

"As I thought," the General shook his head, "It's not good. He's broken his jaw and lost half his tail. I think he may not live."

Then, raising his voice again, he asked Jamaar,

"Shall we get you back to the Master?"

Jamaar just about managed the slightest of nods of his great head before he closed his eyes and drifted into unconsciousness again.

"OK then," the General announced to all of them, "We carry him back on the blanket."

"What blanket?" asked Akk, looking around.

"The blanket that will shortly arrive."

The General looked up to see Forr and Iker returning on the wing with a grey blanket flapping between them.

"Down!" ordered Forr to Iker.

The ravens all stared up as they came in to land. Then Forr started descending through the air faster than Iker and the blanket stretched out.

"Drop!" shouted Forr.

Instead of dropping through the air to catch up, Iker let go of the blanket and it billowed up, pulling Forr sideways. For a moment it looked as though the blanket and Forr would land in the river but Forr flapped his wings so violently, and with all his strength, that he managed to get it under control. As the blanket came down it smothered one bird and landed with one corner in the lapping water. They all watched as the raven under the blanket moved until his head popped out followed by his body and tail.

Forr was out of breath and glowered angrily at Iker. "Why did you let go?!" he snapped.

Iker looked embarrassed, "I... er... I..." he stammered, "But... but you said 'drop.'"

"I meant you, Iker!" Forr said angrily, "I meant you, not the blanket!"

"Well done, Forr," the General said, "That's the way to knock him into shape. Do you think you can train him up, Forr?"

Forr thought, *"No... no way!"* but he knew Iker was the General's nephew and was too afraid to say "No".

"Yes, sir!" he said smartly.

"Good, good," the General nodded, "You seem to be an efficient bird with leadership qualities, Forr. I appoint as *Sergeant* Forr, to be in charge of this important operation."

"Thank you, sir!" said Forr giving his head a little shake as he held it up high with pride.

"Iker," said the General, "Buck up your ideas and do what Forr says!"

Iker looked back glumly without saying anything.

The grey blanket was laid flat on the gravel beside Jamaar. The General instructed all the other ravens to roll Jamaar onto it. There were thirteen ravens altogether, including Sergeant Forr, Akk and Iker who lined up and pushed with all their strength. The General called out repeatedly, "One... two... three... push!" until the injured Jamaar was gradually moved to the very centre of the blanket.

"Right!" shouted the General, "Spread yourselves around the blanket equally."

After a bit of sorting out this was achieved.

"Now grab the blanket on the edge nearest to you with your claws... excellent... now, all together, lift off!"

The ravens all flapped together, and sure enough, the blanket rose ceremoniously and very unsteadily into the air taking Jamaar with it.

"Now take him," shouted the General, "Take him to our Master!"

They flew off through fading light, heading southeast towards the border, while the General, feeling he had done an excellent job, flew in a straight line back to Burney's Hill.

The Dark Wizard Troubler had taken a strong hold in the whole of the Kingdom of Gems through the tight grip of his evil spell. He had become power mad. He was determined to let nothing stop him from achieving his dream of owning an empire that consisted of several kingdoms at least. He felt he had started well in capturing this kingdom, yet he was deeply angry that the Prince and Princess had escaped. This made him cry out in rage at times and kick and smash things in great furies of uncontrollable temper. Not only had they escaped but they had a group of animals that were helping them too and the fact that all these were still free meant that the three gems were still protected.

Often, when he closed his eyes, he would imagine the three shining gems in front of him. There, within reach, was the red ruby, the blue sapphire and the purple amethyst, all in sparkling colours vivid in his mind, etched into his memory. A strong desire for them burned in his heart.

He felt he could not rest, or move on to conquer other kingdoms until these enemies had been dealt with and he possessed the gems. In his mind it was only a matter of time, but the sooner the enemy were killed the better and he was desperate for this to happen. It frustrated him that he could not leave the kingdom without the spell he had cast dissolving, so he had to work from his base in Old

Howard's house. However, it was ideal for his purpose. It was dilapidated and dirty when Old Howard had lived there. Now it was gradually growing darker, dustier and more and more filthy.

So it was with a sense of anticipation, as he looked out of an upstairs window through the fading evening light, that he saw the approach of four of his ravens speeding back to him. He opened the window and leant out into the chilly snow-filled air with enthusiasm. He hoped for, or rather expected, or demanded even, good news. After all he had sent over a hundred ravens, Old Howard and Jamaar to fight for him against his enemies.

He had also dispatched three ravens with special powers to fly right to Wizard Elzaphan's Castle. He had selected them for their courage and fighting qualities and expected them to do well. Surely all these would be enough. He already knew, of course, through the mirror that enabled him to materialize partially in Summertime Kingdom, about Old Howard's struggles to make much real progress. The fact that Old Howard had escaped from his control just added to his problems.

As the ravens swooped down towards the window, there was a great crash from his room downstairs. The Troubler jumped in shock, banged his head on the window frame and cried out in pain. The shadowy black of his eyes deepened in anger. Then there was another crash. He strode out of the room and down the stairs. Just at this moment the four ravens arrived, flew in through the window and followed their master.

The Troubler, consumed with anger, burst into the room downstairs. First he saw in front of him, a great hole in the wall with a pile of rubble of bricks and plaster scattered in front. To his right was Aram, his golden body catching the evening light in bright highlights. Behind the shining gold of Aram was Halo with the cabinet, the one with the mirror that he used for his magic, impaled upon her alicorn. Silver splinters of the broken mirror lay on the floor around her.

"What!" screamed the Troubler at the top of his voice, "How dare you enter here…"

He did not have time to finish his sentence before Aram charged, his golden hooves clattering loudly on the wooden floor. He lowered his alicorn and pointed it straight ahead, but the Troubler moved like lightening and dodged to one side. Aram shot past and through the door. He clattered into the hall as the four ravens came down the stairs and attacked him. The Troubler slammed the door closed and turned to face Halo.

"You," he shouted, glaring at her, "You have made a terrible mistake. Did you think I didn't expect this?"

Halo jerked her head violently in his direction and the cabinet flew off her alicorn and spun across the room directly at his head. Again the Troubler was too fast. He ducked and the cabinet spun past him and smashed into the wall. Gradually the colours were draining out of everything; even Halo had turned to grey instead of her beautiful shining silver.

The wizard took a black compass from around his neck and started whirling it around above his head like a lasso. He let go and it shot across the room and straight at Halo's head. She pointed her magical alicorn at it and dodged with lightening speed. The compass deflected slightly in the air but not enough and it caught Halo on the side of her body. Something stabbed out of the compass and caught Halo's silver skin leaving two parallel scratches. The compass cracked into the wall behind her, embedding itself there. Halo felt her legs go weak.

The Troubler dived for the mantelpiece and slammed his fist down on one end. Immediately, a rope net fell from the ceiling and covered the whole room, except where he was standing. The Troubler glanced behind, hearing sounds of fighting echoing around the hall behind him. He turned back to see Halo struggling, her alicorn getting caught in the net and then her hooves, and then, as his stare intensified the net gathered around her, entangling her in a web of rope, tightening... tightening... until she could hardly move.

She felt that the Troubler was draining her power and knew that she must fight it. Her alicorn was sticking out through the net and she summoned all her wilting strength together and pointed it at the evil wizard. She spoke some words of magic but she was so weak that they whispered out of her mouth and her alicorn could only manage a feeble sizzle. Halo felt the Troubler's sinister deathly presence spreading, engulfing everything around, holding her, imprisoning her in a darkness like the deepest winter night.

No longer disadvantaged by the surprise of the attack, the Troubler felt stronger now. The sounds of the fight from the hall suddenly stopped and he spun around to face the closed door. He was mustering up all his power now to confront Aram. He opened the door to see the unicorn facing him, standing tall and proud, glowing and shimmering with gold, with the four ravens perched up on a high shelf with ruffled feathers and looking terrified. The evil wizard concentrated and Aram felt his dreadful might imposing itself on him, draining his gold into grey, drawing his magic away.

"Halo!" called out Aram.

"I'm trapped!" she replied, "Run, Aram, run!"

Aram summoned all his energy and ran at the Troubler with his alicorn lowered like a knight with his lance ready. His hooves clattered loudly on the wooden floorboards. This time the alicorn hit the Troubler in the side, but only a glancing blow as he jumped sideways with the agility of a cat. Aram could not stop before he had run through the door and back into the room. The floor was completely clear now. The net that had wrapped around Halo had taken everything else with it as well and then lifted up towards the ceiling. It turned slowly, gripping a table, chairs, the large block of gold and Halo.

"Run, Aram, run!" shouted Halo again.

Briefly their eyes met.

"You can't afford to be caught as well," she continued, "Be free to help the others, and save me later. Go now. Run!"

The Troubler entered the room and moved towards the mantelpiece. Aram froze, not knowing what to do, his loyalties divided. He wanted to do both, to fight *and* run; to try to save Halo *and* run free and help the others.

Momentarily, he hesitated and in his confusion he stood still. At the far end of the room the black compass was working its way out of the wall by moving up and down rapidly.

"Run!" screamed Halo.

The wizard slammed his fist onto the end of the mantelpiece again and down came another rope net. At the same moment the compass broke free and began accelerating through the air towards Aram. Aram's powerful rear legs sprung into action and shot him forwards just avoiding the compass that flashed past and sunk into the opposite wall with a dull thump. The net brushed his back as he slipped out and away through the hole in the wall, galloping across the snow with hooves pounding the ground underneath.

He was relieved to feel his colour and the magic returning. He skidded to a halt and turned, snow spraying up in front of him. He looked back through the falling snow and the dim twilight to see the Troubler at the hole in the wall staring at him with his black eyes deep and menacing.

Aram felt the terrible pain of the loss of Halo. He almost let out a howl of agony but managed to hold it back and kept his eyes fixed on the wizard. He wanted to rush back and attack but he knew this could be disastrous. He would have to be cunning and return later at the right time to surprise the Troubler. At least he was still free to do this. He would work out a plan and try to free her later.

He turned and sped off into the snow. The Troubler watched him from the house and his eyes narrowed. He sighed deeply, air clouding out through his thin lips. His pale face was iron-cast with hate.

He turned and looked up at Halo who was unable to move at all in the tight grip of the net.

"I'll deal with you later," he hissed at her.

He walked through the door with the sound of his boots on the wooden floor echoing in the sparsely decorated hall. Pausing, he looked up at the four shivering ravens.

"Well, you cowards," he said threateningly, "Get down here and tell me the news."

The ravens stayed still, too scared to move. He lit a

candle which was on a small table by the wall.

"Get down here!" he shouted, "Now! And tell me the news!"

The ravens jumped at the booming voice and looking even more frightened, they flew down. They perched on the banisters, with one of them, called Rakka, on the end post.

"You know," said the evil wizard with sarcasm, "I thought I asked a question. Yes I did. I'm sure I did, didn't I?"

He moved forwards, lowering his head until his nose was very close to Rakka's beak. He lifted his hand and Rakka cowered away as if expecting to be hit. Then he stroked the quivering raven on the head with a long bony finger.

"Did I or did I not ask you a question?" he asked staring at Rakka intently.

"You did, Master," Rakka said weakly.

"Then be polite and answer."

"The General," Rakka began timidly, "The General and the others are resting, and waiting, in the trees on Burney's Hill. They are waiting for your orders, Master."

"What about the enemy?" the Dark Wizard Troubler snapped, fixing a menacing stare on the raven.

Rakka began shaking.

"They made it to the castle, Master," he said.

"What!" the Troubler snapped, anger rising in him and showing in the harsh expression on his face. He seemed like a volcano ready to erupt. "All of them?" he asked incredulously.

"Yes," Rakka shifted uncomfortably on his feet, his claws clicking on the wooden post, "We think so, Master."

"What do you mean 'We think so, Master'?" mocked the wizard, "Did they or didn't they?"

"They must've, Master," Rakka said with terror in his eyes.

"And Old Howard? What's happened to him?"

"We don't know, Master."

"And Jamaar?"

"Who's Jamaar?" asked Rakka.

"Jamaar, my black dog. Where is he?"

"We haven't seen any black dogs. No, Master, none at all, Master," Rakka replied accompanied by some awkward fidgeting and a few more clicks of his claws.

"Any news," the wizard asked, "Of my three ravens with special powers which I sent to the castle?"

"None, Master," Rakka shuffled his feet uncomfortably.

"I can wait for that," he said angrily. Then, as if talking to himself, he muttered, "It's a dangerous mission, but I'm still in touch with those three. I have plans and they have the character to succeed." Then he glared at Rakka and raised his voice. "Not like some others who seem to have no character at all!"

The Troubler paced up and down the hall a couple of times, wringing his hands together. "How did they get through? How did you let the enemy get through?"

"Well, Master," began Rakka cautiously, "You see, there was a trick... at the river... they played a trick on us... we *thought* we'd killed them... we *thought* we'd killed them all... but then... when we searched for their bodies on Tye water..."

"Stop!" shouted the Troubler looking furious and holding up his hand, "I have found out some of this already... the trick, yes, I heard about this and I don't want to hear it again. It's too painful to listen to. What matters now is that they don't return. They will try to return, of course, but they must be stopped. And the way to stop them is to search for them and then attack."

He paused, and paced up and down again.

"Are all the ravens searching now?"

"Yes, Master. Some are looking out from Burney's Hill, and some of them are scouting."

"Good... good... well that's something I suppose," he said, calming down, "When you get back tell the General that he *must not* allow the enemy back into the Kingdom of Gems. Understand?"

"Yes, Master," said Rakka trying to sound strong and positive.

"Tell the General..." The wizard's eyes narrowed and his jaw tightened with evil power as he hissed the words out, a few drops of saliva spitting out as he spoke. "Tell the General that I will not tolerate failure this time. Tell him you *must not* be caught by them, and you *must* succeed and you *must* kill them."

Rakka was shaking with fear even more now and was so terrified that he could not speak.

"If you fail," continued the wizard, "and make sure you tell the General this - I will give you all, every one of you, a punishment that will make you regret you ever existed!"

There was a pause while the Troubler let his powerful words take effect. The ravens all shivered with fear as they thought about the chilling threat.

As he paused icy tension hung in the air.

Then he continued. "Tell him that the enemy will probably be travelling soon, so work out the possible routes they might take. Then hunt them down and kill them. Now, eat and rest first… we don't want you collapsing halfway there do we? There's food in the kitchen. But I want you out of here by morning light, alright?" They nodded and he shouted, "Now, get out of my sight!"

Rakka took off and flew into the kitchen followed by the other three ravens. The Troubler turned and walked back into the room where poor Halo was bound tightly in the rope net hanging from the ceiling. He slammed the door so hard the house shook.

The thirteen ravens led by Sergeant Forr were carrying the unconscious Jamaar on the blanket and made good progress through the failing evening light. When they set off they were rested and full of energy. They had passed over the Clungberry Fields and were west of Lake Burney when they found themselves beginning to tire and gradually dropping towards the ground as they flew. The weight of Jamaar was too much for them and in spite of them straining with all their might to keep going it was clear that they were fighting a losing battle.

Sergeant Forr immediately took control.

"We'll land down there," he announced, "on the grass bank near that big tree, and then I'll decide what to do."

They saw where he meant, even through the dimming light at the end of the day, and together they all turned slightly, except for Iker who was not listening and carried on flying in the same direction. This meant that he tugged the blanket against the turn of the others. The blanket was torn from his claws making a hole and leaving the edge of the blanket flapping in the wind.

"Iker!" screamed Forr, "Quick! Grab the blanket again! Quick!"

Iker tried to turn in the air and chase the others who were still falling, but he was too slow and too late. With the edge of the blanket loose, the nicely balanced flight of the group had been disturbed, the blanket tilted, and Jamaar rolled from the centre. This disrupted the balance even more and their flight was uncontrollably dragged sideways and downwards.

"Hold on!" shouted Sergeant Forr, with panic in his voice, "Hold on!"

Jamaar was now teetering on the edge of the blanket as the ravens were flapping furiously to tilt it back. Then Jamaar began to roll again and looked as though he was about to fall off. Forr dived in and grabbed the blanket near Jamaar, where it was torn, and stopped the great dog rolling off.

"Hold it steady!" he ordered, but then the torn blanket suddenly ripped further and a piece came off leaving Forr still gripping it as he rose above the others.

Jamaar rolled towards the edge again. Then, inevitably, he fell. There was frantic panic and the ravens rose suddenly as they were relieved of the weight.

Forr, who still had the piece of blanket caught on one of his claws, could only watch from above as Jamaar fell the last few feet and thudded onto the ground.

"Down!" shouted Sergeant Forr at the top of his voice, "All of you! Come on!"

The blanket, now with only a couple of ravens still clutching onto it, had been caught by the wind and billowed up into the air, smothering some of them. They frantically tried to wriggle free but got even more tangled and crashed into the ground in a great screeching bundle. Sergeant Forr landed beside them and shook his head anxiously.

"Get out of there!" he yelled.

Muffled cries and moans came from under the blanket.

"I don't believe it!" he shouted in frustration, "Just get out of there now and let's sort this mess out."

The ravens crawled out while the rest landed and they all gathered around Jamaar, who lay there, a dark shape lying completely still in the dimness of night as it closed in around them.

"Well," Forr began, "Let's hope the dog's alright."

"He'll never survive that fall," said Akk, "No one could."

"He'll be dead for sure," Iker joined in, "Did you hear him hit the ground?"

"We all heard it," snapped Forr crossly.

"Who's the fool who made him fall?" said an arrogant looking raven called Razz, as he stared at Iker accusingly.

Forr turned to Iker in anger.

"How did it happen?" he asked Iker, his voice loaded with sarcasm, "What went wrong? Explain it to me. It was *you*, Iker, pulling the wrong way, wasn't it? So it's *your* fault for killing him! *How* did you get it wrong? Everyone else heard my instruction!"

Iker gazed back at Forr, feeling wronged. He had been thinking about other things and not listening.

"But I… I…" he began but his voice petered out as he could not think of an excuse.

Sergeant Forr stepped towards Jamaar and studied

his motionless body.

"He's dead," he concluded, "And now we'll have to explain that to the General."

He shook his head in despair. He had just been made a Sergeant and this was the first job he had been trusted with.

"Whose gonna tell him?" asked Akk.

"Yeah," growled Razz, "Who's gonna tell him, Forr?"

"You," commanded Forr.

"Huh! No way! You're the great sergeant almighty, you have to do it," Razz retorted.

Forr turned to Akk. "How about you, Akk? Will you tell him?"

"No!" exclaimed Akk in shock, "It's your duty."

Forr shook his head again in frustration because he knew Akk was right. Then Iker stepped towards Jamaar's body and studied it.

"What are you doing?" asked Razz.

"I'm just..." began Iker, stretching his head towards Jamaar, "Look!" he exclaimed suddenly, "He's breathing. It's OK!"

The circle of ravens all relaxed, and moved closer to stare at Jamaar.

"You're right," exclaimed Forr and heaved a great sigh of relief, "I can see him breathing. Well done, Iker," he said encouragingly. "But how did he survive that fall?"

Akk answered. "He's tough, that's how. Look at the size of his muscles... he's a monster of a dog!"

"OK," began Sergeant Forr, now feeling much happier, "I'll go and tell the General that we need two or three more birds to carry the dog." He nodded his beak at

Jamaar. "But I won't tell him that we *dropped* him. He doesn't need to know, does he?"

"No," they chorused, very relieved that Sergeant Forr had decided this.

"And while I'm gone, you might as well sleep. We have a tough journey tomorrow."

On hearing this some of them spread their wings ready to fly off to the nearest tree to sleep.

"Stop!" commanded Forr, and they folded their wings again, "You must stay here to guard the dog."

There were a few mutterings of complaints about this.

"When I get back then *I'll* need to sleep," he continued, "Then we'll leave at first light, OK?"

They eagerly nodded their agreement because the flight so far had exhausted them.

"Akk and Iker. You two go and steal another blanket and make sure it's a strong one... this one's all torn now. Can I trust you Iker?"

Iker looked back and then nodded slowly.

"I wouldn't," muttered Razz.

Forr ignored this and took off towards Burney's Hill and disappeared into the night. A few seconds later he swooped overhead and called out, "Razz, you take first watch... and stay beside the dog all of you."

With a few flaps of his strong wings he flew off again into the darkness.

Chapter 9

~ The Intruder ~

Harris stood on guard at the castle entrance, grasping his beautifully carved wooden post with his feet. It was midnight. His sharp talons gripped into the wood as he looked out through the deep darkness and into the castle grounds. A three-quarter moon shed a pale light onto the grey castle walls at the back, while the front walls, where Harris was on guard, as well as the grounds extending away and beyond the moat, were absorbed in shadow. The drawbridge stretched across the moat in front of him. The night was still and calm and so was Harris, looking stately and dignified as he stared into the darkness.

Absent-mindedly he turned to speak to Quint and then remembered that she had gone to spend a couple of hours overlooking the grounds at the back of the castle. He was used to having her beside him but now she was perched on a high turret where she could gaze down at the moonlit grounds.

Harris was alert. Tonight he felt a strange feeling he could not explain. He could not identify the cause but he felt slightly on edge. The castle door opened behind him. He jumped and jerked his head around.

"Everything alright?" said Wizard Elzaphan as his head appeared around the door.

"Fine, sir," answered Harris, relaxing, "All's well... I think."

"You sound a bit uncertain, Harris."

"Just a feeling... nothing really," replied Harris.

"Well, let me know if you see anything," said the great wizard.

Harris nodded. "I will."

"I'm just going to check with Quint and then I'm going to bed, but wake me if necessary."

Harris nodded again. "I will, sir," he said.

Wizard Elzaphan began to close the door and then opened it again.

"Oh, Harris?" he said.

Harris turned his head to look at the wizard. "Yes?"

"Do you want anything to eat?"

"No thanks."

Wizard Elzaphan smiled kindly. "Good night then, Harris."

"Good night, sir," said Harris.

Harris was alone. He was used to the company of Quint and suddenly he felt a spark of fear arising in his heart. He wished she was with him. He wondered why he was frightened when it was just another night on guard. He knew he was strong enough to meet anything. He would fight with his life for Wizard Elzaphan. Nevertheless, the fear was rising and now he realized for certain that it was the distinct feeling that he was *not* alone, and that he was being watched. He turned his head slightly this way and that as his sensitive nostrils caught a tiny whiff of something. There was a smell in the air, extremely faint but undeniable, an unpleasant, pungent smell. It was so faint that he began to doubt that it was really there. Perhaps he was just imagining it. He turned his head to the door again, wanting to tell Wizard Elzaphan, but turned back knowing that he would be half way up the stairs by now.

Something made him look down at the drawbridge, perhaps a little noise or movement, or maybe just instinct, he was not sure. He jumped off his perch and glided onto the wooden boarded floor of the drawbridge. He looked down through the thin cracks and saw the black rippling water below. Focusing his eyes closer he saw the wooden beams underneath, running lengthwise. He took a few steps and peered down again. Was that a beam or the shape of someone hiding, clinging to the beams underneath? It was impossible to tell from there, and he felt it was probably just his imagination.

He was just about to take off and glide under the drawbridge to look more carefully when suddenly there was a noise of something shaking the undergrowth in the grounds a little distance away. He hesitated and then took off, cutting through the air swiftly and landing in a tree above. The rustling noises came from the bushes directly below and Harris flew down to investigate.

"Hello, Harris," called out Feeni, "Don't worry, it's only me!"

Harris landed beside her.

"Oh, Feeni," he said sternly, looking intently at the brown rabbit, "What mischief are you up to?"

"None," she said in mock innocence, "Why do you think of me like that?"

"You have history, Feeni. You know... things that

have happened in the past. No one trusts you anymore… and Wizard Elzaphan wants to talk to you."

"Me? What about?" she said, acting astonished.

Harris laughed, "Your memory is conveniently short."

"Instead of just talking," she said, suddenly looking up at him with pleading eyes, "Perhaps you could help me out of this."

She shook a back leg, which was caught firmly in some branches of the bush, and winced in pain.

Harris took a step closer to her and said, "Alright, but first tell me… have you seen any strangers in the grounds?"

"Yes," she answered.

Harris straightened his back in surprise.

"Well, who? Describe them to me, and when and where you saw them."

"It frightened me… and it frightens me now just remembering it! It was a great monster with four heads, and twenty-six legs and…"

"This is serious!" Harris snapped, "Did you see anyone? Yes or no!"

"Yes."

"Really. Who?"

"A boy and a girl. And a white hare… yuk, I hate them… and…"

"I know about those. Anyone else?" Harris was getting impatient. He needed to get back on guard. "Tell me now… and no more jokes… and no lies."

"Alright, alright. Where's your sense of humour gone? No, I've seen no strangers, and that's the complete truth. Honest."

Harris lifted his head as high as he could and found

he could just see the drawbridge and the castle door above the leaves of the bushes. One quick glance was enough... all was well. If he had just glanced up a moment earlier he would have seen the castle door gently closing, but he was too caught up in the conversation with Feeni. He bent down and grasped one of the branches in his beak and pulled upwards. Feeni's leg slipped out and Harris let go. The branch sprang back.

"How did that happen?"

"Just running, slipped and got caught. If you were a rabbit you'd know how it happens," she said sounding cross with him for not understanding.

"Alright. You'd better go for now, but if you see any intruders it's your duty to tell me."

She nodded.

"And remember..." he continued, but she turned quickly and hopped off into the bushes. He called after her. "Wizard Elzaphan wants to see you... and soon."

He took off and glided back towards the castle. He swooped underneath the drawbridge and skilfully flew the full length of it to check there was no one there. He flew back along it again to make sure and then returned to his post.

Perched on the high turret at the back of the castle, Quint watched. The gentle moonlight glinted on the golden feathers on the back of her head as she surveyed the grounds below. Her powerful eyes could pick out the slightest movement and twice she had swooped down to investigate, falling in an instant, a mere flash in the night, so fast that no creature could have escaped. Both times it turned out to be small nocturnal animals - a mouse and then a bat. She decided that she must have been watching for about two hours and so she glided around the castle to the front, descending through the warm air to the great door by the drawbridge. She settled on her wooden post. Harris was pleased to have her back.

"Anything?" asked Harris.

"No, it's all quiet at the back. What about here?"

"The same, really. The only excitement was when Feeni got herself caught in a bush…"

Quint looked cross and she shook her head. "Feeni! That stupid rabbit! I don't trust her at all. She's a devious one, she is."

"That's true. Even a simple conversation is difficult with her!"

Quint shook her head again. "I hope you told her that Wizard Elzaphan wants to see her."

"Yes, I did. She acted all surprised and innocent."

"Sounds like her."

"Do you feel… well… something in the air… an uncomfortable feeling?" Harris asked.

"No, I don't think so," answered Quint, looking quizzical.

Harris paused and looked out into the darkness. "Actually, I think it's gone now," he commented.

They both felt uneasy. Quint looked across the drawbridge and into the grounds, "We'd better keep watch with all our attention," she said.

"You're right," said Harris, and they stopped talking and concentrated fully on gazing out into the grounds and listening for any unusual sounds.

Behind them, inside the castle, the intruder moved silently along a hallway.

In Wizard Elzaphan's castle the brave party of travellers slept soundly right through the night. At the sound of a cock crowing Lazuli awoke. The pale morning light was gentle on her eyes as she looked around. Tally was close by, the children in their beds and Joog perched in the silver birch tree. Neville looked comfortable on his blankets.

Amalek woke up next and after a moment she slipped out of bed and walked over to the window. Her wavy hair hung down untidily and she swept it back and hooked it around her ears. She felt refreshed after the sleep, full of energy, and ready to take on anything, even fighting the Dark Wizard Troubler. The bright fresh morning lifted her spirits. The castle's shadow, cast by the rising sun, stretched across the lake in front of her. The brightening sky was clear. Rising up majestically from the still water were the great Daawa Mountains, their snowy peaks painted pink by the sun.

Everything about the view was beautiful. The mirror-like surface of the lake reflected the glory of the mountains in every detail while peace hung in the air above the still water. The scene filled Amalek with joy. The delightful singing of the many coloured birds was joyous. Only the very tops of the trees moved slightly and they seemed to be swaying with joy. There was joy flowing through everything.

"Seph," she called, still looking out of the window, "Wake up and come and have a look at this."

He stirred but stayed asleep. Lazuli got up onto her feet from her bed of hay and took a couple of steps towards him, shaking the floor and he awoke with a jerk.

"Oh, it's you, Lazuli," he said, smiling, "I thought the castle was falling down!"

"Seph," Amalek said again, "Have a look at this."

With ruffled hair he stepped out of bed and walked sleepily over to his sister at the window.

For a few moments they both gazed out and enjoyed the scene. Then Amalek's thoughts turned to her home and she shook her head and sighed.

"I wonder what's happening in The Kingdom of Gems," she said, shaking her head, and turning to Seph, "The snow must be getting deeper and deeper... and what about mum and dad?" she sighed, "Are they still standing there frozen?"

Seph closed his eyes for a second, fighting back the pain and trying to be positive.

"There must be a way..." he said slowly, "A way to break the spell... a way to stop the Troubler and what he's doing."

Amalek sighed again, caught by the image of their beloved kingdom and all the animals and people, and the King and Queen, the town and the palace, all in the power of the evil spell of the Troubler.

"Do you think we can beat him?" asked Amalek.

"Of course we can," Seph began, "I think we just have to try our very, very best. It's like you told me before. We try our best... and that's all we can do. And, of course, we'll have the help of some magic from Wizard Elzaphan."

"We've got to do it!" Amalek looked at her brother with a desperate look in her eyes, eyes that called out for reassurance and encouragement, "Remember how good it was to live there before the spell. *He's* ruined everything!"

"Then we'll have to ruin it for him... and we will," said Seph gripping his sister's hand firmly.

"And look what he's done to Flop," Amalek said, her eyes dampening with tears, "It's horrible!"

Seph gave her hand a squeeze. "I know. To see him like that... but what could have done that to him?"

"Elzaphan said it's poison from a sting."

"Yes, I know," Seph agreed, "But I wonder *what* did it. Wizard Elzaphan said it was a strange poison that he doesn't recognize... he doesn't know what actually stung him."

Amalck shuddered. "It's... frightening..."

Two tears ran down her cheeks leaving damp trails that glistened in the morning sun.

"But we know he was hit by something..." she said, "Elzaphan said that. He said it was something black hanging around the dog's neck, and..." She paused to wipe her tears away and sniffed a couple of times. "And I've been thinking, Seph. That raven who's their leader and they call the General... he had a black compass around his neck. Remember?"

"Yes," said Seph, and then thoughtfully, "Oh, I see. So, perhaps Flop got hit by another black compass. But what does it mean?"

"It must be dark magic..." Amalek said slowly. Suddenly she remembered something. "And when we were watching them from that bush I'm sure I saw the compass moving by itself... it made a jerky movement...

I'm sure it did."

"By itself?" questioned Seph with surprise.

"Yes," she said, "That's the point... it moved by itself!"

"But how?" Seph asked, "This could be important. We should tell Wizard Elzaphan about it."

When they had visited Flop they had been shocked. Simron sat in a chair and Flop was curled up in a basket with a soft blanket for warmth. Miriam was lying on Flop's side. When they knelt down close to him, Flop looked at them below drooped eyelids, with eyes no longer bright and lively, but now dull and sleepy. His head was still swollen. They stroked him and were concerned to feel the bumps of his backbone standing out from his weak, thin body.

Then he recognized them and felt their love, and his eyes lightened slightly. He started purring and for a moment the hope rose in their hearts. It was like the first day of spring as they saw the spark of life shining in him. But their moment of joy was extinguished when he suddenly growled at them and hissed at Miriam. She stayed defiantly where she was and slowly he lowered his head and rested his chin on the blanket. It was as if he was pulled away from himself, away from the real Flop, by some dark emotion and some shadowy mood of hate.

Amalek, with her deep knowledge of animals, was especially sensitive to Flop's feelings. She felt his pain deeply and was hit by his misery, stepping back in shock. She wished there was something they could do for him.

They stayed with him for a while but the mood persisted until he closed his eyes and slipped into sleep.

Now, the memory of the meeting with Flop saddened them whenever they thought of him.

They both looked up when they heard footsteps outside the door. The brass door handle turned and in came the great wizard himself, stooping a little to get through the door with his tall pointed hat and using his staff like a walking stick. He brought with him a wonderful feeling of calm happiness that felt as if it could go on forever. Amalek and Seph immediately felt uplifted.

"Good morning everyone!" he announced with joy as they gathered around him like ants around a pile of sugar, "Did you enjoy the Magic Rooms?"

"Oh, yes!" Amalek and Seph replied together, and the others nodded their agreement.

Lazuli swung her trunk playfully towards the children. Neville waddled towards the wizard and Joog flew off his tree to land skilfully on Amalek's shoulder. Seph reached out and stroked the snowy owl on the back of his head. His feathers felt soft. Then Seph looked back at the great wizard.

"Wizard Elzaphan?"

"Yes?" he replied.

The two children looked up at him eager to tell them what they knew about the black compasses.

"We think we know what did that to Flop," said Seph.

The great wizard's eyes opened slightly wider as he waited to hear more. Seph continued.

"We think that the thing that hit him was a black compass. We saw one around a raven's neck. It must have been the same... it looks like a watch on a chain, but it's a compass... and Amalek saw it moving... making a little jerk."

"That is very interesting and useful to know," he said,

thoughtfully scratching his long white beard, "Yes...
yes... it makes sense... a black compass... yes. I've
come across this before, a long time ago. Compasses
used for evil... as guides. And these compasses, they
move because something lives inside. The compass
carries a creature and protects it. Hides it, perhaps. Now
what small creatures sting? Centipedes, scorpions,
hornets and wasps. And snakes and spiders bite. So it
would be one of these or something like it. But they are
not just ordinary snakes or wasps or whatever... no, they
are infected by the evil of their master and this makes
their sting completely different, and very difficult to
treat."

He looked at the floor as he thought about it. Then he
raised his head and looked at them with a concerned
expression.

"I'm full of hope... and this really helps... but..."

"How is Flop now?" asked Seph.

"He's weak... and growing weaker, I'm afraid. He's
hanging on to life by the merest thread. And he's eating
nothing. But I'm doing all I can." He paused. "It's as if...
the poison, the darkness in him, in his mind... it's
affecting his thoughts and emotions. And he's weak
because he's fighting it. If he wasn't so good-hearted he
would have given in to it quickly and fallen to the power
of the Troubler, and then... well... all his energy would
be used against us. There's a tremendous battle going on
inside him."

Amalek looked anxiously at the great wizard with
sad eyes. "Do you think he'll be strong enough?"

"Well, it's up to him now," he replied, "This new
information, about the black compass, maybe it will help.
We're doing all we can."

Wizard Elzaphan smiled and suddenly looked bright and encouraging as he looked around at their faces.

"Later today you'll be leaving here," he announced, "I have given this some thought... you need a way of travelling that will give you the best chance of getting through." A twinkle now sparkled in the wizard's eye. "But I'll tell you all about it later. First... breakfast."

They followed him to the room where they had eaten the day before. The same waiters and waitress served them. The food was delicious. When they had finished Wizard Elzaphan stood up and spoke.

"Before the hard work of your journey back begins we need to work out some plans. Spark!" he called out.

Spark came running in through the door with his stars shining and his face bright and happy. He sat at his master's feet, eagerly looking up at him.

"Now, Spark, take our guests to the Golden Room. They need a little help with their quest."

"Right!" said Spark.

He trotted through the door and all the others followed.

The dungeons of the Castle were dark, cold and dank. They had not been used for many years and now no one went down there.

Thirty-four stone steps led down to a dingy corridor where fourteen heavy doors, seven on each side, opened into cells. Each door had a small hatch with a sliding cover. A row of wooden-handled torches, evenly spaced along both sides of the corridor, were perched head high in their holders, ready to be lit. The first one, at the foot of the steps, was missing.

The thick dust on the stairs had been recently disturbed by someone descending the steps and moving stealthily along the corridor to one of the cells at the end. The door was open and the flickering flames of the missing torch played on the rock floor and walls. A single sharp cough echoed eerily along the corridor.

Someone had entered the dungeons. In the gloomy cell, the intruder sat on the floor and leant against the wall.

Spark led the way along hallways and through many wooden doors with shiny brass handles that he opened with flying sparks. He led them up and down staircases. Amalek and Seph helped Neville whenever they came to some stairs, carrying him when necessary. Lazuli had no problems fitting through the large arched doorways.

Finally they found themselves climbing up some spiral stairs with narrow windows where bright sunlight poured through in shafts of yellow. This was a tighter fit for Lazuli, who occasionally bumped the walls as she climbed. These were the stairs leading up to the Golden Room and they were long and steep, spiralling up inside the highest turret in the castle.

Spark ran up the stairs ahead and called back to them.

"See you in the Golden Room."

Then he was gone.

When they were over half way up, Joog landed on the ledge by a window above them and looked down. "Come on," he said glancing out of the window, "We're almost there. I can see…"

There was a sudden crash as the window smashed, spraying splintered glass inwards. Joog jumped with surprise and flapped into the air instantly. Something black had burst through and shattered the window.

"Ravens!" shouted Joog as the first one was followed by two more.

Their flight was so fast that in an instant they had circled and flashed out of the window one after the other. Joog began to follow but stopped at the window, landed on the ledge and gazed out after them.

"If they come back," he began, "I'm ready for them."

Seph climbed a couple of steps and looked through the window. "Can you see them, Joog?"

"Not now," he replied, pointing with a claw, "They're in those trees down there. At least that's where they went. I can't see them now."

Another crash made them all look up to the next window. The three ravens exploded through the glass only to circle once and depart again as quickly as before.

Neville's magic scarf had grown longer and was twitching at the end. Amalek and Seph moved up a step to look past Joog and out of the window.

"What are they doing?" Seph asked, "Can you see them?"

"Yes… and get ready!" called out Joog, "They're returning."

"The same ones?" asked Amalek.

"I think so… three of them," Joog said, staring out of

the window and following them with his powerful eyes as they began to circle the tower, "What are they up to?"

Tally hopped up a couple of steps until he was beside Seph. The young hare was inspired by Seph's courage and he nudged Seph's leg. Seph picked him up so that he could see out and they all watched as the ravens circled the tower at a distance and then, with a loud honk that echoed eerily in the morning air, fell down to the trees below.

"What was that about?" quizzed Amalek, shaking her head and spreading her hands.

No one replied. They were all looking around them at what the ravens had left behind; a dark mist which began to swirl around their heads and before their eyes, growing thicker, like mist turning to thick fog in a few seconds. They felt themselves losing sense of where they were and who they were. Their legs crumpled and they slumped down onto the steps. Joog toppled off the window ledge to land softly on his side on a step. Lazuli's great body stopped her falling down as she was jammed against the walls.

They felt they were drifting in the intoxicating substance; the strange dark mist grew deeper and swirled hypnotically around the friends. Their eyelids flickered and drooped. Amalek and Seph felt sleep taking them over and they began to slip into the same dream.

They dreamt they were back in the Kingdom of Gems and were walking along the path leading up to the palace. They looked up at the Round Room. Then the dream turned into a nightmare. The Dark Wizard Troubler stared at them with his terrible black eyes and shouted, "I am your new King!"

The dream melted away and they experienced a

terrible misery which ached deep inside them. All the pain of the imprisoned kingdom fell upon them with crushing weight, filling their hearts. It was the crying of thousands of trapped souls. In a moment, they saw the faces of people and animals they knew, blank faces staring into nothingness, their lives snatched away from them by the Dark Wizard Troubler's spell.

The children could hardly bear it and they felt they were slipping away. Murky sleep fell heavily upon them, like a lead weight into water, and they sensed they were drowning in an ocean of gloom.

The friends lay on the steps like six lifeless rocks, absorbed into the dark power which now possessed them.

The Kingdom of Gems was a wonderland of white with snow swirling and gusting everywhere throughout the frozen land. Before the spell, water from both the Snowpeak Mountains and the Plains of Wilrack used to flow in brooks, streams and small rivers to join the River Gem. This in turn would tumble over the sheer drop to form the Gem Falls with the water crashing dramatically into the river below. All of it was now frozen.

In his attempt to steal the Candara Gems the Dark Wizard Troubler had smashed the sheet of ice that formed from the falling water in order to reveal the Brinscally Cave behind. But now massive new icicles had formed and hung from the high brink of the waterfall to stretch over half way down.

The Brinscally Cave had its own collection of icicles.

They joined and hung down to form a mass of bumpy ice which covered the entrance from top to bottom like a door. There were, however, just a few small gaps in this wall of ice and in front of one of these a lone person crouched with an ice axe laying on the snow close by. The snow blew around the short figure whose face was protected from the cold by a hood and scarf so that only the eyes were exposed to the harsh elements.

Inside the cave the three Candara Gems - the ruby, the sapphire and the amethyst - lit up the far side of the cave. They rested in their places in the cavity carved into the far wall and glowed with luminous beauty.

The figure outside stooped forwards and peered through one of the gaps in the ice. The hole was just big enough for one eye to look through. There was a gasp of excitement and the eye opened wider at the sight of the bright splash of colours on the far side of the cave.

Suddenly, the glow of the gems intensified and grew until the whole cave was lit with their bright coloured light. The eye squinted at the brightness and with a cry of pain the figure staggered back, collapsed into the snow and lay there for a few seconds. The glowing gems faded back to normal and the person regained strength and scrabbled up again. After hesitating for a moment, the figure took a determined stride back towards the cave, snatched up the ice axe and plunged it into the door of icicles. After a few heavy blows, half the ice door had splintered and fallen away, and the figure stepped cautiously in.

At the exact moment when the gems glowed brightly Amalek's head dropped and knocked into Seph's with a bump. They woke. Straight away Amalek jumped up.

"Wake up!" she shouted, "Come on! Wake up!"

At the sound of the Princess' voice, the dark mist dissolved and with it the terrible sense of doom. The others opened their eyes and stared around them in a daze. They all felt as if they had just awoken from a deep sleep and for a moment were unsure where they were.

"Listen," said Seph firmly, trying to fight off the sleepy feeling, "Let's go quickly before they return."

This spurred them all into action. The children picked up Neville between them and they resumed their climb with renewed energy.

Joog hovered above as they climbed, going on ahead to land on every window ledge and look out for ravens.

"Even here..." he said, shaking his head, "Even here the Troubler is still trying to get us... in Wizard Elzaphan's castle! Somehow he has the power."

Amalek looked up at him. "I thought we'd be safe from him here." She glanced down the stairwell nervously but Lazuli was blocking the view down. "What shall we do, Joog?"

"I'll keep watching the windows," he replied, "And you stay alert, and make sure nothing is happening up there."

"Right," said Seph.

"Right," echoed Tally who was still beside Seph and hopping up the steps next to him.

"For this to happen here," Joog said, "I mean those ravens in this castle, it could mean that... perhaps the Troubler is here!"

"He can't be," Amalek explained, "Because of his spell. He'd have to break his spell to come here."

Joog looked serious. "You're right. But... I can't help thinking, you know, that he may have found a way... and if he has, and he's here, then we have an even bigger problem than we thought."

They were nearly at the top now and constantly aware that they did not know what was happening down the steps below Lazuli. They also wondered what they might find at the top of the stairs. When they overcame the pull of sleep and the dark mist they had gained strength and energy to fight for the freedom of the Kingdom of Gems. Experiencing the pain of the entrapped people and creatures made them even more determined to free them. This strong and firm resolve was providing them with renewed willpower and courage. But in spite of this, when they considered that perhaps the Dark Wizard Troubler was waiting for them, or following them, it was a terrifying thought.

"Real strength is found within," said Seph to his sister, "Remember what Simron said to us? That's just what it feels like! The strength is within us, isn't it?"

Amalek looked puzzled, and as they climbed the last few steps she repeated slowly, "Real strength... is found within... I see. Yes... now we know what he meant. Simron was right."

They completed the last few steps and the children put Neville down as they reached the top. Where the steps ended there was a long thin room, like a spacious wide corridor, with an archway with two large wooden doors at the end. The walls were hung with about twenty paintings of wizards and sorcerers. The bright sunshine flooded in through a window near the arched double doors catching a picture frame and reflecting brightly on a shiny, gold door-handle. There were also some golden, decorated letters set in a circle on the door, highlighted by the sun's rays, which read:

THE GOLDEN ROOM

The brightness of the door-handle, as well as the golden letters, shone out in the contrasting dim light of the rest of the room. They all stopped and looked across at the doors.

"Looks all clear," said Amalek, sighing with relief.

"Yes, but…" whispered Joog settling on Seph's shoulder, "I don't know. Remember what happened on the stairs… and there's something strange about this. Can't you feel it?"

"I can," whispered Seph, "It's *his* presence… the Troubler. He's close… I can feel it… all around."

Amalek laughed nervously, and then whispered, "This is silly! We're in Wizard Elzaphan's Castle! It should be safe here…"

"It isn't, Ammey," whispered Joog, "Not at all. And it wasn't safe down there…" he waved a wing down the stairs, "And I must admit *that* scared me… those ravens able to fly right into the castle. This shouldn't be happening."

"So," Seph whispered, "what do we do now?"

"We must watch that window," whispered Joog, "for the ravens… they could return."

For a few seconds they all stared at the window at the other end of the hallway. They only had to walk to the doors but something was holding them back.

Seph shook his head.

"I don't know… that Troubler's presence…" he whispered, "It's something terrible. We must be so careful. If he's around… we have to be ready."

"You're right, Seph," whispered Joog, "We just have to get in through that door and then we're safe. We'll all move quickly together and watch that window, alright?"

The others nodded.

"Here's the plan…" he continued, "Seph and Amalek first…" Tally hopped up beside Seph. "*And* Tally, of course… Lazuli at the back checking down those stairs and then following. And how about Neville on your back, Lazuli, so that he can fly if he needs to?"

"That's fine," said Lazuli.

"But, will my wings fit in this room?" asked Neville.

Amalek looked across the room, "Should do…" she said, "Yes… try them out, Neville."

Amalek and Seph lifted Neville onto Lazuli's broad back and he stretched out his magnificent wings. They just fitted.

"Great," he said, folding them back.

Joog took to the air.

"I'll hover above. Right then… let's go."

The children found themselves creeping cautiously along the hallway towards the door. A floorboard creaked; they paused and then carried on. There was no sound from the Golden Room. As they moved closer the atmosphere thickened. The eerie silence felt oppressively heavy and dull. Amalek shuddered as she felt it growing stronger with every tentative step they took towards the doors. She felt panic arising and it was only the strength of her brother beside her that prevented her from turning and running. Tally crept along beside Seph, his brown eyes wide and alert.

"KYWAY," he thought, *"KYWAY."*

When Prince and Princess reached the window, they looked out to see a strange and frightening sight; the three ravens were standing on the sill and staring in.

Amalek tensed, "What are they doing?" she asked.

"Don't worry," said Joog, "I'll watch them. You go in."

One more step and they were by the doors. Joog hovered above keeping an eye on the ravens but watching the doors too. Everything was quiet and still. The only movement was the silent beat of Joog's wings. Seph slowly reached out his hand towards the brass door-handle.

What happened next was so unexpected that it made Seph jump with shock. Just before Seph's hand grasped the door-handle, it turned. Someone was just the other side of the doors and turning the handle.

They all stared at the door-handle as it turned slowly. The sunlight was still streaming through the window and falling on one of Seph's cheeks. He could feel the gentle warmth in contrast to the chill of fear that gripped his heart. He was completely still. Amalek was completely still. No one moved. They all watched.

The doors began to open. As they looked through the growing crack they could see nothing and when the doors were open wide it was completely dark. It was as dark as a moonless night.

Seph, who was closest to the open doors, took a step forwards. Tally was right beside him. They both gazed into the nothingness. What did it mean? What had happened? Was this the Golden Room of Wizard Elzaphan? Where was Wizard Elzaphan?

Seph reached out his hand and then his foot into the dark.

"Stop!" called out Joog from above, his golden-yellow, owl eyes glowing as they pierced the darkness, "He's in there - look!"

Seph stopped, nearly overbalancing into the room, and found he was on the edge of a sheer drop into darkness. The drop seemed endless. Joog had called out just in time.

The eyes of Amalek and Seph were getting used to the dark now and they could just make out two black dots... even blacker than the darkness itself... and then a form... a black form with black stars... moving slowly...

moving towards them. It was the Dark Wizard Troubler. The black eyes were fixed on them.

"Come and get me!" cried the Troubler, "If you dare! Come on! Or are you too afraid!" Then he called out even louder, "You cowards!"

No one moved.

The Troubler dropped his voice to a sneering hiss. "Don't forget I've got your precious King and Queen in my power... you won't see them again... not alive... unless you come in here. Come on, get me if you can."

"Alright then!" shouted Neville, jumping off Lazuli's back.

"No!" shouted Joog, "Don't go in there!"

But it was too late. Neville had spread his great wings and took off with surprising ease. He started flying towards the open door.

"Stop!" shouted Joog.

Neville was flying straight underneath Joog and above the heads of Amalek and Seph. His long stripy-coloured scarf hung down and blew out behind him and as he flew it brushed Amalek's cheek and she felt it warm against her skin. The brave albatross tucked his wings in, glided through the open doors and into the dark. The scarf glowed brightly and they watched, in amazement, as it wound itself around the Troubler who was totally surprised by the sudden attack.

"Aaahhh!" cried the Troubler, trying to wriggle free as the amazing magic scarf was wrapping itself around him, "Get off me! Get off!"

But the scarf continued winding as it grew longer still. His arms were now held tightly by his sides as the scarf was working its way down his struggling body. His legs were still free and he began to run. He ran straight towards Amalek and Seph who leapt to the side as he came through the doors and into the light of the corridor dragging Neville behind him on the other end of the scarf. Neville just had time to tuck his wings in as he was pulled through the doorway.

"Oh no you don't!" called out Neville, who turned and with a powerful flap flew back towards the door.

He folded his wings and glided back into the darkness. The magic scarf stretched, then shone even more brightly, and then began to unwind. As it unwound from the Troubler's body he began to spin.

"Aaahh!" cried the Troubler, falling to the floor and turning like a top.

At last the magic scarf had completely unwound and the evil wizard was left spinning wildly, a black blur in the middle of the corridor. Neville had disappeared.

"Surround him!" called Seph to the others and they quickly formed a circle around the Troubler.

"When he stops spinning," Joog said calmly and with authority, "Lazuli... put a foot on him... and we'll all help to hold him down..."

Amalek blurted out, "We need a rope or something to tie him up..."

The Dark Wizard was slowing down now and they could see his black eyes looking up at them. Lazuli had padded over and had one of her great feet lifted and ready.

"Get away," the wizard growled at them from the floor, "Get away, idiots! Your out of your depth... little children!"

"Now, Lazuli!" shouted Joog, Now!"

Lazuli placed her foot on top of him and they all move to hold him down, but to their surprise, Lazuli's foot thudded into the floor, and the others crashed and bumped not into the Dark Wizard Troubler, but into each other and Lazuli's leg. The Troubler had vanished and when they stood back to look for him, his shadow lingered. he was gone.

The heavy atmosphere lifted.

Seph looked towards the window and said quickly, "What about the ravens, Joog?"

Joog flew to the window.

"They've gone," he said.

A golden glow lit up the corridor and they looked around to see the Golden Room filled with sunlight. Through the open door they could see the welcome sight of Wizard Elzaphan beaming at them. The stars on his cloak shone and his arms were outspread to greet them.

"Come in," he said, his deep voice warm and welcoming, "Come in to the Golden Room."

Amalek and Seph ran to Wizard Elzaphan and he swept them up effortlessly into his arms. He hugged them both together. They found tears of relief bubbling up in their eyes, but at the same time they were tears of shock and pain at the loss of Neville.

"Oh, Wizard Elzaphan," said Amalek, "Neville's lost."

The wizard just held them with his strong arms of love.

A set of tracks in the snow led away from the Brinscally Cave, dropping down onto Charin Road and then turning south towards Candara. The snow was falling heavily, sweeping across the kingdom in multitudes of large swirling flakes and rapidly covering the tracks.

Something had changed in the Kingdom of Gems. The darkness of the spell had deepened, strengthening its grip on everything living, like a vice being tightened to breaking point. The spell had grown heavier. It had become a power beyond understanding.

Then something happened; something in the air changed. The walking figure felt it and stopped suddenly, looking across the white expanse of the Flatsage Farmlands. At that moment, thousands of birds frozen in mid-air throughout the kingdom, dropped like lead weights. They plummeted into the deep snow, to lie there, possessed by the evil spell and trapped in utter stillness.

Chapter 10

~ The Glyifild Bell ~

The Dark Wizard Troubler lifted a furious fist high above his head but he was too tired to slam it down on the table in front of him, which was just as well because it was covered with shivers of broken glass. He paused and brought his arm down weakly as he crumpled onto his knees and held his face in his hands. He was ready to collapse after his energy-sapping scheme had reached a sudden conclusion and ended in failure.

He felt it was a brilliant idea at the time and was confident that it would succeed, but somehow, once again, the enemy had escaped.

"At least I got the Albatross," he growled angrily as he brushed the broken glass off the table with a loose despairing sweep of his arm. It tinkled gently onto the dusty floor. "But the others…"

His eyelids drooped as he flopped down, his head thudding on the wooden floorboards. He was rapidly drifting away into sleep and as he did he thought about what had happened.

Minutes earlier he had been staring into a mirror he had wrenched off a wall to replace the other one that Halo had smashed. With the help of his three specially-appointed ravens he had visualized Wizard Elzaphan's castle. Then he stared intently into the mirror and concentrated. Time passed until suddenly, to his excited delight, he had been able to materialize there, into the castle, in his ghostly form. It took huge effort and concentration and rapidly sapped his power but it was the most solid he had achieved yet.

Because he was not actually there in person, but only as a phantom, he could not react quickly enough when the albatross had taken him by surprise. If he had not been so solid the scarf would have passed straight through him and not been able to pull him against his will.

"At least," he thought, *"I have made that wretched bird pay. That's one less enemy to worry about."*

However, what he really wanted was the others, especially the Prince and Princess.

At the point where he had stopped spinning and they had all dived on him, the mirror had been unable to sustain the projected image any more and had shattered into hundreds of splintered pieces. He had lost contact with the Castle instantly and the dream of trapping the enemy had gone for the moment, but he still felt it was only a matter of time before he would inevitably succeed.

With these thoughts turning in his mind he drifted off to sleep.

After Amalek and Seph had finished hugging the great Wizard Elzaphan, they slipped down gently onto the cream-coloured carpet.

They glanced around the room. They could see why it was called the Golden Room. There was a golden chandelier hanging in the centre with cream-coloured candles ready to be lit; there were more paintings of wizards and sorcerers in gold frames; there were golden curtains that draped gracefully to touch the deep pile carpet; the carved wooden chairs had gold padding and the wooden furniture had gold fittings. The ceiling was again deep blue with stars of gold and silver, and the walls were the same cream as the carpet. One small cupboard was made entirely of gold.

Wizard Elzaphan sat down in a golden armchair. Leaning against it was his staff and the children watched as he reached for it. His strong hand clasped the polished, dark wood that glinted in the light of the great oval ammolite gemstone on the top which glowed gently. Its translucent colours swirled with hues of reds, yellow, blues and greens.

Amalek looked up at the wizard.

"Neville's gone," she said.

The wizard looked concerned.

"What happened?" he asked.

"He flew into this darkness," she replied, "This room here was just darkness... like endless dark. He flew in and now he's gone."

The wizard looked thoughtful.

"Hmm… endless dark," he said, "And he flew in and disappeared into it?"

"Yes," replied Amalek.

"And the Troubler was in there?" Elzaphan asked.

"Yes," replied Seph, "But Neville pulled him out. Then Neville flew in again and disappeared."

Elzaphan shook his head and sighed, sounding resigned to what had happened.

"He's gone," he concluded, "And his loss… breaks my heart," he said quietly, "But sometimes sacrifices have to be made when things are desperate and a kingdom is at stake. Only the brave are prepared to put down their lives for others."

"Oh no," Lazuli said, her great forehead furrowing with sadness, "It can't be. Won't we see him again?"

"Neville was very brave," said the great wizard earnestly, "He entered into the Troubler's evil, dark mind… but now…" he shook his head, "Well… he can't survive for long, no one could, not in there."

They all looked at Elzaphan wanting to hear some words of hope. The hope was there but it was slim.

"It seems that he's sacrificed his life to save yours. But remember he did it willingly and happily. I know you can see him no longer, and that's the hardest thing."

There was a stunned silence. No one knew what to say. The wizard was clearly upset too. His eyes filled with tears. He stood up and walked over to the window. He stared out for a few minutes before walking back and sitting down again. He looked at them intently.

"Tell me everything that happened, please."

When they had described it all Wizard Elzaphan looked thoughtfully at them.

"I'm certainly glad you came through that test," he said gently.

"Test?" asked Joog.

They were all gathered around the wizard.

"Was that a test?"

"Yes, it was a test," said Wizard Elzaphan, "It was a test in the sense that it was a challenge that you had to overcome... and a very important one. If you had failed... I think all would have been lost. The Dark Wizard Troubler would probably have ruled the Kingdom of Gems for some time... at least his hold would have been much stronger. Also, he may have got a foothold here too. But now that you came through it means that you can head back with the knowledge that you can at least try to challenge this evil, fallen wizard and that you have a fighting chance of success. Well done, this is really excellent!"

"But what happened?" asked Tally, gazing up at Wizard Elzaphan, "What was the dark mist? And the darkness in here? And how did the Troubler disappear?"

"Alright," replied Wizard Elzaphan, "I'll tell you all about what happened. You need to know, but we haven't much time, for you must return to the Kingdom of Gems as soon as possible. Two days ago I noticed three ravens sitting together in those trees over there..."

He waved an arm towards the window, and when they looked out they realized for the first time how high they were. The trees were tiny green shapes far below them, and the birds that flitted to and fro between the trees were no more than dots. Lake Beautiful was far below and stretched away into the hazy distance, shimmering with the light of the sun.

"I've never seen such ravens before," continued

Wizard Elzaphan, "and I knew what they were and that they were sent by the Dark Wizard Troubler with evil intentions for you. Then the other birds came and told me about their black eyes. I knew then that the Troubler was powerful enough to come here, onto Keill Island, even into the castle. This sort of power is extremely rare. I knew I had a major problem."

He paused for a moment and looked around at their attentive faces.

"But he's after you, you see, so *you* had to defeat him to gain strength... and you needed to gain extra strength to have a chance of defeating him and driving him from your kingdom. If I had fought him and defeated him here... and it wasn't actually him but just his projected image... that would not have helped you at all... he would still possess your kingdom... and you would not have gained the strength. Do you follow?"

They nodded.

"Yes," said Joog, "Yes, I see."

"So I had to let him, and the ravens, weave their wicked spells and trust that you would win. It was a difficult choice and thank goodness you did win. It was a chance I had to take and you didn't let me down. It took all my self-control not to interfere and help you. If things had gone wrong then I would have acted, but even then it might have been too late."

He paused again and then continued.

"When your heads knocked together to wake you up," he said looking at Amalek and Seph, "that was no coincidence - oh no, that was providence, a helpful hand from some goodness somewhere... hard to say where the help came from but it would have come from somewhere. And the Troubler is, I am sure, still back in the Kingdom of Gems… the one you met was just a trick of light, and darkness, a very convincing one too, a projection of him… you all fell for it. He was here but only as a phantom as we wizards say. He wanted you to fall into the dark chasm, because if you had fallen in you would have been instantly trapped in the Troubler's mind, and that is not a good place to be. I know I don't need to tell you that!"

He paused while they took in all that he was saying to them.

"So, you did it!" he carried on cheerily, "Well done! Brilliant! You passed the test and gained the strength and resolve to take on the Dark Wizard Troubler! You'll need it… not only has the spell deepened… but there is something else. Something happened back in your kingdom, something has changed there."

His eyes looked distant as if he was trying to work something out.

"I don't know what it was, but something bad happened that sent out a ripple that I felt here."

They all looked up as they heard the sound of flapping wings. At the window, Harris appeared. In his powerful talons he held a terrified looking raven.

"Put it in there, Harris," said Wizard Elzaphan pointing to a golden cage that rested on a small but tall three-legged table in the corner of the room.

The table was so tall that the cage was at head height to the great wizard. Harris swooped in through the open window, caged the tremoring raven and slammed the door closed. It was Jeg, the leader of the three. He jabbed his beak hard at the cage door which rattled the cage, but the door stayed secure.

"You wait," Jeg snapped, "You just wait 'till my

Master hears of this! He'll get you!"

Wizard Elzaphan spoke firmly, "He'll do no such thing. Now you just keep quiet."

Quint flew in clutching another raven.

"Ah, Quint! I thought you'd be along soon. In there with it!"

They all watched the magnificent eagle fly in with the second raven and deposit it in the cage.

"Thank you, you two," said the wizard bending down to stroke the eagles on their backs as they stood on the carpet, "You've done an excellent job."

Jeg and the other raven cackled in mock laughter and Jeg spoke again.

"You can't beat my Master... no way... you just wait..."

Wizard Elzaphan stepped towards the cage, lifted his staff and pointed it towards the ravens. The gemstone shone brightly and sent out a flash of red light which hit the cage. The cage fizzed and sparked with the same red light, shaking the ravens inside. They cowered into a corner.

"Stop! Stop!" yelled Jeg.

"Do what you're told then," said Wizard Elzaphan.

"OK! OK!" shouted Jeg.

"What's your name?" the great wizard asked.

"Jeg!" he shouted from the cage which was still shaking, "Stop! Stop!"

"Alright," Elzaphan said calmly as he lowered his staff and the cage stopped rattling, "No talking!" he ordered.

Jeg opened his beak as if to say something and then thought better of it and closed it again.

"Shall we go back on duty then, sir?" asked Harris.

"Not yet, Harris," said the wizard, "There's one more raven…"

At that moment there was a great commotion of chirping at the window and in tumbled a swirling mass of sparrows. In the centre was the last raven, overwhelmed by the sheer numbers of determined little birds clinging on to it. Wizard Elzaphan pointed to the golden cage and the sparrows put the raven in it with the other two.

Wizard Elzaphan lifted his staff threateningly. "Jeg! Tell the latest prisoner the rules."

"N… n… not… talking," he stammered.

"Good," said the great wizard decisively.

Then he turned to the mass of sparrows, "Excellent!" he exclaimed, "Thank you."

With that Harris and Quint took off and glided out of the open window to return to their guard duties. The sparrows followed with a flurry of fluttering feathers and delightful chirruping. In the cage, the three sad and anxious looking ravens, black as coal, watched with black eyes.

The great wizard pointed at the ravens. "As soon as they had tried to leave the castle and escape, I asked my birds to catch them and bring them here."

The last raven to be caught jabbed his beak defiantly against the bars of the cage. Amalek, who was standing closest, jumped back.

"Stop it!" Jeg ordered.

"Be quiet!" Wizard Elzaphan snapped, lifting his staff again and pointing it at the cage. Again the gem stone shone with red light, the cage shook violently and red sparks flew off it. The three ravens cowered inside and cawed pathetically. Elzaphan lowered his staff.

Amalek nudged Seph and nodded towards something

that had caught her eye. It was the golden cupboard. It seemed to shine more brightly than anything else in the room. Through the glass doors they could see inside, and there, on golden shelves, were rows of little golden pots of different sizes. There was a cluster of golden gloves hanging up and some golden shoes of all different sizes. Then there was a special railing with rows of golden models of animals and beneath these a line of little golden books, which were beautifully bound. Each of the books had MAGIC SPELLS written on the spine as well as Wizard Elzaphan's coat of arms. There were golden rings, necklaces and bracelets draped over golden hooks.

On the lowest shelf were several little golden boxes and some wooden ones of various shapes and sizes. In a golden pot was a group of gold and silver pens just like the ones that Wizard Elzaphan had sent to Amalek and Seph. There were many other things and it was hard to tell what some of them were.

"Well, my friends," said Wizard Elzaphan, "We need to move swiftly and you need a plan for your journey. You must have magic too, so let's see what we can do."

Wizard Elzaphan, followed by all of the others, walked to the golden cupboard, opened the glass doors, and reached inside.

"Here you are," said Wizard Elzaphan to Amalek and Seph, as he reached out towards them with something in his hands. Then he hesitated and looked at them seriously. "These are for you. Take them and keep them somewhere very safe."

He handed them one of the little golden books each and as he did the light glinted brightly on the golden-gilded edges and for a second shone like sunlight on water. Amalek looked at the words on the cover and read them again just to make sure it was really true.

"Magic Spells!" she exclaimed excitedly.

She held the little book in the palm of her hand and studied the front cover. There was wizard Elzaphan's coat of arms. The book was so small that she could close her fingers completely around it. Then she opened it and started reading.

Seph looked at his and studied it, turning it over in his hands with care.

"Magic Spells," he said, "I think these could be very useful on our journey back."

He folded his hand gently around the little book as if holding a baby bird which needed tenderness and love as well as protection. With the greatest of care he slipped it into his pocket and buttoned it up.

"Yes, keep them safe," Wizard Elzaphan said, "They must stay with you. We don't want them to fall into the wrong hands." He paused. "Now... what else I wond..." then he stopped, as if listening, and put a finger to his lips. "I wonder what..." he continued as he crept, without a sound, towards the door, "I should give you next. I think maybe..." he grasped the door handle, turned it, and quickly pulled the door open. As it swung open, Old Howard fell in and collapsed on the floor in front of them all, still clutching the stick he was using to help him walk with his injured ankle.

"You!" shouted Wizard Elzaphan, looking down at Old Howard, "You! I've heard about you! You have betrayed the Kingdom of Gems. And now you're listening at doors... a devious spy working for the Troubler and your own selfishness!"

"Mercy!" cried Old Howard glaring at them with his black eyes, "'Ave mercy on me, please. 'Ee made me do it!"

"You have a mind of your own, don't you?" said Wizard Elzaphan firmly.

"Oy used to 'ave. Now oy don't know any more," and he shook his head in despair.

Not long after he had broken free from the Troubler in the Forest of the Fairies and the evil wizard's voice had faded from his mind, the voice had returned. It was very faint to start with but it still managed to tempt him with more gold and as soon as he had given in to its promises the voice grew louder. Old Howard still did not realize that it was his greed for the gold bar in his pocket that allowed the Troubler into his mind.

Wizard Elzaphan stared at the old man.

"When you decided to turn your mind to evil," began the great wizard, "to pursue your own greed, then you started the chain of events that led you here, and now you are paying the price. It was your decision and it's your fault. And it's led to suffering for others too. Now, get up!"

Old Howard found this quite difficult with his twisted ankle and his heavy, rotund body. Eventually he did manage it and stood before Wizard Elzaphan with a miserable but defiant expression.

"Are you sorry, Old Howard?"

"No! What for? What 'ave oy done wrong? It's 'im," he slipped his hand into his pocket and clutched the bar of gold.

"I see," Wizard Elzaphan said, looking saddened, "I was hoping… still, never mind. Spark!"

Spark leapt up and approached Old Howard growling and showing his sharp teeth. Old Howard stepped back and retreated into the corner of the room, followed by

Spark. He slumped down leaning against the walls and Spark sat in front of him, guarding him with his eyes fixed on his slightest movement. Wizard Elzaphan walked to the other end of the room and opened a cupboard. Inside were rows of walking sticks. He took one out, whispered a few words over it and walked back to Old Howard.

"Take this," the wizard ordered holding it out towards him, "It's a Hadia Stick and can only do you good. Take it now."

Old Howard frowned and looked at it suspiciously, but he did not move.

The stick was made from the strong wood of a hazel tree with three bands of silver around it. The first, near the top, made the rounded handle and had Wizard Elzaphan's coat of arms engraved in it. The second, near the middle, was also engraved, this time with a poem. The third made a strong tip for walking.

"Take it," said Wizard Elzaphan, "It can be your walking companion. You need a stick don't you?"

"Yeah," he replied, sounding disgusted with the offer, "But not that one."

"Take it!" the wizard commanded.

Old Howard slowly reached for it. Suddenly the voice of the Dark Wizard Troubler spoke in his mind.

"Don't take it!" it hissed with desperate malice, "Do… not… take it!"

Old Howard stared at it without moving, his hand stretched out half way towards it.

"Now, take it!" Elzaphan commanded, still holding it out towards him.

Old Howard did not move but just glared at Wizard Elzaphan. There was something obstinate in him, a dark selfish force that resisted the great wizard. Then he heard the voice again.

"Take that and you are finished. Your suffering will be endless."

Old Howard shuddered with fear.

"I won't take it!" he said defiantly and he pulled his hand away.

Wizard Elzaphan's eyes were fixed on him. He had picked up his staff now with his other hand and he thumped it on the floor. The great gemstone glowed with blue light which lit up the whole room for a moment.

"Take it. Take it now," he said.

"Don't!" snapped the voice in Old Howard's head.

"Make me!" Old Howard sneered.

Spark growled and moved slightly closer. Old Howard recoiled further into the corner, still slumped down and leaning against the walls. He bent his knees and brought his legs up in front of him. Spark stepped closer, growled again and barked. For a moment they stared at each other, and then Spark barked again and snapped at his trousers ripping a hole in them.

To defend himself Old Howard took his hand out of his pocket, forgetting he was still clutching the bar of gold and moved quickly to strike at Spark. He stopped as the bar of gold fell to the floor with a clunk and skidded towards Wizard Elzaphan. Old Howard lunged at it. Spark growled at him again and snapped at his hand as he tried to grasp the gold bar. Spark's teeth just caught him on a finger. Old Howard pulled his hand back and cried out.

"Aaah! I'm bleeding!"

He looked at his hand and then back at the bar of gold.

Wizard Elzaphan stepped forwards holding the Hadia Stick out, close to Old Howard.

"Take it," he commanded.

Old Howard slowly reached out and then paused.

"Take it now!" ordered Elzaphan, thumping his staff on the floor again. Blue light made the room glow.

Old Howard closed his eyes and grasped the stick.

"Good," said the great wizard, "The spell is cast now. You have to keep the Hadia Stick with you. It will know when you do anything that may harm others... and then there will be... hmm... consequences for you. If you let go of the stick then you will be in pain and the further you go from it the greater the pain will be. But it is the pain of your own selfishness. When you feel sorry for what you have done and give up your selfish ways then you will be able to let go of it, and move away from it, and feel no pain. It's very simple and it's up to you. Do you understand?"

Old Howard did not answer.

Elzaphan turned to the others and smiled, "That was hard work! He'll be no more trouble to anyone."

"What will happen to him now?" asked Amalek.

"It doesn't really matter... the stick will keep him in order! I think I'll put him in a house in Munden and we'll see what happens..." He looked thoughtful. "But, no, maybe I'd better keep him here for a while... there's an empty hut in the grounds. He can live there."

The great wizard looked down at the bar of gold and then at Old Howard, "So this is how he did it, is it? He played on your greed and tempted you to work for him."

He picked it up and walked over to the open window.

"Harris!" he called. Then he turned to the others. "We don't want this around, but Harris will deal with it."

Harris appeared at the window and landed on the window frame.

"Take this, Harris, and throw it away. It must be thrown away somewhere where it won't be found... hmm..." He thought for a moment, "Yes, I know... throw it in the Tye Water. That's the deepest lake we have."

Suddenly there was a loud shout from behind them. "No!"

It was Old Howard. He had leapt to his feet, gripping his Hadia Stick and looking distraught. "That's moy gold!" he shouted.

He was holding the Hadia Stick and suddenly it whipped through the air and whacked him hard on the bottom.

"Aaahhh!" cried Old Howard.

Wizard Elzaphan laughed and then said firmly to Old Howard across the room, "The gold was yours, but not any more. It caused you nothing but trouble. Can't you see that? You're best rid of it."

He turned back to Harris.

"Take it," he said to the eagle, "Take it now."

"Certainly," Harris replied, glancing at Old Howard as he took the gold bar in a taloned foot, "It will be a pleasure, sir."

"Thank you," said the wizard as Harris jumped off the window frame and glided southwards.

Elzaphan called after him, "Oh, and drop it where the water is deepest."

Old Howard, still clutching his Hadia Stick, dropped his head in despair, muttering, "Thieves! That's moy gold and you're stealin' it."

The stick twitched in his hand and he stopped muttering and slumped against the wall. Wizard

Elzaphan ignored him and turned back to the others.

"Spark," he reached down and patted his dog, "Take Old Howard down to Cedric and tell him that the old man is going to live in that empty hut in the grounds at the back of the castle. He'll know what to do."

Spark growled threateningly at Old Howard until he limped out, his Hadia Stick tapping the floor as he walked.

"Now where were we? Ah yes… what else might they need?" asked the great wizard to himself as he crossed the room again and looked into the golden cupboard, "Hmm… I know… take one of these each," he said as he reached in and handed them a little golden pot each.

"And, now... let's see… what else?"

Much to the delight of the children the wizard reached into the cupboard again. His eyes twinkled with joy.

"Take one of these each," he said.

He passed a tiny star-shaped box to Amalek and an oval one to Seph. They wondered what was inside, and Seph shook his and heard a tiny tinkling sound like the ringing of minute bells. The wizard's coat of arms was embossed on each of the lids.

"You are very fortunate to have these," the wizard said, "They're a new design - smaller, more compact and more powerful than the old ones. I finished the last elements of them only last week. And for each of you… one of these." He handed them a magic pen each, golden for Seph and silver for Amalek. "Of course you know about these already."

"Thank you!" said Amalek and Seph together.

"But…" wondered Seph, "how shall we know how to

use all these things? And when to use them?"

"Oh, don't worry about that." Wizard Elzaphan's voice was calm and deep. "When the time comes to use them, then, and only then, will you know. This you have to trust. Remember in the forest? When you rubbed the magic drop in your fingers?"

The children nodded.

"Well, there you are. There's an example, isn't it? At first you didn't know what to do. And then, when you really needed to know, you knew and acted. Trust and have faith."

Amalek turned to her brother. "Real strength is found within," she said to him, "The Ferryman's secret… it's sort of the same, isn't it?

"I was just thinking that myself," Seph agreed, "The strength within and the knowledge within."

Amalek nodded, "And they both need trust."

"Good," said Wizard Elzaphan, "It sounds as though you're getting the idea. But you do need to read through your Magic Spell books so that you can look things up quickly. And remember that magic must be treated with the greatest respect. Take care and all will be well. Now sit down and we'll discuss our plans during a well earned meal."

Harris flew in a straight line over Lake Beautiful, over the edge of the Forest of the Fairies and on to the long, thin lake of Tye Water. The nape of his neck, where his feathers were golden, glinted in the sun like the gold bar he was gripping in his great black talons. He was able to fly at high speeds, especially with the wind behind him, and he soon found the place where the water was deepest. From above it was easy to spot. It was a rose shaped area where the blue-green colour of the lake was darkest.

He got ready to drop the bar of gold and was surprised to hear a whispering in his mind. It released a sinister sting with each word. The force of it was impossible to ignore.

"Don't drop it," the voice whispered, "Keep it for yourself."

He thought how ridiculous it was, but nevertheless he found himself answering the voice.

"No."

"Why not? No one would know," the whisper snapped back.

"Wizard Elzaphan has told me what to do," Harris replied, summoning up all his strength to withstand the temptation to fly off with it, "I'm going to drop it in."

"No!" barked the voice sounding alarmed and no longer whispering, "Don't do it. Wizard Elzaphan is nothing. Think about it... does he pay you for all the work you do for him? Work for me instead. You'll get gold. And right now you can keep *this* gold... and have more. This can be your first payment. Keep it."

"No, I will not," Harris replied firmly, "Wizard Elzaphan is my master, not you."

Then it crossed his mind that he should fly straight back with the bar of gold to Wizard Elzaphan and tell him about this.

"Listen to me," the voice interrupted his thoughts. Harris felt himself weakening. The voice was somehow pulling him against his will. "You can be rich, I promise you. Keep the gold for yourself."

Harris circled high above the lake. He was tempted. The voice was so strong and persuasive. He could share the gold with Quint and surely it would make her happy.

Then he thought of Wizard Elzaphan and his goodness. How could he betray his trust? The wizard had trusted him when he had asked him to drop the gold in the lake.

Harris summoned all his strength and shouted, "No!"

Focusing all his will and effort he quickly spread the toes of his great feet. The bar of gold fell below him.

A wonderful feeling of relief flooded through him. He felt strong once again, even stronger than before, as he watched the bar of gold tumbling through the air. Then, far below, it splashed onto the surface and was gone, sinking slowly through the water like a feather through still air, until it touched against something hard on the bottom of the lake. It was a massive iron bell, browned and bronzed with rust, tipped onto its side with about half buried under the muddy floor. It was embossed with a coat of arms, the words 'The Glyifild Bell' and a date, 511 Sn.

The bar of gold scraped down the side of the bell and landed gently on the floor of the lake on its end. It slowly toppled over and came to rest, sending a puff of mud into the water.

Harris wheeled around in the air and headed back to the castle.

At the exact moment when the bar of gold hit the surface of Tye Water, the Dark Wizard Troubler jerked in his sleep and for a moment his eyes opened. Something had happened, something had jolted in his dark mind that had shaken him in his slumbers, but at first he did not know what it was. Then he remembered. He had been dreaming that he had been talking to an eagle, a golden cagle, and trying to persuade it to work for him. He had heard the eagle shout "No!" and then he was plummeting, falling head over heels towards a lake. He was so tired that his eyelids drooped and closed.

As he drifted back to sleep he began to dream again. There was nothing but water all around him, and he was sinking down and down, until he hit the bell. A moment later he bumped onto the muddy floor deep underneath a lake and woke up.

Chapter 11

~ Asher & Zipp ~

It was not long after the four messenger ravens had left Old Howard's house when they spotted the fifteen ravens carrying Jamaar. They were travelling in opposite directions, the messenger ravens heading north towards Summertime Kingdom and the others, who were flying lower, were heading south towards Old Howard's house. These fifteen had just crossed the border and were evenly spaced around the edge of the light blue blanket with which they carried Jamaar. The dog was lying in the centre, still unconscious and unaware of what was happening and now covered with a generous helping of snow. The blanket sagged underneath Jamaar's bulk and the ravens found that they needed all their strength to keep going, even with the expanded group of fifteen.

"Hey!" called out Rakka as loud as he could, but the strong, whistling wind that whipped the snow along in great flurries was too loud and the others were too far below to hear. In a moment they were gone.

"What on earth were they carrying?" Rakka asked the others, shouting to be heard as they flew on with the wind.

"Who knows?" shouted another, "Should we follow?"

"No!" shouted Rakka, "We are going straight to the General. No delays. We'd better tell the General what we saw, though."

The group carrying Jamaar had slept right through the night before resuming their difficult flight. With the weight of their load, their flight was slow. At times it seemed that they could only just about stay airborne. They were so exhausted that Sergeant Forr felt he had to order them to take a rest. They were straining to keep going and he was afraid they might drop Jamaar again. The ravens were relieved when Sergeant Forr gave the order to land for a rest.

They descended onto the slopes of the Great Mountain overlooking Lake Clase-Moy. The scene was stunningly beautiful. The persistent heavy snow had steadily built up, layer upon layer, to create a landscape devoid of sharp edges. Everything was smoothed to sweeping white curves which undulated over the mountainside as it fell to the flat surface of the lake. Even the trees were laden with snow and some smaller ones were hidden under massive snow drifts.

The ravens landed in a partially sheltered spot under some trees. Here the snow was thinner and as they landed they lowered Jamaar on the blanket. The weight of the great dog pushed the centre of the blanket into the snow while the ravens walked around him to get warm. They were light enough to walk around on the surface although their feet occasionally pushed through, leaving them sitting on the snow like a duck on water and scrambling to get out. They shook their wings and bodies to get the snow off then gathered around Jamaar. Forr was the first to speak.

"We'd better sweep the snow off the dog else he'll die of cold."

"Is he still alive?" asked Akk, staring at Jamaar.

"If he's not," Razz said crossly, "Then we've done all this... all this effort... for nothing. So he'd better be alive."

"He's not breathing," said Akk.

They all stepped onto the blanket and moved closer until they were surrounding Jamaar.

"OK," said Sergeant Forr staring at Jamaar, "Someone check that he really is dead this time."

Akk jabbed him twice with his beak. There was no response.

"He's dead," he concluded.

"Great!" exclaimed Razz sarcastically, "Well that's really great. So, what now?"

"We go back," said Akk.

"What?" Razz looked astonished, "And tell the General we've failed! You can if you want, but I'm not!"

"Then we go to the Master," said Akk, knowing as he spoke that this was an even worse idea.

"You must be joking!" Razz shook his head in disbelief, "*Think* about it. He'd..."

"Stop!" shouted Sergeant Forr, "No one decides anything except me."

He lowered his head near to Jamaar's muzzle and listened.

Razz tilted his head quizzically to one side and asked, "What are you doing now? He's..."

"Shhhh," Forr interrupted, "He's breathing...just. Get the snow off him."

They felt the burden of failure had been lifted off

them again but they felt so tired that it took them a couple of minutes to brush the snow off Jamaar with sweeping movements of their wings. When it was done Forr spoke.

"This is what we do. We huddle 'round him and fold the blanket right over us. That'll warm him up... it'll warm us up too, *and* we'll be sheltered, *and* we can rest. When we are rested then we complete the journey. Alright?"

They all chorused, "Yes," and nodded their heads.

Soon they were huddled together around Jamaar, tucking their feet under their black feathers and closing their eyes. Two of them had pulled the blanket right over the top of all of them so that they were enclosed inside it. Their breath soon warmed the air inside the blanket and Jamaar's breathing grew stronger. Soon they all began to feel much warmer and stronger and slipped into a pleasing doze. Forr was the first to wake.

"Wake up!" he shouted at the others, "Time to move on."

Forr folded the blanket back so that it was flat again and the falling snow quickly speckled their black feathers. Reluctantly they stepped off the comfortable blanket, stretched their wings and took up their positions again. It took a little sorting out, especially as their feet kept pushing through the surface and they had to struggle to get out. After a while they were evenly spaced around the edge.

"Now," said Forr, "*Exactly* together, on the count of three... take off."

When Iker heard "take off" he immediately flapped his wings.

"Not yet!" shouted Forr.

Iker had risen slightly off the snow but immediately

stopped flapping and dropped down again. Forr was infuriated, but when he spoke he tried to stay calm.

"Iker... Iker... Now listen to me. Listen clearly. No mistakes this time, OK? What would your uncle think, eh? When I say on the count of three I mean it." He jerked his head closer to Iker and stared at him. "*No mistakes!* Understand?"

"Yes," replied Iker sulkily, who felt it was all unfair because he had not woken up properly yet. He shook his young body and stretched out his wings in an effort to be more awake.

"So," said Sergeant Forr, looking around at the others, "Everyone ready?" They all nodded. "Good. On the count of three then... one... two... *three!*"

Iker, who was trying very hard not to make any more mistakes, took off just before *"three!"* which caused an explosion of panic. The others flapped as fast as they could to catch him up as the blanket tipped precariously causing Jamaar to roll over.

"Steady!" shouted Forr, "Find the same level. Quick!"

This was somehow achieved and Jamaar rolled back into the centre of the blanket. They rose slowly through the windy, snow-filled air and flew off in the direction of Old Howard's house. They had been refreshed by the rest, but after a while they felt as exhausted as before, and so it came as a great relief to them all when the house suddenly became visible down below through the dancing flakes of snow.

"There it is!" shouted Forr, "Down!"

They glided down, just clearing the trees at the end of the garden, and landing on the deep snow at the back of the house. The weight of Jamaar pushed into the snow again and as he gently came to rest he stirred and opened his eyes.

"Wha ang I?" he said softly, his jaw still badly swollen.

He shook involuntarily with cold and some of the snow sprayed off him while most of it remained clinging to his matted fur.

Forr rapped on the door with his beak. After a moment the Dark Wizard Troubler opened it.

"Master," said Forr to get his attention.

The wizard was staring out into the snow.

"Master," said Forr again.

"Wait!" snapped the Troubler, "What's happened here?"

He gazed down into the garden with surprise. He noticed that the birds that were frozen in mid-air had gone. An anxious expression wrinkled his face and he strode past Forr and started digging frantically in the snow.

"It can't be..." he mumbled to himself, "Surely... it can't be."

He was terrified that his spell had weakened and the birds had escaped, and this could only mean that everything was free. He was beginning to panic and in a frenzied moment he had dug a deep hole. He found what he was hoping to find; a frozen bird. He stared down at it and touched it with a long bony finger. It was rock hard and just to check he kicked it and it did not move at all. He was clearly delighted but then paused for a moment. It puzzled him. How had it happened? He stood still in the falling snow and wondered.

He quickly reached a decision and it was the only thing that made sense. He decided that it was his power, his strength of will, that had intensified the spell even more. He already felt that his spell had deepened, but this was a revelation. It was now so powerful and heavy that the sheer burden of the spell had torn the birds from the air.

"Ha!" he laughed, "Excellent!"

He walked back to the house, snow whipping past him on the powerful wind, and looked down at Forr.

"Master," Forr said, bowing his large head slowly as if meeting a great king, "We've brought Jamaar back for you."

"Jamaar?" said the wizard surprised, "Where is he?"

"There, Master," and Forr nodded towards the dip in the snow.

The Troubler had been so distracted by the missing birds that he had not seen Jamaar. He took a couple of large strides, looked down into the dip and saw him.

"Bring him in," he snapped.

Jamaar was dragged inside on the blanket, together with quite a lot of snow, and lay there, too weak to move. The wizard kicked the door closed and the sound of the howling wind was dampened abruptly. Jamaar gazed up at his master.

"You look a mess!" said the wizard, "What's happened to you?"

He reached a skinny hand down and gripped Jamaar's jaw, jerking it upwards as he bent down to take a look.

"Aaahhh!" cried out Jamaar as the pain stabbed through his heavy jowl.

The wizard reached down and gripped the compass around his neck.

"And I'll have this back!" he snapped.

He pulled hard, trying to rip it off. The chain held firm and Jamaar's head was jerked into the air and fell back again with a thud.

"Aaaahhh!" cried Jamaar.

"Shut up!" the Troubler hissed, and then he cried loudly, "Another failure!"

He screwed up his face and clenched his fists tightly in sheer anger. He tugged at the compass until it looped free over Jamaar's head. Then he kicked Jamaar as hard as he could.

"You idiot!" he snapped, "I've given you all this strength… as well as this!"

He held up the compass and then flung it at the wall, which it hit with a thud, making a hole right through, disappearing from sight and out into the snow.

"All this strength I gave you and look what happens to you!"

With the impact of the kick, Jamaar passed out again. The wizard turned to the ravens who were standing around Jamaar on the snow speckled floor.

"Go and get that compass, you!" he shouted at Akk and opened the door for him.

A flurry of snow blew in as Akk went out. He returned a few seconds later gripping the black chain in his beak and with the compass, completely unharmed, dangling below. The wizard slammed the door shut after him and took the compass. He hung it around his own neck with the other one where it twitched and jumped about on his chest.

"Keep still!" he bellowed and it stopped moving immediately.

Then he thought for a moment.

"Alright," he said looking at Jamaar, "I need you to

recover and be able to fight as soon as possible. This will help."

He took the compass off his neck and looped it over Jamaar's again where it lay still.

He glared down at the ravens. "Well, what's the story?"

"We don't know what happened to him, Master," said Sergeant Forr.

"No," Akk added timidly, "We don't know. We didn't see."

"We were scouting for the enemy," Forr continued, "And we found the dog… um… Jamaar… by the river. The General organized us… told us… to bring him to you, Master. So we have."

"Yes, yes," the wizard sounded impatient.

He had calmed down now but each word he uttered still felt like a poisonous dart. "That was the right thing to do. Now you must go back to rejoin the army. I have sent orders to the General."

"We are tired," said Forr plucking up courage, "We are so tired. The wind was strong into our faces as we flew, and Jamaar is so heavy. We are exhausted, Master."

"Go now!" the Dark Wizard Troubler snapped sharply.

"We will go, if you s…say so, Master," Forr replied, stuttering with fear, "But we will fall into the snow and die. We have no energy left."

"Alright then, you numbskulls," the wizard sneered, "Eat first in the kitchen if you have to. Then I want you flying back as fast as possible. You'll have the wind behind you but if it turns then fly low where the wind is weaker."

He pointed to the open kitchen door.

"Go in there and eat... now!"

Forr led the way and they all walked along the hall and disappeared into the kitchen.

It was peaceful in the Golden Room. The group of friends, now only five since Neville's loss, had spent some time discussing the plans with Wizard Elzaphan. They chatted as they enjoyed a delicious lunch.

Speaking about the dangerous task that had now become their duty, however, made them apprehensive and fearful. The Dark Wizard Troubler terrified them all and it was this that created a feeling of gloom deep inside them which they could not shake off. They felt safe with Wizard Elzaphan and they wished they could stay with him. Perhaps the problem back in the Kingdom of Gems would somehow go away and everything would be normal again as it always had been. The wizard seemed to read their minds.

"When all this is over I shall come to visit you," he said, "And then the Kingdom of Gems will be free and happy again. But first you have to deal with this Troubler. He's powerful, and his power is growing, so you must go forwards with courage. He must be faced... and the sooner the better. You are the ones who have to confront him. It has to be you."

He paused and looked around at their faces. Then he continued.

"You'll need food and drink for the journey, so these are for you."

He reached behind him to a large wooden chest. He lifted the lid, reached inside and pulled out two rucksacks which he handed to the Prince and Princess. Then he pulled out two more bags that were linked together by two long straps. He swung one of these bags over Lazuli's back so that each bag hung down to rest on either side of her with the straps passing over her broad back.

"They're packed with provisions," he said smiling and looking at the two children, "The cooks prepared these for you earlier. There are some warm cloths and gloves for you too. You'll need them when you get back to your kingdom. Put them on your backs you two."

He nodded at Amalek and Seph who slipped their arms through the straps.

"Now," he continued, "You need to get to the border quickly and without being seen by any ravens. Flying is quicker than walking. Joog can fly... and you must protect the others, Joog. Alright?"

Joog nodded.

"You'll see why this is so important in a minute," he continued, "And the rest of you... well, I have a way of travelling for you that should do the trick."

Wizard Elzaphan leant out of the window and clapped twice. Then he turned to the others.

"Are you ready?" he asked, looking at them with a twinkle in his eye and just the suggestion of a smile.

They nodded.

"Right then," he said.

He reached into the golden cupboard and took out a golden whistle and a small wooden box. He placed the box carefully on a table, then he leant out of the window and blew on the whistle. There was no sound. A moment later two bumblebees flew in through the window, circled around the wizard's head and landed on his shoulder.

"Hello, you two," he said, "I've got an important job for you." Then he said to the others. "We need to make certain... er... adjustments to you. So do not be alarmed. Joog, you come up here please."

Joog fluttered up and landed on top of the golden cupboard.

"Now," said the great wizard, "These changes are only temporary."

He opened the box and dipped his fingers inside. Then with a quick flick of his hand he threw a cloud of golden dust over the four friends and in an instant they began to shrink! Even with Wizard Elzaphan's warning it was a shock. Smaller and smaller they became, until they were as small as insects.

"Asher! Zipp!" called out Wizard Elzaphan, "These good people need to go to the border of the Kingdom of Gems. Take them there as quickly as you can and avoid any ravens on your journey."

Asher and Zipp flew down from the wizard's shoulder and landed gently on the carpet. They looked huge to the children, Tally and Lazuli. Zipp was nearest to them and he looked at them with large eyes. Asher was slightly larger than Zipp and she waved her two antennae in their direction before looking up at Elzaphan.

The wizard knelt down and studied the two bees thoughtfully.

"I think…" he said slowly, "I think that you could do with a little extra speed… as well as strength to carry your passengers."

He picked another golden box from the cupboard, opened the lid and sprinkled a little golden dust over the two bees. They immediately grew to about twice their original size.

"Now," the wizard said gently, "Amalek and Seph… and Tally… you three up on Asher's back."

Seph picked up Tally, and then the two children, with their rucksacks on their backs, climbed onto Asher's furry, black and yellow back, clutching the fur with their hands.

Wizard Elzaphan reached down and with the most delicate touch picked up Lazuli and placed her gently on Zipp's back.

"Now," said the great wizard, stooping down and speaking softly to them, "You'll all be slipping and sliding on there unless we tie you on somehow. And I've got the best thing… the very best thing… golden thread."

He looked into the golden cupboard and took out a golden box. He shook it over them and the finest golden thread fell upon them and wrapped itself right around the bumblebees and their passengers.

"It'll hold you on," explained Wizard Elzaphan, "But you'll find it's light and stretchy and will let you out when you want to get off."

They sank into the soft comfortable fur held on by the magic thread.

Joog turned his head to face the wizard.

"It's a great idea," he said, "But why don't they ride on me? After all I'd be much faster."

"I know," the great wizard said, running his hand gently down the feathers on Joog's back, "I thought of that first... but it would hold too much risk. If you were seen by the ravens, and attacked, well... think of the danger. The tiny travellers would be crushed with one blow, or they might fall off and be hurt... or lost. And if you were injured and couldn't fly then that would be the end of that. This way if you are spotted then the ravens would never imagine that the bees had anything to do with it... they are the perfect way to keep the travellers unnoticed. The ravens probably wouldn't even see the bees, and if they did they'd just ignore them."

Joog nodded, "I see... yes, it's a good plan."

"And your task," Elzaphan continued, "Is to guide them and guard them as they travel... and scout around and keep a lookout for any sort of danger. I know they will have the best possible protection with you there, Joog."

There was a knock at the doors and then they opened. Cedric stood outside. Elzaphan beckoned him over.

"Cedric," he said, "Come in."

"Thank you, sir," said Cedric, stepping into the room.

"And how's Old Howard?" asked Elzaphan.

"Fed up, sir!" replied Cedric, "He's in the hut as you said, but not happy about it or his Hadia Stick... says he hates it. He threw it down but then he was hopping around in such agony that he grabbed it again as quickly as you can say Jicketty Jick! He's grumbling at everything and everyone, but he's grumbling most of all about you!"

Wizard Elzaphan smiled kindly. "Well, I have to say

that the Hadia Stick is good for him. If he's got any sense at all, he'll learn from it."

Cedric stepped forwards.

"I just wanted to say good luck to our visitors," he said.

Elzaphan nodded. "You've come at the right time... just."

Cedric looked around for them with a puzzled expression. "Where are they?"

The good wizard laughed. "Come over here."

Cedric walked over and gazed down in amazement at the bees with their tiny passengers.

"Now, there's a surprise," he said, "But a good idea, of course... a clever way to hide. I feel sure, somehow, that you'll make it through. But nevertheless, I want to wish you good luck."

The Prince and Princess shouted up together, in tiny voices.

"Thank you, Cedric!"

Wizard Elzaphan put a hand on Cedric's shoulder.

"They must go now."

With loud buzzings the two bumblebees took off and flew around Wizard Elzaphan's head.

"Fly through the trees for cover. Now go!"

The bees flew out through the window and Joog followed.

"Good bye!" called out the tiny travellers, "And thank you!"

"Good luck!" shouted the wizard with his head out of the window and his long white hair and beard flowing in the breeze.

Cedric was beside him looking out as well. Together they watched Asher and Zipp descend to the trees below, with Joog close behind them. The bees quickly became tiny dots and then they were out of sight. Joog was visible for longer. He dipped over the cliff and down towards the surface of Lake Beautiful, his strong wings outstretched, until he was too small to be seen.

Wizard Elzaphan wished he could have done more for them, but knew he had to let them go and face the Troubler alone. He had to trust and hope that they would be strong enough.

"Come on, Spark," he said, patting him and scratching him affectionately behind the ears, "How about a walk around the castle?"

"Woof!" replied Spark, wagging his tail.

"I need to speak to Harris," he said, then turning to Cedric, "Are you coming for a walk too?" he asked Cedric.

"I have work to do, sir," he replied, "But I'll walk down with you."

Wizard Elzaphan strode out of the Golden Room followed by Spark and then Cedric and started descending the winding stairs. They had left one door ajar and as their footsteps began to fade away down the stairs it was gently pushed open a little more and in hopped Feeni. Her alert eyes looked bright and black and her ears were pricked up as she looked around the room. She sat back on her large rear paws, lifted her front paws off the floor and sniffed.

Around her neck hung a beaded necklace with several small ornaments hanging on it; there was a black polished stone made of malachite, there was a tiny silver skull, and there was a very small piece of gold. The gold came from Old Howard's bar, chiselled off the corner, but it was the Troubler's plan to bribe her with it. The plan had worked beautifully. Old Howard had tempted Feeni with the gold to help him get into the castle. As soon as Feeni had hung it around her neck the Troubler was speaking to her in her mind, controlling her and able to use her as a channel for his evil powers. He was pleased with this and now he had commanded her to go to the Golden Room.

Feeni paused and glanced behind her where she could still hear the sound of the footsteps growing fainter down the stairs. Then the Troubler whispered in her mind.

"Go on!" it hissed urgently, "Quickly! Set them free!"

Feeni turned to face the room again and responded obediently to the voice, hopping forwards and across the room towards the far corner.

"Hey! Hey, you!" exclaimed Jeg, rattling the cage to attract the rabbit's attention.

The other two ravens had fallen asleep and they woke up with a jerk and looked surprised.

"Hey, you!" shouted Jeg at Feeni, "Let us out!"

Feeni looked up at the cage perched on the tall three-legged table in the corner. "Why do you think I'm here, stupid?" she sneered.

Again the voice commanded in her head, "Stare at the cage... concentrate."

Feeni stared and felt an extraordinary power directed from her to the cage. She had never felt anything like this before and she liked it.

"Concentrate," said the voice.

The cage started to shake and rattle.

"Let us out!" shouted Jeg looking scared, "Quick, let us out!"

"Keep staring…" the Troubler insisted, "Stare with all your concentration."

Suddenly, the cage lifted off the table. A clamour of raucous cawing and flapping wings came from the three frightened ravens. Then the cage exploded apart into three pieces and the ravens were free and fell onto the table in a muddled heap. The top of the cage shot up into the ceiling, bounced off downwards and cracked into Feeni's head. She cried out and collapsed onto the carpet and lay still.

"Good," screeched Jeg, as he disentangled himself from the other two and looked around, "Now, let's get the enemy."

"Where are they?" said one of the other ravens jerking her head around to look behind her.

"If you hadn't been asleep you'd know, Gaaba," Jeg snapped impatiently, "They're tiny and they're on two bees."

Gaaba looked around again, this time for the bees. The other raven called Roon started looking around as well.

"Where?" asked Roon.

"Idiots!" Jeg snapped crossly, "They've gone, but we'll catch them."

Gaaba looked thoughtful. "How can we find two bees?" she asked, "They're too small."

"The owl is with them," Jeg explained, "And it's still normal size, so it's easy to see. We find the owl and we know the bees are close by. And we know they're flying south… due south. So it's easy. But we don't want those vicious eagles spotting us. So we'll fly out and straight down into the trees where they won't see us. Then we'll wait there until we know we can leave without being seen... OK?"

The other two nodded. Feeni lay beside them on the floor. The voice whispered again in her mind.

"Get up, Feeni."

Feeni remained motionless. She had been knocked out by the blow to her head. A trickle of blood ran off her fur, looking bright as it dripped onto the cream carpet.

Roon looked at Feeni. "How did that rabbit do that to the cage?"

Jeg held up his wings in a gesture of puzzlement. "I don't know and I don't care... we're free and that's all that matters."

Roon flew down and landed beside Feeni. "It's not dead... still breathing," he commented.

Jeg looked towards the window and snapped back, "So what? Come on, let's go."

He jumped into flight and flew out through the open window followed by Gaaba and Roon. They dropped immediately, gliding down on the warm air, and landed in the centre of a group of trees below.

"Harris," Wizard Elzaphan said, "I'd like you to make a journey for me."

Harris and Quint were standing on their wooden guard posts next to the great entrance to the castle. Elzaphan had just stepped out of the castle with Spark at his side and was standing in front of the two eagles. None of them noticed the three ravens, Jeg, Gaaba and Roon, descend into the trees behind them.

"Yes, sir," said Harris, "Where to?"

"The Becci Mountains. I want you to take a message to the mountain hares there, but make sure you find an old hare called Hawkeye. It must be him... he is the one who must hear my message... none of the others, whatever they might say."

"Yes, sir," Harris nodded.

"And there's a package too," the great wizard added.

Elzaphan knew that Harris could be relied upon completely.

"And Quint?" asked Harris.

"Quint should stay on guard," Elzaphan instructed.

Quint nodded, her golden neck feathers glinting in the sun. "Yes, sir. Down here?" she asked, "Or on a turret?"

"On a turret. We need to stay vigilant. Those three ravens are safely locked up now, yes... but there may be more on the way. Your journey, Harris, is important... very important and necessary... but get back as quickly as you can."

The two magnificent eagles jumped off their posts, fanning the air with their powerful wings. Quint flew up to the highest turret and Harris sped off across Lake Beautiful towards the Becci Mountains, clutching the package in his talons.

The army of ravens were still resting and recovering in the oak trees on the top of Burney's Hill. They had preened their feathers, removed broken ones and were letting their wounds heal after the battle. They had needed the rest and looked much better for it. Gerr was the first to spot the four male ravens returning with instructions from the Dark Wizard Troubler.

"There they are!" Gerr shouted eagerly, pleased to be the first one to see them, "Look! There! It's Rakka and the others!"

"Good," said the General, "And about time too. I could have sent some wrens out and they'd have been back quicker than these slow coaches."

They landed on the branch below the General and looked up at him with their black eyes.

"Well?" snapped the General, "You didn't go all that way to sit there staring at me. What did he say?"

"I'm afraid, sir," began Rakka, "He wasn't pleased. In fact, he was angry... very angry. He was angry because while we were there the two unicorns attacked him. He caught one and one got away. He said that we *must not* get caught. He said that he could hardly believe that we had let them all get through to the castle and that we *must* get them as they try to return. We *must* kill them."

"Yes," began another, "He said we must search until we find them. We must intercept them as they travel back. He thinks they will be travelling by now and we must work out the possible routes and search."

"And... and..." Rakka began speaking again. Terror seemed to fill him as he struggled to get the words out, then he suddenly remembered something else he needed to say and leapt at the opportunity to avoid what he was going to say. "We saw quite a few ravens carrying a blue blanket with something on it. They were heading across the border towards the Master's house."

"Yes," said the General, "That would be our birds carrying the dog. But blue blanket, you say? Not grey?"

"Hard to tell in the snow, sir," answered Rakka.

"OK, fine. They'll be there by now," the General said, "At least some things are going right. But back to the Master and what he said."

He glared at Rakka making his fear rise again.

"He said that if we fail to kill them... then... then... he will punish us severely!"

This produced a wave of frightened chattering through the mass of ravens.

"Males... and females," the General shouted, trying to quiet the frightened ravens, "We know that he always carries out his threats. We do not want his wrath upon us! So we must rise to the challenge."

The General's compass bobbed as it hung on his chest and he took this to mean that it approved. He continued with increased enthusiasm.

"We are a great army! Let us search out the enemy, and we will not stop until we have succeeded! Are we up for the job?"

"Yes, sir!" they shouted back.

"Will we succeed?" he shouted.

"Yes, sir," they chorused, "We will succeed!"

"Good, that's better!" the General looked pleased, "Male and female squadrons... attennnnnn...tion!" They all sat up straight. "Male and female squadrons... take off!"

They all took to the air and followed the General as he led them off to search.

Chapter 12

~ A White Feather ~

Asher and Zipp had flown as quickly as they could through the trees that grew around the castle and then dropped over the steep cliffs which met the water's edge. Joog could fly much faster than the two bees and so he flew around them, one moment behind and then ahead. Gentle waves lapped against the rocks as they passed over and out across Lake Beautiful. They moved swiftly above the clear, turquoise-blue water and flew low. Occasionally they felt a cool spray carried on the breeze from the crest of one of the waves. This was refreshing, for it was still as sunny and hot as ever in Summertime Kingdom. The tiny passengers found that the furry backs of the bees were warm and comfortable.

Behind them, the castle had fallen away into the distance. It looked unreal in the blue haze of the hot day, and they felt they had left their safe haven behind. They were on their own once more.

"This is scary," Lazuli shouted, "But a great way to

travel!"

Amalek, Seph and Tally, riding on Asher, were not able to hear above the loud buzzings of the bees wings, so Asher had moved closer to Zipp so that the two bees were almost touching.

"What?" Amalek called out.

"Scary, but great," Lazuli shouted again, "My first time flying!"

"What if we're all eaten by some huge bird," Seph shouted, "Perhaps a hungry owl, like you Joog? Or a sparrow... or anything. They could swallow us up in a second!"

Joog replied from below, shouting so that they could all hear, "Wizard Elzaphan warned the birds and animals that we were coming. The only danger is the ravens. We must all keep a look out for ravens."

"I never thought," said Amalek, "that I'd have a ride on a bee. Wait 'till I tell Mum and Da..."

She stopped suddenly realizing that she had momentarily forgotten that the King and Queen were frozen, as still and cold as two granite statues, back in the palace and there would be no point in telling them anything at all. She immediately burst into tears at the thought, drooped her head onto Asher's back and sobbed into her fur.

"Listen, Ammey" said Seph turning to face her, "We *are* going to free them. We are - really!"

He put his arm around her.

"We will do it," he said.

Tally was in between them. "Of course we will," he said.

Amalek felt comforted by their strength and lifted her head to look at her brother.

"Thank you," she said to Seph while stroking Tally on his head, "I just wish they were here with us, and when I closed my eyes I could see them there, completely still, frozen by the spell."

"I know," Seph agreed, "Its best not to think about it. I know what... a song to cheer you up... it'll cheer us all up. I know just the song. 'Summer Days Are Coming'"

He started humming and then singing. Gradually, as Amalek listened, she began to feel better. Her crying stopped and she felt the burden of doubt lift off her with the uplifting words. It was a song she knew well. Tally began to join in with the cheerful song and then so did Lazuli. They sang it over and over as they travelled through the dark shadowy forest

They kept low above the water, the two bees flying side by side, with Joog just below them skimming as close to the surface as possible. When the travellers looked up at the bees wings, they saw the sunlight flashing on them as it divided into a wonderful display of colours. The bees were huge to the tiny passengers and the buzzing was loud as their wings moved at tremendous speed. The warm air whooshed by as they sped along.

They made good progress and as soon as they reached the Forest of the Fairies the bees sped into it so that they were concealed by the trees. The woodland scene surrounded them and made them feel safe as they travelled. The children kept alert and looked around for any signs of danger.

The forest was stunningly beautiful with its undulating landscape where ferns covered the ground in great patches. The bees weaved between the trees with Joog now following, controlling his flight skilfully with a few flaps when necessary and tiny adjustments made to

SUMMER DAYS ARE COMING

The summer days are coming
Can you feel it too?
The humming bird is humming
Wintry days are through.

Every day the sun grows brighter
Giving life to you and me,
Every way your burden's lighter
Soon you will be free.

Autumn falls to winter,
Winter thaws to spring,
Spring leads gently into
Summer's joy to sing.

Every day the sun grows brighter
Giving life to you and me,
Every way your burden's lighter
Soon you will be free.

The heavy weight of trouble
That burdens you today
Will burst like a bubble
To disappear in May

Every day the sun grows brighter
Giving life to you and me,
Every way your burden's lighter
Soon you will be free.

A frown can smooth to laughter
A scowl becomes a grin
Joy will follow after
When happiness begins

Every day the sun grows brighter
Giving life to you and me,
Every way your burden's lighter
Soon you will be free.

the angle of his wings. Every so often he would rise quickly to the tops of the trees and peep out to check for ravens. Then he would drop down again and let the others know that all was well.

However, they were not as safe as they thought. Joog had been spotted earlier as they crossed Lake Beautiful and now they were all being followed. Searle and Urrg flew a few trees behind Joog and the bumblebees, moving cautiously from tree to tree.

"OK," said Urrg quietly as they dodged past a tree trunk, "What happens now?"

"Attack?" asked Searle, keeping her eye on Joog so that they did not lose sight of him.

"Yeah, but owls are vicious creatures... you know, sharp beak and talons... and that one can fight."

Urrg led the way through a gap in some branches. Then Searle caught up again.

"But there's two of us!" Searle sounded surprised, "Surely we can deal with it."

"Yeah, I suppose you're right."

Once again they had to fly in single file through some leaves and branches. This time Searle went first and when they emerged to fly side by side again they had lost sight of Joog.

"It's gone!" announced Searle, "Where is it?"

"Don't panic, don't panic," Urrg said, "It can't be far away."

The trees were growing closer together now.

"There are too many trees," said Searle, "We can't lose it now. We'll have to get closer... come on."

They sped up a little until Urrg said excitedly, "I can see it!"

They were much closer now.

"Look!" whispered Urrg, "Two bees flying with the owl!"

"Oh, yeah!" Searle exclaimed, "What are they doing with him?"

"I don't know but they worry me. Look at them... they're huge bees! Why is he travelling with two bees?"

"I don't know," Searle replied, "But who cares? I..."

"It could be important," Urrg snapped, "They could be... well, I don't know... they could be..."

"Who cares about two little bees? OK, they're big for bees, very big, but still... they're no match for us."

"But why are they flying with the owl?" Urrg quizzed, "I mean... can you think why? It's weird isn't it?"

Searle ignored the question, "Anyway, let's just attack, shall we?" she whispered.

"OK, but hold on a moment. Listen... it's talking to the bees!"

They both listened as they flew cautiously along, hiding behind tree trunks.

"What's it saying?" asked Searle.

"I can't hear... we're not close enough."

The ravens were silent again as they dodged in and out of the trees and tried to hear what Joog was saying.

Searle sighed, "Let's just attack anyway, shall we?"

They were just about to accelerate forwards when Urrg spoke.

"Stop! What's the owl up to?"

Joog was flying upwards to the tops of the trees while the two bees landed on a branch. He quickly descended again. Once more the two ravens could not hear his words as he spoke quickly to the others, so they edged closer.

"There's a problem back there over the lake," said Joog.

"What is it?" asked Seph.

He slid down off Asher's back and stood on the branch.

"A fight…" continued Joog, "It looks like three ravens fighting an eagle. Probably Harris or Quint, I couldn't see, but it looks bad… the eagle's in trouble. What shall I do? The eagle needs help… I think I ought to go, but I don't want to leave you."

"We'll be alright, Joog," said Seph, "Quick, go and help. Before it's too late. Quick!"

"Yes… yes… alright then. I'll be back as fast as I can. Keep flying south and I'll be able to find you."

He rose up through the trees, found a gap and then accelerated away towards Lake Beautiful. Searle and Urrg saw him flash past above their heads.

"I hope he'll be alright," said Amalek to her brother.

Seph smiled. "He's gentle and kind, but get him in a fight and he's as fierce as anyone."

"Yes, you're right," she replied.

Searle and Urrg had edged even closer to the two bees. They had landed two trees away on a branch and had crept along it until they were as close as they could get without being seen. They were peering through a mass of leaves.

Searle nudged Urrg with her wing. "Look," she whispered, "It's the Prince!"

Urrg tried to look through the leaves. "Where?"

"There, stupid, on the branch. He's little… tiny… look, there!"

Urrg moved her head around. "No, I can't see. The leaves are in the way. But, what do you mean 'he's tiny'?"

"He's tiny... you know, really small," whispered Searle, "Must be magic..."

Urrg pecked at the leaves in front of her.

"He's climbing onto the bee!" whispered Searle, "And there's the Princess too! They're taking off!"

"Come on. Let's attack," said Urrg.

"No," snapped Searle, "It might be a trick... or trap of some kind... we don't know where the owl is, do we? It might be watching. I'll follow and you scout around, but keep me in sight. And then, when we're sure that owl has really flown off somewhere, then we get them."

Urrg shook her head in irritation and grumbled, "I can't see why we can't just attack them now?"

"No," replied Searle hastily, "We must check first, then attack."

The bees flew through the trees and Searle and Urrg jumped off the branch. Searle followed the bees and Urrg reluctantly began to scout around the area.

Meanwhile Joog was flying at full speed above the forest towards the fight that was happening half way across the lake to the castle. His yellow eyes were fixed on the ravens with cold intensity. He was focused like a warrior, a hunter set upon his task with all his concentrated energy held taut and ready for action. There was no fear, just pure intent.

In a matter of minutes he was closing in. He assessed the situation. The ravens had the upper hand and were winning the fight. As he sped closer he could see that the eagle was Quint and she was outnumbered and struggling. Roon had managed to catch her by the tail and was gripping tightly with his beak. Quint was furiously flapping her wings in an attempt to shake Roon off and was managing to rise slightly. Gaaba was pecking at her from underneath with her beak and Jeg was trying to grip one of her wings with his claws. It would only be a matter of time before she was overcome.

Joog adjusted his flight and rose. He wanted the sun behind him. He kept his eye on the fight as he manoeuvred silently. When he was ready he dived. The warm air rushed by his white feathers. The ravens were taken almost completely by surprise with only Jeg seeing him.

"Ahh! Look out!" he shouted, looking up and squinting into the sun.

A second later Joog crashed into Gaaba, jolting all the birds sideways and sending Gaaba spinning away and down. Broken feathers spun in the air around them. Jeg abandoned his attack on Quint and turned on Joog. Roon clung on to Quint's tail with determination as he could see that she was weakening. The whole group was now falling.

Quint turned her head. "Joog!?" she exclaimed.

Jeg's harsh voice rang with anger. "Owl! You have made a big mistake! Get lost and let us finish our business!"

Joog ignored the threatening words. He had fire in his eyes. Jeg dived for Joog. With amazing skill, a swift dodge, then a dart and a turn, Joog was behind him. The owl's sharp beak ripped at Jeg's wing tearing off a row of feathers and drawing blood.

The five birds were now a tumbling bundle of feathers as they scrapped with each other. Quint's tail was now free and she held Roon in her great talons and squeezed. There was the sound of cracking bones. She let go and the limp body fell away.

They all plummeted towards the lake, like a meteor falling from the sky. Joog was tangled with the ravens but Quint broke free and was able to break her fall and swoop majestically upwards. She watched from above as a moment later the others hit the water. The splash sent little waves circling out and then all was still.

Jeg plunged the deepest and somehow managed to move his injured wing to swim under water away from the castle. When he bobbed up he was well apart from the rest. He quickly dipped under and swam again.

The lifeless body of Roon rose to the surface first, followed by Gaaba's. The two ravens floated, now still and harmless, on the gentle waves. Gaaba had broken her neck on impact. Quint looked for Joog as she flew down closer to the surface of the water.

"Joog?" she called desperately, "Joog… Joog?"

She scanned the surface anxiously.

"Joog?" Quint called out, louder this time.

"Quint?" said a voice behind her.

Quint turned in the air to see Harris returning from his trip to the Becci Mountains and flying towards her.

"What's happened?" he asked.

"Joog hasn't come up," she replied, "He saved me."

"I know," said Harris, "I saw the fight as I came to help. If only I'd been here in time."

The water was now still. Quint and Harris scanned the surface hoping to see Joog appear but all they could see was a single white feather floating and turning on the surface. Joog had gone.

Hawkeye strained his eyes to see as far as he could. He looked down the sloping mountain where the snow line ended and across the flat land to Burney's Hill. He could only just about see the hill, crowned with a cluster of trees, and anything beyond that was too far away even for his extraordinary eyesight. The cold snow chilled his paws as he sat outside his burrow. He had watched Harris speed away until he was out of sight and now he pondered upon Wizard Elzaphan's message.

He knew he had to act. He still felt like a young hare at heart, although his body was now stiff and old. What he had been asked to do was a challenge and throughout his life he had always welcomed challenges with vigour and enthusiasm. This was his way; to throw his energy into fighting for what was right. Now, however, he wondered whether the energy was in him.

His doubt only lasted a few moments and then he dismissed it from his mind. Now he knew that he would respond to Wizard Elzaphan's message with courage and action. He would do the best he could and if it was too much for him then he would die as he had lived, fighting for what was good and true.

First of all, he would need to call a meeting of all the hares and put it to them and explain the situation.

He lifted a front paw and shook the snow off it. Then he turned slowly and patted the package that Harris had delivered so that it fell into his snow burrow and then he hopped in after it.

In the Golden Room, at the top of the highest turret in the castle, everything was still. Feeni lay without moving. A very small patch of her blood had bloomed on the carpet around her head but now the wound had stopped bleeding leaving a small patch of matted brown fur on the back of her head. Close to Feeni was the broken cage in three pieces. It glinted in the rays of sun streaming in through the window.

Suddenly, one of Feeni's paws twitched. She opened her eyes. It took her a moment to realize where she was and then she was on her feet and alert. Her nose twitched and her ears pointed straight up. She heard something and her ears responded immediately, turning to face the doors. Someone was coming up the stairs.

"Hide, quickly!" whispered the voice in her head. She looked around for a place to hide. The footsteps grew louder and she darted behind an arm chair.

A moment later Wizard Elzaphan walked in through the open doors. He moved towards the window but paused abruptly when he saw the broken cage and the patch of blood. He stared down at the blood and then knelt down to reach out a hand to touch it to see whether it was dry or not. He found that it was dry so he stood up and turned his attention to the broken cage. He picked up the three pieces, placed them on the table and tried to work out what had happened.

He looked back at the blood; this must be blood from one of the escaped ravens. They could have shaken the cage by moving around inside until it fell and smashed apart and one could have been cut by the broken cage in the process. It was strange though because he knew the cage was strong and this could not have happened without the help of some other power. He had badly underestimated the power that these evil ravens must have been carrying with them.

He turned to the open window and leant his elbows on the sill to look out. Leaning forwards, he carefully scanned the trees below for the ravens. Nothing.

Feeni was watching him with one eye peeping out from behind the armchair. She jerked back and out of sight when she saw the wizard turn and look around the room. She was terrified of him because she knew his power.

Elzaphan paused. He had better check the room for an injured raven hiding somewhere. He moved around the room searching and approached the corner with the armchair. This, he thought, would be the best hiding place for a raven. He grabbed the two arms and pulled making the chair slide away from the walls.

There was nothing there.

He bent down to looked underneath the chair.

Still nothing there, so he pushed it back into its place. The great wizard sat down for a few minutes in the chair and thought. He decided he would check with Quint to find out if she had seen anything, so he got up and left the room.

A moment later the chair rustled. Feeni had made a hole with her teeth in the lining under the chair and had forced her way in.

"Get out," whispered the voice, "And then down the stairs."

She dropped out from her hiding place and hopped towards the open door.

In the Forest of the Fairies Asher and Zipp with their tiny passengers were not far from the centre where the trees grew most densely. The great forest was populated by trees of various sizes, from young spindly saplings to rugged old giants with massive trunks. These rose up from the fern-covered forest floor to form a canopy of leaves above, like a high roof which shaded the forest below where the ground gently sloped with dips and hollows. Birds dotted the trees here and there, occasionally fluttering about, and their joyful song blended musically with the sound of trickling streams. This echoed around them in the sweet-scented woodland air. It was a wonderful paradise.

The bees flew together, sometimes one behind the other but mostly side by side.

Searle and Urrg had continued following the bees with Urrg scouting the area and looking for Joog. Every so often she returned to Searle to tell her if she had seen anything. Searle had just landed on a branch because the bees had stopped to rest when Urrg approached.

"Well?" asked Searle.

"Nothing," replied Urrg softly, as she fluttered down to land, "The owl's gone."

She looked at Searle hopefully.

"Good, good," Searle whispered, "That's it then. We attack, OK?"

"OK," Urrg whispered back, looking very eager for action, "At last!"

"Come on!" Searle said and immediately she began to accelerate after the bees.

Urrg quickly followed and together they shot through the trees. In a few seconds they caught up to the bees but in their eagerness they were going much too fast and accidentally flew straight past them.

A flash of jet black feathers passed between the two bees, as if a very strong gust of wind had blown the two bees apart and then drawn them together again. Asher and Zipp bumped together and Amalek slipped, jolted sideways and jerked out from underneath the golden thread.

"Help!" she cried.

She was sliding off Asher's back and grabbed the bee's fur, gripping with both hands and with all her strength. Asher was spinning in the air which made it hard for Amalek to hold on. Seph leant over and reached down for her, stretching his hand out as far as he could without slipping off himself. The rucksack on Amalek's back was weighing her down. Seph strained further.

"Ammey!" he called.

Amalek released one hand from gripping Asher's fur and reached for Seph. Their hands touched. Amalek stretched further but she felt her other hand slipping, the fur pulling through her fingers. Suddenly, with a jerk, she fell.

"Aahh!" she cried.

She swung her arm and grasped the golden thread that looped under Asher's body. The thread stretched as she plummeted into the trees below. Seph watched helplessly. There was nothing he could do.

Searle and Urrg had turned and were now speeding back towards the bees.

Asher and Zipp were both stunned by the bump and they began to descend, spinning around and around in the air like falling leaves, with the others still clinging to their backs and held on by the golden thread. Asher had been pulled down by Amalek's weight on the golden thread which was now released and had sprung up again.

Above them the two black ravens, Searle and Urrg, with beady black eyes had turned. They seemed massive to the tiny travellers.

"They're there!" screamed Searle, "Look!"

"Where?" Urrg asked.

"Down there, stupid," Searle snapped.

They straightened their black bodies, pointed their sharp beaks downwards and fell through the air like hungry vultures upon their helpless prey.

"Attack!" screamed Searle, her voice cutting harshly through the gentle sounds of the forest.

As the black ravens dived Asher and Zipp were tumbling through the air. Searle went for Zipp who carried Lazuli on his back but as she swooped towards them they fell through a thick patch of leaves. Searle lost sight of them and rose again in the air.

"Aaah! No! No! No!" she shouted in frustration.

Urrg went for Asher with Seph and Tally on her back. They were not so lucky. Urrg opened her black beak in readiness. Asher dodged. Urrg missed them but turned quickly, skilfully.

"Aahaa!" screamed Urrg with glee.

They watched in horror as Urrg's wide open, gaping beak approached. Asher tried to dodge again but Urrg followed them. Then suddenly, it went dark and they were inside Urrg's mouth. As fast as a flash of lightening Asher twisted around and plunged her sting into Urrg's tongue.

"Oooowww!" screamed Urrg in pain, and she spat them out with force.

Once again they were falling… falling… plunging… plunging through branches and leaves… twisting and tumbling towards the ground below.

"Fly, Asher, fly!" urged Tally.

Asher was clearly shaken by the speed with which they shot out of Urrg's mouth. She had struck the raven's bill injuring her side and a wing. She was struggling to fly. With a mighty effort, and ignoring the pain, she got her wings moving and halted the dangerous fall.

Searle was now flying around the tree trunks and searching for Zipp and Lazuli. She turned her head this way and that as she flew quietly in the hope of surprising them, her black eyes searching. She perched on a branch in a tree just above the leaves where she thought they had fallen through. Urrg landed beside her with her tongue so swollen that she could not close her beak.

"Where have they gone?" asked Searle in a whisper.

"I don'd dow," Urrg managed to reply.

Searle jerked her head around to look at Urrg.

"Cor, what's happened to you?" she whispered, noticing her tongue.

"It'th thath thtupid bee," said Urrg, forgetting to whisper, "I had them, I did. Then thuddenly thith - thith thearing pain in my thongue."

"Shhh! They'll hear us. Where are the blighters?" whispered Searle looking down and then up, "We had them and now they're gone."

"Well, don'd gib up, keep dookin'. Come on," said Urrg.

"Our Master won't be pleased and it's all your fault!" said Searle.

They had both forgotten to whisper now.

"Our Master deedn't dnow," Urrg said, and then she suddenly shouted, loosing control of her temper, "Hey, blaming me... dats dot fair! Don'd blame me! You didn'd even catch yours ad all. You're de failure."

"But who's ended up with a swollen tongue?" Searle sneered.

"At leatht I caught thomething," Urrg screeched, "You caught do-one and dothing!"

As they argued they grew more and more angry until they began to peck at each other and flap their wings. It turned into a whirlwind of black feathers and screeching, until Searle shouted out.

"Stop it! We must find them! Our Master wants them. And stop shouting!" she shouted.

With this last remark they did stop their shouting and their fighting. They appeared scruffy after the fight, with feathers untidy and out of place. They began to look around again, jerking their heads this way and that in a random sort of way.

They were totally unaware that Zipp and Lazuli were, at that moment, very close. They were inside the tree just behind them. Some fairies had let them into their home and closed the secret hidden door made of bark. The ravens kept glancing around, but it seemed to them as if the bees and their riders had suddenly vanished completely.

"Now where are they?" moaned Searle, shaking her head slowly with disappointment, "They've gone. We had them and now they've gone... they're so small they're hard to see."

"Dey're hiding," replied Urrg, "Dey can'd de far away, can dey?"

"I know," Searle agreed, "They're close by... when I get them they'll wish they weren't so small... I'll swallow them whole, I will. One gulp and they're gone."

"OK, OK," nodded Urrg, jerking her head about,

"Bud don'd dwallow ady bees."

Inside the tree Lazuli and Zipp listened. Staying completely still and silent they peeped out through a crack in the bark. They wondered what had happened to the others. Where were they? And what about Amalek who fell from the back of Asher? The ravens were facing the other way with their tails towards the trunk of the tree and were still excitedly looking this way and that.

At that moment Asher came flying down through the branches, her buzz even louder now due to a tear in the injured wing, and not realizing that the ravens were there. At the same time Amalek was climbing up the stem of a fern. The golden thread had stretched perfectly to give her a gentle landing on the leaves on the forest floor. She still had the rucksack on her back, filled with supplies of food and drink. She reached the top of the fern and poked her head up through the leaves to look around. She spotted the evil ravens high above her in the tree, jerking their heads this way and that to look for them. She quickly dipped down beneath the fern leaves to hide.

Searle and Urrg looked up and fixed their eyes on Asher. They spread their wings ready to attack once more. This time, they felt sure they would get their prey. Then they made their move. With a jump they rose off the branch, but then immediately fell back.

"Aaahhh!" they screamed together as they felt something tied to their tails.

They turned around and pecked frantically at a mass of fine but very strong thread, this time green, which had been fastened tightly to their tail feathers. It was fairy rope made from plants of the forest. A group of fairies had flown rapidly around and around the raven's tails until they were gripped securely.

"Get off!" screeched Urrg, *"Get off!"*

They twisted around and pecked frantically at the threads and some of them began to snap. Then Searle noticed that the threads went into a crack in the tree. She twisted further still and jabbed at the crack with her beak. It stabbed through.

"Look out!" called Lazuli.

Zipp jumped back as the pointed, sharp beak came ramming through but it caught Lazuli in the side leaving a nasty gash. With a wrench Searle pulled out her beak and by this time Urrg had nearly pecked through all the threads.

"Some of them are in there!" shrieked Searle, and with one last hard peck from Urrg the last few threads snapped and they were free.

"Ged dem!" Urrg yelled.

"No," snapped Searle, "We can get them in a minute… we know where they are. What about the others?"

She looked around for Asher.

"Where are they?" she complained.

Asher still had Seph and Tally on her back as they hid on a branch on the other side of the tree. Amalek had slid quickly down the stem of the fern and landed on the leaves that blanketed the forest floor.

"Led's ged dose ones in dere," shouted Urrg, "Come on!"

They turned to the tree again and began diving viciously at the crack with their beaks. Splinters of bark began to fly off and so did some black feathers, probably loosened by the fight they had earlier with each other. The crack began to widen. It was very clear that soon they would be through.

Asher, with Seph and Tally, flew off the branch and around the tree to see what all the noise was about. One peep was enough. They dodged back and landed on the branch again out of sight. Seph already had his Magic Spells book open and was reading from it. He unzipped his pocket and took out his golden, oval box and the little golden pot. He carefully took the stopper from the pot and poured some golden dust from it into the box.

"Asher," he said quietly, as he sat on her furry back, "Fly around the tree again and hover just above the ravens. Quick!"

As he finished speaking he noticed that Asher's eyes were looking slightly glazed.

"Are you alright?" he asked her, but Asher was already taking off and flying around the tree trunk.

Just then the ravens had smashed through the tree and were about to plunge through and attack Lazuli and Zipp.

"Go! Go! Go!" screeched Searle.

"Stop!" shouted Seph at the ravens.

His voice was soft because he was so small but Urrg heard him.

"Shearle!" she exclaimed, turning her head with an angry jerk towards the bumble bee, "Dook! De udder ones!"

Searle stopped in surprise and they both fixed their steely black eyes on Seph who was now standing on Asher's back with his feet apart and holding onto the golden thread for balance. Tally was beside him.

The ravens immediately leapt off the branch to fly straight up at Asher who was clearly becoming weaker. Her buzz was softer and she was only just managing to stay airborne. The ravens were almost upon them. Seph shook the magic, golden box in their direction and the dust flew out into their faces.

"In the name of the good Wizard Elzaphan!" shouted Seph.

"In the name of the good Wizard Elzaphan!" shouted Tally.

"Aaahh!" the ravens cried out together. The golden dust swirled around their heads, sparkling in the sunlight, making them cough and splutter. They blinked and whimpered as some went in their eyes.

"Oh no!" panicked Searle, "I can't see!"

What happened next was an extraordinary sight. First Searle and Urrg seemed to be frozen in mid-air, except that they were shaking and shivering in fear. They screamed and closed their stinging eyes as the spell held them in its power.

"What's happening!" screeched Searle.

"I dunno!" Urrg shouted back, "Do dumding."

"What?!"

"I dunno... dumding!"

As if controlled by invisible hands, they were drawn away from the tree, then stopped again, held in mid-air and turned to face it. With a jerk they were pulled towards the tree moving slowly at first, then, with explosive acceleration, they shot forwards. Their beaks plunged through the bark and deep into the wood of the trunk. It sounded like the thuds of two arrows. They immediately wriggled and struggled with all their energy to free themselves, but they were stuck fast. Their attack was over.

Asher, with her wing faltering, began to lose height, but managed to fly into the crack, while Zipp buzzed down to find Amalek. Soon they were all gathered together in the fairies' den, high up in the tree. The children slipped their arms out of the straps of their rucksacks and then lifted the bags off Lazuli's back. They placed them all together on the floor.

"Well done with that magic dust," said Tally to Seph, "I thought we'd had it that time."

"So did I," said Lazuli, who was bleeding badly from the wound in her side, "Being small is great for hiding but it makes them so huge... I'm not used to meeting creatures bigger than I am!"

Amalek took out her magic silver pen, ran it along Lazuli's cut and it healed immediately. For a moment they lay on the floor recovering.

"I'm worried about Joog," said Amalek, "He said he'd be back soon. Something must have happened or else he'd be here."

Asher had now collapsed on the floor with her legs limp and useless and they all gathered around her. The searing pain from the wound on her side flooded her body. Her large eyes, which usually reflected a wonderful array of rainbow-coloured light, had lost their lustre and dulled to pale colours. She found that she could no longer move and as she looked around all she saw were indistinct, grey shapes. She panicked with fear, but then she felt the wonderful loving presence of those around her and relaxed. Her mind began to drift. The pain fell away.

She felt she was being called by a far-off voice, a beautiful and strong voice, a voice as fresh and new as the woodland dawn chorus that she had always loved so much. The call was irresistible and she drifted towards it as the shapes and voices of her friends faded like mist lifting when the sun breaks through on a new day. She began to feel free.

"What happened?" asked Lazuli.

"It's the sting," said Seph, "She stung the raven's tongue, and bees die when they sting."

"No," Amalek turned to Seph, "No, *bumble* bees don't. It must be other injuries. Look there," she pointed, "On her side."

A ray of sunlight pierced the tiny window and sent a shaft of brilliance into the room and onto Asher's back, lighting up her yellow stripe. Zipp moved closer and looked at her anxiously. Then he saw the wound.

"The magic pen could work," Amalek said quickly, applying it to Asher's side and then to her wing and the effect was, once again, a miraculous healing.

"It's worked!" she cried.

Zipp relaxed as the sense of relief washed away his anxiety. His hope rose. Then the room gently darkened as the sun dipped behind some trees and the ray of sunlight dwindled to nothing. He felt a small hand stroke his fur. It was Seph.

"She's gone," he said quietly, "It's too late now... she's gone."

Chapter 13

~ Nnnnnnnnnnnnnn ~

Zipp followed the fairies as they carried Asher's body to their burial dell deep in the forest. Afterwards he flew back to the tree where the others were waiting in the tiny fairies' room. He was numbed by the shock of Asher's death and was pleased to have the comforting company of the others. The fairies gave them a delicious meal of apple, blackberries, strawberries and cream. The fruit was sweet and the tiniest bit was enough to fill them.

While they were eating, the fairies busied themselves mending the hole made by the ravens. They worked with amazing speed, shaping pieces of bark to fit together and sticking them in place. By the time the meal was finished it was all done.

After the meal the group of brave friends, Amalek, Seph, Lazuli and Tally chatted around the table in the centre of the room as the dusk melted into night. Zipp stared out through the tiny window. It was a square hole in the bark of the tree with no glass.

"A good night's sleep," said Seph, "That's what we need."

"I agree," yawned Amalek, "I'm exhausted. But what about Joog?"

"He'll find us," Lazuli answered positively, "He's got great eyesight, perfect flight and he can navigate anywhere. He knows our direction and he's got that special instinct."

Seph nodded. "Yes, I agree, absolutely. He'll find us… and also when he gets close to us he'll see those two ravens sticking in the tree, won't he?"

"But what if he fought some ravens," commented Amalek, "That worries me. I know he can deal with a few ravens, but it's just if there were too many for him."

Seph stood up and walked to the window to look out. He pondered for a moment.

"I feel, somehow…" he said, "That he's alright."

In this way they remained hopeful that Joog would soon be with them again.

As they chatted, the Prince and Princess started asking Tally about his grandfather, Hawkeye. They asked him to explain the picture on the tapestry in the castle and their life in the Becci Mountains. Tally was full of admiration for his grandfather.

"He was a great adventurer," he said with enthusiasm, "And he was a fighter too. He was the leader against Gugeol when they conquered Summertime Kingdom and other lands…"

"Tally," Amalek interrupted, "Was that when that bell was rung and it cast a spell."

"Yes," Tally replied, "It's called the Glyifild Bell…"

Sadness suddenly dampened his keen young sounds and his voice became soft and began to tremor.

"They killed my parents," he said.

He blinked with tears which trickled onto his white fur. Seph reached out and stroked him on his head.

"But…" Tally continued, "But then Hawkeye defeated Gugeol and set everyone free again. And the terrible bell… the Glyifild Bell… has gone. Lost. You heard Wizard Elzaphan say that no one knows where it is now."

"Well let's hope it's never found," said Amalek decisively.

Tally opened the pouch on his stomach with his paws. This is where he kept maps given to him by Hawkeye for his journey. He pulled out an old folded piece of paper and placed it on the table.

"I haven't told you about KYWAY have I?"

The children shook their heads.

"No," replied Lazuli.

Amalek helped him to unfold the paper and lay it flat and then Tally read it to them.

Keep your wits about you when you act and when you speaK
Your wits will keep you brave but also warY
Wherever you may find yourself, wherever you are noW
Always be alert to meet life's dramA
Your mind and senses open, then your heart will show the waY

After hearing the poem they began to feel tired and decided to settle down to sleep, exhausted by the battle with the ravens, but feeling safe in the fairies den. They kept the miniature curtains open so that Joog could see them if he arrived. There were tiny miniature beds for Amalek and Seph, while the others lay down to sleep on the floor. The mood was subdued and quiet after the loss

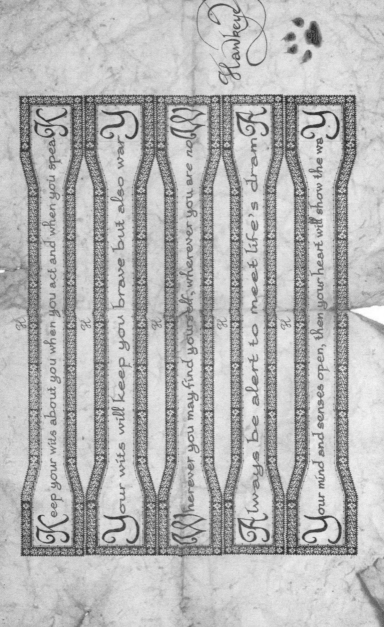

Keep your wits about you when you act and when you speak

Your wits will keep you brave but also war

Wherever you may find yourself, wherever you are nob

Always be alert to meet life's dram

Your mind and senses open, then your heart will show the wa

Hawkeye

of Asher and soon everyone was in a deep slumber except for Zipp. He sat staring out of the window.

The hours passed, midnight came and went, and in the small hours of the morning Zipp was still awake and keeping an eye on Searle and Urrg. From where he was, if he squashed his face against the tiny window as far as he could and looked sharply to the right he could see the end of Urrg's tail feathers just visible behind Searle's body. As he became more and more sleepy he watched Urrg's tail twitching as she tried to pull free.

This went on for some time before weariness finally overcame him and he relaxed onto the floor and fell into a deep sleep. Had he stayed awake but a minute longer he would have seen the tail begin to shake more as she struggled to escape. Then he would have seen Urrg falling when her beak slipped out of the bark, but he was fast asleep.

"I'm free," Urrg said softly to Searle, as she rose up again flapping her ivory black wings. Her swollen tongue was getting better but she still found it hard to speak.

"Nnnnn... nnn... nnnn," said Searle, frantically wriggling to try to get free as well, "Nnnn... nnn... nnnnnnn."

Urrg turned to fly off.

"Nnnnnn!" exclaimed Searle as loud as she could with her beak tightly closed.

Urrg landed on a branch on a tree opposite and wondered what to do. She was starting to feel that Searle's plans were always going wrong and she was tempted to fly off and leave her. Perhaps she could do better by herself.

"Nnnnnnnnnnn!" Searle was now getting desperate.

Urrg decided. She jumped off the branch and glided

across to Searle. She grabbed one of Searle's wings in her beak and pulled, shaking up and down to try to work her beak out of the tree. Searle whined with pain. Urrg let go, spat out a feather and tried the other wing. Searle's beak still stuck fast in the bark and more stifled pained sounds came from her.

Then Urrg tried pecking at the bark where Searle's beak was jammed in. Occasionally she accidentally pecked Searle's beak and Searle would blink in pain and anger and say, "Nnnnnnnnn!"

Urrg decided to try one more really hard peck, but then her beak stuck as well and for a moment there was panic as she flapped her wings and shook her head. After a minute she calmed down and found that without her frantic efforts her beak slid out easily. Then she grabbed Searle's tail and pulled. This finally did the trick and both birds tumbled backwards and down. They landed on a branch and shook their feathers to try to tidy them, but they still looked ruffled and disarrayed. Searle glared at Urrg and stretched her wings out.

"I know you were trying to get me out," said Searle, looking really cross, "But pulling my wings was never going to work. They really hurt now…" Then she looked at Urrg accusingly. "I thought for a minute you were going to leave me there. You nearly flew off, didn't you?"

Urrg shook her head. "No, no! I wath jutht gathering my thtrength to help you out."

Searle gave Urrg a suspicious look. "Alright, but what do we do now? I think we ought to attack!"

"No way!" Urrg exclaimed, sounding shocked, "Dook whad happened to uth lasd dime!"

"But they're sleeping now. It'll be easy. We'll kill

them in their sleep. Come on!"

"No, I won'd! You can if you wand but I won'd be around dis dime do ged you oud of drouble. Dose fairieth have mended de hole dat we made, so we'd have doo thmash our way drough anyway... dey'd wake up... dink about id."

"OK, OK," said Searle nodding, "In that case we watch and get them when they come out."

"OK," Urrg agreed.

"In that case," Searle was looking around, "We need to hide so they come out all innocent and unsuspecting... then we strike. In there would be good."

Searle lifted up a clawed foot and pointed to a patch of leaves in the next tree. They jumped off the branch and flew into their hiding place. They found that they had a perfect view of the fairies' tree house and so they settled down to watch and wait.

A while earlier, after the fight, Quint and Harris had hovered above Lake Beautiful for some time hoping that Joog would suddenly emerge from the water alive and well. After a few minutes, when they felt that all hope was gone because he could not possibly have survived under water for so long, they reluctantly decided that they would have to leave.

Quint sighed, "It's no good... he can't be alive now."

"You're right," agreed Harris sadly.

Quint dropped lower and hovered as close to the surface as she could. Her head was still as she peered into the water.

"I can't see far," she said, "But if he was alive he'd be up by now. No doubt at all. I owe my life to him, you know."

"I know," said Harris who had dropped down beside him.

"We'd better go," Quint concluded, "We need to get back to the castle and tell Wizard Elzaphan what's happened."

They turned and rose. As their powerful wings carried them swiftly towards the castle, the top of a black feathered head surfaced to the south near the shore of the lake. It was Jeg. He had managed to swim just under the surface, using his wings to propel him forwards. It took a huge effort, especially with the injury to one of his wings, but he was determined to escape. He was seething with anger because he knew they would have won the fight if the owl had not joined in.

He looked around briefly, took a deep breath and then dipped under again and swam for the shore. The water became shallow and he felt his feet touch the muddy floor. He stood up and paddled out. Water droplets ran off his feathers, shining like pearls in the bright sun. He shook his body and felt the pain in his wing as water sprayed off all around. He stretched it out and looked at the damage of about a dozen missing feathers and blood oozing from a long jagged cut. Stretching out the other wing, he took off.

With the missing feathers and pain in his wing flying was difficult, but he managed to rise and land in a tree growing close to the water's edge. In anger he pecked hard at the branch. He was still furious that his plans had gone so badly wrong and he was now left with an injury.

He tried to calm down so that he could work out what to do next.

Suddenly, he felt a heavy blow on his side. Something... something white... smashed into his injured wing and knocked him off the branch. He caught a glimpse of a white owl and then he was falling. He tried to lift his wings to fly but only one worked and he plummeted, spinning through the air. Joog followed him down. Jeg crashed into a log, landing head first, and rolled off onto the grass. He lay there motionless.

Joog landed on the grass beside him. He looked at the crumpled body of the raven and knew at once that it was dead. He pushed the raven with his foot to make sure and its head lolled to one side. Its neck was broken.

He flew back up into the tree and landed high up where he had a good view. He felt exhausted. The fight had left him bruised and battered. After he had fallen into the lake he had spotted Jeg swimming away and had decided to follow him. Swimming below the surface was difficult and he occasionally broke the surface for a gulp of air. Now he needed to gather his strength before finding the others. He knew the direction they were travelling in, and he would follow soon, but first he needed rest. He settled down on the branch and closed his eyes.

As soon as Harris and Quint had reported to Wizard Elzaphan and told him what happened to Joog, the great wizard made a decision.

He went straight to find Simron and found him where he had left him, at the top of one of the turrets keeping watch with Cedric. They were looking east through the battlements.

"Change of plan," said the wizard appearing in the open air after climbing the winding stairs.

They both turned to face him and saw the concern on his face.

"Is everything alright?" Cedric asked.

"No," said Elzaphan, "It's Joog, I'm afraid. It was a fight with some ravens… he saved Quint, and the ravens were beaten, but he's gone. He fell into the lake and didn't come up. He died a hero's death fighting for another."

Simron stood up and stepped towards the wizard. His cloak fluttered in the warm breeze.

"What can I do?" he asked.

"You'll have to go," replied Elzaphan.

"Go?" asked Simron.

Wizard Elzaphan scratched his chin under his long white beard. "Yes, I want you to go with the Prince and Princess back to the kingdom of Gems. Now that Joog is no longer with them they'll need you."

"Yes," the hooded Ferryman nodded, "I'll go, of course. But what about you here?"

"I'll be alright," Wizard Elzaphan smiled, "There's danger, yes, but not for a while I think… I hope. Have you seen anything?"

"No, nothing."

"So there you are," said the great wizard, his voice decisive, "I'll need you later on when the threat comes closer. The creeping desert in the east is on the move in the Kingdom of Moone, I know, and it's moving in our direction… but it's still not far from the coastline there. And to the west it's still no more than rumours and suspicions… something's definitely stirring in Gugeol, no doubt about it… but we have time."

"So," Simron said, "When do I go?"

"Today. As soon as possible. You'll have to find them and catch them up… but for you that's no problem. They are young and their task is daunting. Maybe it is too much for them… and I am deeply concerned because the Troubler's power is growing. I felt something happen in the Kingdom of Gems this morning… something bad… and I keep thinking of the Candara Gems. I think he may have them… he may have found a way to steal them and have them in his possession now."

Simron shook his head. "If you're right then this is even more serious than we thought. If he *has* got the gems… then his power would be multiplied… it's a terrifying thought."

"So," the wizard continued, "You see why they will need you with them. You need to eat and then go."

"Yes," Simron said, and looked out over the turret again and then pointed, "I'll go that way… back the way I came. The current of the Sween will be behind me. That will speed up the journey."

"Good," Wizard Elzaphan smiled, "Come now and have a meal first, and then you must go. There's no time to lose."

He turned to Cedric. "Can you keep watch a while longer?"

"Of course, sir," he replied, "And may you travel well, Simron. I'll watch you from here."

Simron followed the wizard down the stairs. He ate his meal quickly and then set off, rowing eastwards, with his powerful strokes, across Lake Beautiful. When he was clear of the cliffs he looked up to see Cedric looking through the battlements. The bow of the boat cut swiftly through the water and with the boat pointing directly at the estuary leading into the River Sween.

When Joog awoke it was nearly midnight. The silver moon looked down from a black velvet sky where thousands of stars shone and twinkled. The air was warm and still. Joog opened his eyes and lifted his head in shock. He did not expect it to be nighttime, not at all, but he realized straight away what had happened. He only intended to rest briefly to gather his strength so that he could fly off and find the others but he had been so exhausted that he had fallen into a deep sleep. He stretched his wings out as far as he could and then shook them. They felt stiff and bruised.

He needed to act quickly. He had to find the others so he looked up at the stars to plot his flight to the south. He told them to fly due south and he knew he was not far from where they all entered the forest together. He would fly south and zigzag until he found them. He jumped off the branch and flew towards the trees, gliding smoothly in the moonlight.

He flew straight into the forest, remembering where they had been when he left them, and then he began to search.

Finding two bees in the dark seemed like an impossible task but his eyes were superb in the night and also he realized that they would be looking out for him. He listened attentively for the sound of voices or the buzz of a bee. If they were resting then hopefully they might see him but if they were all sleeping this could be a problem.

After a while, he saw something above, silhouetted against the moon, that made him fan out his feathers in front of him to stop. He landed gently on a branch. At times like this he was glad that his soft feathers enabled him to fly silently.

He felt his heart beating in his throat with excitement and fear. On a branch close above, almost hidden among some leaves, were two ravens. The moon above them highlighted their angular black shapes. Joog kept completely still, hoping that he had not been seen, and stared up at the sinister-looking birds.

For a minute nothing happened.

Then Joog heard them talking.

"I've been thinking," said one.

"Yeah, what?" asked the other.

"I've had enough of all this, Crayle. You know... trying to be heroes and fighting. I'm old and tired. I'm ready to retire."

Crayle sighed and fidgeted on his feet.

"Jum," said Crayle, "How can you say that? We're in the army. It's in my blood. We're at war, fighting against the enemy. How can we stop now?"

"Easy," said Jum, "We just fly off somewhere and live in a tree. Like that lovely tree near Munden."

"What?!" exclaimed Crayle, so shocked that he slipped and almost fell off the branch. He flapped his wings and regained his balance, turning his head so that he could look at Jum with his one eye, "Not be in the army? What are you saying?"

"I'm saying we're too old," sighed Jum, "Don't you understand? You're always trying to be like a young bird again! I'm tired... we're tired... and as for the General! The General just treats us like dirt, doesn't he?"

This time Crayle was quick to agree. "You're right there, but to leave the army... I couldn't do that! Anyway, if we did, which we *will not,* we'd have nothing to do anymore. It's a stupid idea."

"It's not stupid..." Jum said, "What's wrong with it? We just fly off somewhere and live a quiet life... you know... find a nice tree like that one near Munden... that was perfect, the sort of home I've always wanted. Then we could live there and relax..."

"But... but..." began Crayle, so shocked that he could hardly speak, "No, definitely not! It wouldn't be right. And stop going on about that tree in Munden all the time. We must find the army again. If the General realizes we're missing and then sends out a search party to find us... well, imagine the trouble we'd be in! No, *we* must find them and join them again unnoticed and then do our bit in the war against the enemy."

"But, dear..." complained Jum.

"No buts..." Crayle snapped decisively, "I've decided. And I can't talk anymore now because my eye's hurting."

"But your eye's missing, Crayle! How can it be hurting?"

Crayle was getting crosser now, "Well it is, OK?" he snapped.

"You always say that..."

Joog silently jumped off the branch and continued searching. His priority was to find his friends not to fight two old ravens. He had soon left the sound of their voices behind as he zigzagged through the forest.

Some distance away, across the border, the Kingdom of Gems was absorbed in the depths of night. The snow had thinned now and was fluttering down lightly in small, dancing flakes. There were a few gaps in the clouds where every so often the silver moon would peep through to throw down its gentle light for a moment until the drifting clouds would hide it once more.

The spell had created an eerie, sinister atmosphere throughout the land and when darkness fell this seemed to deepen into a tangible heaviness that hung in the bitterly cold air. Everything was painfully gripped by the Dark Wizard Troubler. His spell had trapped all creatures so that none of them could move or make a sound. It was as if there was no life there at all because everything that had once filled the kingdom with the rich colourful variety of daily activities was suspended in frozen timelessness. This wonderful kingdom, once teeming with life, now seemed dead.

In the dark silence, however, there was one creature moving. Approaching Old Howard's house, and now about to enter the garden, Aram moved stealthily through the grey snow-bound scene. His hooves made a very quiet shud… shud… shud as he placed them one by one into the snow. He walked carefully forwards with a look of determination and concentration on his proud golden face.

He had decided that he had to make an attempt to find out what had happened to Halo and at least try to free her. He knew that the night was the ideal time because it gave him less chance of being spotted, so he had ignored as best he could the eerie heaviness and had set out bravely on his quest. He could hide in the shadowy darkness and hopefully reach the house, then look through the windows first and see if Halo was there. If he saw her he would then have to decide what to do next.

Shud... shud... shud.

He moved closer, lifting one leg at a time and placing it gently down. His striated alicorn was glowing very slightly to show him the way but not brightly enough to be seen by the Troubler from the house.

As he came closer to the house he slowed down even more. He would have liked to make no sound at all, but that was impossible. In the silence even his breathing seemed too loud. As he moved he inhaled and exhaled the chilly air, blowing out two misty clouds from his nostrils. He slowed his breathing to make it softer and dimmed his alicorn to the slightest glow. Now he was almost silent and he was sure that only someone very close could have heard him.

Suddenly the moon shone through a gap in the clouds lighting up the garden for a brief moment and then it was dark again, but in those two or three seconds he had seen something out of the corner of his eye that sent a shiver of fear through him. Something had moved quickly, to his right, a shadowy figure perhaps, but as he turned his head to see what it was, the blanket of darkness returned. He stood still in shock with his golden heart beating faster in his chest.

He tried to see through the night and the lightly falling snow, gazing blindly into the thick darkness where he had seen the movement. Then he heard a swishing sound and the moon came out again. There, only two steps away, was the Dark Wizard Troubler, his gaunt white face staring straight at him with his penetrating black eyes filled with menace. The wizard was swirling a black compass above his head, holding the end of its chain.

"Where's Halo?" demanded Aram.

"Oh yes, that!" sneered the wizard, the cutting venom in his voice sent a shiver of fear through Aram. "She's quite safe, she is. I wouldn't worry about her if I were you... ever again."

"I want her back," Aram demanded firmly, holding his fine head up in defiance, "I want her back now."

"Oh, I'm so sorry," the wizard hissed back, heavy sarcasm drooling from each word. The compass was still whirling in the air just above his head. "That won't be possible. Not at all. No. Definitely not." He scowled at Aram with hate in his twisted expression. "She's not available right now."

"What do you mean?" snapped the golden unicorn, "Where is she?"

"She's unavailable, so to speak..." the Troubler began, swirling the compass even faster now, "I'm not going to..."

Before he could finish his sentence, Aram leapt at him. The wily wizard dodged and with a lightning-quick sidestep he slipped out of the way. Aram landed in the deep snow and turned quickly to face his foe. The Troubler lunged at him just as the clouds covered the moon, and it was dark again. Aram saw him just in time and leapt to the side and kicked out with his front leg.

"Ahh!" cried the wizard.

Aram's hoof had hit his hand making him drop the compass. It plummeted into the snow.

"You vile creature!" cried the wizard, "I'm too powerful for you. Give in while you can…"

The moon came out again and for a second they glared at each other. The compass had fallen onto the snow in between them. It had sunk in a little but was still clearly visible. It was closer to Aram. He lifted his front leg and placed it on the compass, his hoof pushing it downwards into the snow. He felt it twitch and then it jerked upwards, breaking free and forcing him to stagger to one side. Aram nearly toppled over but managed to regain his balance. The compass rose out of the snow and flew by itself towards the Troubler's hand. He caught it skilfully and began to swirl it above his head again by the chain.

The evil wizard seized the opportunity just before the moon went in again and, moving now like a hunting cheetah eager to catch his victim, he dived at Aram. He let the chain go, aiming it towards Aram's alicorn. The chain caught on the alicorn and the compass now swirled around it making the chain wind around and around until it was gripping tightly around the spiral horn. Then he grabbed the black compass and pulled.

Aram tried to pull back, straining his neck muscles, his mighty legs forcing into the snowy ground, but the power he was fighting was too great and in a moment he was dragged, skidding in a circle around the wizard. His legs were being hauled through the snow and sending fine sprays of it into the air. A moment later, his feet left the ground and he was lifted into the air as if he weighed nothing with the Troubler now swinging the chain around his head like a lasso. Aram was whizzing around and around in the air with the black chain still gripping his alicorn. He started feeling dizzy and kicked his legs viciously in an attempt to free himself, but the wizard just swung faster.

Suddenly the chain released itself from his alicorn sending him flying up... up high into the air in the direction of the town of Candara.

Aram felt the cold snow-filled air against his tumbling body as he rose high above the town on the wind. As he turned in the air he first caught a glimpse of Candara below. Then he was looking up and for a split second saw the dark cloud above the town, and then down again at Candara. He realized he was heading straight for the cloud and was just entering it when a sudden gust of wind jolted him sideways and down. Then, as he started falling, he saw, to his astonishment, a sight both wonderful and shocking at the same time. Halo was in the cloud, her silver body catching the moonlight and rippling with strength as she ran along above him.

"Aram!" she shouted, "It's me!"

Then Aram was falling, "Halo!" he cried, "I'll save you!"

She shouted something back, but he was already out of earshot as he tumbled towards the ground. He knew he was strong, but could he survive a fall like this? Certainly, the thick snow was like a soft cushion, but he was falling so fast. He concentrated hard and his alicorn began to glow. The land rushed up to meet him, looking dimly grey and barely visible in the darkness. His alicorn glowed brighter still and began to slow him down. He crashed onto the snow-laden roof of a house, slid down on his back and dropped to the ground, skilfully twisting around in the air and landing on his strong golden legs, bending them to absorb the impact. He sank into the soft snow. Aram shook himself and a mixture of snow and golden sparks sprayed off his long golden mane.

He stood in the deep snow. During his fall most of the snow that had settled on his head and back had been blown off him but now flakes began to powder him again. A single tear rolled from each eye as he thought of Halo trapped above. He was shaking, not with cold but with the emotion of a broken heart. Would he ever see Halo again? He shook his head slowly in despair. For a moment he felt tempted to collapse into the snow and just lie there until the snow covered him. How could he free her now? He felt that the Dark Wizard Troubler was just too powerful and the task overwhelming. He was too weary and dejected to fight.

He looked up at the cloud above and strained to see Halo. The moon came out and through the falling snow he saw a glint of silver in the cloud. Something stirred in him. A spark of pure love lit him inside, lifting his heavy heart. At that moment hope was reborn, like a dying fire rekindled by a puff of air, and he knew that he would not give up. He could not give up.

He started walking, wending his way along Nathan Avenue, and lifting his legs high with each step he made through the deep snow.

"What shall I do now?" he wondered.

The Dark Wizard Troubler was certainly in control and he knew that to face him alone again was too dangerous, far too dangerous. This evil troubler was stronger than he had expected. Aram knew he would have to wait until the others returned, that is if they did return. Then, together, perhaps they could defeat him somehow. The good thing was that he was still free and able to fight again, and as he thought about it his spirits began to lift further.

Yes, he would wait now until the others returned. He could do nothing about Halo at the moment but at least he knew where she was. He realized that the Troubler had intended to throw him right into the cloud as well and maybe he thought he had succeeded. Without the gust of wind he would be trapped there now.

He walked along Nathan Street passing motionless snow-covered figures and animals. There were no birds suspended in mid-air now. It was like a ghost town. The spell had stolen the life of Candara. He turned right into High Street and crossed over the bridge. Then he turned right again and approached the tall Spindley Tower. He entered the house that adjoined the tower and looked past the horse that was frozen in the hall. He glanced up and there was John Chardley, the bee keeper, half way up the stairs and also completely still.

He turned and pushed the door with his hoof, closing it on the snowy nighttime world outside.

The Dark Wizard Troubler was now back in Old Howard's house and sitting in the smelly old armchair. His feet were stretched out in front of him and crossed at the ankles, and his wiry hands were clasped behind his head. The wounds on his hands, where he had lost a thumb and forefinger while trying to steal the Candara

Gems, had now healed. A wry smile curled the corners of his thin lips. Around his neck hung the black compass on its chain.

"You did well," he said to the compass.

He unclasped his hand and patted it. The compass gave a little jump in reply.

He was feeling content with himself after the confrontation with the golden unicorn and he was taking great pleasure in running his victory over and over in his mind. He had really enjoyed this one and he laughed out loud at the thought of the unicorn creeping up and trying to attack him. He shook his head at the sheer insolence of it, especially when he remembered the golden unicorn demanding the other one back.

Then he pictured in his dark mind, the unicorn thrown high into the air and heading for the cloud prison. He felt proud of this; not only the whole idea of the prison, but also the way that he had sent the golden unicorn up there to join the silver one. Unfortunately he had missed the best bit due to the darkness and the falling snow, but he imagined it anyway; the unicorn entering the cloud, finding he could not get out, and running up and down, probably with the other one, trying to find a way to escape. This delighted him and his smile spread across his face lifting the corners of his black eyes.

He leant his head back and closed his eyes. In his imagination he saw the three shining gems just in front of him. His desire for them rose, together with the frustration of not being able to get them. The wounds on his hand began to ache intensely as he remembered the terrible moment when he had touched the ruby.

"Not yet," he thought, trying to force the pain out and focus on the future, *"But soon. Very soon I'll have*

them. It won't be long now."

He opened his eyes to get rid of the image that was too painful to endure. A single candle lit the dingy room with the flame dancing in the draft.

"Dog!" he called out. Jamaar got up from his rug in the corner and padded over. He had almost made a complete recovery due to the help of his master's magic, although his broken jawbone had healed slightly out of centre leaving his lower jaw sticking out a touch to the left. The bruising and swelling were all gone.

"How are you feeling, dog?"

"Better, master, much better now," Jamaar growled, then he frowned and looked cross, "But my side still hurts from when you kicked me."

"Are you blaming me for that?" the wizard glared at Jamaar intently.

The candlelight flickered in the chilly room.

"No, master, I was only..." started Jamaar regretting that he had mentioned it.

"Because, *you* made me do that!" the wizard interrupted, "You failed and that angered me. Of course it did! You were lucky that's the only punishment you received!"

He raised his leg as if to kick him again and Jamaar cowered away towards the wall.

"No, master!" he cried, "I know. I shouldn't have failed. I won't let you down again."

"Alright," the wizard grabbed Jamaar by an ear and pulled him away from the wall, "I want you to stay alert. Remember you are guarding this house once again. You are now a guard dog once more. Alright, Jamaar?"

"Yes, master," Jamaar answered timidly and he slunk away into his corner and flopped down dejectedly on his rug.

Jamaar had been too frightened to ask for food so it was a surprise when the Troubler left the room and returned with a massive bowl of food. He was pleased to find that for the first time since Simron had hit him with the oar, he could eat without any pain. As he leant over the bowl to eat, the black compass swung on the chain around his neck. He devoured the food quickly, wagging the remainder of his tail now and again. Then the Troubler threw him a large bone and he opened his mighty jaws and crunched into it.

It was dark in the cloud above Candara. Halo had seen Aram fly past the cloud and was thankful that he had not entered it and been trapped there as well. But then, as she strained her eyes to watch him fall, she was filled with terror. With the thick falling snow and the dark night, she had soon lost sight of him. She feared that he had crashed to his death and she hung her head in deep sadness. The scratches on her side that she had received when the black compass hit her had caused a numbness which had now spread to most of her body. She had known that she would not survive long, and now the loss of Aram was the last straw. Despair swept through her, making her shake, and she let out a heartbroken wail.

She glanced down again through tear-filled eyes at the place where she thought Aram would have landed. Suddenly, moonlight dimly lit up the land below. Something caught her eye; for a second, a star-point of gold light shone, glinting clearly in the night. Something stirred in her. Hope was ignited in her heart, and like a single spark that can burst into flames, so her love was alive and strong once again.

Then she felt the numbness fading away from her body. She turned to look at the scratch marks on her side but they were gone.

The fifteen ravens led by Sergeant Forr had passed The Snowpeak Mountains and were approaching the border in an untidy arrow formation. They had eaten well in Old Howard's house but they were still exhausted after carrying the heavy Jamaar on the blanket. They tried to sleep before they left but they were too afraid of getting into trouble with the Dark Wizard Troubler so they huddled together in a corner of the kitchen listening for him. When they heard him moving around they left quickly and began their journey back.

The wind had turned and so they were flying low, where the force of the snowy blast was slightly less powerful. They were all very relieved when they crossed into the warm, still air of Summertime Kingdom. Sergeant Forr, who was taking his turn flying at the point of the arrow, rose higher and all the rest followed.

"That's better!" exclaimed Akk.

"Let's take a rest," suggested Iker.

"You're always wanting to rest, Iker," snapped Sergeant Forr. "And sleep. Anyway… I'll decide when we rest."

All the others groaned and complained in low

mutterings. They felt shattered through all the flying and lack of sleep.

"Come on, Forr," sighed Razz, "I'm resting now… whatever you say. We haven't slept all night!"

"As it happens," Forr began quickly, not wanting a mutiny, "I think we *should* rest now. But this is the last one before we report to the General, OK?"

"In that case," Razz said, "It had better be a long one."

There were more mutterings, this time in agreement. They landed in a huge redwood tree, dotting the very top branches with black. They were on the edge of Juran Forest and all around them echoed the beautiful sounds of the dawn chorus. They quickly settled down and went to sleep.

Chapter 14

~ The Candara Gems ~

In Summertime Kingdom the dawn chorus welcomed the new day. It was bright, clear and warm. The happy sound of singing birds filled the Forest of the Fairies. On the top of the tree where the travellers were sleeping, a thrush sang loudly but they were so tired and sleeping so comfortably that they did not wake. They slept until late morning.

Amalek woke up first. Her eyelids flickered open and closed as she got used to the light. Momentarily, she wondered where she was, but then she smelt the sweet scent of wood and remembered that she was sleeping in a tree. Looking up she saw some fairies flitting in and out of the window.

She lay in bed and watched the fairies flying skilfully as they worked. They were about her size and she could see clearly all the details of their appearance. Their faces were child-like and smooth-skinned, some with golden hair in a mass of curls and some with dark hair hanging straight and blowing out behind them as they flew. Their bodies were slim and light. They shone gently, leaving a faint trail of light behind them when the moved. Most extraordinary of all was their transparency. She could see right through them, for their bodies and clothes were as transparent as their delicate wings. Occasionally, they laughed with high voices as they flitted about happily. They did not talk at all but communicated with gestures and expressions.

Princess Amalek tried to count them but they fluttered around so quickly it was difficult. She decided there were about ten, perhaps eleven or twelve.

The room was round because the walls were on the inside of the tree trunk. Beams of sunlight lit up the room in patches as they streamed through the tiny glassless windows and thin cracks in the bark.

For a few minutes she let all the things that had happened tumble through her mind. Then she began to think about the future and a knot of fear formed in her stomach. The task in front of them was daunting. She wanted to curl up, pull the bedclothes over her head and stay there. Perhaps she could fall into sleep and forget all about it all.

She made an effort to lift herself out of the darkness of her thoughts. Her worries and fears were pulling her down and it took all her strength to stop her thinking. She took three deep breaths and then another three. Gradually the strength arose and she swung her legs out of bed. She quickly dressed and walked over to the window.

"They've gone!" she exclaimed.

Seph stirred in his bed.

"Oh, Ammey," he said sleepily, "You've woken me up… and I was just in the middle of a good dream."

Amalek was still staring out of the window.

"But, look!" she said, "They've gone."

"What?" asked Seph, sitting up.

"The ravens," Amalek leant out of the tiny window, "I can see the two holes where their beaks were stuck."

Soon, the travellers, now reduced to five, were awake and looking out of the windows at the morning scene, soaked in summer sunshine. A round table draped with a tablecloth sat in the centre of the room and at one side a flat wooden wall cut across the curve of the bark. In the flat wall two square doors had been made. With a click the right hand door opened, two fairies flew out and one of these opened the other door. A handle on the flat wall was turned by the other fairy. There was a rattling noise and after a moment, through the open door on the left, they saw a lift descend carrying a collection of plates and bowls laden with food. Breakfast had arrived.

The fairies busied themselves carrying the food from the lift and laying it out on the table. There was yoghurt flavoured with gooseberry juice, honey, and wooden bowls with pieces of many different fruits. There was sweet dew to drink.

"What shall we do?" asked Seph, "Those ravens are probably waiting for us to come out."

"Yes, it's a problem," Amalek acknowledged, looking thoughtful.

Her planning mind was working now, thinking about their situation and searching for a solution. They needed a plan.

"We need to go…" said Seph, "But it's too risky… too dangerous especially without Joog to protect us."

Tally looked anxious. "Where is he?" he asked.

He stood up on his back legs, placed his front paws on the bark and tried to look out through the window. He was not tall enough, so Amalek picked him up.

"We don't know what happened to Joog when he flew off to help the eagle," Seph said, "But if he is looking for us... well, we'd be hard to find, wouldn't we?"

"That's true. Let's hope he's on his way," Tally said, turning to him, "So, what do we do now?"

"Hmm..." said Amalek, "Difficult. Let's eat and perhaps we'll think of something."

They were just turning away from the window when Seph stopped. He had seen something.

"Look!" he exclaimed quietly, "Over there in those leaves... it looks like... deep black, and there's a feather sticking out."

Amalek stared at the patch of leaves.

"You're right," she said, "It's them. Oh no!"

"But it's good," Seph commented, sounding positive, "Now we know where they are. That's much better than guessing."

An urge took hold of him and he reached into his pocket. He pulled out a round pebble which he had picked up on the shore of Blue Lake and took aim at the ravens.

"Stop!" exclaimed Amalek grabbing his arm.

She did not stop the throw completely but changed the direction so that the pebble flew just below the ravens, hit a branch and fell to the ground. Seph looked at his sister crossly.

"That would have hit," he snapped, "What did you do that for!"

"They might be asleep," she said defensively. Then her voice hardened and she took the air of explaining something obvious to a little child. "That would've woken them up and then they might have attacked."

"Or I might've killed one," he retorted, "You hadn't thought of that!"

Amalek shook her head and said scornfully, "Of course I had. You've forgotten how small we are and how tiny that pebble is! That wouldn't hurt a fly!"

"It would hurt a fly!" he snapped.

"No, it wouldn't!" she stated.

Seph glared back and opened his mouth to argue further but then he hesitated. It was an awkward moment and he closed his eyes to calm down. He realized that he was wrong.

"Alright," he conceded, backing down reluctantly, and then smiling, "I suppose you're right…"

"I am right," she stated sharply.

"You don't have to be so bossy about it," he retorted, "I've said you're right, haven't I?"

There was a moment when the argument could have flared up again. Seph felt he had been told off as if he was a naughty little boy and Amalek felt she was right to do it. However, in the pause they both realized how silly it was. There were far more important things to deal with. Together they reached out with both hands and lightly touched their fingertips of each others hands three times, turning their hands over each time. It was a small action but it was a gesture they used for their friendship. It cleared the air and they both felt much better.

Seph smiled.

"Sorry," he said.

"So am I," said Amalek, smiling back, "Come on… let's eat."

They gathered around the table and began to eat.

Meanwhile Searle and Urrg were perched in their

hiding place in the next tree. They looked very scruffy, with several bent feathers sticking out at strange angles. Urrg's tongue had partly recovered from Asher's sting but it was still swollen. They had watched until early morning but by then they were so tired that they had both drifted off to sleep. Searle was the first to wake.

"Wake up Urrg!" she said quietly, jostling Urrg with a wing, "Wake up!"

"OK, OK," said Urrg, opening one eye sleepily, "Whad's all de hurry?"

"We're meant to be watching, remember?"

"Oh, yeah," Urrg responded sullenly, "For a moment I'd forgoden aboud all dat. I feld free. Id's such a hassle isn'd id? I think I mighd just give id a miss and fly off somewhere and…"

"You can't do that!" exclaimed Searle, but still talking very softly so they would not be overheard, "We're so, so close."

Urrg opened the other eye as well and looked out through the leaves. "Are de enemy sdill in dere?"

"Yes," Searle replied, "We're lucky they didn't escape when we were sleeping. I can hear noises… talking… just about."

"Whad are dey saying, Searle?"

"I dunno. I can hear talking but not the words… it's them. It's not fairies because all those stupid fairies ever do is laugh and giggle. It's definitely the enemy…"

They both listened for a moment, tilting their angular black heads first to one side and then the other.

"OK, then," began Searle, "The plan remains the same. We wait 'till they come out… and they have to come out some time… and then… we attack, we attack them hard, we kill them."

"OK den," agreed Urrg, sounding resigned rather than keen, "OK."

Inside the tree the five friends were just finishing breakfast. Amalek had been searching her mind for a way, a plan of escape.

"I wonder about that," she said thoughtfully, pointing towards the lift, "Where does it come out?"

They all looked towards it. The door was open, swung outwards on hinges, and inside they could see the square wooden area with nothing inside. A couple of fairies moved towards the open lift door, one taking hold of the handle and the other beckoning to them to get in.

"It's worth a try," Amalek said, "It may be another exit."

"Good idea," acknowledged Seph.

"Alright. We'll go first," Amalek said, "Seph and I... and Tally could fit as well. If the lift comes down empty then you follow us up, Lazuli, and then Zipp."

"Right," agreed Lazuli, "But don't forget the bags."

The bags of food and clothes were lying on the floor by the wall. Seph picked up his rucksack first and slid his arms through the straps. Then he helped Amalek put on hers and together they hung the last two bags over Lazuli, the straps on her back supporting a bag on either side.

Amalek and Seph stepped into the lift. Tally hopped in after them and sat between them. There was plenty of room. The fairy started turning the handle and the lift jolted into motion. It rattled upwards. They passed the kitchen, then another room and finally the lift stopped at a door which opened straight out onto a branch. They were high up near the tops of the trees. They cautiously stepped out onto the branch, looked around and then leant over to look down.

"Look!" whispered Seph pointing, "The two ravens... there they are... hiding in those leaves down there."

"Great," Amalek smiled, "It's worked. Send the lift down for the others."

They closed the door and the lift began to descend. When it came up again and the door opened they saw Lazuli. The lift was sent down once more to collect Zipp who just about managed to squeeze in without any room to spare. He looked thankful to crawl out onto the branch. The golden thread was still around his furry body. He lowered himself by bending his legs to help them climb up. Amalek heaved herself up first, gripping the golden thread. Seph then passed Tally up to her. It was obvious that Lazuli was too heavy to get up in the same way. Amalek had already got it worked out.

"Can you hover by the branch please, Zipp?" she asked.

Zipp's wings buzzed into life and he dropped off the branch and hovered right beside it. Lazuli stepped on, followed by Seph. They were all now nestled into his fur with the thread holding them on.

Tally looked around, his brown eyes reflecting a sparkle in the sun.

"It's a beautiful day for travelling," he said.

"Let's go, Zipp," said Seph.

Zipp started flying forwards and in a moment his wings were a blur of movement as his buzz grew. Then, with a little more effort and a louder buzz, he rose back up and past the branch.

Down below Searle and Urrg heard the distinctive sound of a buzzing bee and jerked their heads upwards.

"A bee!" shouted Searle, "It's a bee! Come on!"

They both leapt off the branch with such eagerness that they tried to fit through the same gap between two branches. For a moment they were stuck.

"Ahhh!" cried Searle, "You idiot!"

The leaves shook as they wriggled frantically. A second later they broke free and flapped their wings furiously to fly upwards and chase the bee. The delay had given Zipp time to fly through the trees.

"Down, Zipp!" called out Amalek, "Quick, drop down."

Zipp dipped down through the leaves and branches. When they were just above the ground they carried on flying southwards through the forest.

"Hey!" said a voice behind them.

The children turned. Flying behind them, and closing in fast, was Joog. Joy flooded the hearts of the tiny travellers. The Prince and Princess beamed at him and Tally did a small hop on Zip's back.

"Joog!" shouted Seph.

Joog caught them up and flew just above them.

"How are you all?" he asked.

"We're fine," replied Amalek, "Just about. How about you?"

"I'm alright too. It was just a little matter of dealing with a few very determined ravens. But I'll tell you all about it later."

The forest sang with bird song as they threaded their way in between the tree trunks and chatted about what had happened to them.

High up in the branches Searle and Urrg were hunting.

"Where are they?" asked Searle as they searched.

"Gone," sighed Urrg, "Dey've gone. How can we

hope do find a bee? A diny bee is doo small do find."

"Urrg, stop grumbling. You go down there and look in through the window to make sure that they've gone… we need to check that they were on the bee… and I'll carry on looking up here."

Urrg did as she was told. When she looked into the fairy's tree house all she could see were two fairies who pointed at her and giggled. She flew back up to join Searle again.

"Dey've gone," she announced.

"Follow me," commanded Searle who began flying quickly southwards.

Urrg followed and then moved up so that they were flying side by side through the trees.

"Whad's all de hurry?" enquired Urrg.

"The hurry is that I've got a new plan," said Searle.

"Listen, I think I've had enough of you and your plads!" Urrg sounded thoroughly fed up, "I can make plads doo, you know!"

Urrg landed near the top of a tall tree which stood slightly above the rest. Searle landed beside her. In front of them the forest stretched away like the waves of a great ocean.

"This whole thing was my idea," Searle snapped, "So therefore, I should make the plans. Anyway, why are you so grumpy? Cheer up!"

"Look, Searle," Urrg said wearily and sighed, turning her head to stare at Searle, "We are exiled from de army… oudcasd and presumed dead… de enemy caughd us yesderday and we were lucky do escape dat! I've spend mosd of de nighd sduck do a dree like a sdupid idiot! My beak feels sdrange and doesn'd fid dogether properly adymore and my dongue sdill hurds like adything! Somehow de enemy have dricked us and escaped again... and dey're doo small to find! *And* half my feathers feel derrible and dey won'd lie flad! And you say cheer up! Ged losd!"

"But we can't give up. Not now!" Searle said, sounding frustrated, "Think of what our Master would do to us!"

This made Urrg shake her head in despair and a shiver of fear ran down her body. She sighed again.

"Why did you have do mention thad?" she said, "I'm drying to forged him. He frighdens me more thad adything."

"Well then?" Searle queried, "How about a new plan?"

Urrg sighed yet again. "OK, OK. Bud your plad had bedder be a good one dis dime."

"Good, that's better," Searle began, "To start with we don't try to fight the enemy."

Urrg nodded with relief. "Thank goodness for dat. Go on."

"We try to get something of theirs. A bit of their clothes, or better still something magical, like a wand or something... whatever they've got. Then we take it back to our Master and he will be pleased. The General will turn up with nothing, the old fool, and we will be promoted and get rewards!"

Urrg nodded hesitantly in approval. "OK, but where are dey?" she said, "We don'd dnow, and besides dey're so small, we'll dever find dem."

"Urrg!" Searle said enthusiastically, "Just stop thinking of problems. Listen to me. What *do* we know?"

"Aboud whad?"

"About the enemy, stupid. We know that they will

probably cross back to the other kingdom where they entered. That's useful to know, isn't it?"

Urrg nodded.

"Also, the magic that keeps them so small - will it last into the Kingdom of Gems? I doubt it. More useful knowledge. So... therefore... we go there, to the border, and watch and wait."

"OK," said Urrg slowly. The things Searle had said made sense to her and she was beginning to feel slightly more positive now. "Yes... well... OK den."

Searle rose above the trees so that they could fly more easily and Urrg followed.

"Look! There they are!" cried Searle suddenly.

They both gazed into the summer haze to see the great flock of ravens searching over the Clungberry Fields. Together Searle and Urrg dropped through the air and landed in the top of a tree.

"We don'd wand do be seed by dem," said Urrg.

"Forget about them for the moment," said Searle, and Urrg was pleased to obey, "They can't see us from there."

Searle thought for a moment turning her head to one side.

"The other thing is..." she said after a while, "The three gems."

"Whad gems?" asked Urrg.

Searle looked at Urrg and wondered whether to share the knowledge she had. She decided not to tell her everything, but she could not resist saying something about it. "You know the three Candara Gems that protect the Kingdom of Gems?"

"No," Urrg looked quizzical.

"Well there are..." Searle took on an air of superiority. "There are three gems... special gems. They protect the kingdom, and they're hidden. Well," she lifted her bill slightly higher in the air, "*I* know where they are. *I* know where they are hidden," she announced triumphantly.

"So whad?" Urrg retorted, determined to be unimpressed.

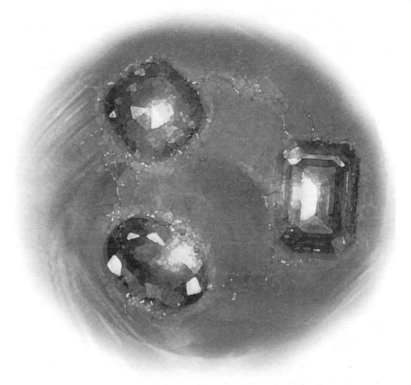

"So what?" Searle exclaimed, "They protect the whole kingdom, that's all. And you say 'So what'! The Master sent me and another raven to find them and we did. They're magical. We couldn't take them then because..."

"You and who?" interrupted Urrg.

"Me and Gerr... but that doesn't matter. What matters is that, when the time comes, we can get them! Then you won't be saying 'So what?' will you?'"

"Where are dey den?"

"I'm not telling you *that*," began Searle with the same air of superiority, "You do not need to know yet, OK?"

Urrg chose to ignore the question. "Whad happed dow?"

"We fly to the border," Searle replied.

"But whad about dem?" Urrg asked nodding towards the raven army.

"We are skilful enough," began Searle, "To avoid being seen by them. We skirt around them. Come on."

Searle spread her wings and got ready to take off.

"No," Urrg said defiantly, "Led's waid undil dey're nod so close. Dey're bound to move on."

Searle folded her wings. "OK... we'll wait a little, but we need to get going soon."

Joog led the way as he glided gracefully in and out of the trees, always making sure that Zipp could keep up. The bumblebee followed, skilfully avoiding even the slightest brush of a leaf which might have knocked off his tiny passengers. As they travelled through the Forest of the Fairies they were thankful to see no more black ravens.

The trees gradually thinned until they could see through them to the Great River Sween. They passed through the last few trees and then they were flying over its flowing waters. The summer sun was warm on their backs. Bright sunlight flashed on the little waves beneath them as they dropped to just a few feet from the surface where it was cooler.

They approached the southern bank where the trees reflected in shimmering shades of green. Flies danced around them in the air. They looked huge to the tiny travellers. Then they passed between a pair of gigantic hovering dragonflies who stared at them with massive, multicoloured eyes.

They were nearly at the southern bank when they heard unwelcome sounds coming from the south. It was the unmistakable cawing of ravens, not just a few but many, their harsh noises shaking the gentle air, turning the pleasant, relaxed atmosphere of a summer's day into a dark threat. Their sounds carried a cruel and ruthless edge to the ears of the travellers, which made them tense with fear.

Then they could see them, through the trees on the southern bank and above the Clungberry Fields, a dark swirling mass, looking down to search the land below. Some were swooping down to investigate further and then rising again to join the circling group.

"Keep low," shouted Joog who had risen slightly above Zipp, "We'll have to fly low. Really low."

He quickly dropped until he was just a few inches above the water and Zipp did the same.

"Follow me," said Joog, turning east, "We'll follow the river this way and then turn south across the Falwell Fens. It's the best route to take. It's more direct and also they'll expect you to be travelling on land, of course, so they won't be looking there. No one can walk across the fens."

"The only thing is," began Amalek, "Those two ravens. They may have told all rest about us being small and riding on a bee."

Joog turned his head to talk to the others as they flew.

"True, but if they did know about that they wouldn't be looking for us in the Clungberry Fields... they'd be searching in the forest. So, they don't know yet."

Joog paused.

"But remember this..." he continued, "We must not land on the fens for any reason. There are no trees there and only a few bushes... mainly reeds and rushes... but fall in and you'll sink into the mud."

They flew above the water, shielded by patches of trees on the southern bank. After a while the trees ended and they turned south, leaving the river and flying across an area of grass and bushes towards the fens. When they reached the fens they kept as low as possible, almost skimming the taller reeds as they passed over. The water-bound land was completely flat and without trees. Stagnant water reflected the blue of the sky in patches and lines among the gray-green of the reeds and occasional bushes. They felt exposed. Looking to their right they could see the army of ravens and this spurred them on to travel as fast as possible.

Behind them, flying eastwards over the Great River Sween, were Searle and Urrg. They were shielded by the trees and were also trying not to be seen by the army of ravens. When they reached the end of the trees they turned south as well to head across the Falwell Fens.

"Down, down!" said Searle, "We mustn't be seen."

"OK, OK," replied Urrg impatiently, "But I dought I daw domething move... out dere, righd oud dere... I couldn'd dee whad id was... id's doo far away, and I can'd dee id now… but domeding…"

"Get down," snapped Searle.

Urrg dropped down until they were both skimming just above the grass at speed.

"What did you see, then?" asked Searle.

"I… I… Oh id's so hard do speak! My dougue! I don'd know wahd id was. Domeding moved out dere… a bird, maybe. Maybe id was de owl."

"Let's head straight for it then, just in case."

Ahead and over the fens, Joog was flying behind Zipp so that the bee could set the pace. He was constantly scanning all around when his powerful eyesight spotted the two ravens. They were just black shapes far behind them, but he recognized the style of flight, as well as the angular raven shape and the intense black. They were heading straight towards them.

"Ravens coming!" he exclaimed.

"Where?" Seph asked.

"Behind us… look back there! towards the river. It's two I think. Quick, into that bush!"

They were fortunate. They had just passed over a small bush and so they quickly turned back and dived into it. There was hardly room for Joog and not much cover from the leaves.

"This isn't going to work," said Joog, "They'll see me and then catch you… I'll go."

"No…" Seph replied quickly. He was looking back at the approaching ravens, "Just keep still. Anyway they're almost here now. If you fly out now then they'll see you and might find us too."

Searle and Urrg were flying side by side as they loomed closer. They were talking as they flew.

"Where was it?" Searle asked.

"Domewhere here," Urrg replied, "Perhaps a bid furder."

"There's nothing here, is there?" Searle nodded her beak forwards, "Look... nothing."

Urrg was more worried about the army of ravens which they could see to their right, still searching over the Clungberry fields

"We should have waided longer," said Urrg, "Dey'll see us."

"No they won't," replied Searle, "We keep low and it'll be fine. We must get to the border."

Urrg was terrified of being seen by the General. "Led's hide," she suggested, "Look, dere's a bush. We'll hide dere undil de army's moved on."

The bush was right in front of them now.

"Led's hide," repeated Urrg.

"No," said Searle.

In their indecision they were heading straight for the bush, skimming quickly above the reeds.

Inside the bush the travellers tensed.

"They're going to crash into us," whispered Amalek.

At the last minute Searle swerved one way and Urrg the other and they shot past either side of the bush.

Joog turned to look out through some leaves. "Have they seen us?"

After the two ravens had passed the bush they flew side by side again and their wings touched. They lost control. Urrg fell while Searle recovered.

"Help!" cried Urrg.

She rolled over in the air and one wing caught on some reeds, swinging her around slightly and down. Her feet channelled through the water.

"Help!" she cried.

Then she dipped further and one of her wings was dragging in the muddy water.

"Help me, Searle!" she screeched.

She skimmed the surface in panic, scrabbling with her legs and trying to shake her wings free. Suddenly she hit a large tuft of thick grass which knocked her upwards and above the water. She was out, regaining her flight and in a moment up beside Searle again.

"Idiot!" said Searle angrily.

"Danks for helping," Urrg grumbled.

From the bush the six travellers watched the ravens fly on.

"They've gone," said Seph.

Amalek sighed loudly with relief and looked at Joog.

"But why aren't they with the others?"

"It's a bit strange," Joog commented, gazing after them as they flew into the distance, "I wonder what they're up to?"

Seph remarked, "Perhaps they're the same ones we met in the forest."

"Maybe it was them, they looked tatty enough!" laughed Tally.

They watched as the ravens flew into the distance and then out of sight.

"Let's go," said Joog.

Zipp took off and led the way with Joog, his beautiful soft-feathered wings cupping the air below as he glided close behind.

In the icy snowbound Kingdom of Gems, the Dark Wizard Troubler's spell asserted his will by holding the whole land prisoner. Before he entered the kingdom he had fixed his heart on being the lord of this land and his plan had been successful. He knew he was ruler here now and he was delighting in the feeling of power. His masterstroke, the spell, had been executed perfectly and now he had his prize. He was the lord.

From time to time he thought about how to extend his rule to other kingdoms, but he would wait because there were just a few matters to be dealt with. First he had to kill the Prince and Princess and their companions, and then steal the Candara Gems. He had expected that he would have been able to get rid of these last remnants of opposition by now. They were just the last flames of a dying fire and they would soon be extinguished for ever. It was only a matter of time.

The Troubler thought he was in full control of this frozen land but while he wallowed in his glory and planned his next move another force had awakened. He was completely unaware of it. He knew that his spell had strengthened and tightened its grip but he associated this with his growing strength.

Not far away in John Chardley's house Aram also knew that something had changed. He had felt it the day before. He was planning his nighttime attempt to free Halo when it happened. First he felt a glow of strength inside followed quickly by pain, as if something precious had been lost. It was like witnessing an evil action without seeing it or knowing what it was. Then a crash had made him spin around in shock. He had seen the frozen, frost-covered John Chardley falling down the stairs. It was like a statue tumbling down, crashing into

the wall and coming to rest once again on the floor. At
the same time all the bees, frozen mid-flight, had fallen
like little stones, rattling on the wooden boards.

He thought it must have something to do with the
Dark Wizard Troubler and it left him even more
concerned for Halo. After his attempt to rescue her he
knew at least that she was alive and there was nothing
else he could do at the moment.

The memory of the change he had felt the day before
haunted him and he knew that he had to make a journey.
He looked out through the window in John Chardley's
house. The snow had deepened since the day before and
was now almost half way up the window pane. Then he
noticed that something had changed. The birds that had
previously dotted the air, frozen completely still in flight,
had gone. Like John Chardley they had fallen, and they
were now lying under the snow.

He glanced up but the snow-filled air hid the cloud
that hovered over the town and trapped Halo. He turned
away and decisively walked to the door, his golden
hooves clattering on the wooden floor. He pushed the
door handle down with his alicorn and it opened to the
icy world outside. He pushed through the piled up snow
and stood for a moment gathering his strength.

It was an arctic scene. The snow cascaded down in
large flakes which swirled and gusted around the strong
unicorn. His mane sparked with gold as the fierce wind
pulled and shook it violently. He held his head forwards,
blinked and took a step.

Journeying would have been extremely difficult for a
horse but for Aram it was reasonably straightforward.
The magic of his alicorn cleared a pathway through and
he trotted along it. The snow blew excitedly all around

him but he could still travel at a fair pace. Before long he was passing between the little hamlet of Charin and Blue Lake. The bridge over the River Gem could hardly be seen under the deep snow but he knew that this was his landmark to turn to the west. He could see where the frozen river lay under the snow, looking like a flat path of white, lower than the surrounding area. So he walked along the river with a growing sense of anticipation. He feared the worst.

A few minutes later he approached the amazing sight of the Gem Falls, now hanging with giant icicles instead of tumbling water. He approached closer and stopped outside the Brinscally Cave. He stared for a moment at the entrance. The left hand half was a sheet of solid ice but the right side had been smashed away. Small icicles were forming again but it was immediately clear that someone had been in there recently.

Stepping up to the entrance he knocked away the newly forming icicles with his alicorn and placed a hoof inside. It echoed slightly as it rapped on the rock floor. Then he moved in.

He knew what he was looking for and walked to the back of the cave. Gazing into the cavity hewed out of the back wall, his heart sank. His eyes confirmed what he had expected. The Candara Gems were gone.

Chapter 15

~ Spies ~

Riding on a bumblebee was exhilarating for the four riders. Amalck and Seph, with Tally in between them, were sitting just in front of Lazuli and were held on safely by the golden thread. The warm air rushed past them, blowing the children's hair. Zipp stayed as close to the ground as he could and Joog glided close behind with the occasional flap of his white and brown-speckled wings. To the left they could see Burney's Hill crowned with the cluster of trees and beyond that, in the hazy distance, the snow-peaked Becci Mountains.

Amalek was clasping her tiny MAGIC SPELLS book and every so often she would look at it. She flicked through the pages, scanning the words and noting the chapter headings. There were many diagrams too. Each spell began with, "What to do if…" followed by a description of the magic and what things you needed in order to do it. Then there were further notes with more information, for example, what to do if the spell you are trying to cast does not work.

Tally looked at the mountains and was reminded of his home there in the labyrinth of snow-burrows and wondered about his grandfather, Hawkeye. In his mind he could see him and imagine him telling his wonderful bedtime stories. The love between them was strong and Tally hoped with all his might that they would meet again. He knew that Hawkeye was old and his days were numbered and suddenly it crossed Tally's mind that Hawkeye could have died while he had been away.

The thought brought a deep sadness to Tally, and just like a shadow cast over a shining lake steals away its lustre, so Tally felt his bright young heart paled by the misery of impending loss. His grandfather had brought him up with love and guidance and Tally was filled with great respect for him. Then Tally heard a voice.

"Tally."

He looked around, the furry edges of his long ears fluttering in the air, but all he could see was Lazuli's large body.

"Tally," the voice said again.

The tone was gentle and smooth as if rising from the depths of the earth. It seemed to sound all around him. It was his grandfather's voice. No doubt about it. Tally turned to Seph.

"Did you hear that?"

"What?" asked Seph.

"My grandfather?" Tally looked up brightly at Seph, "My grandfather's voice. Did you hear it?"

"No," said Seph, looking puzzled, "Nothing."

"KYWAY," said Hawkeye. There was urgency in his voice. "Don't forget. Don't forget the meaning. Live the meaning… now."

Tally's sadness melted away. His grandfather's voice

was rich and clear and he followed the instruction immediately. He opened out his senses. His nose twitched with life. He was alert.

"Are you alright?" asked Amalek.

"Yes, fine," said Tally, hesitating to listen for the voice again but it had gone, "It's just that I hear my grandfather sometimes… speaking to me. It's fine."

Seph looked down and smiled. He reached out and stroked his soft fur on the back of the young hare's head.

"What does he say to you?" he asked.

"Good things," Tally said, "Always good things. He says KYWAY… which I told you about."

"That is good advice, Tally," Amalek commented, "It's exactly what we need to do… all of us."

She glanced to her right where they could still see the swirling mass of ravens searching over the Clungberry Fields.

They were now passing over the southern edge of the fen and the ground beneath them was gradually changing to grasslands. Here the land undulated gently with a rolling terrain covered with grasses, flowers and herbs. A few trees grew in small clusters as well as in isolation. Now they felt safer with the rises and falls of the grasslands providing some cover so that they were much harder to see. They made good progress as they flew, still keeping as low as possible to the ground below and landing occasionally to rest. Soon they caught sight, some distance ahead, of the dark smoking line of the Great Crack to the Centre of Ruddha.

The great flock of about a hundred ravens, spurred on by the screaming commands of the General, was intent on searching the area beneath them thoroughly.

"What's that down there?" barked the General who was flying slightly higher than all the rest.

Several ravens looked up nervously.

"You…" he snapped crossly, "You with the stupid-looking beak."

One raven immediately flew up closer to the General. She had a beak that fitted together so badly that she knew straight away that the General was addressing her. As she rose she opened her beak to reply.

"Where… d… do… y… you…" she stammered.

The General looked at her with arrogant disbelief.

"No! No! No! Why are you flying up! I want you investigating down there!"

She turned, saying meekly, "Sorry, sir," and she dived down, not knowing where she was supposed to be looking.

"Under that tree!" he yelled.

She did not know which tree he meant and started flying down towards the wrong one.

The General looked around for Gerr and saw him flying back after scouting around as the General had commanded.

"Gerr?" he called out.

In a moment Gerr was by his side, as eager as ever to please the General. He was still hoping to be promoted to a position of authority in the raven army.

"You go down there Gerr, OK?"

"Yes, sir," replied Gerr brightly, "But why, sir?"

"I thought I saw something move… under that tree… could be the enemy," he said, staring down.

They were flying around in small circles together.

Gerr dropped from the sky to investigate. He flew around the tree and then rose again to the General.

"Just a grazing cow, sir," he reported with enthusiasm.

"Well don't sound so happy about it," the General snapped.

"No, sir," Gerr said, trying to be serious. Then he added perkily, "And there's something I've been meaning to tell you, sir."

"Now is not the time, Gerr," snapped the General, "This search is not just a casual fly around the park… it's *very* important."

"But, sir," Gerr persisted because he thought that what he had to say might impress the General, "This *is* important."

"Let me be the judge of that."

Gerr still persevered, "It's *very* important, sir."

"OK, Gerr, go on then. But be quick about it and it had better be worth me listening to."

"I know where the Candara Gems are," Gerr announced proudly.

The compass around the General's neck jumped and he lowered his voice, "The gems, Gerr… did you say the Candara Gems. I've heard all sorts of rumours about them. What do you know about them?"

"Well, sir," Gerr replied eagerly, "I know where they are hidden and I know they're really, really important and I know that the Master wants them. We went into a cave and found them there…"

"You went into a cave?" The General was very surprised, "And saw the gems? The *Candara* Gems you say?"

"Yes, sir." Gerr's lively speech bubbled excitedly out of him. "You see, we were sent there to find them and we did and it was the Master who sent us…"

"The Master sent you?!" the General interrupted, even more surprised. He was so surprised that he forgot to flap his wings and dropped slightly in the air. Gerr immediately dropped too and the General started flapping again. "When was this?"

"Ages ago," replied Gerr, "Before the Master sent us out to get the enemy."

"That's a real honour, Gerr," said the General, "It's an honour for any raven… to be picked by the Master for a job like that! I've heard that the gems are powerful… and they're dangerous too. But… Gerr, you say 'we were sent'? Who's 'we'? Who went with you?"

"Searle, sir… it was just the two of us… just Searle and me."

"Searle?" repeated the General, again surprised, "That's ridiculous! Why did he pick her? She rebelled against my command!" He shook his head. "But she's dead now and just as well. You're telling me she had the honour of being picked by the Master… and then she goes and betrays my trust. Well, she got what she deserved. Anyway, Gerr, go on. Tell me more. Where are the Candara Gems kept?"

"In a cave behind the Gem Falls… we had to dive through the water and find the way in and Searle was scared but I wasn't and I found the way in and… "

"Ah… clever!" the General nodded, "A cunning place to hide them. Behind a waterfall where no one would think of looking. Did you see the gems, Gerr?"

"Yes, sir. They're really bright… they just shine so brightly. But, well, sir, it was really bad in there, in the cave, we got a bad, bad feeling… like someone was watching us. And when I tried to steal one of them it did this to my beak."

Gerr tilted his head to show the General his damaged beak.

"I noticed that crack." The General flew slightly nearer to Gerr and studied it closely. "A gem did that? How? What happened?"

"I pecked the gem, the red one… just the slightest of pecks, and there was a big flash. A great big flash…"

"That's because they're powerful and dangerous, Gerr… very powerful and very dangerous. And the Master wants them for the power. Huh! That'll teach you to peck something like that!"

"But I was trying to steal it, sir," Gerr said defensively.

"I see," the General nodded, "OK. Go on, Gerr. What happened next? Did you steal one?"

"Well, no. There was a great big flash, like I said, and it did this to my beak. The gems are protected in some way… by something that you can't see. But you can certainly feel it… my beak hurt for ages. Then we flew back to tell the Master."

"What else?" the General asked, "What else do you know about them?"

"They're protected but also they protect the kingdom… the Master told us… and they protect everyone who lives there, I think. And everyone who lives there protects the gems, as long as they're all alive, or free anyway… like not caught or anything. At least I think that's right. And that must be why it flashed when I touched it."

"I see… I see," the General said, nodding his head

and thinking about it while the compass turned and twitched as it hung down on the chain. "Anything else?"

"No, sir."

The General and Gerr were still circling as they talked.

"All this about the gems," the General said, "It doesn't help much now... but later on when we return to The Kingdom of Gems this knowledge could be useful. When the enemy are dead then we can get the gems for the Master. That's right, isn't it Gerr? They have to be all dead or trapped, and then we can steal the gems, yes?"

"Yes, sir. That's right, sir."

"Then when we get the gems," the General sounded very happy at the thought of it, "Then we'll present them to him and he'll be pleased with us. Imagine that! You did the right thing to tell me, Gerr."

"Thank you, sir," Gerr said.

The General looked at Gerr, "So... carry on with the search then. Don't hang around here. Search... search... search."

Gerr fell away from the General again and glided low over the ground.

With all their busy searching the General did not notice Crayle and Jum fly slowly out of the Forest of the Fairies and join the searching group.

Aram was standing inside the Brinscally Cave and looking out. He was stunned by his discovery of the missing Candara Gems and his mind kept turning. He was confused. He was unsure what he should do next because it seemed impossible to work out what had happened. He kept turning to look at the cavity in the back wall of the cave with the three indentations where the Candara Gems were supposed to rest. This is where the ruby, the amethyst and the sapphire belonged and as he thought about it he felt the deep sense of loss that sat like a lead weight in his stomach. Someone had stolen the gems.

Who could have stolen them? The Dark Wizard Troubler kept coming into his mind, but it could not possibly be him. He knew that if any of the inhabitants of the kingdom were still alive or free then the gems were protected. But maybe the Prince and Princess and the others had been killed or trapped and the Troubler was the thief. Each time he thought of this it sent a shiver down his spine. However, he had realized that there could be another explanation which lifted his spirits with a tiny spark of hope because it meant his friends could be alive.

There was a chance.

There was another way that the gems could have been stolen. An inhabitant of the kingdom *could* steal them, whereas an intruder could not take the gems or even touch them. It was the answer he hoped for, and although it was a slim hope he clung to it as if he had been thrown a lifeline.

If this was the explanation it was a startling surprise because they had assumed that everyone in The Kingdom of Gems had been frozen and trapped by the spell. Who could this person be? However much he thought about it the mystery remained.

There was another problem. If the Candara Gems

were taken from the kingdom not only would the kingdom lose all its protection but Aram and Halo would lose their magical power and would turn back into statues. Aram shook his head at the thought and stood still pondering what he should do. Then it came to him.

"I must be there for them when they return!"

He should be ready at the border. There was nothing else he could do here now. He needed to be at the border for the Prince and Princess when they returned, if they returned. He had no idea whether they were still alive but something told him that they were. It was an instinct, a feeling, a deep inner knowledge which he knew he could rely on.

He had given Prince Seph the unicorn whistle to blow and he would hear that and follow the sound, but the closer he was to them the better. He was halfway to the border anyway and if he left straight away he could be there soon.

He stepped outside and into the blizzard. He shook his mane and a flurry of golden sparks flew on the wind. He looked magnificent as he stood for a moment gathering his strength like a race horse waiting for the start. Then he lowered his alicorn to clear a path in the snow in front of him and burst into action. He broke into a trot, then a canter and finally a powerful gallop, speeding down the slope to Charin Road, then turning north towards the border.

"Look!" cried Seph, pointing ahead, "The border!"

They were still flying low above the grasslands but had risen to pass over a small hill. From the higher land they could clearly see the border where the sunny hot weather ended and changed into the spellbound winterland of the Kingdom of Gems. A wall of snow tracked the borderline, which appeared from the distance like a line of white. Lake Burney, which sparkled brightly in the late evening sun, was on their left. Between them and the border was the Great Crack to the Centre of Ruddha with thin wisps of smoke rising up and curling from its deep crevices. Soon they were passing over it.

"This brings back memories," Amalek sighed, her face tensing as she recalled her fall into the crack, "And not good ones." Then she pointed. "Look there, Seph. There's the bridge… or what's left of it."

Just along the crack, to their right, they could see the broken Marrin Bridge, no longer spanning the chasm, its jagged, splintered remains hanging from each side. Amalek shuddered as she remembered her fall into it.

A moment later the crack was behind them and the border was looming closer and closer. When they looked behind and to the west, over the Gooseberry Woods, they could see the army of ravens, searching in small groups of ten or so, flitting everywhere in an effort to succeed.

Then they heard the roar of a bear coming from deep in Juran Forest where the towering redwood trees stretched away to the east. Joog had explained when they were travelling to the castle that a fierce territorial war between bears and wolves had been fought there for many years.

Zipp seemed tireless as they kept up a steady speed until, as darkness closed in, they finally approached the border to the Kingdom of Gems. He was flying just below the height of some tree tops when he dropped out of the air and landed gently in some long grass beside the border. Joog followed, landing and then looking down at them. The riders, the Prince, Princess, Lazuli and Tally, slipped out from the protective hold of the golden thread, off the furry, stripy back of the bumblebee and landed softly in the grass. Zipp realized he had completed his task and needed to return to the castle, so he took off straight away.

The blades of grass towered above their heads as they looked up to wave at Zipp who was circling above them. The low evening sun lit up the tops of the grass, but where they were, dwarfed by the smallest plants like tiny insects, they were shrouded in shadow.

"Good bye!" they shouted to Zipp, "And thank you!"

"Be careful of the ravens!" shouted Seph.

The tiny group of travellers watched as the bumblebee, huge to them, turned in the air, and with a quickly fading buzzing sound, headed off back towards the castle. He would report to Wizard Elzaphan.

"Right," asked Lazuli, "Now what?"

She was expressing the thought that was in all of their minds. They were at the border and so it was time to turn back into their normal size. They were surrounded by the tall grass which seemed to them like a thick and tangled jungle. Through gaps in the grass they could see the wall of snow which rose up like an immense mountain, white and bright in the blazing sun. Across the border the falling snow rushed chaotically in a strong wind.

Joog looked down upon them.

"Come on," he said, "You lot have to grow back to your normal size."

Amalek smiled up at him. Wizard Elzaphan had instructed her to read her magic book and then consult it when they got to the border and she had been looking forwards to it.

"Hmmm..." she said with her bright blue-grey eyes twinkling.

She already had the little golden book of magic spells in her hands and she opened it.

"Page thirty-seven, chapter sixteen," she said quietly.

She held it up and pointed to the chapter title.

Size Changes

"Size changes," she read.

Joog said happily, "There we are. It sounds easy."

There were a few moments of silence while Amalek carefully read page thirty-seven.

"Stand in a circle everyone," Amalek instructed the others.

Seph stood opposite his sister and Lazuli opposite Tally.

"Now stay very still - completely still."

Joog watched. She unbuttoned her pocket and took out her golden star-shaped box, held it in the palm of her hand and flung it high into the air. It rose slowly, as if in slow motion. From the points of the star fell fine golden threads which attached themselves to the very top of their heads. The magic star-box kept rising slowly and as it rose the threads rose too which pulled on their heads. There was a jerk and the four brave friends found, to their astonishment, that they were being stretched. They had soon grown to about half their normal height but had become as thin as rakes.

Just then they heard the beat of wings above, a moment of shadow and two flashes of black in the sky. They glanced up.

"Its ravens," cried Amalek, her voice high and shrill.

"Make us smaller then," squeaked Seph, "Quick!"

Amalek quickly looked into her magic book again as they continued to grow.

"No… we'll have to carry on now we've started this."

Joog flew around them.

"I don't think they saw us," he said.

The golden threads were still pulling them up, stretching them, until they were back to their normal height but extremely thin. Their arms and legs were stretched out like spaghetti.

"Help!" called out Lazuli, in a voice that was as squeaky as a mouse.

"Oh, Amalek," Seph squeaked, "Has the spell gone wrong? What shall we do now? Have another look in the magic book. Quick!"

They were still standing in a circle and before Amalek had time to find more information in the book, the magic star-box started swirling around them with the golden threads, no longer attached to their heads, brushing on their cheeks and tickling them on their necks. The star-box was circling faster and faster, and they found they were growing fatter… and fatter… until, to their great relief, they were, once again, their normal size and shape.

As they looked around, the piled up snow over the border was now waist-high to the children. The smooth whiteness stretched away through the greyness of the falling snow and to the misty shapes of the mountains. Between them and the mountains, standing out clearly against the bright whiteness, were the two black ravens, with their heads turned towards the five companions as they circled around them. They were keeping a distance and watching until, suddenly, with the low sun behind them to make them hard to see they swung around and flew directly towards the group. In a moment they were bearing down on them at speed. Their beaks were pointed forwards, ready for action.

"Attack!" shouted Searle.

"Get down!" shouted Joog, "Everyone get down!"

They all flattened themselves on the ground behind the wall of snow. The gold star-box was still in the air just above them, gently spinning as it fell slowly to return to Amalek.

"Get that box thing!" cried Searle to Urrg, "Do it for the Master. He will be pleased with us."

Urrg swooped, beak open, ready to catch the star-box that glittered and flashed by itself in the failing light. The star-box rose suddenly but Urrg followed it. She opened her bill and caught it, but with her still swollen tongue the box slipped free. The box opened and the five friends, watching from below, heard a loud gust of wind come from it. Urrg was blown head over heals, flapping frantically and leaving a trail of black feathers floating in the air behind her. Higher and higher went the poor screaming raven until she was a small black dot. Then she disappeared into the gathering darkness.

Joog took to the air. He still had some magic gold ink on his leg to protect him from the spell. Above him the star-box snapped closed just as Searle, who had been close behind, dived in. She closed her powerful bill around the star-box and held the lid firmly closed.

Seph grabbed a pebble from his pocket and threw it at Searle. It cracked into the magic box with a flash, and then shooting off and then falling to the ground. Searle was knocked sideways by the blow and then she was off flying as fast as she could across the border and over the snow-covered land of the Kingdom of Gems. She was heading back to her evil master, the Dark Wizard Troubler. Joog was following and catching up but then turned and headed back to the others.

Amalek stood up and watched as Searle flew away gripping her golden magic star-box in its beak. Urrg dropped down from above to fly beside Searle and they soon disappeared into the grey mass of falling snowflakes. Amalek wondered if she would ever see it again and shuddered at the thought of the Dark Wizard Troubler touching it. She remembered Wizard Elzaphan's warning not to let them be lost or stolen. There was nothing that could be done about it now.

Joog flew out of the driving snow and into the warm air, swooping down and landing on Seph's shoulder.

Seph reached up to stroke Joog on his wing. It was damp with melted snow.

"I thought you were going to catch it, Joog," he said.

"Well, yes..." Joog explained, "I definitely could have but I thought it might have been a trick. You know, to draw me away from you... so I thought it best not to risk it... and to return to you. But that was a great throw, Seph."

Seph nodded. "Thanks, Joog. It was *so* close!" He looked around. "There don't seem to be any other ravens around though."

Joog scanned the area along the border and behind them.

"I think you're right," he agreed, "But we'd better take cover anyway."

"It's getting dark," said Tally, "That will help us hide."

He was looking up at Seph. Amalek had been gazing across the border. She reached down to pick up Tally in her arms so that he could have a better view above the wall of snow.

"That…" she said with a shiver and nodding towards the Kingdom of Gems, "that looks tough… cold wind, deep snow… it'll be hard to travel in that!"

"Yes," Joog said calmly, his golden eyes expressing kindness and wisdom, "For you land creatures it will be difficult."

Tally was looking wide-eyes across the border.

"Lovely snow," he piped up.

"I'd forgotten, Tally," said Joog, "Of course snow is your home."

"Yes, but it's not as deep as this!"

"It's the deepest snow I've ever seen," continued Joog, "Before we set out we'll rest first… sleep the night and then get going in the morning before its light. That way we'll be refreshed and still have the darkness to hide us."

"Where shall we sleep?" asked Lazuli.

They looked around for a suitable place. They needed to be comfortable but hidden. There was a group of half a dozen trees very close by, so they headed for it. They sat in a circle on the grass under the trees and began to think about the next step of their journey - crossing the border and entering the Kingdom of Gems. They felt the tense energy of anticipation sitting in their stomachs like a heavy weight. It was the feeling of impending doom. They knew that the task that lay ahead was filled with danger and that success could be the sweet reward, but just as likely, or perhaps even more so, were the dire consequences if they were to fail.

The Prince and Princess opened their bags and passed around some food and drink. There were bottles of flavoured water, bread, a selection of fruit both fresh and dried, some small cakes, some ghicky nuts, some tunroot and other tasty things all carefully packaged in jars and boxes.

As they ate and drank they talked. They needed to discuss and clarify their plans before sleeping. They also needed to feel rested and strengthened to face the dangerous journey ahead. They would wake early, before dawn, and make an early start.

"Male and female squadrons stop searching and gather!" boomed the General as he landed in a tree in Gooseberry Wood.

Gerr was one of the first to land. He had, as always, stayed close to the General. During the search over the Clungberry Fields he had tried to impress the General with his skilful flight and enthusiastic searching. He was desperate to be appointed as the General's second in command. So far, however, all his efforts did not seem to be working.

Soon the whole flock had landed and the tops of the trees, now dark in the failing light, were speckled with their jet-black shapes. The General shook his wings and folded them by his sides. He turned to Gerr.

"Where are those fifteen?" he asked, "The ones who flew off carrying the dog. Surely they should be back by now."

"Well, yes, sir," Gerr replied, "Unless our Master has detained them for some reason."

The General nodded slowly. "You could be right, but I don't see why. It's a nuisance. I like to have a full army under my command."

He turned to address all of the birds and raised his voice.

"Did anyone see anything?" he asked.

They all shook their heads and there was a collective cackle of "No"s.

"Not a thing?" questioned the General, but the response was the same.

Then Crayle piped up, "It's getting too dark to see."

"Sshh," said Jum nudging him with a wing to stop him talking.

"That's only because your eyes are failing. Or I should say… eye!"

A cackle of laughter rippled through the group. The General paused, looked at them disapprovingly, and then continued.

"Well… we won't let nighttime stop us from finding the enemy!"

His compass gave a little jolt and began to glow, shedding an eerie dim light around him. A chorus of impressed "Ooo"s and "Aahh"s flowed through the group of ravens. The General puffed out his neck feathers proudly. His compass, the symbol and sign of his leadership and superiority over all the others, was now making its presence seen even in the dark. This made him feel important and in control.

"Perhaps they've not reached here yet, sir," said Gerr.

"Or," the General growled, "They may have got through. We cannot tell. *How* can we tell? This is most frustrating."

"Shall we search by the river, sir?" asked Gerr.

"No," said the General decisively, "If they *have* gone past somehow then we need to catch up. If they haven't got here yet we can still catch them at the border, so we need to go to the border now."

"I did see something earlier, sir," said Gerr.

"What?" snapped the General.

"Two ravens, heading towards the border, sir!"

"What?" The General looked shocked. The compass moved again and glowed slightly brighter. "*All* the ravens should be here. All of them. There are none native to Summertime Kingdom, so who are they?"

"Perhaps our Master sent them, sir," said Gerr keenly.

"You and your 'perhaps this' and 'perhaps that'!" snapped the General impatiently, "But no, I don't think so. The Master would've told us. They must be deserters. But… but I did a role call this morning. There were eight missing and all accounted for. Crayle and Jum were missing then, but I just assumed those two useless old birds were sleeping as usual."

Then he suddenly glared down at them intently and snapped crossly, "And I see you've chosen to join us again. It's not behaviour fitting for an army, is it?!"

"N…no, sir," blurted Crayle.

The General shook his head as if in despair and then carried on. "And the other six missing ones are the six killed in the battle. Did you check properly that they were dead, Gerr?"

Gerr looked twitchy at this remark and his voice sounded nervous, "As you said, sir. There were no signs of life, sir."

"How do you know?" barked the General.

"Well…" Gerr ruffled his feathers uncomfortably, "No movement, sir."

"OK… OK," the General was holding back his temper, and the compass was now pushing against his chest feathers, "It is clear what must have happened. At least two have escaped… well… deserted. Either they were knocked out by the fall and came round later, and then they should have returned to us straight away, or… worse still… they pretended to be dead. This is very…" and suddenly his temper snapped and he screeched out loudly, "Frustrating!"

There was a deathly hush. All the ravens looked at the General, their black eyes reflecting the light of the compass like stars in the night. The compass pushed into the General harder and he calmed down again.

"OK… so… any ideas?"

Gerr was first as usual. "Perhaps they were spies for the enemy, sir, who have now deserted!"

"Now, Gerr…" The General seemed impressed by one of Gerr's suggestions for the first time. His compass gave a jump. "I suppose if you keep guessing enough you're bound to be right in the end. I think you may have come up trumps for once! Mmmm, interesting. Spies! The spies I've suspected for some time."

There was murmuring through the great audience of ravens.

The General continued, "That would explain how the enemy seem to have always been one step ahead, wriggling through our claws, always slipping out of our grasp just when we think we've got them. Yes, spies who have been among us. Now, who is not with us now who was with us before?"

"Searle and Urrg, sir!" said Gerr smartly.

"Yes! Well done, Gerr," the General raised his voice in excitement and Gerr was very pleased to have been complimented by the General.

The compass glowed more brightly. Then the General paused and looked thoughtful.

"*And...*" he continued, "*And* the other four. Searle and Urrg *and* the other four, yes? I agree that Searle and Urrg are the primary suspects due to their disruptive behaviour, but there were four others weren't there?"

He looked at Gerr who nodded.

"So it could be any two of those six, couldn't it?"

"Yes, sir," Gerr nodded.

"Now, who were the six who fell in battle? Searle and Urrg. And I remember from the role call this morning that Farr and Liggi are missing. And who else? Anyone remember who the other two were?"

"Tab fell," called out one.

"And Kaaj," called another.

"So we know the six," said the General thoughtfully, and pleased by the way he was thinking it through so logically, "We know all their names. And it seems that two of those are the spies. Maybe more!" He looked shocked at the thought of this possibility. "Maybe all six! But certainly at least two are flying around thinking they are as free as mayflies to do whatever they want."

He paused and turned his head on one side as he tried to work out what to do next.

"Spies…" he thought aloud and shook his head.

There was a moment when no one spoke.

"Right," the General said, suddenly sounding decisive, "There is a way to find out. Who's the fastest flyer?" the General asked the whole group.

"Decc," called out one, and this was echoed by most of the rest as they cackled in agreement about this.

"Ah yes, Decc," the General acknowledged, searching the group with his eyes, "I've noticed how well you fly. Some of these could learn a thing or two from you. Where are you?"

Then he spotted him.

"Come here," he ordered.

Decc flew off one of the trees and landed on a branch just below the General. Even that small manoeuvre was done with skilful ease. He appeared young and strong with well-groomed black feathers shining blue and green where the glow of the compass reflected.

The General looked down at Decc. "Fly at full speed to the trees on top of Burney's Hill, and check the casualties of the battle. You remember where they were?"

"Yes, sir."

"Check the bodies if they are still there. Count them, make sure they are dead, identify them, and then report back to me. Understand?"

"Yes, sir."

"Then, go."

Decc jumped off the branch, accelerated quickly and flew off into the night straight towards Burney's Hill. Half an hour later he returned and landed on the same branch.

"Well?" asked the General.

"Four dead bodies there, sir," Decc said crisply.

"And now," the General looked around at the group who were all staring at him, "Let's find out who the traitors are. Who are the four dead bodies, Decc?"

"Kaaj, Farr, Liggi and Tab," Decc said precisely.

The General was clearly pleased. "That's it!" he

exclaimed, "It must be Searle and Urrg."

Again the compass gave a little jerk.

"They pretended to die. You saw *two* ravens, didn't you, Gerr? And only two?"

"Yes, sir," said Gerr, "I saw two, sir!"

Gerr felt very pleased with himself. At last some of his suggestions had impressed the General, and also he was the one who had spotted the two ravens and started the whole investigation.

"We *know* who they are, Gerr," said the General, "It all fits! Six ravens missing... four confirmed dead... and two seen alive. And these two are also the devious rebellious ones who have stirred up the two attacks on the males. I have been wondering who was behind those stupid ventures." His voice was loaded with hate for Searle and Urrg. "In my mind there were always two primary suspects... and now evidence points to them without doubt."

Then he suddenly turned his head with a jerk towards a female sitting close to him and she jumped with surprise as he spoke to her. "It was Searle and Urrg who organized the attacks on us, wasn't it?" he snapped angrily.

"Yes, sir," she answered timidly.

"Searle and Urrg... the two ravens seen," he continued, his glowing compass once again jiggled excitedly around his neck, "Yes, it fits perfectly! Well done, Gerr! They've been tricking us and passing on information to the enemy all the time. No wonder we couldn't catch them. And now you've seen the two traitors heading back to the Kingdom of Gems to mislead our Master no doubt. We must go to him, tell him what's been happening and expose the spies."

"Shall we go now, sir?" asked Gerr.

"Immediately," the General answered. He seemed happier now that he thought he knew what was happening. "And on the way we will continue the search for the enemy. Remember, our priority is to find and kill the enemy, so we search thoroughly all around here before we head south. And you, Gerr, you have done well. Very well!"

Gerr swelled with pride and sat up slightly taller.

The General looked down at him. "You're either a complete idiot or a genius, but I'm prepared to take the chance with you. It may be rash, but I don't care because we have just uncovered the devious work of two cunning spies, and you saw them, suggested they are spies, and then suggested who they are, Gerr. So I am going to make you my assistant, my second in command. You are now Colonel Gerr!"

There were some mumblings of surprise from the others. One said, "Why him?" and another, "I'm as good as him... better."

"Thank you, sir!" Gerr somehow sat up even straighter with pride. "I won't let you down, sir!"

"You had better not. Now male and female squadrons... attennnnnnn...tion! Male and female squadrons... take off!"

They all took off together in the darkness and started circling though the warm air and scanning the land below. Crayle and Jum swooped down to the nearest tree. Jum quickly settled on a branch while Crayle misjudged flying through a gap and disappeared in a mass of leaves. The leaves shook as he panicked, flapping his wings in an attempt to free himself. After a moment of violently shaking leaves his head popped out and he looked around for Jum. He saw her and flew out and down, managing to land beside her.

"Are you OK?" she asked him, looking at his ruffled feathers with a mixture of concern and amusement.

"Fine," he replied curtly, breathing heavily after his fight with the leaves.

"Shall we sleep?" asked Jum.

"No, not yet."

Jum shook her head and sighed.

"What then?"

"Look," said Crayle in a matter of fact sort of way, beginning to recover, "I'm fed up with the General... you're fed up with the General. The way he speaks to us is... unprofessional."

Jum nodded, "That's true, and that's why I want to leave the army. I'm fed up with it."

"OK, then," Crayle announced, "OK. We leave."

Jum was stunned.

"At last!" she exclaimed with glee, her voice soft and loving. She leant towards him and snuggled up against his feathers. "Thank you, Crayle. I must say you've been testing my patience recently..."

"And..." he interrupted, turning his head so that he could look at her with his one eye, "We become spies."

"What?!" Jum cried out with shock.

"I said... we become spies."

Jum raised her eyes to the night sky and leant away from him. "I know what you said. It's just that I can't believe it. Us... work for the enemy. No way... what if..."

"No, no, no," Crayle interrupted her again, "We spy for us, but we don't tell anyone."

Jum looked puzzled, "Eh?"

"We will be independent and free... no one will know... no one will be rude to us like the General... we will disappear from the army and no one will care."

"Well I definitely won't care! But why can't we just fly off somewhere?"

"Don't be silly, Jum. I've always wanted to be a spy... working on a secret mission... here's our chance. We spy until we have some important information."

Jum was feeling sullen again after the elation of thinking they could leave the army altogether.

"Oh, Crayle," she sighed, "All that talk of spies has put this stupid idea into your head. And if we pretend to be spies... then what?" she asked.

"We don't *pretend!*" snapped Crayle, "We become *actual* spies. *Real* spies. Then we report... and here's the masterstroke... we report to the Master himself! We spy for him!"

"Oh, Crayle," she sighed again, "Why can't we just fly away from it all."

"Because," he paused to think, "Because... because we just can't, that's all. It would be wrong, OK?"

Jum sank down on the branch and closed her eyes.

"Think of it, Jum," he said, "We'll have the best of both worlds... no General, which is good... but we're still fighting the war, which is also good."

Jum kept her eyes closed.

"So, let's go," he said, "Let's go now."

Then he shouted as if it was a great announcement, "To the Kingdom of Gems. Under the cover of these trees. Come on!"

He jumped off the branch with surprising energy and circled around the tree.

"Come on!" he cried to Jum, "Let's go!"

Jum reluctantly joined him in the air and they flew off together, through the trees.

Chapter 16

~ Lake Merlode ~

The Troubler was sitting in his chair in Old Howard's house when he suddenly jumped up.

"Come here, Jamaar," he announced, "Come here and listen."

Jamaar jumped up from his corner and padded over at once. Eerie candlelight flickered in the chilly room. Jamaar stood at his master's feet wagging what was left of his tail. He looked eager for some action.

"Yes, master," he said.

"We have something to do," the wizard hissed, "Something important, and I need you to help me. It would have been good to have Horrik helping too, but she's gone... do you know anything about that?"

The question shocked Jamaar and he could not help a hint of fear appearing in his brown eyes. He glanced down to hide it. "No," he answered.

The wizard leant forwards in his chair. When he spoke, his words were like poisonous darts.

"Look at me, dog!"

He reached down with both hands and pulled Jamaar's head up until their eyes were just a few inches apart. Jamaar felt a sharp pain in his jaw and groaned.

Then the wizard snapped, "Now tell me! Where is she?"

"I don't know, master."

The wizard glared. "But she followed you... I saw the tracks, dog. Now, tell me what happened. Tell me the truth!"

Jamaar had regained his composure. He had been dishonest for so long that he knew exactly how to play this one. It was simple; show nothing, deny everything. The candlelight flickered.

"I don't know, master," he said calmly, "I don't know... honestly. I didn't know that she followed me and I don't know where she is, master."

The wizard was still gripping Jamaar's head and stared into his eyes for a moment.

"Alright... alright," he hissed, "But it is strange... very strange. I want her back. If anything about this does come into that rattle-brained head of yours then tell me, won't you, dog?"

The wizard shook Jamaar's head.

"Yes, master," said Jamaar, wincing with pain, "Of course, master."

"Now, Jamaar," the wizard said, letting go of the great dog's head, "We have a journey to make. We are going to the palace."

Jamaar shuddered. Last time he was out in the snow

he had nearly died. He had never felt so cold in his life.

"Now…" the wizard continued, "I'll get us both some food to give us strength and then we go. Alright?"

"Thank you, master," said Jamaar, "I am hungry. But why are we going there?"

"It's something that has to be done," the Troubler spoke harshly, "You'll find out when we get there."

After they had eaten they set off into the icy, frozen world outside. The deep darkness of the night had engulfed the kingdom. The howling gale drove the snow hard into their faces and the force of the wind slowed them down, but this was not the main problem for them; it was the depth of the snow that made travelling so difficult. The continuous falling snow had built up layer upon layer until it was waist high to the wizard in most places. Here and there it had drifted even deeper. The smooth, white covering extended everywhere throughout the kingdom, transforming it into an arctic wonderland.

When they finally arrived in Candara Palace, the wizard slammed the door closed and collapsed with exhaustion in the hall. After a while he struggled to his feet and sat on the lowest step with the muscular Jamaar lying on the floor nearby. The wizard was the first to speak.

"It's so dark," he said, "We need a lamp."

At this the compass around his neck started to glow and then jerked and tugged at him. He stood up, and following the tugs and pulls of it, he moved to a cupboard. He opened it and could see inside by the light of the compass. On the lower shelf was an oil lamp and a box of matches. He lit the lamp and lifted it by the metal handle as the flame grew and spread its light.

The surroundings became clear but everything

around them was colourless, afflicted by the draining power of the Troubler's presence and showing only shades of grey.

"Right, Jamaar," he said, "Let's go."

With renewed strength in their legs they started climbing the stairs that led to the Round Room. Jamaar's black compass was now glowing as well. The evil wizard carried the lamp to light the way. Their breath puffed out in vaporous clouds. The chill of the Troubler's frozen heart accompanied him like a shadow everywhere he went.

The palace was cold and dusty and the heavy nighttime atmosphere hung everywhere in the chilly air, but to the Troubler and Jamaar this made them feel comfortable. It was the heavy atmosphere of the Troubler's spell. It was his own selfish presence, which he had created, and it had seeped into every plant, rock and building in the kingdom. It covered everything like a shroud for the dead. It had taken over the land.

"Jamaar," said the Troubler, his thin icy voice echoing up and down the stairs.

"Yes, master," Jamaar replied from behind him.

"We're nearly there now," he said as they reached the top of the stairs, passed through a room and started climbing the winding stairs up the turret to the Round Room.

They soon reached the top where they saw the cook on the landing, covered with a white sheen of frost. She was still in exactly the same position as when she sneezed.

"Come on!" said the wizard.

Jamaar trotted obediently behind his master. As the wizard walked past the cook he patted her gently on the head, disturbing some of the dust that had settled there.

"Sweet dreams," he said to her.

They entered the Round Room. The light of the lamp cast long shadows that moved eerily as the Troubler crossed the room. He headed straight for the Queen who was also covered with frost. She was frozen exactly as she was when she sneezed and the spell struck her; her hand gripped the porridge spoon with her head dipped and her nose next to the spoon. He fell upon one knee in front of her in mock respect. Then he took her frozen hand gently in his and kissed it.

"Your Most Royal Majesty," he said with fake reverence, "Madam is cold. Would you like a shawl?"

Then he stood up and moved over to the frost-covered King.

"Ha!" he said, a gruesome smile spreading across his face. Then he knocked on the King's forehead as if it was a door. "Anybody in?" he asked mockingly.

The King stood completely still like a statue, frosty and dusty. He stared blankly, blindly, immovably frozen by the spell.

"No?" ridiculed the evil wizard, "What a pity. Still, never mind." He paused. "Jamaar?"

"Yes, master."

"Do you think that a King who can't do anything should be ruling a kingdom and living in a palace?"

"No, master," replied Jamaar joining in, "Definitely not."

"Or a Queen who is also useless?" he glanced at the Queen as he uttered the harsh words.

"Oh no, master, definitely not. No doubt at all."

"Right then," the wizard said as he strode over to the windows and opened them wide, "They'd better leave!"

"But they'll be hard to move, master," growled Jamaar remembering when he had to use all his strength to lift just the frozen rat.

"I know," the wizard said coldly, "My spell is even stronger now. I'll have to weaken it... just a little... but not too much. I don't like to do it for these offending pests, but it's the only way."

"Master," began Jamaar, "Why don't you release them completely from the spell and then I could kill them?"

"Too risky, dog," snapped the wizard.

"Why?" growled Jamaar, who was disappointed by the wizard's reaction because he was hungry after the journey.

The wizard shook his head. "It just shows how little you know about these things. The release of the spell could spread and get out of control. Spells and their dissolution are hard things to handle. Also something might go wrong... they might escape, dog, then where would we be? No, it's best to keep them frozen. Leave these things up to me."

He stared at the King with an icy penetrating glare and began whispering the necessary spell.

"OK, let's try."

Together, with the Troubler pushing and Jamaar pulling with his teeth, they managed to drag the King to the window. They hauled him up, resting him briefly on the window frame and then dropped him out. He plummeted through the icy snow-filled air, tumbling gently as if in slow motion and then crashing heavily into the snow way below.

The Dark Wizard Troubler stared at the Queen, whispered the spell, and then they dragged her to the window. In a moment she was falling from the high turret. She landed beside her husband, snow spraying up like a frothy wave hitting a rock. They were both unharmed because they were frozen solid by the spell and the deep snow cushioned their fall. Then the Troubler and Jamaar pulled the door off its hinges and threw that out of the window as well.

"What's that for, master?" asked Jamaar.

"It'll be a makeshift sledge," hissed the wizard with a cunning look in his eyes.

"And what do we use it for, master?" asked Jamaar.

"To get rid of them, of course," snapped the wizard, "Come on, dog, let's go down."

The wizard grabbed the lamp and they left the Round Room and started descending the stairs.

"You know this kingdom well, don't you, Jamaar?" hissed the wizard, "Where can we dump them where they'll never be found?"

Jamaar thought for a moment and tilted his great head on one side.

"I do have an idea," Jamaar said, looking pleased.

"Well?" snarled the Troubler, "What is it?"

As they descended the stairs Jamaar explained his idea and the wizard zealously approved.

"Great idea, Jamaar!" he chuckled.

At the bottom of the spiral stairs they had to pass through a room, along a corridor and then down the main stairs to the hall. At the foot of the stairs the wizard hesitated.

"I need some rope, Jamaar," he said, "Try in the cellar."

Jamaar remembered the way down to the cellar and descended the steps to look for some rope. The Troubler held the lamp at the top of the steps. Jamaar started looking and sniffing around when he heard the wizard call down to him.

"And an axe to cut it with."

Jamaar found an axe hanging up with a row of other tools and a roll of rope in a dusty corner. After two trips up and down the stairs Jamaar had dropped the rope and the axe at his master's feet. The wizard unwound a stretch of rope and cut it off with a single blow with the axe, which he left embedded in the floorboards.

A moment later they emerged through the great front door of the palace into the falling snow. Even with the lamp, it took them a moment to find the two frozen bodies and the door because they had sunk into the deep snow.

The Dark Wizard Troubler stared at them. He had judged it exactly right.

"Look at them, Jamaar," he sneered, "Helpless… trapped… under my power. And yet we can move them."

Jamaar pushed the King with one of his large paws. "You're a great wizard, master," he growled.

The Troubler smashed two holes in the door with the heel of his boot and threaded through the piece of rope. Together, pulling and pushing with all their might, they managed to load the King and Queen onto the door and then the rope was tied around Jamaar. The powerful dog toiled along through the thick snow pulling the sledge. The Troubler followed and chuckled with glee as he thought about where they were going. It was perfect.

After passing out of the palace gates they turned left along a path that took them into Silvermay Forest. The journey would be tough because of the deep snow, but at least it was not as deep here as it was out in the open.

"Keep going, dog!" shouted the evil wizard.

The lamp was just strong enough to light the path in front of them for a few steps and the falling snow looked like grey insects dancing in the thin air around it. They passed through trees, mostly silver birch, but they were both oblivious to the beauty of these delicate trees that were laden with snow upon every branch. Jamaar's load was very heavy, which made his walking particularly laboured. It was not only the weight of the load but also the rough surface of the door and its heaviness that made his travelling so difficult. After a while Jamaar started complaining.

"Master," he grumbled, "It's too heavy. Let's leave one of them here and then come back for it later."

"No," the wizard replied sharply, "We press on."

"But, master…" pleaded Jamaar stopping and sitting down.

"I said, 'no', dog! I've given you all this extra strength, now use it! We'll rest a moment and then we'll get going again."

They paused in the falling snow, which speckled the wizard's black cloak and clung to Jamaar's fur. After a minute the wizard was getting impatient.

"Let's go," he snapped.

Jamaar stood up, strained forwards and pulled. The door jerked into motion and they were on their way again.

For an onlooker it would have been hard to tell if his load was two bodies or two statues, because they were so still and frozen. After a while the path came to a fork. Jamaar hesitated, pretending he was wondering which way to go in order to take another needed rest. He was extremely tired. He sat down and let the rope go slack behind him.

"What's the matter now?!" shouted the Troubler, his frozen breath forming fleeting clouds before dissolving into the thin air.

"I'm not sure which way, master," growled Jamaar, "It's all this snow. I think it's that way. No, that way. Um... I just need a moment to remember."

He looked from one track to the other a few times. Then, as if he had suddenly remembered which fork to take, he stood up and started walking again. The rope tightened, the sledge jolted into movement and they turned to take the right fork. After a couple of bends they were moving downhill. The path weaved its way through the trees and then levelled off. The Troubler strode with determination etched on his face and his great boots ploughing through the deep snow.

Eventually they arrived, and when the evil wizard saw the place he gasped with pleasure as he spotted a glint of silver, dulled in his presence but still shining. Jamaar had led him to the Silver Well.

"So, there *is* silver in my kingdom as well as gems and many other riches!" he said greedily to Jamaar, "I can have this moved... all this silver. I'll return for this later."

Snow was piled up against the sides of the well, especially where the wind had driven it, and it lay on the top of the circular wall like a thick cushion. Silver showed through here and there on the sides of the walls which made the Troubler grin with pleasure as they unloaded the King and Queen.

The two compasses, one hanging around each of their necks, were glowing gently, and with the light shed by the lamp, they could see what they were doing. The falling snow was lit up in the yellow lamplight, whirling around them like a swarm of bees. As they worked, their breath puffed out in misty clouds and disappeared. They first heaved the King onto Jamaar's broad shoulders and then tipped him forwards onto the wall of the well, where he balanced precariously.

The Troubler knew he could not kill anyone when they were frozen by his spell; they were beyond life and death, suspended in limbo, forever existing yet unable to act in any way. But the King and Queen, well, he wanted them out of the way; out of his sight. He felt uneasy with them around, even in their frozen condition and he wanted to remove the slightest possibility that they could ever awaken.

"And now, my lady!... no... I should say... Your Royal Majesty, it's your turn. Are you ready, dear?"

Together they hauled her to the other side of the well. They forced her up onto the wall so that she was balanced on her feet opposite the King. Timelessness held her as her hand gripped the porridge spoon with her head dipped towards it. The falling snow settled on them as the Troubler enjoyed the sense of power. He was about to strike a blow to establish himself even more securely as the King and ruler of the Kingdom of Gems. He felt that after he had disposed of the King and Queen his hold on the land would tighten. For a few seconds he paused to savour the moment. Eager anticipation filled his cold heart.

"Now," said the wizard, "To strengthen the spell again to its fullness."

He moved close to the Queen and whispered the spell. Then he walked around the well to do the same to the King.

When he spoke again his words were loaded with sarcasm. "Your Most Gracious Majesty... my heart bleeds to say goodbye." Then he lowered his voice to a sinister deathly hiss, "Goodbye... forever."

He gave the King a hard push with both hands and began to rock him backwards and forwards. Then, with an extra hard push, he watched with glee as the King fell over the circular wall leaving just a puff of snow in the air. The King was gone, tumbling down and down into the depths of the well.

"Get out of that!" the Troubler exclaimed down the well, and he roared with sinister laughter as he looked at the Queen, "We don't want His Majesty getting lonely do we?"

He walked around the well to kiss her on the hand.

"Good bye," he ridiculed and he pushed her with two hands but his feet were slipping in the snow.

"Jamaar," he said, "Help me with this one."

Jamaar put the top of his head against the Queen and together they pushed with all their strength until she began to rock. They managed to increase the rocking motion until she began to overbalance. In eerie slow motion, in the shadowy colourless night, she began to tip and then topple headfirst into the well.

Jamaar jumped onto the wall and peered down while the Dark Wizard Troubler leant over the side and also looked down.

"It's a long way down there, master," said Jamaar.

The wizard slapped his hand on top of the well in glee, sending a cloud of snow spraying off. "This well is deeper than I thought... perfect."

He rubbed his hands together.

"It's a job well done, Jamaar, very well done. It's a

job completed. They have gone."

The evil wizard stood still and ran his hand around the top of the silver wall with greedy delight. A handful of snow collected in his hand and he pushed it into the well, watching it fall. Then he rubbed his hands together again in satisfaction. Jamaar stood on the wall gazing down into the dark depths of the well.

"Good... good... good," said the Troubler, "They have gone... forever!"

He felt that this was an important event. He had tightened his grip on the kingdom and began to stride off in the direction of Old Howard's house, pushing through the deep snow. After a few steps he stopped and then turned back to fetch the lamp. He paused to look at the well. He felt greedy for the silver and pleased by the task he had just completed. Then he kicked the snow with excitement and it sprayed out in front of him.

"Yes!" he cried, "This gets better and better! The King and Queen gone. I am certainly now the new King!"

Then he noticed something on his boot, something that had caught there when he kicked the snow. He reached down and picked it up; it was a small black velvet bag, the one that belonged to the compass Jamaar had stolen from Darsan Lopery. He looked at it closely. It was wet from the snow, but running around the edge was the silver-threaded pattern and when he saw it his jaw dropped and he gasped in surprise.

"What's this, Jamaar?" he asked, sounding utterly astonished by the find.

"I don't know," Jamaar answered immediately from where he was standing on the well wall.

"You know nothing about this, dog? Nothing at all?"

Jamaar shook his head, "Nothing, master."

"No, you wouldn't," whispered the evil wizard to himself, "But what on earth is it doing here?"

He brushed off a few flakes of snow which had just landed on it and studied it closely. He shook his head in disbelief and then stuffed it into his pocket.

His eyes looked distant as he tried to fathom it out. Where was the compass that belonged in the velvet bag? And who owned it? He instinctively suspected that Jamaar knew something about it, but now was not the time to find out. Later he would make him talk. His greedy black eyes focused on the glittering shiny silver of the well reflecting in the lamplight and thought again of how he would return for that silver later on.

"It's mine," he had muttered to himself.

He walked around the well so that he could reach out for the lamp. Just then Jamaar slipped on the ice and snow on the top of the wall. The short remainder of his tail brushed the lamp, knocking it over. It plummeted down the well just before the wizard closed his hand around the handle. They both looked over and saw the walls of the well light up as the lamp descended until it disappeared way below. Now the only light to see by was the pale glow of their compasses.

"You stupid dog!" shouted the Troubler.

In his anger the wizard hit Jamaar around the back of his head with his hand, making him slip again. The great dog began to fall into the well, but somehow, as he fell, he managed to hook his front paws over the wall and hang there. He scrabbled with his back legs against the smooth silver to get out. The Troubler took a step around the well to get close to where Jamaar was hanging on but his paws began to slip.

The wizard moved with speed, but just as he had reached out for Jamaar, one of the dog's back legs gripped and his head and body rose up. However, the weight shift made him lose his balance and his paws slipped back off the slippery wall. He had lost his support and again he began to fall. As he fell, his chin cracked against the wall, jerking his head back violently and knocking him out. The Troubler, acting with selfish instinct, grabbed at the compass that was around Jamaar's neck but missed and caught the end of one of his paws in his fingers. Jamaar's weight was far too great and Jamaar slipped out of his grip and fell limply into the well.

The Troubler gazed down into the depths and watched as Jamaar fell into the darkness.

He shrugged dismissively and thought, *"Stupid animal. It's his own fault for being so clumsy. But the compass... now losing that is frustrating... extremely frustrating."*

He looked at the Silver Well. It had stopped snowing and for a brief moment the moon shone through a break in the clouds. He brushed some snow off the wall and stared in admiration at the silver shining in the moonlight.

"I've lost a dog, a stupid dog... and a compass, which is a serious loss," he thought, *"But I've gained all this silver!"*

He slipped his hand into his pocket, felt the velvet bag and pulled it out to inspect it again. There was no doubt what it was for, no doubt at all. The size and material of the bag was exactly right and the pattern of the silver thread was unique. But whose was it and how had it got there? Most intriguing of all, and most worrisome, was the fact that the compass was not there inside it. His dark mind swirled with these questions as he turned and strode off.

The return journey was much easier because he could walk in their freshly made tracks. For a while he was absorbed in his thoughts about the mysterious compass but he soon became frustrated when he found he could not work out what had happened. So he turned his mind to his immediate plans. The problem of the Prince and the Princess still haunted him like an annoying thorn in his foot. Everything else had gone so well and he now felt he was the new king of this kingdom.

"I want the Candara Gems," he thought, *"But I must deal with the enemy, the Prince and Princess... and the others. I must get rid of them all... then I can take the gems... at last. The ravens can kill them, and no doubt they will, but what if they don't?"*

He pondered upon this question as he emerged from Silvermay Forest and turned onto the path leading up to the palace. Then suddenly he stopped when an idea struck him. A distant look came into his eyes and an evil smile curled his thin lips. He had thought of a way of taking the situation into his own hands.

"Yes," he said to himself, nodding with anticipation, "Good... good... good... the Candara Gems will soon be mine."

Now he knew exactly what he would do next to further his plans. The snow began to fall again and soon it was swirling around him as he started walking with firm resolute strides up to the palace.

Horrik had heard the splashes of the King and Queen falling into the lake at the bottom of the well. It surprised and intrigued her. A feature of her new underground life in the tunnels was the almost complete silence. The only sounds were the constant hiss of the distant sound of flowing water, and the far away screech, which she had heard again, several times. Each time she heard it she cringed inside. She was a huge, powerful creature who was rarely afraid but there was something about this sound that sent a shiver down her spine. It was the sound of something in great distress, something so filled with suffering that it seemed unbearable. Horrik was unnerved when the tormented screech echoed in the distance.

Apart from these screeches and the running water it was a soundless world. Down here nothing moved. There seemed to be nothing to make any sounds.

When the first splash happened she had been sleeping in Serinta's Cave. She woke up and lifted her large, scaled head. She was not sure whether she had dreamt it but then she heard another splash. Now she was alert. Maybe something she could eat had fallen down the well or down another well somewhere. She was very hungry.

The sounds had echoed along the tunnels and Horrik could not tell where they were coming from. She was completely lost. She no longer knew how to get to Korum's Cave and Lake Merlode under the Silver Well. She stayed still and listened, her long forked tongue slipping in and out of her mouth, sensing, smelling. Then there was a third splash, much softer, and finally another louder one. She decided to have a look around and so left the cave to head off down a tunnel in what she thought was the right direction.

In the labyrinth of tunnels where she found herself, to the west of the Silver Well, there was no flowing water. Normally, before the spell had frozen everything above, water would gush through, filling Lake Merlode first, and then coursing its way through many tunnels to the great Eastern Synamian Ocean. But now, as there was no rain to filter down through the earth and fill the underground streams, the tunnels were mostly dry. There were still a few pools, puddles and damp patches and for Horrik these were a life saving source of drinking water.

She spent some time hunting through the tunnels by the glowing light of the black compass. Her hunger was growing and she was just beginning to feel the weight of disappointment fall upon her; there was nothing to eat. Then something brushed against her tail. She whipped around and snapped with her great jaws, catching something small and furry in her mouth. It was a bat. She devoured it with one swallow and then stayed still for some time, watching by the light of the compass and hoping that more bats might fly past. No more bats came but at least she knew that there were others living down in this underground world and that it was just a matter of finding them.

Then a thought struck her.

"How had the bat avoided the spell? Why wasn't it frozen like everything else?"

She did not ponder these questions for more than a moment. She just hoped there were more. If she could find a cave full of bats then she could have a proper meal instead of just an appetizer. She would have a hunt later on but now she would return to her cave. She had made a special effort to remember the way back and soon she was scrabbling along the rocky surface in the right direction. Entering Serinta's Cave, she passed the gold-streaked wall and moved beside the patch of fern. Feeling tired and hungry she flopped down to finish her sleep.

In the tunnels to the east of the Silver Well there was still a healthy supply of water flowing from Lake Merlode. Ramoy's Canal was straight, but the other smaller ones zigzagged catching all sorts of debris, bits and pieces left by adventurers and broken roots as well as branches and leaves that had fallen down holes. All these floated in the water. In due course, as the water level of the lake dropped, these underground streams too would dry up. Day by day the water level was dropping, but for the moment there was a reasonable flow. It was in one of these underground rivers, to the west of the Korum's Cave that Jamaar was floating.

The great dog was still alive, but only just. The blow when he hit the wall of the well had knocked him out and he had remained unconscious ever since. In his fall he was helped by his great strength and also by the black compass around his neck. It pulled and tugged around his neck as he descended so that by the time he hit the surface of the lake at the bottom of Korum's Cave he was falling tail first. After he plunged in, the compass pulled him back up to the surface, where he floated and then it had kept his nose above the water.

He was still unconscious. Within a couple of minutes the water drew him into the underground River Towes, which flowed eastwards out of the lake. The water was just deep enough to carry him along until he met a sharp bend where he bumped into a rock at the water's edge. The compass chain around his neck caught on the rock.

The chain pulled tight around his throat and Jamaar started to choke.

Soon his breathing stopped and the life began to drain out of him.

A soft click echoed in the tunnel. The back of the compass opened and a creature, glowing gently with soft light, began to crawl out. Two large pincer-bearing arms appeared first. Then the head, with two eyes on the top and five more pairs just below those in a line. Next its flat, slender body crawled out on eight legs. The body was divided into two tails which were five-segmented and arched over its back. Each tail ended in a bulb-like poison gland with hooked needle-like stingers. Two pairs of wings lay flat on its back. It was a small flying two-tailed scorpion.

The scorpion scuttled up the chain and onto the rock, moving quickly and with extraordinary precision. Its bone-hard claws clicked on the metal of the chain and then the rock. It easily found the clasp and, gripping the chain with one of its pincers, it undid the clasp with the other. The chain and compass swung down into the water, held at one end by the scorpion, and Jamaar was freed.

He drifted again on the flow of the underground stream. His broad chest heaved as his lungs desperately sucked in air. Then his body rolled in the water and his mouth and nose dipped under. He coughed and spluttered violently which brought him around and he opened his eyes. It was dark. He was barely conscious and so weak that he could hardly move. He did not know where he was and panicked.

With great effort, he scrambled in the water, splashing and lurching onto some debris floating at the side of the tunnel. His front legs and head hooked over a log, which pulled it loose from the side and drew it out into the flow of water. Jamaar could now breathe freely but the effort had been too much and immediately he passed out again.

In this way Jamaar was carried eastward on the log, deep under the ground.

Back down the tunnel the scorpion used both its pincers, moving them rapidly to gather in the chain and haul the compass out of the water. It fixed the chain firmly by winding it around a sharp corner of rock until the compass hung just clear of the water. It waited a few seconds while the water drained out of the compass and then it climbed quickly down the chain. When it was half way down, the chain slipped with a small jerk and the scorpion stopped. The compass dangled by its chain, just brushing the surface of the flowing water.

The scorpion waited for a moment, completely still. The chain held firm, so the scorpion carried on climbing down and slipped into the black compass. It clicked shut.

Aram had found the travelling to be tough. The first part of his journey was straightforward, as he cut across the northern tip of Blue Lake and then headed for the Snowpeak Mountains. His magic alicorn opened up a path in the snow in front of him as he galloped like the wind. When he first entered the great mountain range he could still gallop, but as he approached the higher mountains the difficulties began. The snow became much heavier and was far thicker. It had been swept by the blizzard into great drifts, some of which towered above Aram in huge white mounds. His alicorn served him well, helping to clear the snow ahead but it lay in such quantities that he had to slow down and force his way through. At times he even created tunnels through the great drifts.

Once he had passed through this region he had been able to speed up once again and make good time. When he reached the slope of the last mountain, he paused to rest and look towards the border. The blizzard was too thick for him to see far, with white flakes rushing in a madness of frantic motion around him. His golden body heaved as he drew breath in and then blew out streams of misty air from his nostrils.

He needed to rest and stood there for a few minutes to recover, turning so that the driving wind was behind him. His long mane shook as it was blown fiercely forwards around his head, sparkling with a sprinkling of gold specks which disappeared in the driving snow.

After a little while he felt stronger again and sprung into action with renewed strength. Now there was not far to go. He began to drop down the last slope and towards the flat Northern Borderlands.

In the dark attic of The Old Mill in Candara, someone moved. A tightly clenched hand opened, releasing the sparkling brightness of coloured light. The three Candara Gems were quickly smothered in a cloth and hidden under the floorboards.

In Summertime Kingdom, Sergeant Forr and the other fourteen ravens were so exhausted that they had slept through most of the day. They were perched in the highest branches of a huge redwood tree in Duran Forest. They decided there was no need to rush back to the army where the General would force them to go straight into action, so they planned to report to him the next day. They would rest and doze until they felt strong again. Sergeant Forr was not in agreement but the others made him agree. Now it was night again and they were at last beginning to feel stronger.

"Now that we feel better," said Forr, "We'll report back to the General."

"No," said Razz, "We all agreed, remember? We report tomorrow."

"Look, who's in charge here?" snapped Forr.

"You… if you like," said Razz, "But you're out voted. What do you say all of you… stay or go?"

They all answered 'Stay', except for Iker who was fast asleep.

"That's decided then," said Akk, joining in.

Sergeant Forr suddenly turned his head on one side to listen to something.

"Sshh," he said.

They all heard it now. It was the sound running feet, pounding the ground and getting louder. Someone was running fast from the north and towards the border. They peered through the darkness.

"Can't see a thing," said Razz, "It's…"

"Sshh," Forr interrupted.

The pounding feet began to grow softer.

"Right," said Forr, "This could be important. We follow."

"But…" argued Razz, "it could be nothing… just someone running."

"We follow!" snapped Forr, trying to force his authority upon them, "We follow now! OK?"

With more grumbling they reluctantly agreed, probably because they felt stronger and sensed that this might lead to some action. Iker was still fast asleep.

"Iker!" Razz shouted.

He still did not wake up.

"Leave him here," said Akk, "He's useless anyway."

"We can't just leave him here, can we?" piped up one of the others, "He's the General's nephew! What will the General say?"

"And…" said another, "when he finds out, what will he do to us?"

"Don't be stupid," said Razz, "Everything Iker does goes wrong… remember he nearly killed the dog. He's more trouble than he's worth. He's only in the army because he's the General's nephew… he's useless."

"I know, but…"

"We'll make up some story," suggested Razz, "You know… like he just flew away or something. Come on Forr. Iker's a bad egg."

Sergeant Forr reluctantly nodded his agreement feeling more and more that he was being bullied into decisions by the strong-willed Razz.

"Let's go then," said Forr, and he tilted his head to one side to listen to the sound of running feet but they had faded into the distance, "Soon we won't be able to hear enough to follow."

"We can't already," stated Razz, listening, "Can't hear a thing."

"In that case…" Forr began, "We'll have to guess and try to find it."

"What about Iker then?" asked Akk.

Razz shook his head.

"I thought we'd decided that," he growled, "We leave him here, OK?"

Forr was still reluctant but felt bullied into the decision. "OK, we leave him here."

They took off and flew in the direction of the footsteps, leaving Iker fast asleep on a branch.

Joog had kept watch in a tree through the night as the other four friends slept. Before dawn, he woke them. They felt refreshed and ready to move on. Lazuli slept standing up and was next to a tree trunk while the children and Tally slept on the grass. They had slept close to the border of the Kingdom of Gems, where the snow wall marked the change from one kingdom into another.

They were embraced by the warm air beneath a clear sky where thousands of twinkling stars and a pale moon, now falling in the sky, looked down upon them. A short distance away across the border the freezing cold snowbound land was cloaked in heavy darkness.

"What's that?" said Tally suddenly, his ears pricked and alert.

They all spun around to look into the darkness of the trees. Joog flew silently down from the branch where he had been perching and landed on Lazuli's back. Someone was approaching. The sound of feet pounding the ground close by, running feet, hurrying towards the trees and in their direction, made them all stare anxiously. Darkness covered everything, especially under the trees where the pale light of the moon could not reach.

Amalek glanced at Joog and whispered, "What shall we do?"

"Keep still," he replied, "It's too late to hide."

The running steps had already entered the trees, slowed to a walk and then stopped. The five friends gazed into the shadows. They were on edge. Everything was still. They heard the slightest of sounds which pulled their attention to one of the trees. Then something moved and a hooded figure stepped out.

"Hello," said Simron, pulling his hood off is head, "That was quite a challenge catching up with you."

Relief flooded through them and they relaxed. Then Simron saw Joog.

"And Joog!" he exclaimed, "We thought you'd died in the fight with the ravens."

"Ha!" Joog laughed, "You don't think I'd let some ravens get the better of me, do you?"

"No," agreed Simron, "Harris and Quint were sure about it... but I did wonder. I'd like to hear what happened."

Amalek smiled at Simron. "It's so good to see you."

They all felt the joy of meeting him again. Seph stepped forwards and hugged him. Simron wrapped his arms around Seph, patting the boy on his back with his dark-skinned hand.

"Great to see you," Seph said, "but you scared us! We couldn't see you by that tree at all! How do you do it?"

"Sorry about that," Simron laughed.

Joog lifted his wings and held them out like arms. "He's a Master of Disguise... he can't help it."

Seph let go of him and stepped back. Simron turned to Amalek and hugged her. "How *did* you catch up to us?" she asked.

"I travelled by river and then across Lake Burney. Mind you, I had to row fast... very fast. Then I jogged to here from the lake."

Joog was still on Lazuli's back. "It's great to have you with us," he stated, "But why? We thought you had to stay with Wizard Elzaphan."

"Elzaphan was concerned," he replied, "When he heard that you were lost, Joog, he sent me... well, in your place. And now..." he turned to the Prince and Princess, "You've got both of us."

"Which is wonderful," Amalek said, smiling at him.

"I agree, but…" began Joog, "perhaps, now that you know that I'm here you should go back… with the danger threatening there he may need you."

"I don't think so," replied Simron, "There's no immediate danger in this kingdom, whereas the situation across the border there," he waved an arm in the direction, "its getting worse. Elzaphan feels that the Dark Wizard Troubler's power is strengthening… his grip on the kingdom is tightening. The spell is stronger now than ever, and he fears that he may have stolen the Candara Gems."

This news stunned everyone there.

"But… how?" said Seph, "He can't. We're alive and that protects the Gems…"

Simron nodded, "That's true… but with his power growing, who knows what he can do?"

There was a pause while everyone pondered the frightening implications of Simron's words.

"We should get going then," said Joog, "But let's eat first."

"Yes," agreed Amalek, "A good breakfast to build up our strength before we go. Who'd like some?"

She quickly took out an array of jars and packages and laid them on the grass. Seph did the same. Then they reached their hands into the bags that Lazuli had been carrying and drew out several bottles of flavoured water.

"I'm glad I came," said the Simron, "It looks like quite a feast."

They started handing the food and drink around. Lazuli was standing and reaching down with her trunk for food while the others sat down on the grass.

Amalek handed a jar to her brother. "Here you are,

Seph," she said.

"Thanks," he said, taking the jar eagerly and then looking at it, "Hey… ghicky nuts. Yuk!"

"But they're good for you," she laughed.

"Yes, I know," he acknowledged, "But they taste disgusting!"

He took one out, placed it on the lid which he held in one hand, and then flicked it at her. It bounced off her forehead and onto Tally's back. Tally shook his back until it slid off.

"Thanks," he said eating it, "Keep them coming!"

They all laughed.

"Sshh!" said Joog suddenly.

They stopped laughing at once and looked at Joog. He was looking through the trees and along the border to the west.

"Look!" he whispered urgently, pointing with a wing, "Ravens!"

"Keep still," said Simron.

Two ravens were crossing the border side by side. They passed across and plunged into the falling snow in the Kingdom of Gems. In a moment they were gone.

Joog looked around. "There don't seem to be any more… but the sooner we go the better. We mustn't lose time. Over there we'll be shielded by all the snow."

They packed up the remaining food and drink in the bags. They slipped the bags on and began to walk quickly together to the border. Joog glided just above them, keeping a sharp lookout for any more ravens. The sky was now showing the first signs of dawn, the horizon glowing with light and drowning the last few stars.

They stood and gazed through the twilight and across the border at the amazing sight of falling snow being swept past on the driving wind.

Joog landed on Amalek's shoulder. "Come on… let's go," he said, "Those ravens will be reporting to the Dark Wizard Troubler soon."

He shook his wings to tidy his snowy-white feathers and then looked at Seph.

"I've just remembered something. Have you got that whistle that Aram gave you, Seph?"

"Joog!" Amalek exclaimed, "Of course. Aram said to blow it and he and Halo would come."

"Yes, it's here," said Seph, taking the little golden unicorn out of his buttoned pocket, "Right then."

He carefully unscrewed the alicorn, put it to his lips and blew. No one heard anything. He blew again. Still no sound.

"Perhaps it's like one of those dog whistles," said Amalek, "It's so high that only unicorns can hear it."

They all gazed eagerly into the dark snowy scene of Kingdom of Gems. What if Aram and Halo could not hear it because of the howling wind? They waited patiently, Seph blowing the silent whistle every now and again.

Then they saw something in the growing light. An area of greyness was approaching. It was clear that a cloud of snow was being thrown up by someone approaching. It must be the two unicorns rushing to greet them, this seemed certain, but somehow they all felt uneasy. Their nerves were on edge again. They could feel a dark presence, an unsettling threatening atmosphere. It was the feeling that the Dark Wizard Troubler had brought with him when he had first entered the kingdom. It sent a chilling shiver through them.

They thought they heard the pounding of hoofs as

they peeped cautiously and hopefully over the wall of snow. The snow-cloud was approaching fast, but whatever it was making it was still hidden from their sight. It stopped a little distance away and the snow-cloud began to settle. They stared as the snow thinned and gradually, in the slow-gathering dawn, they began to see a shape. It was a tall black shape, a figure silhouetted against the falling snow behind, a dark figure standing tall and still, a figure with two legs and a hat on its head.

"It's a wizard's hat!" said Amalek in fear, "It's him, the Troubler."

"I don't think so," said Joog, his powerful eyes seeing clearly, "It's too pointed," Joog observed with his powerful eyes, "Too pointed to be a hat. And look..."

The figure turned slightly. Two legs turned into four and to Joog it was clear now that it was a unicorn.

"It's Aram," he announced.

"Then where's Halo?" Seph said, "Can you see her, Joog?"

"No... I don't think so. But Aram's moving again. He's heading straight for us. I think he's seen us. Blow again, Seph."

Seph blew the magic whistle again.

Their emotions were mixed and confused. At once they felt relieved but also concerned. Seeing Aram galloping towards them was wonderful, but where was Halo? They still felt the dull ache of something evil around them, something stifling and disturbing that seemed to be closing in on them like a slowly descending mist.

Aram was close now, when suddenly several things happened together. The sky darkened, not in Summertime Kingdom where light was gathering as dawn broke, but just across the border. Seph impulsively stepped towards the border to cross and greet Aram. As he jumped across Amalek shouted to him, panic in her voice.

"Don't jump!"

It was too late. He was already leaping off the ground and over the wall of snow. Suddenly, as he crossed into The Kingdom of Gems, he stopped in mid-air. His head, shoulders and body down to his waist were across the border, but were utterly still and immediately snow began to settle on him. The lower part of his body was still in Summertime Kingdom and for a moment his legs kicked frantically before going limp. The spell had claimed another victim.

"Seph! No!" shouted Amalek in despair.

Joog took off from Amalek's shoulder and flew close to Seph.

"We forgot the magic ink," Amalek cried, "It must have washed off his ankle." She looked terrified, and then sighed deeply. "He should have thought…"

Tally was by Amalek's feet. "What do we do now?" he blurted out.

Joog glided back to the others, landing on Amalek's shoulder.

"The spell must be stronger now," he said, "He didn't even sneeze! We'll have to…"

At that moment Simron spotted something, turning his hooded head to look back into Summertime Kingdom. "Look!" he said urgently, pointing behind them.

They turned to look. Heading their way, still some distance off but closing fast, was a swirling mass of ravens, the raven army, like a multitude of wild autumn leaves.

"And look there!" added Joog.

Much closer, and also flying straight towards them, were the small group of ravens led by Sergeant Forr.

"Oh no!" Tally exclaimed.

It was not the ravens but something else that had taken Tally completely by surprise. He was pointing with a paw at a dark cloud just across the border. It had dropped low above the snowy surface in the Kingdom of Gems. He cowered back with his brown eyes wide with terror.

Amalek and Joog saw Tally's face and spun around to look. They caught their breath in horror as an icy fear ran through them, chilling them deep inside. Glaring at them from inside the cloud, was the Dark Wizard Troubler. His evil black eyes were intently fixed on them, those eyes that concentrated all the hate and anger that could ever possess anyone.

Amalek's eyes met his. She felt weak in the presence of such evil power. She was being drawn in by his dark mind, sucked into a world that was murky and cold. She sank to her knees. The world began to swirl out of control.

"Turn away," said a calm voice behind her. It was Simron. "Turn away and fight his power with all your strength. Turn away now."

She summoned all her inner strength and fought but she already felt trapped, as if she would never be able to move again. The Troubler stared at her with steely intensity as the cloud drifted closer. Then she heard him speak in a half whisper. Each word was as clear as if he was right beside her and stabbed into her like an icy blade.

"Welcome, little girl," he hissed, "Welcome to *my* kingdom."

...CONTINUED IN BOOK 3 OF THE TRILOGY ~
THE GLASS PRISON

Bonus Story

This is a short story related to The Kingdom of Gems trilogy. This story takes place prior to any events in the trilogy itself.

This is an example of one of the stories you will receive by being part of the KOGworld™ membership.

Make sure you are a member of KOGworld™ so you don't miss out on other short stories like this.

~ The Dark Moon ~

Snow fell thickly on the peaks of the Becci Mountains. It swept and gusted through the chilly air as if it was excited about the beautiful scene it was creating. Just below the peaks was the perfect place for mountain hares to live and a group of them had made their home here. For them it was a white paradise. They had built a series of burrows in the snow, connected by a labyrinth of tunnels so that they could move around easily from burrow to burrow.

Night fell as gently as the snow and gradually the hares fell asleep. However there was one burrow which was still busy with life.

"Come on, you young scamp," said Hawkeye to his grandson, "The neighbours will be complaining again if you don't quieten down now."

Tally raced around the burrow twice more and then sat down. He was just eight months old and about half the size of Hawkeye. He looked cheekily at his grandfather.

"You should make thicker walls, Gramps," he said, "It would be easy... I'd help... we could do it now... I'll..."

Hawkeye watched him speed around the burrow again and laughed at the wonderful enthusiasm and energy of the young hare.

"Thicker walls!" he exclaimed, "That's one answer, yes! But the other way is for you to go to bed when it's time, isn't it? Don't you think that's a better solution?"

"Yes, Gramps," Tally replied, sitting down again, "Can I look in your chest then?"

Hawkeye's old wooden chest was filled with interesting things for a young hare with a sense of adventure. Apart from the old maps, there were candles, pens and all sorts of other things. There were also strange diagrams which Tally did not understand at all.

"No, Tally," Hawkeye said, "It's just not the right time for looking in my chest... it's bedtime now... well, past bedtime."

"Will you tell me a story then, please, Gramps?"

"Of course," said Hawkeye, who enjoyed telling him stories as much as Tally enjoyed hearing them, "Into your burrow then."

There was a small burrow off the main one and this was where Tally slept. When Tally's parents had been killed and Hawkeye had taken on the responsibility of bringing him up, Tally had been a tiny baby and Hawkeye had dug out this burrow for him. At first it was spacious for the tiny hare but now that he had grown he could only just fit in. It made a snug bed which he liked.

He reversed in, lay down and looked out keenly with big brown eyes.

"I'm ready," he announced. He loved his grandfather's stories. Sometimes Hawkeye told a true story about adventures that had happened to him and at other times he made up a stories to entertain the young hare.

"Alright," said Hawkeye, "Would you like to hear a true one which I've not told to you before?"

"Yes, please!" exclaimed Tally in anticipation.

"Well, alright, here we go."

Hawkeye paused and took a breath.

"I was young… a little older than you… about two I think. The story I am going to tell you is about an important event. It was important for me… I learned a lot on that day… but it was also important for the whole of Summertime Kingdom.

"You already know about the time when a Troubler invaded the kingdom... that's what the poem called 'The Bell' was about. Remember?"

Tally lifted his head and nodded. It was one of his favourites and he had heard it many times.

"Well, the story I am about to tell you happened about twenty years after that terrible invasion... when they rang the Glyifild Bell to cast the spell and take over the whole of Summertime Kingdom." He paused to work it out accurately. "Hmm… now let me get this right… it was… yes… um… twenty-three years after the invasion… so the spell had been holding the kingdom for twenty-three years! Now… a little sum for you to help you with your education. I was two then and now I am seventeen, so how long ago did this happen?"

Tally looked up at the roof and then screwed his eyes up as he tried to work it out.

"Fourteen years!" he announced proudly.

"Nearly," said Hawkeye.

"Fifteen then!"

"That's right. Well done."

Hawkeye shook his head with sadness as he remembered the difficult times.

"The whole kingdom was shrouded in darkness..."

"It's in the poem," said Tally, "It says - the sun forgot to shine."

"That's right," continued Hawkeye, "The spell was so powerful that the whole kingdom was cloaked in semi-darkness. You could see the sun in the sky but only just, as if through a thick mist. But what was worse was the dark moon. It was deep black and pierced the mist like a ray of light would. And that black moon created a dark, dark mood which was like a constant dull ache throughout the land. It was a terrible burden that squeezed the life out of everything. And whenever this ache weakened and began to lift they rang the Glyifild Bell again and the dullness returned. It held the kingdom like a vice. And you remember from the poem who did this terrible thing to our kingdom, don't you, Tally?"

"A Troubler," piped up Tally.

Hawkeye was almost whispering now and his eyes moistened with tears. "A Troubler, yes," he said, "And the Troubler came from... Gugeol."

He paused for a moment to calm his emotions, then looked at Tally and carried on.

"The spell of the Glyifild Bell held the whole kingdom prisoner. Animals and people still moved around, talked and did all the usual things but they were in a dark dreamy state. They were irritable and lethargic, always picking arguments and sleeping a lot. They would do the minimum they needed to do and then go to sleep.

"Soon after the invasion the Troubler killed the king... that was King Tefan, a good man... and the Troubler took the throne. He then went around the land with his gang of thieving barbarians, doing whatever he wanted. He ransacked the homes of ordinary folk and creatures, taking gold and silver and anything he found of value. They were destructive too... violently breaking things as they searched for things to steal. They burnt some houses right to the ground in Munden and Butterknowle... the people there suffered very badly.

"Anyway, the spell effected me as well, of course, but because it had already been around for twenty-one years when I was born, it was normal for me. I felt bad all the time, like everyone else and I did not know what happiness was! It was like living in a cloud where there was no love. It was a living nightmare! But then one day, as I said, when I was two, something extraordinary happened. I remember it now as if it were yesterday.

"It was night and I was all by myself on the lower slopes of this mountain as I nibbled on some grass. I was mean, irritable and unhappy, so much so that I did not even enjoy the grass I was eating.

"I pricked my ears up when I heard voices and the sound of a horse's hooves thudding on the ground. As they approached I felt frightened and this feeling grew as they came closer. I wanted to run off but I was too terrified and could hardly move. Somehow I managed to slip into a bush and from there I looked through the branches and watched.

"The sounds became louder until, in the dim light, I saw them. There was a human on a horse, both looking at first like black shadows in the darkness. The horse was trotting and as it came closer, I saw that around its legs were four wolverines, two on either side and running beside the horse... they were the largest wolverines I had ever seen. They looked fierce and angry with saliva dribbling from their open mouths.

"Stop!" the human ordered.

His voice was harsh and evil, cutting through the night like a chill in the air and the animals all stopped immediately. They were right next to the bush I was hiding in.

"There's nothing here," growled the man, "Just Mountains. Why has he sent us over here anyway?"

"For valuables," said the horse.

"I know that!" snapped the man, "But there aren't any here are there? Not here, in the mountains."

The wolverines and the horse looked around.

"See," the man said, spreading his hands out in front of him and looking around as well, "No buildings... no people... no valuables. There may be animals here, yes, but they rarely have many things of value. Animals are often hard to find anyway... they hide like cowards in holes in the ground and up in trees."

"We can find them," growled one of the wolverines, "And we're hungry."

"Yeah!" rumbled another wolverine, "Let's go for animals... then we can eat them for food *plus* steal their valuables."

The man screwed up his face with the tension of working out what to do and looked down at the ground, considering what the wolverines had said. The horse shuffled its hooves on the grass.

This is when I recognised the man... and it gave me a shock. It was Jarm Shorplen, a man from Munden, who was well known even to us hares because he was the mayor of the town. He had turned traitor and was working for Gugeol.

"No," he concluded, "I'm fed up with this! Let's go!"

He shook the reins of his horse and it reared up and neighed, its front legs slamming down, one hoof passing through the bush and just missing my head. I jumped out and found myself staring into the eyes of a wolverine.

"Look!" exclaimed the wolverine, "Food!"

I summoned all my strength to run off. I forced my back legs down and leapt away from them, only to bump into one of the other wolverines who had cut off my retreat. I scrambled away from it and looked around. I was surrounded. I cowered down beneath the four slavering creatures.

"We'll share it," growled one of them, "A quarter each."

"Yeah... rip it apart."

"Alright," said another, saliva dripping from his mouth, "But I reserve one of the back legs... they're delicious."

They all moved in closer.

"Stop!" shouted Jarm, "Are you stupid! If there's one here, then there must be lots more nearby. It can lead us to them. Then you can eat one each... or more... and they're bound to have some valuables."

The wolverines were ravenous and ignored him. I felt a searing pain in my back leg as teeth sank in. I cried out in agony.

"Stop!" Jarm shouted again.

The wolverine released my leg from his jaws in order to speak. I collapsed and decided to pretend to be dead. Maybe it would give me an opportunity.

"Listen," said the Jarm impatiently, "We can follow its scent... easily... and then we'll find the others."

The wolverines were fighting to hold back their desire for food.

"Yes," one of them said, "Alright then... but this one looks dead already."

Jarm laughed. "Probably the shock of looking at your ugly face. Eat it then, if you must. But it will have left a scent so afterwards we find the others."

The wolverine opened its jaws again. I saw a glisten of its white teeth as I looked into its slavering mouth which bore down upon me. There was nothing I could do to escape, so I attacked, jumping up on my good leg and thumping into its nose. It yelped and stepped back. The other three moved in, growling ferociously, and I knew that this was the last few seconds of my life. There was no escape now.

Suddenly, the wolverines stopped. They had sensed something and looked up. I looked too. Striding towards us was a tall wizard, glowing with light. He clutched his staff in one hand and on the top, a huge gemstone shone with changing colours; red changed to blue, then green and yellow and then other colours. The horse reared again with terror in its eyes and blowing noisily through its nose.

"Let the hare go!" ordered the wizard.

"Attack!" shouted Jarm.

The wolverines abandoned me and leapt towards the wizard. The wizard stopped and pointed his staff towards them. A bright blue flash shattered the night and lit up everything around. I'll never forget the terrified blue faces of the wolves as they cried out and then dropped to the ground and lay there whimpering.

"Get up!" shouted Jarm.

The horse was backing off and Jarm was tugging at the reins but having trouble controlling it.

"Go!" screamed Jarm.

The horse turned, the wolverines jumped up and together they raced off into the night.

I flopped down and felt the throbbing pain of my injured leg filling my mind. Blood dripped down my white fur from the wound and onto the grass. In a moment the wizard was looking down at me. He knelt down and noticed my injured leg.

"Hello, little fellow," he said, "You were in a bit of trouble there."

Suddenly, I was feeling very strange. I was feeling something I had never known before but it made me smile, and then laugh. In the presence of this wizard, the dreamy mood of misery had gone and in its place was... happiness. I had never been happy before and it was wonderful! For the first time ever I felt free.

The wizard smiled and then studied me intently from under his white bushy eyebrows, noticing my change in emotions.

"Is that better?" he asked.

"Yes," I replied, surprise in my voice, "Much better."

His staff glowed again, this time yellow. I felt the pain in my leg fade away.

"That's amazing!" I said to him, "My leg... it feels fine now."

"Try walking," he said.

I got up and found that it was a little stiff but after a few steps it loosened up.

"Thank you," I said, "But who are you?"

"I'm Wizard Elzaphan," he replied, "And what's your name?"

"Hawkeye."

"Well, Hawkeye," he began, "I have come here to help this kingdom. To try to drive out Gugeol from here... if that's possible. They have no right to be here."

"I'll help," I offered.

"Good, Good," he said, "I was hoping you'd feel that way. I don't know my way around this kingdom, so to start with, will you be my guide, please?"

"Yes," I said.

I knew I was in the presence of a great wizard and I would do anything for him.

"Thank you," he said, "and can you take me to your home where I presume there are more hares living."

"There are many more of us," I replied, "and I can take you there now."

We began the walk together up the mountain and I couldn't help glancing up at Wizard Elzaphan and at his staff, glowing gently with a rich blue light. A moment later, it began to rain and each drop became a little blue lantern helping us to see the way.

After some time we reached the snow-line and moved into the falling snow. I hopped in front showing him the way to my home where all the other mountain hares lived in a labyrinth of snow burrows.

As we were travelling we chatted. This was the beginning of a wonderful friendship between us."

Hawkeye looked at Tally and smiled to see that he had fallen asleep. He wondered how much of the story he had heard but knew that he could always tell it again the next night.

He smiled at his grandson and then crept to the other side of the burrow and settled down to sleep.